THE GIF P9-EDY-115

The smell of pine, the f   nth
of a burning fire, the taste of eggnog, and the sight of gaily
wrapped presents. It's Christmastime, and what better way to
celebrate than with three charming novellas of joy and good
cheer by three of Zebra's most popular Regency writers.

Dawn Aldridge Poore tells the charming story of two wonderful little girls who bring love and laughter to a Christmas
romance. Nina Porter brings Christmas to the country, where
a shy young miss finds true love in the arms of a dashing
viscount. And Alicia Rasley relates the true meaning of
Christmas in her tender story of a young mother and an unexpected love.

So enjoy this special season and take pleasure in these three
romantic Regency stories, which will warm your heart at the
merriest time of the year.

A Touch of Christmas

Dawn Aldridge Poore

Nina Porter

Alicia Rasley

ZEBRA BOOKS
KENSINGTON PUBLISHING CORP.

Table of Contents

THE CHRISTMAS RING

by

Dawn Aldridge Poore

Chapter 1

Kate looked in the mirror and tried to practice. "Barton, will you marry me?" She tried again. "Barton, will *you* marry me? Barton, *will* you marry me?" It still wasn't right. "Barton, will you marry *me?*" She turned and made a face at her best friend, Sophie. "I'm not sure I can do this. What if he says no?"

"He probably will," the imperturbable Miss Page told her. "Barton Rush isn't the marrying kind."

"Well, it isn't as if I *want* to marry him, anyway," Kate said, sitting down in a low chair and pulling one of the twins up on her lap. "All I need is for him to say that we're going to get married."

"He probably won't do that, either," Sophie said, looking at one of the twins carefully smearing paste on her fingers. "Which one of the twins is that? Mary or Megan?"

"Megan," Kate answered automatically. "The one eating the colored paper is Mary. Mary, stop that this instant!"

"I don't know why you just don't let Nurse Freeman take care of them. Heaven knows they've ruined enough gowns for you." Sophie picked a fleck of colored paper from her skirt and brushed away some imaginary dirt.

Kate looked at her stubbornly. "I like taking care of them. I'm the only mother they have." She sighed. "Which brings me to my present predicament."

Sophie laughed and looked at the clock. "And brings here, you hope, part of the solution to your present predicament. It's time for me to leave you now, so you'll have time to get yourself and the girls ready for Rush's arrival. Didn't you say he was coming at three?" Sophie paused as she reached for her gloves and reticule. "Why Barton Rush, Kate? Surely there are many more amenable men out there. You could have taken either Baxter or Clarke. Both of them offered for you last summer."

Kate put Megan down on the floor and handed her some more paper and paste. "You miss the point, Sophie. I don't want to get married; I merely want to be engaged while Sandford's here. Barton's the only man I know well enough to ask such a thing."

Sophie laughed. "You may not know him as well as you think. Have you seen him lately?"

Kate looked at her in surprise. "No, I haven't, not in a year or more, but I've known him since we were children. Why do you say such a thing? Has he changed?"

Sophie sat back down. The only thing she loved better than hearing gossip was telling it to someone else. "Kate Caldwell! I can hardly credit my ears! I thought everyone had heard about it since it was the on-dit of last Christmas."

"Don't you remember? We spent last Christmas in the country because the twins had measles. I didn't hear anything."

Sophie smiled gleefully. "Then you didn't know! You haven't heard about Rush chasing Amalie Armitage last winter. The on-dit was that he fell madly in love. Even went so far as to follow her and sing songs to her. She told Rebecca Ashe that he swore he'd kill himself if she didn't marry him. She feared for his life."

Kate was incredulous. "That can't be true. I own I haven't seen Barton for a year or so, but he couldn't have changed that much."

"He did." Sophie's voice was sure. "Miss Armitage was

10

on the dangle for someone richer and she turned Barton down flat. Of course, nothing else worked out for her and I think her father was fit to be tied, although I heard she does have someone else on the string now. I don't know who." Sophie tapped Kate on the arm with her reticule. "I'm telling you, Kate, Barton Rush is a burned man. He'll never marry after making such a fool of himself."

"I can't believe it, Sophie. Barton would never act that way. I've known him for years."

"Love makes men do strange things," Sophie declared. "You may want to have another plan."

"I suppose so." Kate sighed. "Sophie, do you think you could come spend Christmas with us in the country? No matter whether or not Barton agrees to pose as my fiancé, I'm going to need some help dealing with Sandford. Robbie's going to be there, of course, and if he decides to help by pretending to be my fiancé, Barton, too."

"I'll try my best." Sophie laughed as she turned to leave. "From what I hear of Sandford since he's returned, you're going to need all the help you can get."

"Spoken like a true friend." Kate grimaced as she walked Sophie to the door.

"That's what friends are for." Sophie gave her a quick kiss on the cheek. "I'll be back tomorrow to find out what happened."

Kate went back into the drawing room to check on the twins. They were busy pasting colored paper on the side of her best footstool. "No, no." She sat down to show them how to make pretty chains and Christmas flowers from the paper. Finally, they had a flower each, a bit lopsided but still a flower. She stuck the flowers in their hair and got to her feet. It was time to get ready. She couldn't see the clock, but it had to be almost one.

Kate gathered up the bits of extra paper and stood there, looking at them, wondering a dozen things: What would Barton be like now? Would he agree to pose as her fiancé? Could she even manage to ask him? Would Sandford be duped by the whole thing? Right now, the ideal solution seemed to be to give up the whole harebrained scheme and flee to Germany to join Mama and Papa. It was more than tempting, although it probably wouldn't solve anything. Sandford would just follow them there.

The sound of the knocker interrupted her thoughts and she realized one of the twins was crying. Megan was trying to paste Mary to the sofa. Whoever was at the door would be taken care of by Waters, since no one was expected until Barton arrived at three. Kate separated the twins and tried to clean the paste off Mary's face, who was eager to help by rubbing her face all over Kate's gown. Streaks of colored paper accompanied it, and as Kate tried to hold Mary, the paste on her fingers stuck in the child's hair. Mary began to howl.

"Another charming family interlude in the Caldwell household." The voice held a hint of laughter to it.

Kate whirled about, scattering bits of paper and dragging Mary around with her. "Barton! Whatever are you doing here? You weren't supposed to be here until three."

Barton Rush stepped into the room, tall and elegant in immaculate buff and dark blue. His plain black boots gleamed in the reflection from the fireplace. He stripped off his gloves, holding them and his cane in one hand while, with the other, he snapped open his watch and closed it again. "It is three."

"Oh, my Lord!" Kate looked around. The room was a mess, she was a mess, the twins were more than a mess. They were covered with bits of red and green paper, as was the end of the sofa. Kate closed her eyes. Things were already falling apart, she thought. She had planned to have the twins dressed and looking angelic, the room quiet and peaceful, and herself looking her best. She reached up to smooth back her hair and realized she had bits of red and green paper stuck to her hands. Kate took a deep breath. Surely Barton wouldn't hold this against her. After all, they knew each other so well.

"Do come in, Barton. I'll ring for some tea." She gestured toward the sofa, then saw it wouldn't be at all suitable, as it, too, was covered with little bits of paper and a pair of scissors. Barton laughed and sat gingerly in a chair, checking the seat first.

"Come here, young ladies, and stand where I can see you," he said to the twins. To Kate's surprise, Megan and Mary marched over and stood in front of the chair. "How you've grown!" he said, looking at each of them seriously. "Are you Megan and you Mary?"

The twins looked at one another, giggled, and each pointed to the other. "Then I suppose I must have that backward," Barton said with a laugh as Kate rang for Nurse Freeman. "You must be Mary and you must be Megan."

"You were right the first time. They're only five, and they already love to confuse people." Kate looked down at her gown and her hands. "We're making Christmas flowers."

"I don't mind waiting if you want to get the paper off your hands." Barton grinned, glancing at her from head to toe. "And perhaps out of your hair. If you feel comfortable with it, though, it doesn't bother me at all."

"I'll ring for tea and be right back." Kate gave him a grateful look and helped Nurse Freeman gather up the twins. Upstairs, Riggs was waiting for her.

"I saw him come in," Riggs said anxiously, fumbling with Kate's laces in her hurry. "I have everything ready, but it'll take at least a half hour to get you ready."

"I have five minutes." Kate bent down so Riggs could toss a clean dress over her head. Just get the paper and paste off."

Riggs took more than five minutes but still less than ten before Kate ran out of her room and back to the small drawing room where Barton waited. Her tangle of rich auburn hair had defied their best efforts, and Riggs had finally just bound it up with a ribbon to match Kate's deep green dress. At least all the paper was out, although her hands were stained with

13

red and green spots where the color had run when she had tried to wash off the paste.

Barton was sitting comfortably. He had moved the paper and scissors from the sofa and was sitting there, his feet propped up on the footstool, the tray of tea and macaroons in front of him. "Ah, there you are," he said, starting to get up.

Kate motioned him to stay seated, then sat beside him and poured each of them a cup of tea. "Most domestically cozy," Barton said with a grin. "It's too bad you've never married, Kate. Some men would love all this comfort."

She thought it might be an opening. "Would you?"

He shook his head as he looked at her. "I think not. I almost fell into the leg shackles last year but managed to escape. It was such a close call that I think I'll avoid that trap for several years, if not forever. Marriage is not for me, Kate."

"Oh." She couldn't think of anything else to say.

Barton laughed. "What? You're not going to do like every other woman in the world and try to convince me that marriage is the natural state for men?"

"No." She groped for words. "Some marriages work well. Look at Mama's and Papa's, for example."

Barton sipped his tea and thought about it for a moment. "Yes, I own they're devoted to each other and their marriage is ideal for them. However, you must admit that they're so devoted to each other that there's been little room for you, Robbie, or Carleen." He looked at her as a flicker of pain crossed her face. "I'm sorry, Kate. I thought you might have gotten over Carleen's death by now. How long has it been? . . . Five years?"

"Yes, five years," she said with a sad smile. "And I have gotten over it, for the most part." She paused. "You're right about Mama and Papa, you know. I didn't realize you were so perceptive, Barton."

He laughed and put his teacup on the tray. "I've changed

14

in the years since we played together, Kate. I'm eight and twenty now, and I hope I've gained a little knowledge of people and the world. Lord knows that kind of knowledge is acquired the hard way.''

He glanced at Kate, and she could almost repeat what he was thinking: He was eight and twenty now and she was almost five and twenty—on the shelf, by any standards. Marriage was a logical thing, even if only the pretense of a marriage. There was a long pause and Kate realized it was now or never. She took a deep breath.

''Barton, we've been friends for all these years,'' she began, then searched for the right phrase to continue.

''Since you were old enough to toddle and visit Barfield House.'' He looked levelly at her, his brown eyes meeting her green ones. ''What is it, Kate?'' He took her cup from her fingers and held it. ''I knew when you wrote and asked me to stop by today that you needed something, and I felt it must be important. You know I'll do whatever I can for you if you need me.''

''Barton, will you marry me?''

The cup crashed to the floor. *''What!''*

''Barton, will you marry me?'' She looked right at him. ''Not *really* marry me. Just pretend you're going to marry me, and just for Christmas. We can call everything off right after Christmas, I promise. I'll put it in writing if you want me to.''

Barton stood, walked to the mantel, and stared into the fire for a moment. He turned and ran his fingers through his glossy hair. ''All right, Kate, let's have it. Just what the devil is going on?''

She paused. ''It's a family thing,'' she said, trying not to cry. ''Robbie thinks perhaps we can work things out with Sandford, but that's only a chance. I can't take that risk with the twins, Barton. I'll take them and run away first. We can go hide in America.'' She didn't say anything else.

Barton sat back down beside her, after stepping neatly over

15

the discarded Christmas flowers. "Well, you certainly seem to need my help about something, but I'm still a little confused." He paused and waited, but Kate said nothing. "Kate," he said, touching her hand briefly, "don't you think I deserve to know all the particulars before I make up my mind?"

She looked at him with hope. "Then you'll do it?"

"I didn't say that, Kate. What I said was I need to know what's going on. Now tell me and, I promise, it will go no further."

"I know you well enough to know that." Kate rang for another teacup and picked up the pieces of the dropped one. As soon as they were alone, she poured more tea and turned so she could watch his face as she spoke. He still looked the same, perhaps a trifle leaner, and in his hair there was a thread or two of gray that hadn't been there before. She had always thought him handsome, although Carleen had thought he usually looked angry. His face was strong, and he had dark eyes and heavy eyebrows. To Kate, his most redeeming feature was his smile. When he smiled, his face softened and he even had a dimple on the right side. His mouth was well shaped and had a tendency to quiver at the corners when he was amused, which was often. She'd always liked that about him.

"You've stalled long enough," he said now, the dimple appearing in his cheek. "Or did you mean to make me wait until I'm replete with macaroons and in a good humor?"

Kate laughed. "I thought you were always in a good humor. I'm just trying to think of the best way to say this. I suppose I should start at the beginning.'

"Usually the best place." He leaned back against the sofa and smiled at her.

"Sandford's back from India," she began bluntly.

"Sandford? Your brother-in-law's cousin? He inherited the title and estates after William died, didn't he?"

Kate nodded. "Yes, and now he wants to take the twins

16

away from me . . . from us. I know that isn't the beginning, but that's why I'm all to pieces.''

"With reason. Why does he want to do that?''

Kate sighed. "Now for the beginning. You recall that when Carleen died, the twins were only three weeks old. William was distraught and felt he couldn't care for them, so he gave them to Papa and Mama—and to me—until he could decide what to do. Then a year later, he was killed in that fall from the top of his house.''

"I recall that. There was a question as to whether it was an accident.''

Kate looked at him sharply. "I didn't know anyone knew that. It was suicide, since he didn't want to go on without Carleen, but officially it was ruled an accident to avoid embarrassment to the family.'' She bit her lip to keep her emotions in check. "Before he did that—committed suicide, I mean—he made his will leaving an allowance for upkeep of the twins, but he named his cousin their guardian.''

Barton raised a dark eyebrow. "That I didn't know. I always assumed your parents were the guardians since Sandford was in India.''

"He didn't even come home for the funeral,'' Kate said bitterly, "and we haven't heard a word from him in the years since Carleen and William died, except a note asking us to take care of the twins and keep an account of our expenses. He said he realized William had left some money to take care of the girls, and we'd have an accounting and settlement when he came to London.''

"And now he's here.''

In spite of her best efforts, Kate started to cry. "Yes, he's back and he wants the twins. He wants to take them away.'' She mopped ineffectually at her eyes with the back of her hand. "That's why I need a husband, Barton. Or rather, need to say I'm going to have a husband.''

He pulled his handkerchief from his pocket and wiped her

eyes, then gave her the handkerchief. "I don't see that you can do anything, Kate. A husband certainly won't help you."

She plucked at his sleeve. "Yes, yes, it will, Barton. I'm not telling this very well." She paused and swallowed hard. "Sandford says he's going back to India and taking the twins with him. He said the reason is that I take care of them by myself. He knows Papa and Mama are in Germany most of the time on government business, and he says the twins aren't getting the proper upbringing because they don't have a father in the house."

Barton frowned. "That won't wash. If they're with him, they won't have a mother in the house. I don't recall Sandford being married."

"He isn't, but he told Robbie that he had made most of his fortune and that it was time for him to look around and select a suitable bride. If the twins were with him, they'd have both a mother and a father. That's why I need to produce someone to marry and do it in a hurry, Barton. Robbie, the goose, invited Sandford and whoever it is he's considering as his bride to Falwell Hall for Christmas. Robbie's planning to be there and his idea was to show Sandford what a wonderful family atmosphere we have for the twins."

Barton smiled, the dimple dancing on his cheek. "Wonderful family atmosphere aside, you want a husband for insurance."

"Exactly." She put her hand on his. "If I had someone there and said we were engaged to marry, then Sandford couldn't say a thing. I need to show him the twins have parents, but Mama and Papa won't be home for Christmas, so they can't be parents for the twins then, and Robbie's not married."

"And even if he were, Sandford might not like to think of Robbie as a parent for the girls." He laughed again. "Not that Robbie isn't a fine person, of course."

Kate sighed. "Of course. I know what you're saying and

I agree. Sandford could hardly think that a dasher and a gamester like Robbie would provide guidance for the girls.''

"You're too harsh on the boy. After all, he's just enjoying London life a little. We all do.''

It was Kate's turn to raise an eyebrow. "Boy? Whatever are you calling him, Barton? Robbie's thirty.''

"But a young thirty.'' The corners of his mouth quivered, then he became serious. "I don't know, Kate. I'm really not interested in posing as anyone's husband-to-be. For the past year, everyone in London has heard me swear off women forever. I don't think it would work. If Sandford's talked to anyone at all, he'll see right through it.''

"No one will know, Barton. I swear it.'' Kate could see her careful plan crumbling. "We'll be at Falwell Hall. I'll introduce you to Sandford as my intended, and as soon as he leaves, we'll go our separate ways. No one will ever know.''

Barton ran his fingers through his carefully barbered hair. "Kate, we've been close friends for a long time. I . . . I wish I could help you. You don't know how much.''

She looked at him steadily, but her voice was shaky. "You won't do it, then?''

There was a long pause as he got up and paced around the room. He stopped by the fireplace and looked at her. "It isn't that at all. I didn't say I wouldn't, Kate.''

"You didn't say you would, either, Barton.'' She sensed a chink in his hesitation and hurried on with reasons. "There shouldn't be any problem with it, I promise. No one will know anything about our plan except Robbie, and he certainly won't say anything. He loves the twins as much as I do.''

He sighed and sat back down beside her. "I know that.'' He paused a minute. "As I told you, I almost got married last year. At any rate, I proposed to . . . to a young lady. Did you know that?''

Kate shook her head. "No, I didn't know about it then.''

The corner of his mouth quivered, but his voice was cynical. "I flatter myself in thinking it was such an on-dit."

"I was in the country," Kate blurted out. "I didn't hear a thing."

"However, I take it that you've heard since then?" Barton's smile was twisted.

"Just today." Kate wished she could avoid the truth, but she had never been one to tell a lie. Robbie could do it with ease, as could Sophie, but Kate had never been able to lie. Every time she tried it, even if it was just a tiny white lie, she always looked, as Papa said, as if she had just killed someone's sheep.

"To be blunt, Kate, I made a fool of myself in front of all of London."

She risked a soft smile at him. "I don't know any of the particulars, Barton, and I don't need to know them. Since you hesitate, I won't press you about this. We're friends, we always have been, and that's all I need to know." She sat forward and put her hands over her eyes. "If you can't pose as my fiancé, do you know anyone who would? I could pay someone if I had to, but not much. Papa left some money before he and Mama went abroad."

"Good God!" Barton reached out and pulled her hands from her face, holding both of them. "I had no idea you'd go to such lengths, Kate. Surely the situation can't be that desperate."

"It is. Sandford's going to take them away. I know he is. Robbie thought if we had him at Falwell Hall for a while that he'd see how happy the twins are, but I know that won't be the case. He'll take them away." She paused. "Please, Barton. I said I wouldn't press you, and I won't, but please think about it. You're my only hope. I know this sounds like some crack-brained scheme, but if Sandford takes the twins, I don't know what . . . I don't know how I can . . ." She stopped, fighting back tears. "Please."

He turned her hands over to look at them, the red and

green spots from the paper dotting her palms. "All right, Kate. I'll do it." He spoke quietly.

"Barton! Oh, Barton!" She hugged him fiercely around the neck. "Thank you, thank you! I'll do anything you ever want me to do, Barton. During my whole life, all you'll ever have to do is tell me what you want and I'll do it. I promise."

He removed her arms from around his neck. "I'll remember that, Kate," he said with a grin. He stood and moved away from her, then smiled as he spoke, his dimple deep. "I have a terrible feeling that I'm going to regret this. With my luck, it'll probably be in the newspapers tomorrow." He straightened his coat and looked down at her. "When are we supposed to leave for Falwell Hall?"

She smiled at him. "Tomorrow. But if you can't go then, that'll be all right. Robbie, the twins, and I are going tomorrow. Sophie—that's Sophie Page, you remember her—is going to try to join us."

"And the villain in this whole charade? When does he arrive?"

"On Monday. And he's leaving to return to London the day after Christmas. That gives us a little more than two weeks."

Barton ran his fingers through his hair. "I have some loose ends to tie up in the city. I don't think I can get there until after Monday. I'll do whatever I can to get there earlier, but I'm not sure when I can arrive. Will that be all right?"

Kate stood beside him feeling a rush of gratitude. "Any time would be wonderful." She paused, struck by a thought. "You didn't have other plans for Christmas, did you? I wouldn't want to interfere."

He gave a short, harsh laugh. "Really, Kate, you know my family better than that. What do we ever have in common except a last name? I haven't seen or spoken to any of them in months."

There was no way to mend this. Kate could have bitten off her tongue, but the words were out. Instead, she smiled broadly at him. "I remember as children that you always wanted to stay with us at Christmas, Barton. Now we can make this one Christmas you'll always remember."

He grinned at her and reached inside his pocket for his cigars. "That's exactly what I'm afraid of. I'll do my best, you know, but I think I have to agree with Robbie this time." He paused at the door. "A little more than two weeks . . . almost three weeks. Kate, it'll never work. Take my word for it. It'll never work."

Chapter 2

That evening, Kate was surprised in the middle of her packing by a visit from Robbie. She and her brother were close, even though he had lived in his own lodgings for several years. In their parents' absence, he considered himself responsible for Kate and the twins and stopped by often to check on their well-being.

"Have you heard from the parents?" he asked as he gave his caped greatcoat to Waters.

"A letter last week and a box of gifts for everybody that I'm supposed to take to Falwell Hall."

"That's all?"

Kate nodded. "You know Mama and Papa. They love Germany, especially at Christmastime." She paused. "I did think they'd try to get back home for Christmas this year. The twins would love to see them."

"Do they know about Sandford?"

Kate walked in front of him to the drawing room and rang for some tea. "I wrote them, but I don't suppose they've had time to get my letter. They'll probably come straight home when they hear. In spite of all their traveling, they dearly love the twins and wouldn't want Sandford to take them, I know."

"Nobody wants that," Robbie said, tossing his arm around his sister's shoulder and giving her a hug.

"Except Sandford," she said glumly.

They paused as the tea tray was brought in. There was nothing on it except cups, milk, sugar, and tea. "Something to eat would be nice," Robbie said plaintively as he sat down. "I haven't had anything since morning."

"I see I'm to take care of you again," Kate said, laughing. "Very well, brother. Since I know exactly what you want, I'll go fix you a tray with my own hands."

Robbie grinned as he grabbed one of her hands. "Red and green splotches and all. You're a good sister, Kate."

Kate waved him away and, with a grin, went to the kitchen to see what was there. She brought back a tray heaped with cold meats, cheese, bread, fruit, and pastries and a bottle of wine. "I see your appetite is still up to snuff," she said with a laugh as he helped himself. She handed him a cup of tea as they heard the knocker. In just a moment, Waters was at the door, announcing Barton Rush.

Kate ran over to greet him, holding out both hands. "Barton, is anything wrong? You haven't changed your mind, have you? Robbie's here right now and we can talk about it."

He laughed and tucked her hand under his arm as they walked to the drawing room. "No, I promised and I'll see it through. I just wanted to talk." They walked into the room and Robbie waved a cold chicken leg in their direction.

"Barton, come in and join us. Have you had anything to eat?"

"No, but I don't really want anything. I've got to go to Wrexham's for a midnight supper."

"Better have something." Robbie offered him some cheese. "Have you ever been to Wrexham's? I have, and I can tell you that you'd be wise to eat before you go. The man's such a clutchfist that he won't give you enough to last until breakfast." Robbie finished his chicken leg and started peeling an apple.

Barton looked at Robbie in wonder. "How does he do it?" Barton asked. "Since I can remember, he's eaten everything

24

in sight. Your parents probably stay abroad in self-defense. They'd never get anything to eat if they stayed here.''

Kate laughed. ''I think you may be right. And still, look at him. He's not much bigger than a flagpole.'' It was true. Robbie was famous for eating prodigious amounts but never gaining weight. If anything, his tall, thin frame seemed to grow leaner and more wiry with every passing year.

Barton sat down, accepting some cheese, an apple, and a cup of tea. Then he looked at Kate. ''Have you told Robbie about our conversation?''

She shook her head. ''No, he hasn't been here long.'' She grinned. ''It's taken that whole time for me to make sure that he's been supplied with enough food to see him through until midnight.''

''Listen to her, will you?'' Robbie bit into a tart. ''What conversation?'' he asked in alarm. He put down the half-eaten pastry and looked at them. ''You didn't! Lord, Barton, you actually promised her you'd do it? When she told me she was going to ask, I told her you'd never do it.'' He looked at Kate in admiration. ''How on earth did you do it? I can't believe it!''

''Weakness on my part,'' Barton said with a sigh. ''And a few tears on Kate's.''

''You always did have a soft spot for Kate when she cried,'' Robbie said, waving his knife. ''I remember that she made good use of that on occasion. She could call up the tears on command.''

Barton looked sideways at her in surprise. ''Is that true?''

''Of course not. Robbie, how could you say such a thing? I never cry.''

''Except when necessary,'' Robbie said with a laugh. He ducked as Kate tossed a grape toward him, catching it and popping it in his mouth.

''Barton has agreed to help us,'' she told him, ''even though he doesn't think it will work. I told him it would. All we have to do is make sure we all say and do the same thing. We *must* show Sandford that the twins have a good home.''

"Easier said than done.'' Robbie spoke around bites.

"That's what I thought.'' Barton leaned back against the sofa and reached for his cigars, offering one to Robbie. Kate poured each of them a glass of wine and they lit their cigars, both of them thoroughly comfortable. "Now,'' Barton said, "let us talk. Since I'm going to have to play the part of affectionate suitor, I thought I should stop by and discuss exactly how this should be done. And I brought this.'' He pulled a small jeweler's box from his pocket and opened it. "Only sightly used,'' he said ruefully, taking a ring out. It was a beautiful square sapphire, a deep, rich blue, surrounded by diamonds. "See if this fits, and if it doesn't, I'll have it fixed.'' He tried, but Barton couldn't keep the bitter edge from his voice.

Kate tried to lighten the moment. "Wouldn't you, as the affectionate suitor, like to put it on my finger?'' She smiled and lifted her finely arched brow in question.

Barton grinned. "You want the whole thing, don't you? The next thing I know, you'll be wanting me to get down on one knee and declare my innermost feelings for you.''

"I did that once,'' Robbie said, "and felt like a damn fool. Lucky for me, I managed to stop myself before I actually offered for the chit. I don't know what came over me. Too much whiskey and too much moonlight, I think.''

Barton reddened slightly and there was an awkward pause. "It's a lovely ring, Barton.'' Kate reached out to take the ring and put it on.

Instead, he took her hand in his and slipped the ring on her finger. It was just a little snug going over her knuckle but fit perfectly once it was on. "There. If you don't mind wearing it, I thought you'd better have an engagement ring. I wouldn't want Sandford thinking I couldn't get you a ring. If he gets there before I do and you tell him you're engaged, that's probably the first thing he'll look for.''

"He'll think Kate's snagged a prime 'un," Robbie said. Kate threw a pillow at him.

Before Barton left, they had concocted a story. Since Barton and Kate had known each other for ages, it would be easy to make references to their past. Their story would be that they had been friends for years, and only recently this friendship had blossomed into something more substantial. They decided that they would tell Sandford they planned a very quiet summer wedding, and that Barton wanted to adopt the twins if Sandford would agree. Then, as soon as Sandford left to return to India, they would quietly drop the whole thing and no one would ever know anything about it. Finally, Barton rose to leave.

"Both of us are indebted," Robbie said. "I know the twins probably mean more to Kate than they do to me, but I like having the little hellions around." He smiled a sad smile. "Besides, they're all we have left of Carleen."

"We all miss Carleen." Barton smiled back. "I've thought about it for years, and I finally decided that the reason you, Carleen, and Kate were so close was because your parents were away all the time. You had to rely on each other." He paused as though to say something else, but stopped and merely said good night.

As the door closed behind Barton, Robbie gazed at his sister in admiration. "I apologize, Kate. Granted, I still think it's a crack-brained scheme, but I do believe it might just work. I had my doubts, but Barton's the very one to carry it off." He stirred up the fire with the poker, then sat back down and lit another cigar, making himself comfortable. Robbie gave his sister a piercing look. "He doesn't know about you and Sandford, does he?"

Kate blushed. "No, and neither does anyone else except you. Not even Mama or Sophie. And I don't ever expect anyone to know about it." She pinned him with a look. "Besides, there's really nothing to know except that I made a complete fool out of myself."

27

"I wouldn't go that far," he said mildly. "Still, it won't bother you to have Sandford around, will it?"

Kate met his eyes levelly. "I'm sure Sandford doesn't even remember me, Robbie. I was a temporary dalliance while he was visiting. He may even have thought a mild flirtation was the way to make himself agreeable to the little sister of his cousin's future wife." She frowned. "That's all it was—a mild flirtation, a passing fancy. I'm sure he forgot all about it, and I assure you that I have as well." She averted her eyes and looked into the fire.

Robbie gave her a quick glance but said no more. He smoked his cigar in the quiet, then got up to leave. He gave Kate a quick kiss at the door. "I was going to wait a day or two before going to Falwell Hall, but since Barton isn't coming down for a while, I'll go with you tomorrow." He grinned. "You know what a sacrifice that will be on my part."

"You can ride outside the carriage," Kate said with a giggle. "The last time you rode with us, I recall, one of the twins cast up her accounts all over your new waistcoat."

"Waistcoat, new watch, and two fobs." He laughed. "I'll ride alongside. That way I can escape if I need to."

After he left, Kate went back to the dying fire and sat down. The sapphire on her finger caught the firelight and gleamed. The ring felt heavy, and Kate imagined for a moment that it was really hers. Robbie's question had brought up thoughts she had long ago suppressed. They had been in the back of her mind, nagging, since she had first heard from Sandford, but she had denied them. Now the memories were back in detail.

She closed her eyes and remembered the time she had first met the man who was now the third Baron Sandford. He was then only William's younger cousin, Hale Trelawney. Kate had found him fascinating. She had been seventeen then—a very naive seventeen—and he had been years older, almost five and twenty, he had told her, and had already been to India once. He had flirted with her and she had fallen in love with him with all the fervor of a seventeen-year-old. Looking back, she could see that a mild flirtation was probably only a way for him to pass the time while he stayed at Falwell Hall for the wedding; the only other girls there were Carleen, his small cousins, and a sister.

Her cheeks flushed red as she remembered the rest. He was to leave the day after the wedding, and that late night Kate had seen him walking in the garden alone. Full of romantic notions, she had gone down to talk to him. Between the moonlight and the wedding and the flowers, she had embarrassed herself beyond any imagining. Kate had practically thrown herself on him and told him she loved him. He had smiled and talked to her, telling her he was a man while she was still not grown. He had called her a "dear little child." Kate still cringed at that memory. Worse, he had told her that he planned marriage someday and had hinted that he planned to wed a wealthy woman. Quite obviously, that was not Kate.

She had fled in tears. Besides Trelawney, no one else would ever have known had she not run into Robbie at the top of the steps. She was crying and didn't see him. He demanded to know what had happened, jumping to conclusions and threatening to call the scoundrel out. Kate had had to confess her folly. She didn't know which was the most humiliating: declaring herself to Trelawney or having to confess it to Robbie.

Her brother understood. He had sent Kate to bed, advising her to forget it because Trelawney was going to India and she'd never see him again. Robbie had been halfway right. Hale Trelawney was gone from Falwell Hall before she got out of bed the next day. And she had never seen him again— until now. Robbie had kept his promise and had never mentioned her humiliation again until tonight.

Was her scheme more than just a ploy to save the twins? she wondered. Did she want to flaunt Barton just to show Sandford that she had forgotten him? Those were questions

Kate didn't want to face, especially not tonight. With a sigh, she made sure the fire screen was in place and went upstairs to finish her packing.

The trip to Falwell Hall was uneventful. Kate got several inquisitive looks from the staff about her ring, while Riggs made several references to it. Since Kate didn't want anything said in London, she decided to wait until they were at Falwell Hall before she explained the ring. Servants' gossip always spread like wildfire through London. Thinking of her promise to Barton that no one would ever know, she realized this would be almost impossible to keep. Riggs would know, the servants at the Hall would know. The twins would know.

Maybe, she thought with a sigh, as the carriage rattled along the frozen road, just maybe Barton had been right. Looking at the scheme in the cold daylight, it seemed as if it wasn't going to work. She wrapped a fur robe around the twins and settled them down, trying to get them to sleep for at least a few miles of the journey. It took a little while, but as soon as they were asleep, looking like angels, Kate thought again of the difficulties they faced. It wouldn't work and Sandford would want to take the twins away. She and Robbie could always take the twins and run to Germany, where Papa would do something. She'd tell Barton when he came to Falwell Hall. It wasn't fair to put him through this. Maybe she could invent a fiancé in Canada, someone in fur trapping who appeared only once a year. Kate sighed. Sandford would believe that for all of five minutes.

"Why so glum, little sister?" Robbie asked, riding up beside the carriage. "This is your favorite season and your favorite weather."

Kate tried to smile, but it was a chore. True, Christmas was her favorite season. Papa and Mama loved the German Christmases, having taken Carleen, Kate, and Robbie to Germany for Christmas when they were young. They had brought so many German customs back to Falwell Hall that their celebrations were the best of both the German and the English

Christmases. It seemed as if every year they added something new, and every year each new tradition made Christmas better and better. They had adopted the German custom of giving presents, along with the wonderful custom of having a tree covered with decorations and candles. When Papa came from Germany last year, he had brought them dozens of little candleholders for their tree. This year they were going to have the best tree ever, and Kate had boxes and boxes of presents to give the family and the staff. She should be excited beyond measure, but she wasn't.

Falwell Hall was ablaze with candles when they arrived. It was clear and crisp outside, with just a flake or two of snow blowing around and the ground just whitened. Inside, everything was cheerful. The housekeeper, Mrs. Wallace, had done as Kate had instructed: The house was empty of Christmas decorations. Kate had wanted the twins to be able to participate in the decorating since they enjoyed it so much. Too, there was the very real possibility that this might be their last Christmas at Falwell Hall.

"We're home! It's Christmas!" Mary and Megan shrieked together as they ran to the tree. "Look at all the candles! When can we decorate, Kate? Have we got a big tree?"

"Tomorrow, I promise," Kate said, holding them in a bear hug. "We'll start on it all tomorrow. And we'll have a huge tree, too!"

"Presents, too?"

Kate nodded as Robbie came in, shaking a few flakes of snow from his hat and coat. "Kate, when I invited Sandford down, I wasn't sure when we'd arrive, and . . . well, I really wasn't sure about the date. I know I told you he'd be here in a few days, but . . ."

"What are you saying, Robbie?" She quieted the twins.

"You're not going to have much time to get ready. I just talked to Wallace. Have you talked to Mrs. Wallace?"

Kate shook her head and grabbed for a twin, who was waving the poker dangerously close to Papa's Chinese vases.

"No, other than to compliment her on how well the house looked. She's gone off to see about supper. What's this about Sandford?"

Robbie squirmed. "I thought I'd asked him down for a few days from now, but he sent word to Wallace that he and his party will be here before eight." He pulled his watch from his pocket and glanced at it. "That's about an hour."

Kate felt her jaw drop and the poker fell to the floor, right on Robbie's foot. He yelped, but she didn't seem to notice. "An hour! Robbie, are you sure? The twins need to be bathed and fed, the house needs one last polishing, I need . . ." She shooed the twins out with Nurse Freeman. "He can't come now. I'm not ready."

Robbie picked up the poker, replaced it, and limped to the sofa. "Too bad. He'll be here in an hour and, according to Wallace, so will his guest—no offense, but I assume this is the horse whose teeth he's checking—and her mother, along with assorted maids." Robbie leaned back and smiled at her.

"Horse?" Kate glared at him. "Robbie, that's a terrible thing to say. I'm sure he plans to marry the lady or he wouldn't be spending Christmas with her. And her mother."

Robbie shrugged. "Who knows? At any rate, he's bringing someone here." He paused and looked at Kate. "Perhaps this short notice is the best way. You won't have time to dread it." He laughed as she gave him an evil look and went to find Mrs. Wallace, to see if there would be enough places set for supper.

Mrs. Wallace, in her usual efficient way, had already made arrangements. "Wallace told me to expect them," she said, going over the arrangements with Kate. "Will that be all?" She caught a glimpse of the sapphire on Kate's finger and her eyes widened. Kate took a deep breath. This would be the first hurdle.

"My . . . my fiancé will be joining us for Christmas," she said stiffly, her voice trailing off at the end. "I believe Miss

Sophie Page will be here as well. Please put her next to my room.''

Mrs. Wallace looked at her in complete shock. "Your fiancé? Miss Page and''—there was a pause—''your *fiancé?*''

Kate finally found her voice. "Yes, Mrs. Wallace. My fiancé. You remember Barton Rush, of course. Please put him in the room next to my brother's. He will, of course, have his man with him, so please arrange for that as well.'' She tried to look at Mrs. Wallace, but the woman's eyes were the size of teacups. Kate looked at the floor instead. "Thank you for taking care of everything, Mrs. Wallace, and I'm sure you'll do your usual efficient job. I'll be upstairs changing, so please inform me when the guests arrive.''

"Mr. Rush and Miss Page—they'll be here this evening as well?'' Mrs. Wallace's voice was full of curiosity. Wearily, Kate realized that she wouldn't have to say anything else to anyone. In less than five minutes, word would be all over the house that Kate was engaged to her old friend Barton.

"Miss Page will be here later; Mr. Rush wasn't sure. He'll probably arrive after Monday.'' Kate realized she was sounding abrupt but couldn't seem to help it. All she wanted to do was run somewhere and try to compose herself. Saying the word *fiancé* had been more difficult than she had thought it would be, and as she had feared, she had been unable to look Mrs. Wallace in the eye as she had told the tale. How on earth had she ever imagined she could carry it off with Sandford? She rushed up the stairs and closed her chamber door behind her, sagging against it. "Why can't I just lie the same way everyone else does?'' she asked aloud. "Just one simple lie? I'll never manage to do it.''

The clock struck and she realized she didn't have time to worry about it. Quickly, she rang for Riggs and explained the situation.

Riggs outdid herself. She dressed Kate in green and threaded gold, with green ribbons through her mass of auburn hair. Wisps of curls escaped here and there, but overall the effect was charming. Kate always had trouble keeping her hair in place and had finally settled on a style that would accommodate her wayward locks. It was as though her burnished curls had a will of their own. But much as she wanted to make sure she looked her best, she didn't take the time to check her appearance. It was more important to see that the twins looked perfect for their first appearance in front of Sandford. They simply had to make a good impression.

Nurse Freeman had the twins dressed in white and they looked beautiful. They were spotless and their curls, so like William's dark hair rather than Carleen's auburn, shone in the lamplight. Nurse had put white and red ribbons in their hair and they looked like Christmas angels. Kate had only a moment to give them a quick kiss and hug before Mrs. Wallace came to get her and tell her that Sandford's carriage had arrived. "Tell us a Christmas story," Mary said, holding on to Kate's fingers.

"I want to hear a story, too." Megan grabbed her other hand. "How the animals talk. That's a good story."

"Later." Kate firmly removed their hands from hers. "I promise I'll come back later and tell you a Christmas story about how the animals talk. Right now, I just want you to sit still until your uncle gets here. Behave yourselves."

"We will," they said together, returning to their toys.

Kate gave them one more glance, then hurried down the stairs to where Sandford and his party were just coming in the door. She recognized him instantly. If anything, the intervening years had made him more handsome than ever. He looked up and saw her approaching. "Miss Caldwell—Kate—how delightful to see you." He held out a hand to help her down the last step. She started to reply as he held her hand and glanced down at the sapphire on it. There was a question in his eyes that she ignored.

"It's good to have you with us," she said, wondering just how much to say to him. Where was Robbie when she needed him?

Sandford smiled at her and then turned his attention to the two women just coming in the door. He held out a hand to one of them and she came toward them, her hood falling back. She was one of the most beautiful women Kate had ever seen and she recognized her at once. To Kate's horror, she was looking right into wide blue eyes the color of sapphires . . . eyes that had made every male in London fall to his knees.

Sandford took the lovely's arm possessively and turned to Kate. "Kate, I'd like to introduce a very dear friend of mine, Miss Amalie Armitage."

Kate felt her heart stop and crash.

Chapter 3

Robbie swept in from behind her just as Sandford made the introductions. "Miss Armitage," he said gallantly, bending his tall, lanky frame over the lovely's hand and kissing it. "I can't tell you what a pleasure it is to have you with us for Christmas. Surely we don't need presents since we have you."

Kate stared at Robbie. This was why he was such a popular figure around London. He'd be welcome anywhere if he managed to flatter all the ladies in such a manner. He was almost as effusive in his welcome to Mrs. Armitage. He gave Kate a nudge with his elbow as he stood back up. "Sandford," he said, putting his arm on Kate's and drawing her up beside him, "it's good to see you again."

"Yes." Sandford regarded them from blue eyes that Kate had once thought were the most beautiful blue she had ever seen. Now they were merely a clear, pale blue and it seemed to Kate that they held a hint of ice.

Kate found her speech and welcomed Miss Armitage and her mother, then greeted Sandford. She forced herself to look right into his pale eyes and smile. She saw nothing there—no recognition, no embarrassment. Perhaps, she thought bitterly as she turned to lead them up to their rooms, all the recognition and embarrassment was in her eyes.

Sandford was assigned the room next to Barton's, while

Miss Armitage and her mother were in the rooms across the hall. Kate regretted putting Miss Armitage where she did, but there seemed to be no help for it now, the only other presentable room being Sophie's. There would be an empty room, anyway, as Barton would never stay at Falwell Hall with Miss Armitage here.

Sandford turned at the door to his room and looked at Kate. This time she was sure there was ice in his gaze. "How are the children?"

"Fine." She was pleased that she managed to answer him with a steady voice. "Would you like to see them?"

He glanced down at his clothes. "As soon as I change. Would that be possible?"

"They'll be ready."

As soon as his door was closed, Kate sped to the nursery. Nurse Freeman was sitting in a rocking chair in front of the fire while the twins, still immaculate, were playing quietly with some animal figures. "We're making the animals talk," Megan said, pretending to move a cow into some shredded paper. "This is hay."

"Good." Kate knelt down beside them. "I'm going to introduce you to your guardian later. I want both of you to be on your best behavior. Is that understood?"

Both twins nodded, then returned to their play, Mary making what she thought was a donkey noise as she moved her figure. "No, silly," Megan said. "The animals say real words at Christmas, don't they, Kate?"

"Yes, animals talk at Christmastime," she answered absently. "Now remember, you're on your best behavior when you meet Sandford."

"Don't you worry about a thing," Nurse Freeman said, sipping her tea and propping her feet on a footstool in front of the fire. "I'll watch after them."

Kate left, still worried. So many things could happen. One catastrophe had already happened: Amalie Armitage. Kate told herself that the first thing she had to do was write Barton

37

and tell him that Miss Armitage was here and was with Sandford. Barton wouldn't come if he knew, but she had to inform him in time to save himself the embarrassment. She went to see Robbie.

"You're right; you've got to let him know," Robbie said. "I realize you were in the country when the—what shall I call it—the contretemps happened between Barton and Miss Armitage, but I was in London. It was quite the talk for days, and I have to credit Barton for staying there and holding up his head as though nothing had happened. Still, I don't think he'd want to be here."

"Sophie told me that he . . . he . . ." She groped for words.

"He made a cake of himself in front of half the ton," Robbie said with a sigh. "Hell, it could have been me. It could have been any man in London. The Armitage chit led him on, led him to believe an offer would be accepted, and then publicly embarrassed him. The worst part of it all, I believe, was that he truly cared for her."

"Does he still?" Kate asked dully. She could only imagine the pain such a rebuff would cause a proud man like Barton Rush.

Robbie looked at her strangely. "I don't know. I'm really not a confidant of Barton's. Just speaking as a man and using my own feelings as a gauge, I'd say he probably does."

"Then I have to write him and tell him. That means he won't come here, and I'll have to concoct some new story for Sandford." She glanced down at the large sapphire ring on her finger. "Oh, good God, Robbie! I've already told Mrs. Wallace and Riggs."

Robbie frowned and poured himself a drink. "That can be scotched, I think. Tell both of them that it's a secret."

Kate sat down on the sofa, thoughtful. "I told Mrs. Wallace to ready a room for Barton—the one next to yours. We could say that Barton had some family matter which kept him from coming. Everyone knows Barton's family doesn't get along, so that would be reasonable. We could tell Mrs. Wallace that it's to be kept quiet, and I don't think she'd say anything. I know Riggs will keep her silence.'' She walked over to the desk. ''The sooner I write, the better, I suppose.'' She gave Robbie a wistful look. ''It almost worked, didn't it?''

''We can still manage to convince Sandford not to take the twins, don't you worry.'' Robbie sat and watched her write, the fire casting golden glints in her hair and reflecting like a prism from the diamonds surrounding the sapphire.

''There,'' she said, standing and sealing the note as she frowned. ''Robbie, I hope you're right about Sandford, but I don't feel overconfident. I'm going to be ready to take the twins and Nurse Freeman and run to Germany if I have to.''

''That wouldn't work, Kate. If Sandford really wanted to, he could come after you and take the twins. The law is on his side, you know.''

''I don't want to hear about it.'' Kate got up and went to find Wallace, so he could send a footman with the message first thing in the morning. Barton would know in plenty of time.

Sandford was coming down the stairs as she turned around. He looked rather as William had—dark hair, blue eyes, tall and well-built. But whereas William had been pale, Sandford was bronzed dark by the sun, and whereas William had been kind to a fault, Sandford had a rakish, devil-may-care attitude about him. If there was kindness, it was hidden. He had been fine looking years ago, but now he was more than that: He was the most handsome man Kate had ever seen. No wonder Miss Armitage, who could have her pick of any man in London, had set her sights on Sandford. As if that weren't enough, rumor around London was, according to Robbie, that the man had made a fortune in India before he inherited the title. It seemed as if everything he touched turned to gold, although as Robbie had quoted, ''the story is that he watches every penny.''

Sandford smiled at her, a trifle awkwardly, and Kate realized that he remembered her earlier humiliation in every detail. She couldn't look him in the eyes. "Do you want to see the twins now?" she asked, starting to go up the steps past him.

He touched her arm briefly as she went by him and she stopped. "Kate—it is all right if I call you Kate? We are cousins in a way, and as I recall, at one time in the past we were friends."

She wanted to tell him no, because she needed distance between them, but Kate found herself looking right into his eyes. "Yes, of course. That is, feel free to call me Kate."

He smiled at her, a rather satisfied smile. "And we're still friends?"

Kate turned her head and looked at the top of the stairs. "Of course. Is there a reason we wouldn't be?" She forced herself to look at him and smile. She knew he was going to say something else and she wasn't ready for a discussion with him, so she moved away quickly and ran up the stairs to the nursery. "I'll bring the children right down," she called back over her shoulder.

In the nursery, Nurse Freeman was still sitting in her rocker, her feet propped on her footstool, but now she was sound asleep and the twins were nowhere to be seen. Kate shook Nurse until she woke up. "Bless me, child, what's the matter?" Nurse Freeman glanced around, still groggy.

"The twins? Where are Megan and Mary?"

They looked all about, but the pair were not to be found. Finally, Kate noticed that their scarves, coats, and mittens were gone as well. "They must have gone outside," she said, grabbing Nurse Freeman's cloak from behind the door and throwing it over her shoulders.

"Impossible." Nurse Freeman was firm. "They'd never go out after dark. They know better."

Kate paid no attention to her protests. "Go down right now, get my brother, and tell him to come up here. On no

40

account let Sandford see you." She took Nurse Freeman's arm and walked with her to the stairs. "Hurry. Sandford wants to see the girls."

Nurse Freeman's eyes widened and she started down the stairs, then stopped and dashed back up, rounding the corner so fast that she almost ran into Kate. "He's standing down there," she gasped, "looking right up the stairs. That man, I mean. Sandford."

"Then go down . . . no, I'll do it. I'll go down the back stairs and get Robbie. You go down and tell Sandford that one of the girls did something—tore her dress or lost a shoe or something."

"Oh? Which one was it?" Nurse Freeman frowned. "I didn't know one of them had done that. I'd wager it was that Megan. I can't keep her dresses mended."

Kate took a deep breath. "Nurse Freeman, nothing happened. You're just going to tell Sandford that to give me some time to find the twins."

"You mean I'm going to tell a *lie?*" Nurse Freeman was horrified.

"Just a small one," Kate said, giving her a small nudge toward the stairs. "Tell Sandford that and then come back upstairs. Don't talk to him." She knew Nurse well enough to realize that Sandford could have the entire family history out of the woman with two or three well-placed questions. Perhaps even one question would do it.

As soon as Nurse began her wobbly way down the stairs, Kate dashed across the hall and ran down the back steps. She hurried through the kitchen and across the back hall the servants usually used, almost knocking down Mrs. Wallace and a maid. She didn't stop for explanations, but dashed right into the drawing room where Robbie sat, smoking his cigar. "They've disappeared!" she gasped as she closed the door behind her and propped herself up against it. "Sandford wants to see them and I can't find them anywhere. Their coats and mittens are gone!"

41

Robbie leaped to his feet and tossed his cigar into the fireplace. "I'll help you look."

Kate grabbed his arm. "No, you entertain Sandford. He's out in the hall with Nurse Freeman right now."

"Nurse Freeman?" There was horror in Robbie's voice. "Good God! There's no telling what she might say! I'll get him and keep him in here. Bring the twins in as soon as you find them."

Robbie and Kate dashed out the door together, Robbie heading for the hall and Kate running around to go out the back door. Along the way, she dragooned Wallace, two footmen, and a maid to help her search. "Be as quiet as you can," she told them as they fanned out across the yard. "I don't want to alert Sandford." She surveyed the empty yard. "Remember to look carefully. Those two could be anywhere," she added.

"Megan! Mary!" Kate tried to keep her voice low as she called. The snow was picking up and she had no idea which way to go. Finally, Wallace called to her and pointed to two sets of tracks just barely visible on the whitened ground. "The pond? Oh, good heavens, Wallace, you don't think they've gone to the pond, do you? We've got to hurry." Kate tried to run, but the slick soles of her shoes caused her to slip on the flagstones of the path. She landed on her derriere with a thud. The pain was intense, but she couldn't take time to assess the damage as Wallace helped her up. She tried to hurry toward the pond, limping and hanging on to the bushes.

"This way," Wallace said, taking her arm. "They've veered off here and headed for the stables."

The stables were dark in the snowy night. The tracks led right into the door, but Kate couldn't see a thing inside. Wallace held up the lantern and the light first glinted off their eyes. Both of them were huddled in a corner of a stall, burrowed in some hay.

"We were listening hard," Mary said, blinking.

"And they didn't do it," Megan announced, standing up.

42

"No, you said they would and they didn't. We listened."
Mary stood and marched over in front of Kate and Wallace.
"We were quiet and everything."

"They didn't do what? Who didn't?" Kate tried to bend
down to get to their eye level, but her hip was already sore.
Instead, she bent at the knees. "What are you talking about?"
She gasped as Wallace moved the lantern so she could see
better. "Look at you two! You're both filthy!"

The twins ignored this. "The animals didn't talk, Kate.
You said they always did at Christmastime and we came to
listen. Well, it's Christmastime and they didn't say a thing."

Kate gritted her teeth to keep from yelling at them. "It
isn't Christmas yet, that's why."

Mary considered this. "Do you mean we have to wait until
the very day?"

"Yes, you have to wait."

"Until the very day?"

"Christmas Eve!" Kate shrieked, her control snapping.
"You have to wait until Christmas Eve!" She got back on
her feet and grabbed a twin in each hand. "Let's get back to
the house and clean you two up. I told you not to get dirty."

"We didn't," Megan said, looking down at her dress and
shoes. "It's just hay and some other muck."

"That's manure," Kate said wearily, "and it's all over your
shoes and the bottoms of your dresses." Both girls seemed
to have stepped into horse droppings and the fragrance was
overpowering. They all hurried into the kitchen, where Kate,
Mrs. Wallace, and the maids stripped the girls and washed
them off while Nurse Freeman brought down clean dresses
and shoes. Even working as fast as possible, Kate reckoned
it had been above half an hour since she had promised Sandford she'd bring the girls to him. She fervently hoped Robbie
had been able to concoct some sort of plausible story.

Herding the girls in front of her, she almost ran all the way
to the drawing room. Sandford and Robbie were there, sitting
in front of the fire, smoking. Kate lined the girls up for in-

43

spection, and as she held her breath, they curtsied politely. Sandford looked at them and nodded. "And which one is which?" he asked.

"Mary," said Megan.

"Megan," said Mary.

"Very good." Sandford nodded sedately, as though he were speaking to adults. "Have you started your lessons yet?"

Lessons? Kate panicked. She should have thought of lessons before. She had taught the girls a little French and some notes on the piano, but they hadn't had any formal lessons.

"Oh, yes," said Mary.

"But I haven't," Megan added.

Sandford raised an eyebrow and looked at Kate. She knew exactly what he was thinking: Someone has been remiss in teaching these children the proper lessons and manners. He looked back at the twins. "Do you know who I am?"

Both girls nodded. "You're going to marry Kate," Megan announced.

Mary looked at her in disgust. "No, that's not right. He's the one who's going to marry the lady with the blond hair." She looked back at Sandford. "Isn't that right?"

Kate leaped forward in horror. "Now, girls, that really isn't important. This is your guardian, Baron Sandford. He's your father's cousin."

The girls thought about this for a moment. "Is he your cousin, Kate?" Mary asked. "If he's our cousin, then he should be yours."

"No, he isn't my cousin." In desperation, she turned to Robbie, but he was only sitting there, looking highly amused. Kate scowled at him; this was no time for humor. "The girls need to eat and go to bed now," she announced. "I try to make sure they eat and go to bed at the same hour every night. That's very good for children, you know."

Sandford nodded again as she gathered up the girls and prompted them to say their good nights, then started out. Before they could get to the door, however, Miss Armitage and her mother came in. "What dears," observed Mrs. Armitage.

"I adore children," Miss Armitage said. "Come here, you beautiful girls."

Megan curtsied, but Mary looked hard at her hands. "Kate, I think I have manure under my fingernails," she announced, holding up her hand for inspection. "Look. Is that manure?" Horrified, Kate snatched the two girls up and hustled them out of the room. She could hear Mrs. Armitage exclaiming behind them in offended accents. All too well, Kate could just imagine what she was saying.

As bad as the introduction of the twins had been, the evening was worse. When Kate got back to her room, she discovered one reason Robbie might have been chuckling: Kate had a large, dirty patch on her gown where she had fallen, and her shoes hadn't escaped the trip to the stables, either. Both heels were covered with bits of hay and manure. When she had Riggs help her remove the dress, she discovered a large, purple bruise on her hip. She didn't have time to soak in a tub and certainly didn't want to smell like liniment, so she had to endure the soreness throughout the evening.

As painful as sitting was, Kate decided it was only the third worse thing of the evening. It was difficult to rank the other two: One was having to sit at the table and listen to Mrs. Armitage prose on and on about the virtues of her beautiful daughter while making the occasional remark about other children who ran wild. This last was always said with a significant look in Kate's direction. The other was having to watch Sandford gaze in admiration at Amalie Armitage. That wouldn't have been so bad if he had looked elsewhere once in a while, but neither he nor Robbie could seem to take their eyes off her. Miss Armitage blossomed under the attention and flirted outrageously with both men. It was, Kate thought glumly as she poked at the food on her plate, a good thing Mrs. Armitage talked to her, even if it was about the twins' careless behavior. She would have been completely ignored otherwise.

Everyone went to bed earlier than usual, since the visitors were tired from their journey. Kate slipped out of her room and went to check on the twins. They were asleep in their beds, looking like little angels, their dark hair spread out on their pillows. She felt a lump in her throat as she gazed upon them. Never would she let Sandford take them away to India! No matter what she had to do or where she had to go, she wouldn't let it happen. She reached over and touched Megan's hair, silently promising both of them.

The next morning, the snow was still blowing around. Not much more had accumulated, but the air was cold and the wind was whistling around the corners of the house and rattling the windows. Miss Armitage and her mother elected to stay in bed. Kate had trays of muffins, jam, and chocolate sent up to them, and she had the maids check the fires in their rooms. The longer she could keep them out of the way, the better.

She didn't have as much luck with Sandford, however. Kate had decided to take breakfast with the twins in the nursery. While they were all gathered around the low table, Sandford walked in, his bulk darkening the doorway. When he came into the room, he seemed to fill it up.

"Are you lost?" Mary asked before Kate could say a thing.

Sandford shook his head and found a somewhat larger chair to sit down in. "I was looking for the nursery and I presume this is it."

"It is," Megan said, biting into her muffin and talking with her mouth full, "but grown-ups never come here. They eat downstairs."

Sandford looked around the nursery, his gaze settling on each item as though assessing it. Kate mentally followed him, cringing at each thing that was scuffed or dirty or not completely perfect. She could almost see Sandford's mind in the

46

same way that Robbie had told her others did: an account book with debits and credits.

He walked over to the window and looked out at the snow. "I went downstairs and there was no one there," he said, turning and smiling at them. The smile was every bit as Kate remembered, and it transformed his whole face. For an instant, she could see a hint of the boy he once was. "Perhaps, Kate—you do remember that you said I could call you Kate?"

"I remember." Kate felt the beginnings of a blush under her fair skin and fought it down.

"Fine," he continued, "and you must call me Hale." He didn't wait for her answer but looked at the twins. "Since we're going to know each other, would you like to call me Uncle Hale? My sister's children call me that, so I'm accustomed to it."

Megan and Mary tried out the address a few times, then went back to their breakfasts. Sandford turned to Kate with a rueful smile. "So much for my importance. Would you like to go down with me and have some breakfast? I hate to eat alone."

She returned his smile and agreed. First, she made sure the twins were going to be dressed properly and instructed them to have Nurse Freeman read them a book. At least Sandford would realize they were familiar with books.

The twins, however, weren't excited at the prospect of a book. They had more important things planned. "Will there be enough snow to make a snowman, Kate?"

She shook her head. "No, the snow's just blowing around and it's cold outside." She laughed at their disappointment. "We'll get our decorations for the hall instead. We need to get holly and mistletoe and pick out our tree. Then we'll gather our decorations and get ready to trim the tree when it's cut. We've got all those pretty new candleholders Papa sent from Germany. Do you remember that you said the trees there the year before last looked like trees with stars on them?"

47

"Candleholders?" Sandford asked as they went to the breakfast room, where breakfast waited on the sideboard.

"It's a German custom. I think you'll find Christmas here is more German than English. Mama and Papa have always loved the German Christmas and we've adopted some of the customs. We always have a tree, and this year we're trimming it with small brass candleholders Papa bought in Cologne. We also exchange gifts with everyone." She paused. "We realize that you and the Armitages didn't know about our custom, so please don't feel obligated to give any gifts. Your presence here during the holiday is enough."

He looked at her. "Did you get gifts for us?"

"Small tokens, that's all. Papa likes to say that it's the thought that counts, not the gift." She sat down at the small table opposite him. She had gotten herself a cup of coffee to drink while he ate. Kate really didn't want even that and she toyed with the handle of the cup as they talked. Her ring caught the light and gleamed.

He reached out and took her fingers in his. "I take it that this is an engagement ring?" He touched the smooth surface of the sapphire. "Quite a beautiful ring. He must be an exceptional man."

The sapphire looked huge on her finger. Kate snatched her hand back and put both hands down in her lap. "He is. That is, it isn't really . . ." She realized she didn't know what Barton was planning to do. Would he take her advice and stay away because Miss Armitage was here, or would he feel duty-bound to fulfill his promise? The Rushes were known far and wide for keeping their promises, no matter how inconvenient. It would be just like Barton to feel that he had to come to Falwell Hall simply because he had promised to do so and thought Kate was depending on him. She had tried to assure him that he didn't need to, but who could predict what Barton would do? She had thought she had known him beyond question, but after learning about his disastrous relationship with Amalie Armitage, she realized she didn't know him at all.

"Perhaps we can go into details later," Kate said, jumping up. "Right now, I need to see about Wallace's plans for the tree. I also have to make sure he knows where there's some holly and mistletoe for us to gather. Christmas just isn't Christmas without holly and mistletoe and evergreens." She realized she was chattering aimlessly, but at least it filled up the silence and she didn't have to lie about Barton.

Wallace, bless him, had found a fine stand of holly and some bits of mistletoe close enough to the ground to shoot down, so he took his gun along. Kate and the twins bundled up and took scissors and baskets to get the holly. Kate made sure they all had their gloves, not so much for the cold as to ensure that the prickly holly leaves wouldn't scratch them. The best holly bushes were a distance from the house, and the day was just perfect for thinking about Christmas. It was cold and the snow was blowing, but the sun was shining behind the scattered clouds, giving everything around them a glitter of diamonds. The twins ran and jumped, laughed and played. They had been out half an hour or so when Sandford joined them.

"I need to get acquainted with my charges," he said with a grin, "and what better time?" Kate put him to work cutting holly, the twins making sure he cut only the branches with the most berries. "I'm extraordinarily glad," he said as they walked back to the house with full baskets, "that Wallace elected to shoot down the mistletoe. As picky as those twins are about their Christmas decorations, I'd be climbing the tallest trees around."

"They know how to keep you busy," Kate said with a laugh as they went inside and put their baskets in the hall. The twins gathered around the holly, looking healthy and happy, their cheeks glowing from being out in the cold. Kate glanced up as Amalie Armitage and her mother came down the stairs.

"You'll ruin their complexions by letting them stay out in the cold, my dear," Mrs. Armitage said with a frown. "Take some advice from someone who knows how to be a mother: Start them early on watching their complexions. Now would be a good time."

Miss Armitage came down and stood beside Sandford, touching his arm possessively. Kate looked at her pale perfection: her skin porcelain with just the right touch of pink, her wide blue eyes, and her blond hair dressed to perfection. She had set all this beauty off with a deep blue gown that echoed the color of her eyes. Kate thought of sapphires when she looked at her. She glanced down at the ring on her finger. No wonder Barton had chosen it for Miss Armitage. The ring was her color.

Forcing herself not to stare at the beauty, Kate turned and caught a glimpse of herself in the hall mirror. She looked like a hoyden. Her hair had blown from beneath her hat and was flying in wisps around her face, her green eyes sparkled, and her face was ruddy from the cold wind. She didn't look at all cool, poised, and beautiful. Sandford probably thought the twins would end up looking and acting just as she did, when he obviously preferred them to look and act like Miss Armitage.

Kate started to thank Mrs. Armitage for her advice when the knocker sounded. Wallace was right there and opened the door as Kate turned to see who could be visiting.

There was a moment of frozen, stunned silence as Barton Rush walked in.

Chapter 4

Barton paled visibily as he saw Amalie Armitage, and Kate quickly stepped in between them. She grasped Barton's hands and pulled him inside. "Barton, what a pleasant surprise! I didn't think you'd be here. That is, not yet."

Wallace shut the door behind them as Barton's man directed a footman to carry in the baggage. Barton gave the assembled company a glance, then put his arm around Kate's shoulders. "How could I stay away?" he asked with a smile. Kate hoped she was the only one who saw that the smile didn't reach his eyes.

Kate paused for an awkward moment, then made the introductions. Halfway through, it occurred to her that Barton probably knew Sandford as well as she did. It was a certainty that he knew Amalie Armitage better than she did.

Sandford nodded as they shook hands. "It's been a while, Rush. Good to see you." Amalie wasn't so subtle. She smiled at Barton and touched his arm in the briefest of gestures. "What a surprise, Barton. I'd have to say I didn't expect to see you here." She gave Kate a look that could mean any one of a dozen things.

As Kate told Robbie about it later that afternoon in the library, she paced the floor and frowned. "You should have seen her, Robbie. She looked at me as if I really weren't worthy to be in such company, much less have Barton here."

"Perhaps it had something to do with Barton standing there with his arm around your shoulder. Nice touch." Robbie's voice was dry.

Kate gave him a sharp look. "What do you mean 'nice touch'? I'll have you know that everything was proper."

Robbie laughed aloud. "Feeling guilty, Kate? I didn't mean *touch*. Still, how did the lovely Miss Armitage like the scene?"

Kate tried to suppress a grin but gave it up. "Not above half, I thought. I suppose it did look strange. I was all wind-blown and red in the face from the cold, and still had on my coat, scarf, and mittens. Miss Armitage looked perfect, while I looked a complete fright. Remind me to thank Barton."

"Have you asked him why he came after you wrote him?"

"No." She paused, as there was a noise in the hall. "You know the Rushes. They all have a reputation for doing whatever they promise to do. I wish he hadn't done it."

Robbie leaned back in his chair and lit a cigar. "You have to admit that it should make for a very interesting Christmas. Did you get the tree trimmed?"

"Not yet. Wallace hasn't even cut it." Kate sighed. "By the time we got Barton settled in, Wallace brought a letter from Sophie telling me she couldn't come, and then the twins had to be fed and so on. We were going to do it this afternoon, but by the time we carried in the holly and mistletoe, it was too late for the tree."

"Good. You can waste another day searching for a tree and then yet another trimming the thing." He grinned. "I didn't know you were sly enough to think up that many activities, Kate." She started to retort, but there was a knock. Both of them turned as Barton opened the door and peered around the edge.

"Come in and join us, Barton," Kate said. "I believe we may need to talk."

"Actually," Robbie said with a laugh, "we're gathering our forces in order to survive the evening."

52

Barton sat down beside Robbie and gratefully took a glass of wine and a cigar. "I believe that's a good idea." He glanced at Kate as he lit his cigar and smiled. "I apologize for my . . . my fumble when I got here, Kate, but I was surprised."

Her eyes widened. "Didn't you get my note?"

"What note?"

Kate closed her eyes. "I sent you a note as soon as I realized that Sandford's . . . uh . . . guest was Amalie Artimage. I didn't want to put you through . . . through an agonizing holiday. You were doing enough for me without that complication."

"Your note's probably waiting for me in London. I had Ransom pack early and join me on the road so I could get here early. I didn't even go back home." He grinned at her. "Well, Kate, it seems there's nothing for it now except for the two of us to give the performances of our lives." He leaned back and savored the cigar. "Has Sandford offered for Amalie yet?" He lifted an eyebrow. "Just asking out of curiosity, of course."

Kate and Robbie looked at each other. "Neither of them have said anything, but I don't think so," Kate declared. "From a remark or two Mrs. Armitage dropped, I'd say she expects an offer . . . and soon. Amalie seems sure of it, but I've heard no talk of an engagement."

"From what I've heard, Sandford's probably checking her father's account and ledger sheets before he offers." Robbie chuckled. "He won't find much there to warrant an engagement."

"I suppose as far as engagements go, at least we're one up on them." Barton laughed as Kate blushed to her hair.

She was saved from having to answer when the door burst open, and the twins ran in and climbed onto her lap. "Is there enough snow for a snowman yet?" they asked in unison.

Megan slipped and almost fell, but Barton caught her. He

put her on his knee where she could face Kate. "There, is that better?" he asked.

Megan nodded solemnly as she regarded him. "Are you another uncle?" she asked. "We've already got a new one."

Barton raised an eyebrow. "No, I'm not an uncle. Do you need another one?"

"What do uncles do? How many are we supposed to have?" Mary asked disinterestedly. "Kate, is there enough snow for a snowman yet?"

"Becky Fletcher has five," Megan said.

"Five snowmen?" Mary was derisive. "She does not. *Nobody* has five snowmen." She pinned Barton with a glare. "Do they?"

"Not five snowmen, you silly." Megan was superior. "Becky has five *uncles*. She told me so."

"Anybody can have five uncles." Mary dismissed this as not worthy of consideration. "Kate, is there enough snow for a snowman?"

Barton threw back his head and laughed. At Megan's and Mary's perplexed looks, Kate and Robbie started as well, just giggling at first, but then joining Barton as he laughed.

"What a pleasant little family scene. We heard you laughing all the way out in the hall." Miss Armitage and Sandford came across the room and joined them. "Do the girls come down from the nursery often?" She sat down across from Barton and gave him an arch look. "You look quite elegant with a child on your lap, Barton."

He gave her a brief smile as Megan slid to the floor and went to stand by Kate. "I like children. That was one of the reasons I came this Christmas. I felt it was time for the three of us to get acquainted."

"The three of you? You and the two children?" Miss Armitage looked puzzled. "Why should you get acquainted with children, Barton? I would hardly think someone who frequents the best clubs of London would prefer spending time in a nursery."

Barton lifted an eyebrow and looked at Kate. The corner of his mouth was quivering and she could see a trace of his dimple. He was actually enjoying this! "Hasn't Kate given you our news?" he asked.

"News?"

"So you're the one," Sandford said. "I noticed the ring on Kate's finger."

Miss Armitage glanced down at Kate's hand and immediately recognized the ring as the one she had spurned. Her body stiffened and she gave Barton a tight smile. "Very nice, Barton. It resembles a piece I've seen before."

"I daresay you have," Barton said lazily, offering Sandford a cigar.

"Do put away those awful things," Miss Armitage said, fanning the air in front of her. "How you men can stand those obnoxious things is beyond me. They smell terrible and give the whole house such an odor. It even gets in one's clothing and hair." She looked at Kate. "Don't you object to those things in your house?"

Kate glanced at Robbie and Barton puffing contentedly on their tobacco and then at Sandford, who had stopped in the act of putting a flame to the tip of his. "Actually, I rather like them," she said.

"Grandfather smokes them," Megan said.

"We tried one once, but it made us sick," Mary added, much to Kate's horror.

"Good heavens!" Miss Armitage's tone clearly gave her opinion of Kate as a parent. "Children smoking cigars!"

Barton chuckled. "I didn't know little girls did that sort of thing. I remember the first time I smoked a cigar. I thought I was going to die immediately and didn't care. In fact, I recall thinking that the sooner I died, the better."

Sandford lit his tobacco and laughed along with Barton. "I imagine most of us have similar stories. I almost set the stables on fire."

55

"But these are girls!" Miss Armitage sputtered. "One might expect that sort of behavior from boys. But from *girls!*"

"It made me sick," Mary said, "and Megan, too. She threw up."

Megan nodded. "All over Kate."

Before anyone else could comment, Kate jumped to her feet and gathered up the girls. "I think it's time for you two to go back upstairs. I'm sure Nurse Freeman will read you a nice story." She risked a look at Sandford but couldn't see his expression. He had his head bowed and his shoulders were shaking.

"Nurse already did that," Mary announced. "She read two of them." She paused. "She even told us a ghost story. Kate, did you know that Mad Jack Rackham walks the moors at night and kills children who don't behave?" Mary's voice was as matter-of-fact as if she were discussing the weather.

"Yes," Megan agreed with relish. "And he's bloody all over and has long, bloody fingernails and a long, black beard."

"A long, black beard that drips blood." The twins looked at each other and nodded. "And a knife." They nodded in agreement again. "That's for really bad boys and girls."

"Enough!" Kate snapped. "Let's go upstairs right now." She herded them toward the door.

"But you promised we could decorate." Mary started to cry. "Can't we decorate? You *promised*, Kate."

Barton came to her rescue. He stood and walked over to them. "Why don't we all decorate? I've never decorated for Christmas before and I'd like to see just what I'll have to do next year." He turned and looked at the others. "Wouldn't the rest of you like to join us?"

Robbie hesitated until Kate glared at him. He put his cigar in the dish he kept beside his chair just for that purpose and sighed. "Of course. Nothing like turning the house into part of the Black Forest to induce a little Yuletide cheer."

Sandford and Miss Armitage decided to join them, and

they all went into the hall to begin. "I always let the twins tell me where to put things," Kate explained as Miss Armitage raised an eyebrow.

"Really?" she said with a significant glance at Sandford.

Megan and Mary were already into the basket of greenery. "Are we going to decorate the stairs like last year?" they asked Kate. "Can we use ribbons and candles?"

Kate sent Mrs. Wallace for the candles and holders she had put aside, and the decorating began in earnest. Miss Armitage declined to participate after she stuck her finger on a holly leaf and dropped a spot of blood on her dress. "You'd think she'd cut her whole finger off," Robbie whispered to Kate as they bent to pick up some evergreen boughs Wallace had brought in.

Mrs. Wallace brought them a surprise she had procured— a full branch of mistletoe covered with waxy white berries. "I saw it and knew you had to have it here," she told Kate. "I wouldn't let Wallace shoot it down for fear he'd ruin it. I had to make him shinny up the tallest tree around. Thought he'd never stop complaining." Wallace gave her a disdainful look as Kate took the mistletoe and thanked them.

"There's enough mistletoe here to send all of London into an embrace," Barton said as he picked it up. "You'll need to split it into sections."

They did just that, summoning a footman to get a ladder, then fastening ribbon-festooned balls of mistletoe in the main hall at the foot of the stairs, in the drawing room, and outside over the front door. There was one small sprig left, which Robbie picked up. "I'm going to put this one in the library, since I stay there most of the time. Who knows," he said with a grin. "We may have company and I'll have need of this."

"Everyone needs a dream," Kate called after him, laughing, as he and Megan went off to put the mistletoe in the library. Sandford, Miss Armitage, Barton, Kate, and Mary were left in the hall. Kate looked around, satisfied. There

57

was greenery up the stair railing, tied on with cheerful red ribbons; there was greenery over the doors, the tables were decorated with holly and candles, and Mary had insisted on putting some greenery and Christmas bells from Germany on the front door.

Barton went around and lit the candles in the decorations as night fell outside. Then he came back to stand between Mary and Kate, lightly putting his arm around Kate's shoulder. "My first decorated Christmas." He grinned as he looked down at Mary and took her hand in his. "Very nice. I think I'll do it every year."

Robbie and Megan came back into the hall from the library. "Look." Megan pointed to a ball of mistletoe and greenery hanging from the ceiling on a red ribbon. "Kate's standing right under the mistletoe."

Kate looked up and saw that she, Mary, and Barton were right under the mistletoe. "You know what that means," Robbie said with a grin.

"That means I'm going to move." Kate made a face at him and started to step aside, but Barton held her. "I think I'm going to enjoy all these Christmas traditions." He laughed and, before Kate knew what was happening, kissed her lightly on the cheek, just beside her mouth. She jumped back, her face flaming, and looked first at Barton, then at the others. Barton was grinning, his brown eyes dancing with delight. Robbie and Sandford were also laughing; Miss Armitage's face was chiseled in ice.

Mary pulled at Barton's hand. "I'm here, too."

"You're bringing up a true female, Kate." Barton laughed as he bent and kissed Mary on the forehead.

Megan ran over. "Me, too."

Mary shoved her sister out of the way. "You're not under the mistletoe. It doesn't count if you're not right under it."

Megan solved that by pushing Mary aside and grabbing Barton's hand. "Now I'm here."

Mary started to hit Megan, but Barton stopped the battle

by taking each twin by the hand. "Right under the mistletoe?" He looked up. "So you are," he said seriously, "and I'm delighted." He kissed Megan on the forehead as well.

"How very charming," Miss Armitage said, sounding bored. "But I would never have thought you so fond of children, Barton. I find it quite surprising. In all the time I've known you, you've certainly never expressed an interest in children."

"You didn't know me very well, Amalie."

Miss Armitage and Barton exchanged looks, and the tension was thick in the air. "Why don't we go have some chocolate?" Kate asked to fill the silence.

"Chocolate?" Miss Armitage echoed, giving her an amazed look.

"Why not?" Barton said, turning to her. "Decorating's dashed hard work." He smiled down at the twins. "Would you two like to join us?"

Miss Armitage's "Well, *really!*" was drowned out by the twins enthusiastically yelling out "Yes!" Kate risked a despairing glance at Sandford. From the disapproving frown on his face, she decided that he didn't particularly appreciate this approach to child rearing.

Kate rang for chocolate while Barton led the way to the drawing room, holding a twin's hand in each of his. Inside, the air smelled of candles, the aroma of burning wood from the fire, and the spicy scent of the greenery. Barton sat between the twins as Kate poured chocolate. Mary tried to sit on the floor, but Barton merely had to look at her and she primly sat back down beside him, on the edge of the sofa. To Kate's relief, both the girls were using their best manners, remembering to say thank you and behaving perfectly. She looked at Barton and he grinned at her. She smiled back and dared to relax a bit. Perhaps this would work after all. It would be difficult to carry off the charade and perhaps Barton might like to concoct a story about having to go home for

Christmas, but his presence even this long at Falwell Hall might be enough to convince Sandford.

The girls eventually grew tired and went upstairs. Kate left instructions for Nurse Freeman not to let them out of her sight. She was too preoccupied to worry about dressing for supper, but Riggs was excited. "I knew you'd want to look special for Mr. Rush," she whispered as she threaded green and gold ribbons through Kate's hair. "A handsome man he is, too." She glanced down at Kate. "And to think that you never let on about him. Never a word!"

"That looks perfect, Riggs," Kate said hastily, standing. She reached up to smooth back a stray curl and the ring gleamed in the mirror, the deep blue looking all wrong against her skin, hair, and amber gold silk gown.

Supper was a silent affair with only the barest of conversation exchanged. Kate gave up and ate in silence after several attempts that went nowhere. The rest of the evening was as much of a disaster. Miss Armitage complained about the cigars until the men decided to forgo them. Robbie kept walking around picking up things and putting them back down. Kate knew he wanted his customary cigar and port after supper. Sandford finally suggested cards, and he, Miss Armitage, Barton, and Robbie made up the foursome. Kate and Mrs. Armitage sat to one side. Mrs. Armitage felt it her duty to use this opportunity to give Kate the benefit of her expertise as a parent, and she spent the entire evening giving volumes of unwanted advice. It seemed Mrs. Armitage was worried about the twins being unable to procure husbands because the girls were such hoydens.

"They're only children!" Kate exclaimed. "They won't need to think about husbands for years."

"It comes sooner than you think." Mrs. Armitage nodded sagely and looked at her daughter sitting with the three men. "I've planned for my daughter since she was a babe. The best of dancing masters, the right gowns, the right friends. It's never too early to start." She began outlining a plan for the twins, starting immediately and culminating with finished young ladies when they were of marriageable age. Kate was more than relieved when it was time to go upstairs to bed.

Riggs brushed her hair until it shone, then braided it, all the while informing her how the household was all in a dither about the engagement with Mr. Rush. According to Riggs, everyone was surprised but knew it had been bound to happen sooner or later. After all, hadn't she and Mr. Rush been friends for years, hadn't their parents been friends for years, and wasn't he just a handsome man? Kate twisted the heavy ring on her finger and couldn't look at Riggs in the mirror. She knew that Riggs would be able to read the truth in her eyes.

After Riggs left, Kate wandered around her room, feeling guilty. She paused in front of a framed sketch of Carleen and William. The two of them were in the garden, holding hands and laughing together. Sophie, a talented artist, had captured them in a few strokes of her charcoal. "Oh, Carleen," she whispered, "I'm doing this for you and the girls." She paused. "No, I'm doing this for me as well." She turned to the mirror and touched the spot on her cheek where Barton had kissed her. That had been completely unexpected. He was only, she told herself, trying to make Miss Armitage jealous. That was all. He really didn't want to do it.

She paced around the room, with each turn getting more disgusted with herself for playing a part in such a lie and for dragging Barton into the deception. Finally, she decided to go down to the library and read until she got sleepy. She put on her warm, heavy dressing gown and the knitted woolen slippers Mrs. Wallace had made for her last Christmas. The slippers made no sound on the floor and stairs as she descended.

The fire was still burning in the library and Kate caught the smell of cigar smoke. As she closed the door behind her, someone got up from the chair in front of the fireplace. All Kate could see was a silhouette. "Robbie?" she asked, although it certainly didn't look like her brother. Robbie was tall and thin, and while this man was tall, he was well built. "Barton? Is that you?"

"Sorry to disappoint you," Sandford said, the tip of his cigar glowing in the dark. "I couldn't smoke earlier, so I thought I'd come down for a cigar before I went to bed. I'd have to say that your brother keeps excellent stock." He put a candle from the table into the fire to light it, then lit the others. Only then did he see that Kate was in her dressing gown. He raised an eyebrow in question. "I believe Barton's gone to bed."

Kate looked down at her dressing gown and clutched it tighter. "I didn't come down to meet Barton."

"Of course not."

"I certainly did not!" She was furious. "I certainly don't make it a habit to go around meeting men after dark." Unbidden, the memory of the time she had sought out Sandford to tell him she loved him came flooding back. She had sought him out after dark. What must he think of her?

He smiled at her, a curiously gentle smile. "Couldn't you sleep, either?"

She shook her head. "I came down to get something to read. I thought I had a book in my room, but I didn't. Sometimes I like to come here and curl up in that chair to read."

"The chair is yours." He gestured toward it. "Just let me move my port. I helped myself to a glass."

Kate sat down stiffly. "Take all you want." There was an awkward pause. "Are you enjoying your stay so far?"

He nodded, sat down in the chair beside her, and puffed on his cigar. "Very much. I'm amazed at all these Christmas customs. I never knew the Germans were so imaginative."

"Just don't get Papa started on Germans or Germany. He loves all things German." Kate laughed.

"I should say the same about Indian things, but I'm really not that charmed by the country. There are some wonderful things there, but I'm an Englishman at heart. I was planning to return to India because of my business interests there, but I may just stay in London." He paused. "Kate, I think we need to talk about the children."

Kate felt herself stiffen. "They're happy children. Your only complaint was that they had no father to guide them. If . . . when I marry Barton, they'll have a father. He . . . he'll be good with them."

"Are you going to marry Barton? I had the feeling you were as surprised by his appearance here as . . . as Amalie was."

"Of course I'm going to marry Barton!" She looked straight into the fire, for she could not meet his eyes. There was a silence. "Are you going to marry Amalie Armitage?"

He reflected on this while he puffed on his cigar. "I don't know. I haven't offered for her." He paused. "Her father and I have some business dealings together, so it would be convenient."

"Convenient?" Kate stared at him in amazement. "Convenient? Sandford, I'm surprised at you."

He gave her a quizzical look and put his cigar down in Robbie's dish. "Yes, convenient. I know you think all marriages should be like William and Carleen's. They were, I'd have to admit, very much in love—even, one might say, too much in love. To a degree, I'd like to fall in love and have someone love me in that same way, but I don't think it will happen to me. At least not again."

"Again?"

He smiled at her in the glow of the candlelight. "Once a lovely young girl declared she was in love with me. At the time, and for several reasons, I felt it was impossible for me to enter into any . . . uh . . . type of entanglement. However, I've thought about it over the years and realized I should have made an arrangement with her father. She would have devoted her life completely to me."

Kate's cheeks stung. "I was very young then, Sandford.

That was only a youthful indiscretion. I had forgotten all about it." She looked away from him and into the fire again.

"Had you?" The words were soft.

She couldn't look at him. "Of course. And as to devotion, you're entirely mistaken. I'm not at all the kind of person who would devote my whole life to someone."

"You've devoted your life to the twins."

Kate stared right into his eyes. She could be completely truthful here. "So I have, Sandford, but that's different. The twins needed me; they still need me. They could never survive if they were in a home where they weren't loved."

"I take it you're talking about me and the type of home I might provide for them. What makes you think I'm incapable of love?"

Kate got the impression he was talking about two things at once. "You are, I'm sure. And no, I really wasn't thinking of your home." She groped for words. "Amalie Armitage," she blurted out. "I don't think she could love the twins."

"Ah, we're back to Miss Armitage." He leaned back. It was his turn to stare into the fire. "One of the reasons I was interested in coming here, Kate, was to see if you still had feelings for me."

"Then why did you bring Miss Armitage?"

"You wouldn't be jealous, by any chance, would you?" He grinned at her.

"No." She couldn't look at him again. She really wasn't sure if she was jealous of Amalie Armitage or not.

He sighed, picked up his cigar, and looked at the tip. "I don't know exactly why I brought her. For one, she invited me to spend Christmas with her family, and when I said I was coming here, she managed to invite herself." He lifted a candle and relit his cigar, then puffed on it. "I could have said no, but I didn't. I brought her for comparison purposes, I suppose. I'd been seeing her in London, and thought perhaps she and I would have a future. Financially, it would be the perfect match for me."

Kate didn't know how to answer this, so she said nothing.

"When Rush got here, I was surprised to discover you two were engaged. I made some discreet inquiries about you when I first got to London, and no one mentioned it."

"We kept it very quiet." A log on the fire popped and fell to embers as Kate watched. "We're rather private people."

"I know enough about Rush to understand that he's well to grass but not wealthy. Do you care for him?" he asked bluntly. He snuffed out two of the candles so the room was darkened. There was only the glow from the two other candles and the light from the fire. Kate was glad he couldn't see her eyes.

"That's a rather private question," she said. "Barton and I are old friends. We've known each other for years and—"

"Do you care for Barton?"

"Of course," she snapped. "Barton's a wonderful person."

He sighed. "I'm sure you know that he offered for Amalie last Christmas. She tells me he gave her a ring, a large sapphire surrounded by diamonds." He looked pointedly at the ring on Kate's finger. "She kept it for two days and never wore it. She said she kept it more to spare his feelings than because she wanted it. Evidently, he declared himself in front of half of the ton. But you knew all that, of course."

"Of course, and it really isn't relevant." She stood and held the lapels of her dressing gown close, her thick braid of russet hair across her shoulder. "The important thing to me is your decision about the twins. As their guardian, please think about what's best for them, Sandford. That's all I ask."

He stood beside her and tossed the last of the cigar into the fire. "I will." He looked down at her face in the firelight as though deciding whether or not to say something. "Miss Armitage—Amalie—says Barton is marrying you on the rebound, Kate. I want you to think about that. I don't want to see you hurt. I've had years to think about you and what you said to me so long ago. I'm sorry I wasn't able to accept what

65

you offered me then. Things would be different now. All I'm asking you is to be sure how you feel about Barton and,'' he added, ''how Barton feels about you. Amalie thinks he's still very much in love with her. I don't want to sound cruel, but please consider what I've told you.''

''All right.'' He was much too close to her, and she could remember that long-ago night as if it were happening now. He looked the same, smelled the same, and she felt just as if she were seventeen again. She took a step back, running into a table covered with holly. The holly slid off and she tried to catch it, sticking her hands with the thorns on the leaves.

''Oh!'' She dropped the holly and looked at her hands.

''I'll get it.'' Sandford knelt to pick up the holly. ''Kate . . .''

''I've got to go wash my hands,'' she said hastily, dashing for the door. She ran up to her room and leaned against her closed door, gasping for breath, not from the exertion but from the welter of emotions that made her chest feel as though it would explode. She put her hands over her face and felt them sticky and wet. Looking down, she saw that they were covered in tiny pricks from the holly leaves, many of the spots bleeding. She washed off the blood and put some salve on the spots, then sat down in front of her own fire.

It was only then that she realized she hadn't gotten a book to read, but there was no way she was going back downstairs to risk facing Sandford again. Instead, she did the next best thing. She crawled into her bed and pulled the covers over her head.

Chapter 5

The next day, the twins were ready early. In fact, they came knocking on Kate's door just at daylight. She sat up groggily in bed, wondering what was wrong as the two of them threw the door open and ran inside, climbing up on her bed. "Today's the day we get the tree and trim it," Megan said, cuddling next to her. "Can we keep the candles lit all day?"

"We can't see them burning in the daytime," Kate explained, yawning and making room for a twin on either side of her. They crawled under the covers and curled up next to her. "It's still dark outside, girls. Don't you think we should wait until this afternoon, or at least until we can see to pick out a tree?"

Both of them shook their heads. "You promised today."

Kate thought a moment. "Yes, and we will today, but first we have to eat breakfast, and then you have to let Nurse Freeman read a story to you. By that time, Wallace will be ready to go with us." She smiled down at them. "I told you that the two of you are big enough now to begin your lessons. Isn't that wonderful?"

They lifted their heads and looked at each other.

"No," Mary said.

"No," Megan agreed.

"You don't do lessons," Mary told her.

"So we shouldn't have to, either," Megan said.

The twins nodded in agreement.

Kate laughed. "Yes, but when I was your age, I did. I don't take lessons now because I finished them a long time ago. Just think: You'll never know how to read, write, do sums, speak French, or play the piano if you don't take lessons." She looked at her little watch on the table beside the bed. "Why don't we try to sleep another hour or so, and then we'll have breakfast. Right after breakfast, I promise I'll get Wallace to hurry. We'll go out to the woods in back and pick out our tree. Then you can have your story, and we'll trim the tree this afternoon." They made faces at her. "You can stay in my bed and sleep with me this morning."

To her surprise, they all went back to sleep. When Kate awoke, the twins were still sleeping. She carefully crawled out of bed across Megan and gathered up her clothes. She didn't ring for Riggs, but dressed herself instead and tried to do something with her hair. It was going every which way this morning. She finally just tied it back with a ribbon until Riggs could help her. Then she picked up her shoes and tiptoed out, closing the door behind her as she stood in the hall in her stocking feet.

Barton came out of his room as her door clicked into place. He looked at her, from the ends of her flyaway hair, down past the shoes in her hand, to her stockinged feet. "Running away from home?" he asked with a grin.

Kate propped one hand against the wall as she hopped on one foot and tried to put her shoe on her other foot. "The twins are in my bed asleep. I was trying to get out without waking them." She wobbled and fell into the wall.

"Here, let me." Barton laughed and took the shoes away from her. She leaned against the wall as he knelt and slipped them on her feet.

Miss Armitage came out of her room at that moment. "On your knees already, Barton?" she asked, giving Kate's appearance a disapproving glance.

Barton's face reddened as he stood. "Good morning, Amalie. I see you're your usual pleasant self this morning."

To Kate's surprise, rather than being insulted, Miss Armitage pouted prettily and walked closer to Barton. "What a bear you are in the mornings, Barton." She smiled at Kate and lifted an eyebrow. "I do hope you don't plan to talk to him in the mornings. He told me once that he wasn't fit for conversation until he'd had his morning coffee." She smiled archly at Barton. "Is that still correct?"

Barton moved to Kate's side and tucked her hand under his arm. "I've reformed. My morning disposition is as sunny as yours, Amalie." He smiled back at her. "We're going to breakfast. Would you like to join us?" He hesitated, then out of politeness, Barton offered his other arm to Miss Armitage. She took it readily and monopolized him all the way to the breakfast room, chatting incessantly about the latest doings of the ton. Kate felt like a hopeless provincial.

Robbie and Sandford were already at breakfast, the latter expounding on the excellent financial opportunities available in India. "Any man can make his fortune there if he watches for openings and seizes them," he was saying. "Of course, there are opportunities here as well, especially if a man is careful about buying shares and, of course, making the right connections and marriage. The importance of the right marriage can hardly be underestimated. As for myself . . ." He looked up as the three of them came in, frowned slightly, then rose as Robbie did. "Good morning." His greeting took in all three of them. "You're looking particularly fine this morning."

"Thank you. I knew this gown was one of your favorites." Miss Armitage held out her hand to Sandford and sat beside him. "Blue is my favorite color." She glanced pointedly at the sapphire on Kate's finger, then patted the place beside her. "Do sit here, Barton. I'm famished for some talk of the ton. I've given you all my news. Have you heard anything new?" She gave Sandford a flirtatious glance and batted her eyelashes. "All Sandford wants to discuss is 'Change or the fluctuating price of grain. Dull stuff."

"Without it, there'd be no ton." Sandford smiled. "Actually, it's fascinating once you get into it. Robbie and his father dabble on 'Change." He turned to Robbie. "I suppose your father knows what and when to buy, since he's got an ear in the government."

Kate was scandalized. "Papa would never do that! That would be dishonest." She turned to Barton. "Wouldn't it?"

Barton laughed. "Unethical, perhaps. I really don't know about the illegality. I suppose it depends on the circumstances."

Miss Armitage tugged at Barton's sleeve. "Do leave off this dreary talk and let's discuss something of importance." She took the coffee Sandford handed her. "Barton, are you going to Wrexham's do on Twelfth Night? Sandford's promised to take me."

Barton hesitated. "I really haven't thought about it. I suppose if Kate stays in the country, I'll probably stay here."

"And miss the do of the season?" Miss Armitage's eyes widened.

"If it's up to Wrexham's usual standards, it'd be well to miss it," Robbie said dryly. "The man's such a clutchfist that he won't even hire a decent band."

"And the refreshments." Barton rolled his eyes and looked at Robbie. "You were right the last time, you know. I think Wrexham's gotten worse lately instead of better."

"I heard he'd lost a pile of money on some speculation in the Bahamas," Sandford said. "The on-dit was that he was trying to recoup. He had some partners who lost money with him, but I don't know who they were." He paused as he buttered his muffin. "I suppose you could locate them by watching to see who's trying to sell the family jewels."

"Or who's trying to marry a daughter off to money," Robbie added with a grin. "Untold sons-in-law have had to bail out unfortunate fathers. I've had some close calls myself."

70

"That's ridiculous," Miss Armitage said sharply. She turned to Sandford. "If you don't leave off this dreary talk, I'm going to have a tray sent up and eat with Mama."

Sandford patted her hand. "My apologies. Robbie tells me it's going to snow tomorrow. Would you like a sleigh ride?"

"Mama says the cold is bad for my complexion." Miss Armitage smiled prettily. "What can we do today?"

Sandford looked at Kate. "What do you have planned today, Kate? More holly and mistletoe?"

Kate laughed. "No, I promised to trim the tree today. That'll probably take all day."

"Actually," Robbie said, "the way the twins decorate, trimming the tree takes about an hour and cleaning up the mess takes all day." Kate smiled sweetly and kicked him under the table.

"What the devil?" said Sandford, glancing down quickly as Kate realized she had made contact with the wrong shin. He looked quizzically at Miss Armitage and a slow smile crossed his face. He patted her hand again, his fingers lingering on hers. Miss Armitage smiled back sweetly.

Kate excused herself as soon as possible and went upstairs to the nursery. The twins were up and had already eaten. They were ready to start on the tree. "Wallace says it's still too wet and cold to go out for the tree, so we have an hour or so." She swooped both girls into her arms before they could protest. "So as a treat, I'm going to begin your lessons myself."

"You are?" The twins looked skeptical.

"Of course. I've had lessons and know exactly what to do. First, we're going to read a story and talk about your letters and numbers," Kate said, sitting down at the table with them. "Then I'll teach you how to write some letters."

"I'd rather go get the tree," Megan said. "I'd wear my mittens and not lose them. I promise."

"Lessons." Kate was firm and drew the girls next to her at the table. She couldn't get too close because the chairs were small, but she went through the alphabet and numbers up to ten. It was difficult, since the twins kept interrupting her to ask if the lessons were over yet so they could trim the tree.

"You said we could," Megan told her.

"Yes, you did," Mary agreed.

Nurse Freeman dozed in her chair by the fire.

"I know I did, and we're going to as soon as Wallace is ready, but first you need to learn the alphabet. I want you to be able to recite it to Sandford."

"Our uncle? Do we have to have him for an uncle, Kate?" Mary asked.

"We don't want him," Megan told her. "We decided we'd rather have someone else. We thought Ben down at the stables would make a good uncle. He says all kinds of interesting things."

Kate had heard Ben say some of his more interesting things on occasion and looked at the girls in horror. Ben was a past master of profanity—not around others, of course, but now and then one could hear him off in the back of the stables cursing to himself. He had been here for time beyond telling—Kate couldn't remember a time when he wasn't around—and had to be in his eighties by now. He had been here even when Papa was a boy, so there was no removing him or correcting his language. Besides, as Papa had once explained to her when she was a small girl and had quoted a colorful passage she had overheard, Ben didn't really know what he was saying. His profanity had become such a habit with him that he seldom even knew he was speaking. Now that he was old and deaf, things were worse. He couldn't hear others around him and he couldn't hear himself, so his words were loud and clear.

Still, the girls shouldn't be hearing such things. Kate looked at them sharply. "What kinds of things? When have you been down to the stables? Don't you know you shouldn't go there without my permission?"

Mary looked at her solemnly. "We went back to see if any of the animals were talking yet. I know you said we had to wait for Christmas Day, but we thought we'd better make sure."

"I didn't say Christmas Day," Kate said automatically. "It's Christmas Eve. The animals are supposed to talk then."

Megan turned to Mary. "I told you so! I told you so!"

"Hush now. When did you go out to the stables? I do not want you wandering around the grounds unless someone's with you." She took a hand in each of hers and regarded them with what she hoped was a stern look. "You've got to be on your best behavior while Sandford's here. Do you understand?"

They nodded and smiled at her like little angels. "Kate, can we go get the tree now?"

Kate gave it up and closed the alphabet book. "Let's go find Wallace and get the tree. Get your mittens."

"And trim it, too?"

She looked down at them and laughed. "After the midday meal. Trimming the tree is our afternoon job."

Megan and Mary danced around. "Tonight we can light the candles and it'll look like stars in the sky."

Megan suddenly stopped and looked at Mary, then at Kate. "Maybe we need a tree in the stables, so the animals will know it's Christmas and then they'll talk." She took Kate's hand as they walked down the stairs. "Just how do the animals know it's Christmas, Kate? Does somebody tell them?"

There was a chuckle behind her. "Yes, Kate, how do they know?" Barton came down the stairs behind them. "That's one question I've always wondered about myself."

"It's perfectly simple." Kate groped for an explanation as Barton picked up Mary and swung her around. Megan held out her arms and Barton bent down and picked her up as well. "Heavy little things, aren't they?" he asked in surprise as they went on down into the hall. "You haven't answered

73

our question, Kate. Has she, girls? How do the animals know it's Christmas?''

Kate gave him a disdainful look. ''There's a calendar in the stables. Ben keeps it on the wall right in front of them.''

Barton whooped with laughter as he put the twins down on the floor. ''And I suppose you provide one in the barn and sheepfold and dovecote as well. Can't let them miss the day, can you?''

Kate was saved from answering by Wallace's appearance, accompanied by a footman carrying an axe. They got their coats and Barton decided to join them. ''I've never been tree hunting,'' he explained, taking Megan's hand as Mary took Kate's and they went off behind Wallace.

Wallace led them to the tree he had selected, but the twins, after walking around it, decided it wouldn't do at all. Barton and Megan found one that everyone deemed suitable, and they cut it and put it on a wagon. Kate let the girls ride to the house in the back of the wagon with the tree.

''Are they always this excited?'' Barton asked, laughing, as he waved to the girls. Mary was almost hidden by the tree.

''Most of the time. I'm sorry if they bother you.''

He turned to her in amazement. ''Bother me? Kate, this is wonderful. I've always hoped for . . .'' He stopped awkwardly. Kate smiled up at him, thinking about Barton's family. They were not close at all and she knew Barton had always wanted a family like hers.

''They are wonderful, aren't they?'' she asked with a smile. ''Now our only problem is to convince Sandford of that.''

Barton laughed and took her hand in his. They walked together behind the wagon until they got to the house, where Barton, much to Megan and Mary's delight, supervised the unloading of the tree.

''There,'' he said, proud of his handiwork as he looked at the tree. ''That should stand until after Christmas.''

Megan pulled at Kate's gown. When Kate looked down,

Megan was frowning. "Kate, *do* you have calendars in the dovecote?"

"I'm sure Ben takes care of that," Kate answered vaguely. "Now, what do you think of the tree?"

The tree was wonderful. Papa had loved the German custom of having a decorated evergreen tree and they had had one for years, but this was the best one of all. It must have been twelve feet tall and was full and bushy. The needles gave off a spicy scent that mingled with the cinnamon and potpourri Kate kept in the room.

They had just gotten a good start on trimming the tree when they were joined by Sandford, Miss Armitage, and her mother. Mrs. Armitage sat down by the fireplace and began working with her wools, while Sandford and Miss Armitage decided to join in the tree trimming.

On the floor, Kate spread the paper flowers and chains of silver paper the twins had made. "What's this, Kate?" Robbie sauntered into the room. "Getting ready to set the house on fire again?"

Kate blushed furiously as she moved to stand by the fireplace. "That was an accident. You really shouldn't bring up such things every year, Robbie."

Robbie leaned back against the fireplace and grinned. "It's too good to keep. When was it, Kate? Three years ago? Four?" He laughed and put his arm around Kate's shoulders. "It was wonderful. Kate wanted a tree with candles just like one we had seen in a little town in the Black Forest, so she tied candles to the tree and lit them. Naturally, the candles fell and set the tree on fire. We had to have the whole drawing room repainted and get new curtains."

"Well, we needed to do that anyway." Kate squirmed out of his grasp. "Mama was looking for an excuse to get rid of those awful blue curtains." She turned back to look at the tree. "This is a perfect tree. Papa sent us an angel to put on the very top. Which one of you wants to do that?" Her glance included the three men. "Or do I have to call a footman?"

She pinned Robbie with a look, but he waved her away. "You know I'm all thumbs. Get Barton to do it. He's the agile one here."

Without waiting for his answer, Kate handed Barton the angel. "Now all you have to do is get on a chair and put the angel firmly on the very top. While you're up there, you can put one or two candleholders on the top limbs."

Barton held the angel and looked up at the top of the tree. "It must be ten or twelve feet," he said. "Do you have a chair I can stand on?"

The only chair close by was the one used at the small French secretary on the side of the room. Kate had always thought it was more for ornamentation than use, but she pulled it out and placed it next to the tree. Barton put his handkerchief over the upholstery, then climbed onto the chair and leaned toward the top of the tree. "I can't reach it," he said. "Besides, I think the very top is going to have to be trimmed a little so the angel can fit down over it and not fall over." He jumped down from the chair.

"It'll take forever to get a ladder," Megan said wistfully. "Could you get another chair?"

Barton patted her on the head. "We'll do it. Don't worry." He looked around the room and pointed to a small footstool by the fireplace. Megan and Mary ran to get it while Robbie handed him a small pocketknife. The girls put the footstool on the chair and Barton settled it firmly on the seat, then clambered up on the chair and then the footstool. "Just right," he announced, leaning over with the pocketknife in his hand to trim the top spike of the tree. Megan and Mary waited right under him, holding the angel.

Barton cut the spike, then handed it and the pocketknife down to Kate. He stooped to get the angel from the twins and the footstool teetered dangerously. "Be careful," Kate warned as he straightened up.

"Don't worry," he answered with a grin at her, the dimple in his cheek dancing, "I never fall." He leaned over to put the angel on the tree, placing it firmly down on the top spike so it seemed to float over the tree. Kate handed him two of the brass candleholders and he clamped them firmly in place in front of the angel.

"There," he said, looking down at Kate and the twins. "I told you that I never fall." He bent his knees to grasp the back of the chair just as the flimsy French chair broke completely apart. Barton went sprawling on the floor with a heavy thud.

There was a shocked silence for a moment as they all looked at him. He was motionless on the floor. Miss Armitage rushed to his side, knelt, and took his head into her lap. "Barton, speak to me! Are you all right?" Kate stood, her arms around the twins.

Barton opened his eyes and looked right into Miss Armitage's wide blue ones. "I'm just fine," he said groggily. "I can't believe I fell. I never fall."

Kate gathered her wits and knelt at his other side. "You didn't fall; the chair came apart."

"French furniture," Barton said weakly as he sat up and felt his head. "Does everything seem to be where it's supposed to be?"

Kate laughed and put her hand on his arm. "Yes, you look fine. How do you feel?"

"I feel . . ." he began.

Miss Armitage threw her arms around his neck. "Oh, Barton, what a scare you gave all of us! You could have been killed! All because of a stupid tree!"

To Kate's relief, Sandford came over and took Miss Armitage's arms. "Don't distress yourself, Amalie. Come over here and sit down."

Mrs. Armitage took her daughter by the arm as well. "Come over here and sit with me, dear." She turned and gave Kate a meaningful glance. "Her sensibilities are so developed that an episode like this quite oversets her."

In spite of Barton's protestations, even Megan and Mary

agreed that the tree trimming should be put off for an hour or two until Barton felt like joining them. "I'm really fine," he said, watching as Sandford and Mrs. Armitage led the distraught Amalie out the door. "There's absolutely nothing wrong with me."

"Except a lump on your head the size of a chicken egg," Kate said.

"And worse," Robbie added, "a rip in the back seam of your coat. Now *that's* a disaster. Heads can be mended, but coats . . . seldom to never."

The twins decided to play nurse and take care of Barton until he could help finish trimming the tree. They made him sit down and covered his knees with a robe, then crawled up on either side of him and proceeded to entertain him with their picture books.

As a matter of courtesy, Kate went to check on Miss Armitage. She was in bed, her mother hovering anxiously beside her. "She's quite overset," Mrs. Armitage reported. Kate looked at the bed. Miss Armitage was propped up against her pillows, sipping chocolate. She looked as healthy as ever. "Oh, Mama, do call Sandford in. He's the only one who can cheer me up when I feel this way," she said, her voice trailing off weakly.

"I'll go find him and send him to you," Kate said, trying hard to keep the annoyance from her voice. If there was one thing she couldn't abide, it was missish, fainting females.

She found Sandford in the library, sharing a cigar with Robbie, and sent him up to Miss Armitage's room. The more she thought about things, the angrier Kate became. She paced the room, picking up things and putting them back down. Finally, she picked up a bowl of pinecones and slammed it back down on the table. "Did you see that? Did you just see that? I'd *die* before I'd make such a cake of myself!"

Robbie blew a cloud and regarded her. "Care to enlighten me? I'm not really sure what I'm supposed to have seen."

Kate wheeled on him. *"That* . . . that *brazen* . . . that

78

brazen *woman!* That's what! Here she spurns Barton last Christmas, makes him the laughingstock of the entire ton, and then look what she does. Did you see her dash over there and cradle his head in her lap as if they were . . . they were *engaged* or some such! It was disgusting!''

Robbie thought a moment as he regarded the glowing tip of his cigar. ''You're right. You're his fiancée. *You* should have dashed over to him and cradled his poor broken head in *your* lap.'' He ducked as Kate tossed a pinecone at him. ''As I recall, dear Kate, you didn't even faint. At the very least, you could have fallen to the floor beside him.''

Instead, Kate fell into the chair across from him. ''Be serious, Robbie. This could be a catastrophe. This woman is just toying with Barton, trying to make Sandford jealous. I know it.''

''How do you know?''

She glared at him. ''I just know. Women know these things, Robbie. The only problem is that men don't. Barton is probably in there right now planning to resume their romance. He probably thinks the chit has finally come to her senses and wants to marry him.''

''It more likely that he's in there fighting off the twins,'' Robbie said dryly. ''After all, he's a wounded man. How could you leave him alone with them? A trial by fire, perhaps?''

''You're as bad as Sandford,'' she said, leaping to her feet. ''Barton and I happen to be the only ones here who really appreciate how well behaved the twins really are.''

Robbie's laughter followed her to the library door. Kate turned around there and did a rather unladylike thing, but one that was very satisfying: She looked at him and stuck out her tongue.

All was quiet as she approached the drawing room. She pushed the door open further and looked inside. There was Barton with a twin on either side of him. The furry robe was pulled up around them, and all three of them were asleep in front of the fire.

Kate tiptoed into the room to look at them. The twins were curled up in Barton's arms, their picture book open on the floor where it had fallen. Barton was holding them both. His cravat had either been untied or become untied, the torn jacket had been tossed on a nearby chair, and his head was bent to one side. Kate smiled as she looked at them. The twins looked like little angels, while Barton . . .

His lashes swept his cheeks and there was a faint half-smile on his face. A curl of dark hair had fallen onto his forehead, touching an eyebrow. Kate looked at him and felt a surge of emotion rush through her. Since childhood, he had been her very best friend. She couldn't analyze all the emotions she felt as she gazed upon him and the twins. Then her anger rose again, recalling how Miss Armitage had hurt him and that she would probably do so again.

Kate began to turn, as much to hide her emotions as to stop herself from reaching out to brush the hair back from his forehead. Instead, she smiled briefly at the three of them and tiptoed back out of the drawing room, softly pulling the door closed behind her.

Chapter 6

The rest of the afternoon was spent trimming the tree. Everyone agreed that it was the most beautiful tree ever. They didn't light the candles until after dark. Kate let the twins stay up and watch for a while as the candles flickered, glinting off the little brass candleholders and the small painted soldiers and angels Papa had bought the year before. "Tomorrow can we put the presents under it?" Mary asked sleepily. She had crawled onto the chair beside Barton and curled up next to him. Megan was almost asleep in Kate's lap.

"We'll begin. I don't have all mine ready," Kate said with a smile.

Barton looked at them lazily. The light from the candles and the glow from the fireplace gave his skin a golden cast, and his eyes looked very dark, almost black. "What's all this about presents? You told me that you exchange gifts, but I didn't bring any. Who's going to help me with that?"

Mary nodded and curled up even closer under Barton's arm. "We'll help. We know all about Christmas."

"I, for one, think this is really overdoing things," Miss Armitage said. "I really would prefer some entertainment in the evenings." She looked pointedly at Kate. "Perhaps we could have a play or a treasure hunt." She looked around the room, dark except for the candles on the tree and the fireplace. "Cards would certainly be better than sitting here admiring a tree. After all, if you've seen one tree, you've seen them all. One evergreen is much like another." She got up and paced around the room. "Sandford, would you like to play cards?"

"Anything you wish. We make two, but we need four."

Miss Armitage turned to her mother, who was once again working with her wools. "Mama?" She looked back. "Barton?"

He glanced down at Mary, just closing her eyes. "I hate to disturb her."

Miss Armitage had no such qualms. She shook Mary awake. "You really could ring for the nurse, Barton.

Mrs. Armitage nodded. "Children should be put to bed right after their suppers. It aids in digestion."

Kate looked at Sandford, who was taking in this exchange, a serious look on his face. She couldn't defend herself without making an issue of her method of caring for the twins. Stung, she stood and picked Megan up, then took Mary's hand. "I'll take them to bed. Go on and play cards, Barton."

As Kate left the room, Miss Armitage took Barton's hand and led him to the table, while Sandford lit all the other candles in the room. Kate stopped Wallace in the hall. "Will you please snuff all the candles on the tree. I'm afraid they might catch fire. The others are playing cards and might not watch them closely."

Wallace nodded. "We certainly don't want to catch the curtains," he said.

After Kate put the twins to bed, she started to go back downstairs, but the more she thought about Miss Armitage's possessive attitude toward Barton, the angrier she became. The last thing she needed to do was anger Sandford by making some sort of scene, so it was easier to stay in her room. She crawled into bed and read until she was sleepy.

The next day there was enough snow on the ground for the sleigh to travel. Evidently, Miss Armitage had put aside her qualms about the cold ruining her complexion as she planned the trip and invited Barton along. Mrs. Armitage, Miss Armitage, Sandford, Barton, and Robbie all went. Kate begged off with a headache. Robbie knew she was not telling the complete truth since she stared at the tips of her shoes the entire time she complained about her head. He laughed and pulled a lock of her hair as he went out.

"Do you want me to stay with you?" Barton asked, remaining behind a moment. Kate shook her head no. "I don't particularly want to go," he offered, but again she declined. Still, when she saw that Miss Armitage had placed herself in the sleigh between Barton and Sandford, Kate felt a moment of regret. Barton was too good for the likes of Amalie Armitage, she thought to herself. She was just toying with him, attempting to make Sandford jealous. Suddenly, Kate stopped and stared as the sleigh pulled away. There was another possibility: What if Miss Armitage was using Sandford to make Barton jealous? Was it possible that she cared for him? Did she regret her refusal of his proposal?

Kate's thoughts were interrupted by a tug at her skirt. "Kate, can you help us?" Megan and Mary were holding their colored paper and some scissors.

Kate sat down in front of the drawing room fire. The air was spicy with the smell of evergreens. "Now what do you want to do?" she asked the twins as they sat in front of her.

"We want to make Barton a present but we don't know what he'd like. We thought about a picture."

Kate nodded seriously. "A good choice. Perhaps we could make a penwiper for him as well. I think he'd like that."

They spent the next hour or so cutting colored papers and gluing bits and pieces down. The girls had wanted a picture of themselves, but after Kate persuaded them that would be extremely difficult if not impossible, they settled on a picture of the beautiful tree with the candles all lit. Barton would love it, she assured them.

They heard the sleigh riders returning before they finished

and quickly stuffed their papers, glue, and scissors under the nearest chair cushion. "It has to be a surprise or it doesn't count," Mary said, poking the edges under the cushion. They hid everything just in time, as Barton, Sandford, and the Armitages came in and dashed over to the fire to warm themselves. Megan and Mary stood guard in front of the chair to make sure no one sat down on it.

"It's unbelieveably cold out there," Barton said.

Miss Armitage put her hands up to her face. "My poor complexion. I must be chapped beyond belief." She turned to glare at Sandford. "I told you I was freezing, but nothing would do you but to continue until we crossed the bridge. No matter that I may never look the same."

Sandford bent low over her hand. "Nothing, my dear, can mar your exquisite beauty." He winked at Kate as he stood back up.

Miss Armitage was somewhat mollified. "Draw a chair up for me so I can warm my feet." She put a hand on Barton's shoulder and leaned on him as though she were unable to stand any longer.

Sandford reached for the chair Megan and Mary were guarding.

"No!" they both cried at once, and stood squarely in front of it. "You can't have this one."

Sandford stepped back and gave them a surprised look, which turned into a hard stare. Kate tried to step into the breach. "The twins aren't being rude," she said quickly. "It's just that they don't want a repeat of yesterday's accident. That particular chair isn't glued well and has been known to fall." This was an out-and-out lie, and she couldn't meet Sandford's eyes. She concentrated on a point of the woodwork directly over his head. "We certainly wouldn't want Miss Armitage to fall." She turned to the twins. "Would we, girls?" She was horrified at the bad example she was giving them.

The twins looked at her in puzzlement, as did Sandford.

"It looks all right to me. I don't think it'll fall." He reached again for the chair, and this time Megan grabbed his arm and bit him on the wrist. Sandford jerked his arm back, and to her horror, Kate saw a perfect semicircle of teeth marks on his skin. Sandford whitened and his mouth went into a hard, thin line. "Kate, I haven't said anything to you even when I felt these children were running wild all over the house, but this is too much. I demand that this child be whipped and I want it done right now."

The twins' eyes became as large as saucers. "Whipped?" They looked at each other. They had never been whipped in their lives.

"Whipped?" Kate asked faintly.

"Yes, whipped." Sandford's voice was icy. "Children should be taught some manners. They should also be restricted to the nursery. These children seem to have the run of the entire house."

Kate tried not to break into tears in front of everyone. She gathered up the twins and started to lead them out. "Our picture!" Mary wailed, trying to get back to the chair as Kate dragged her to the door. "I want our picture!" Kate paid no attention to her, pulling the two of them out the door and shutting it behind her. She didn't dare say anything until she had them safely in the nursery and that door closed behind her as well. Only then did she collapse on the floor, put her head down on the small table, and give in to tears.

The twins tried to console her, but Kate couldn't stop crying. He was going to take them away from her, she just knew it. He thought she wasn't fit to take care of them, and they would be taken to a strange land and restricted to a nursery. If she ever saw them again, they wouldn't be the happy Megan and Mary she knew and loved.

She didn't hear the knock at the door. Mary opened it and Barton came inside. He closed the door behind him and sat down on the floor beside Kate. "I brought these," he said, putting the scissors, glue, and colored paper on the table.

The paper was bent, creased, and torn in places. "Our picture," Megan moaned, picking it up and sticking her finger through a hole.

Kate mopped at her eyes. "It was a present for you," she said, trying not to cry again. "They wanted to make you a picture of the tree."

Barton picked it up and looked at it carefully. "It's a beautiful tree. Would you finish it for me?" He handed the ragged paper back to the twins. "I'd like to have it.

"He's going to take them away, isn't he?" Kate asked dully.

Barton put his arm around her shoulders and wiped her eyes with his handkerchief. "I don't know. I think there still may be a chance. I thought I might talk to him." He looked down into Kate's eyes. "That story about the chair just didn't work, did it? Frankly, Kate, you just don't do well with fabrications at all." He laughed and she grinned weakly at him. "That's better. Now let's see a smile." He gave the twins a serious look. "Megan, Mary. I think we need to talk about some things." He looked back at Kate. "With your permission, of course."

She nodded and they waited in silence for a moment. Then Barton turned to her. "Kate, why don't you go put some water on your eyes while I talk to the girls? Then perhaps we could plan something this afternoon."

Kate stared at him for a moment, then left them alone. She paused outside the nursery door and tried to listen, but couldn't hear anything. The only thing she achieved out of that was having Robbie catch her in the act. "Kate, the paragon of virtue, listening at doors," he said with a grin. "I came upstairs to see if you've flogged the hellions into submission yet."

In spite of herself, she laughed. "Barton's in there doing it," she told him. "Not whipping them, of course. I think he's giving them what-for."

"No better person," Robbie said, drawing her away from

the door. "Miss Armitage has decided to take the entertainment of our group into her own hands. There's to be cards tonight, a trip to the Abbey tomorrow followed by more cards, and a trip to the village after that. I'm sure she has a long list of local attractions."

"Probably all of them followed by an evening of cardplaying."

Robbie nodded. "If I were Sandford, I'd be on watch about that. She seems to have the same penchant for cards her father has. And," he added, "the same luck."

Kate looked at him sharply. "What do you mean?"

Robbie shrugged. "I'm surprised Sandford doesn't know. Her father was one of the ones in that scheme with Wrexham that went bad. As if that weren't enough, Armitage has had a monumental streak of ill luck at the gaming tables. When Lady Luck deserts a man, everything goes bad." He shrugged. "On-dit is that he's lost everything they have and she's on the lookout for a rich husband. I told you she was looking."

"Yes, but I didn't know they were under the hatches." Kate paused. "Poor Barton."

Robbie gave her a curious look. "What do you mean 'Poor Barton'? He managed to escape. I'd be tempted to say 'Poor Sandford.' " He paused a moment, then chuckled. "That should be quite a tug-of-war, shouldn't it? Sandford, stingy as he is, trying to hang on to every penny and the Armitages trying to lose it all at the gaming tables and on 'Change. London will enjoy that."

"Stingy? I know he's always talking about money, but is he really stingy?"

Robbie looked at her incredulously. "What's this, Kate? You're usually the one who notices these things. You must be so worried about the twins that you're not paying attention. Yes, stingy. Clutchfisted. All the man thinks about is money. I'm surprised that he hasn't tried to mend his fences with you, thinking that you're a better prospect than Miss Armitage.''

Kate blushed furiously and Robbie stared at her. ''He has! Lord, what gall!'' He started to say something else, but Barton came out of the nursery and walked toward them, smiling.

''The twins have been verbally flogged, if that's anything. They gave me their solemn promise never to bite anyone again.'' He laughed. ''You should have heard their reasons.'' He paused and looked somber. ''They really don't care for Sandford at all, Kate. I do believe I'll try to talk to him.''

''They don't like him because they know he doesn't like them,'' Kate said with a sigh. She put her hand to her head.

''Headache, little one?'' Barton asked, putting his hand on her shoulder. ''Why don't you lie down a while? Everything will work out.'' He smiled at her and went on down the stairs. Kate glanced at Robbie and saw the speculative look in his eyes as he stared at her first, then at Barton, rubbing his chin slowly all the while. She dashed into her room before he could comment.

Kate kept the twins in the nursery that night, on the premise that out of sight was out of mind. As Robbie had said, Miss Armitage took charge of the evening, and she, Sandford, Barton, and Robbie played cards. Kate sat a while with Mrs. Armitage, then pleaded a headache and went to bed.

The next few days went much the same. Miss Armitage had a trip planned every day and cards set up every evening. Kate usually excused herself from both. She spent her time with the twins instead, and whenever Barton could, he joined them. They went ice-skating and walking in the snow. They gathered more evergreens and holly, and made a snowman that looked quite lopsided. The wind blew their snowman down the next night and they spent the better part of one morning getting it propped up again. The twins put holly around its head and dubbed it the Christmas snowman.

Kate tried every way she could to keep the twins away from

both Sandford and the Armitages, but she was running out of ideas. When the next day dawned and there seemed nothing else to do, she resolved to take the twins shopping in the village. At least that would take up most of the day. To her surprise, Barton met them in the hall, dressed for the weather.

"I was invited," he said with a grin, looking at her. "After all, I have some shopping to do as well." He took Megan's hand and went out. "I thought the carriage instead of the sleigh," he explained, handing them up. "Most of the snow seems to have blown off the road during the night. It's not very icy, but it's rock-hard and this wind is too much for a sleigh."

"Did the Christmas snowman blow over again?" Mary asked, peering over his shoulder. "I don't see it."

"We'll fix it when we get back," Barton said. "I think we're going to have to pour some water on him to freeze him to the ground." He changed the subject to the shopping trip as he tucked the furry lap robes around them. He even promised they could eat at the inn. The twins shrieked.

"Enough!" Kate put her hands over her ears. "We'll go back home if you don't behave."

The pair hushed immediately and Barton looked at her in admiration. "How on earth do you do it? I'm putty in their hands." He gave her a strange look and raised an eyebrow. "It must be something females learn from birth."

Kate laughed with him, but she wondered if he was talking about the twins or about Miss Armitage. Privately, she thought it was Miss Armitage. She had seen Barton looking at her several times during the past two days. Each time, he had had a rather strange expression on his face. Kate couldn't define it. It looked as if he were perplexed rather than besotted. Kate had finally concluded that he was trying to define his feelings for Miss Armitage.

For her part, Miss Armitage was flirting outrageously with both Sandford and Barton. If she hoped to make Sandford fall in love with her, it didn't appear to be working. He seemed more angry than in love. This bothered Kate, since the very last thing she wanted at Falwall Hall was Sandford in an angry mood. From what she knew of him, his temper had always been volatile, and if provoked, he could decide in an instant to take the twins away.

"A penny for your thoughts." Barton interrupted her reverie.

Kate looked back from staring at the landscape and managed a smile. "My thoughts are hardly worth that," she said, trying hard to appear cheerful.

The carriage stopped in the village and they were soon going from shop to shop. The village was small, and to Kate's dismay, everyone there seemed to know that she and Barton were engaged. There were many congratulations, and the vicar's wife, Mrs. Linwood, whom they met when they went to eat, inquired coyly about a wedding date. When Kate stammered, the woman came right out and asked if they would be getting married at Falwell Hall or in London. "So Linwood and I may make our plans," she explained.

Barton took Kate's arm. "Quite probably here," he said with a smile that completely won over the vicar's wife. "As I'm sure you know, Kate and I prefer the quiet life in the country."

Kate watched glumly as Mrs. Linwood left her meal uneaten and scurried out the door to spread the word.

"Heavens," Barton said with a laugh, "I'm an on-dit again."

Kate looked at him, then at the twins. They were busy trying not to get bread and butter all over themselves. "I'm sorry, Barton. I don't know why I thought this would work. I promise I'll make it all up to you someday."

"Make what up?" Megan asked, bits of butter falling on her dress.

"Don't talk with your mouth full," Kate said.

They walked the village after lunch, splitting into twos or sometimes threes so the purchases would be a surprise. The twins were curious about Barton's parcels, but he was firm. "Not even a hint," he told them with a laugh. Of course, they were just as secretive about his present. After much consultation, the twins and Kate had decided on presents from each of them—a paperweight, a book, and a silver bookmark. The twins had originally preferred getting him a box of sweets, but Kate convinced them that the other presents would last, and every time Barton used them he would be reminded of this Christmas at Falwell Hall.

They got home late, the shopping trip a complete success. When they paused in the hall to sort the packages, Kate realized she had left one of hers in the village. "I think I left it on the floor at the inn," she said with a sigh. "I was so overset about Mrs. Linwood that I didn't keep up with my things. It's probably gone by now."

"I doubt that. I'll go back and get it if you wish." Barton put his parcels aside. He seemed to have several.

Kate shook her head. "I'll have Wallace send someone later. I don't want to put you out." She helped the girls gather up their various packages and sent them upstairs. "You've done enough today by just taking us. On behalf of the girls, I thank you."

He scooped up his packages. "It was my treat. I've never taken a bevy of females shopping before and it was an experience I wouldn't have missed." He paused at the foot of the stairs and looked back at Kate. "Besides, I did have my shopping to do." He laughed. "I think this idea of presents is a custom I could learn to like as much as the twins do."

Barton was not to be found at suppertime and Kate held the meal for half an hour. When he did not appear, they began without him. They heard him come in partway through supper, and Kate left her place at the table to go see about him. She stopped in the doorway in surprise. He was muddy, his coat was torn, and there was a scratch on his face. He grinned sheepishly at her and handed her her parcel from the inn. "I went back to get it for you," he said. "I was in a

91

hurry to get back to change for supper, and my horse stumbled and fell.''

Kate touched his arm. "Are you hurt?"

He shook his head. "No, but my horse hurt his leg. After I crawled out of the ditch, I found him and had to walk him back. I put him in the stable and rubbed him down as best as I could.''

"Ben will take care of him. He's excellent with horses."

Barton frowned. "When he returns. He's gone to visit his sister. I didn't want the stableboy to touch the horse until Ben had a chance to look at him. He should be back in an hour or two.''

Kate grinned at him. "He'll be back fussing and fuming about how you don't know how to treat horseflesh."

Barton smiled back. "Fussing and fuming probably isn't quite an apt description. Cursing and ranting are probably more like it." He looked over her shoulder into the dining room. "At any rate, I think the horse is all right. I'm going to change, but I don't think I can be down in time for supper.''

Kate put her arm through his and walked him to the bottom of the stairs. "I'll have a tray sent up, and then you can eat and join us in the drawing room later."

Barton looked down at her strangely, then looked back to the dining room door, where Sandford and Miss Armitage were staring at them curiously. "Fine," he said, hesitating only a moment. Then he gave her a quick kiss on the forehead and went up the stairs.

"Very touching," Miss Armitage said acidly as Kate came back into the dining room.

"You know how these young lovers are," Robbie said as Kate sat down beside him. She blushed furiously and glared at him as he laughed.

Chapter 7

Sandford was quite attentive to Kate as they went to the drawing room after supper. He made it a point to sit beside her, much to Miss Armitage's annoyance. As soon as Barton came down, Miss Armitage devoted herself to talking to him. To Kate's surprise, she found herself glancing at Barton and Miss Armitage continuously. She was finally able to put a name to the emotion she felt and was horrified to realize that she was more than a little jealous. So much, in fact, that she had a difficult time listening to Sandford talk about his latest decision on his investments. Robbie sat by the fireplace, looking from one couple to the other and, every now and then as he caught Kate's eye, grinning.

"I asked you a question, Kate," Sandford said with annoyance. Kate forced herself to turn and give him her undivided attention. "Exactly how much," he repeated, "do they cost per year?"

"What? What costs?"

Sandford gave her a disgusted look. "The twins. Exactly what do you spend on their upkeep per year? I know William left them an allowance, but your father told me to keep it. It's quite a tidy sum now." He frowned slightly. "The status of the allowance is unclear, but I think the girls could be kept for much less than the amount William left. After all, how much could two small girls cost?"

"We've never calculated the costs," Kate said coolly. "We don't consider the children in the family in the same light as bank notes."

"You're a woman, so of course you wouldn't," Sandford said easily, giving her a smile. "But I'm sure your father has calculated it. I was quite surprised when he wrote and told me to keep the allowance. Of course, I haven't touched it."

"But you'd have to spend it if you took the twins to live with you."

Sandford shrugged. "They *are* my responsibility." He paused. "Mrs. Armitage seems to feel they would benefit from a good boarding school. I've sent out inquiries but haven't heard anything about the cost. Do you have any idea what a good boarding school would cost for them? The initial costs—that is, what it would cost me now—might be greater, but in the long run, I think as they grew older, it would be cheaper for them to board year around."

Kate felt the room spin slowly around and closed her eyes. "What's the matter, Kate?" Sandford asked in alarm, holding her hand. "Are you ill?"

"Probably caught a chill from being out shopping all day," Mrs. Armitage said, pulling at her wools. "I wouldn't dare let a daughter of mine be out such hours. Very bad for the constitution."

Kate felt as if she would scream if she stayed another minute. She got to her feet as Barton came over to her. "Do you need to rest, Kate?" he asked anxiously.

She pulled away from him. She didn't want to speak to anyone, not even Barton or Robbie. "No. I mean yes, I do feel terrible," she said, stumbling blindly toward the door. "I'm going to rest." She fled from the room before anyone could stop her.

As she went up the stairs, Kate heard Mrs. Armitage talking. "Young girls just can't go cavorting all over the country all day. It sets a bad example for the children, too. Children see; children do. They'll come to the same thing, mark my words.''

Kate ran up the rest of the stairs and slammed the bedroom door behind her before bursting into tears. Boarding school for the twins! She'd take them and hide in America first. There had to be some way to protect them.

"If you married Sandford, at least you could watch them. He doesn't love you at all, but you have a better portion than Miss Armitage." The words came right into her head, almost as if someone had spoken them. "No," she said slowly, "I couldn't." But, she realized as she dropped into a chair, she could—and would—do it if she had to.

Kate worried and fretted, pacing the floor for what seemed like hours until she judged that everyone had gone to bed. Then she slipped out into the hall and knocked softly on Robbie's door. She wanted to tell her brother what Sandford had said and try to discuss the situation with him. There was no answer. He must still be downstairs, she decided, probably in the library smoking yet another cigar in front of the fireplace.

As she passed the drawing room door, Kate smelled cigar smoke and heard a noise. Robbie must be in there. She pushed the door open. "Robbie," she called as her eyes adjusted to the dimness of the room. There was only the light from the fire throwing a soft glow into the room and she could see someone standing there. "Robbie?" She blinked her eyes and, to her horror, realized it wasn't Robbie. It was a couple standing in front of the fireplace, almost embracing. They wheeled at the sound of her voice. It was Miss Armitage and Barton.

"Kate!" His voice sounded strangled.

Kate was trying to speak when she felt a hand on her shoulder. "Did you call me, little sister?"

Robbie was behind her, solid and dependable. Kate wanted nothing as much as to melt right into him and have him support her, but she didn't dare break down in front of Amalie

95

Armitage. She forced a smile. "I just wanted to talk to you a moment." She looked back at Barton and Miss Armitage and smiled again. "Sorry to interrupt you."

Barton rather unceremoniously left Miss Armitage and rushed across the room. "You didn't interrupt us," he said hastily, taking Kate's arm and pulling her into the room. "We were just . . . just discussing the weather."

"A good topic," Robbie said with a chuckle. "I think we might find it rather frosty from now on." Kate glared at him, but Miss Armitage laughed as she came to stand beside Barton.

"You may be right," she said archly, "but I rather think it may be warmer than usual." She drifted toward the door. "Indeed, it may." With a tinkling laugh, she left them in the darkened room.

"I know what you're thinking, Kate . . ." Barton began, but she stopped him.

"Don't bother, Barton. I know how you feel about Amalie Armitage, and I certainly wouldn't have asked you to play in this farce if I had known she would be here at Falwell Hall." Kate looked down at the heavy sapphire on her finger and pulled it off. "Here," she said, offering him the ring, "you may need this."

He held her hand and put the ring back on. "The ring stays where it's supposed to be."

"I'm not sure this is where it's supposed to be." She started to take it off again, but Barton held her hand and she relented. "All right, Barton," Kate said. "But don't let your sense of duty get out of hand. I don't hold you to your promise at all."

"Such nobility, such sacrifice," Robbie remarked with a chuckle. "You sound like one of those heroines in novels, Kate. I didn't think you had it in you."

"Oh, shut up," she snapped, not bothering to conceal her irritability. "I came down here to discuss something serious with you, and all I get are remarks about . . . about . . ."

She spluttered, searching around for the perfect word but not finding it.

Robbie lit a cigar and offered one to Barton. "I'm always ready for serious discussions, Kate. Do go on."

She looked quizzically at Barton as he sat on the sofa and drew her down beside him. "I'm sure you're going to talk about the twins, and I feel I'm involved enough to be part of the discussion." He grinned as Robbie lit some candles. "The scamps grow on you, don't they?"

Kate nodded and took a deep breath. "Sandford wants to put them in boarding school. Permanently."

"Now?" Barton frowned as he looked at her. "Surely you must be mistaken, Kate. They're far too young for boarding school."

She shook her head and the tears she'd been suppressing came welling from her eyes. "No, that's what he said. He thinks it might cost more now, but in the long run, it'll be cheaper to board them permanently, year around."

"Here, here." Barton mopped at her eyes with his handkerchief, then pulled her next to him and kept his arm around her shoulders. "He's probably just talking, exploring one possibility or another."

"No, he means it. You were right, Robbie. The man's a complete clutchfist. He'd really do it if he thought he could save a shilling."

Robbie gave a harsh chuckle. "I've begun to think that his reputation doesn't do him justice. He's more than just a penny-pincher." He reached over and patted Kate's hand. "Would you like for me to talk to him?" She nodded and he continued. "If all else fails, we'll petition the courts. That may be a long shot, but it'll be worth a try. At least it'll tie things up for a while."

Kate sat up and rubbed her eyes with her fingers. "There's one other option," she said slowly. "I could marry him. On a strictly cash basis, I think my portion is larger than Miss Armitage's. Sandford would appreciate that. At least I would always be with the twins." She felt Barton's fingers tense on her shoulder.

" 'On a strictly cash basis'?" Barton put his hand under her chin and turned her face toward his. "Kate, my dear, I think you've been talking to Sandford way too much." The smile faded as he looked into her eyes, a worried frown between his brows. "That's really no answer, Kate. In the first place, you don't . . ." He dropped his fingers and averted his eyes. "I don't know how you feel about him, so I really can't address that aspect."

Kate felt herself redden. "I don't care for him at all. Most of the time, I don't even want to be around him. When I was seventeen, I thought he was dashing and adventurous, but now he seems to have the heart of an account book."

"Seems isn't the right word, Kate," Robbie said dryly, puffing on his cigar. "He *does.* Never saw a man more concerned with debits and credits."

Beside her, Kate heard Barton release his breath slowly, as though he had been afraid to breathe. He touched her hand and smiled at her again. "That settled, there's no reason for you to even entertain such a thought. It would solve absolutely nothing for you. Sandford would still have the authority to do whatever he wished, Kate. You'd have less protection than you have now. Now, you've got your father, your brother, and me."

"Thank you, Barton, but I don't want to draw you into our problems," she began.

Robbie blew a cloud in her direction and grinned. "Seems to me that he's already right in the middle of them," he said with a laugh. Kate ignored him.

"As I said, thank you, Barton," she continued, "and I don't want to involve you any further." She glared at Robbie. "Is *that* satisfactory?" He laughed and she went on. "I've thought about this thing with Sandford. Barton, you need to get on with your own life, and Robbie will marry and have children of his own someday. The twins are my responsibility. No, it wouldn't be ideal, but a marriage with Sandford would solve most of the problem."

Barton shook his head. "Sandford could still do whatever he wished to with them."

"He could," Kate agreed, "but I could do some things as well," she said with a shaky laugh. "If I worked at it, I could make his life a living hell. Would that be enough?"

"At what cost to your own life?"

She looked at Barton in surprise. He had a strange expression on his face, a look that she couldn't decipher. "Does it matter?" she asked quietly, standing. Kate glanced at Robbie, hoping to tell Barton that he was free to pursue Miss Armitage, but somehow it didn't seem the time or the place. Instead, she turned toward the door. "For all his ranting about responsibility, I really don't think Sandford wants to be bothered with the twins at all," she said as she paused in the doorway. "They're too much of an expense. He feels obligated to take them because William named him their guardian, but he really doesn't know what to do with them."

"I know," Barton agreed with a smile. "He seems to view them as something to put a value on and tot up on a ledger sheet." He chuckled as he looked at the end of his cigar and relit it. "Don't worry about a thing, Kate. I have the glimmerings of a plan."

"I hope it's better than Kate's scheme," Robbie said with a laugh, blowing smoke her way.

Kate made a face at the both of them and went up to bed.

The next morning, the twins were up and tumbling on her bed well before their usual hour. "Uncle Barton's going to London," they announced, "and asked us if there was anything we wanted."

"Uncle Barton? Girls, you shouldn't call people familiar names unless they ask you to do so." Kate struggled to a sitting position and pulled a twin down on either side of her.

"He asked us to," Mary said.

"That's right," Megan chimed in. "He's an uncle anyway,

he told us, so he certainly didn't mind having us call him that.''

''Did you say he was going to London?'' Kate sat bolt upright, last night's scene with Barton and Miss Armitage flashing through her mind. Perhaps Barton was leaving because of Miss Armitage. Perhaps because of her. Perhaps because he wanted Miss Armitage and couldn't court her under Kate's very eyes. There were dozens of possibilities. ''Has he gone? I really need to speak to him.''

The girls looked at each other behind her back. ''I don't think he's gone yet, but he was almost ready to leave.''

Mary nodded. ''I think Mrs. Armitage wanted him to do something for her. He was having to wait until she wrote something out.''

''You two wait here for me.'' Kate scrambled out of bed and looked at herself in the mirror. ''On second thought, go down and ask Barton to wait until I speak to him. I'll hurry.''

The twins tumbled out of bed and ran out the door, their nightgowns flapping around their feet. ''I hope they don't run into Sandford,'' she thought to herself as they slammed the door behind them, their bare feet making slapping sounds on the floor. ''He'd think they were perfect hoydens. Again.'' With a sigh, she looked down at the heavy ring on her finger, twisting it so she could see the sapphire in the morning light. No matter which way it was turned or which light it was viewed in, it was always the color of Miss Armitage's eyes.

Quickly, she rang for Riggs, but nothing went right. Her dress looked terrible; her hair kept falling every which way; and the more she hurried, the longer things seemed to take. She squirmed so much that Riggs let the brush slip and all Kate's hair fell down again.

Megan dashed into the room, still barefooted, still in her nightgown. ''Uncle Barton's ready to leave,'' she announced. She looked strangely at Kate. ''Why are you getting all dressed? It's just Uncle Barton.''

Kate fought the blush she felt flaming her cheeks as she

100

snatched up a ribbon and tied her hair back carelessly. "I know that, but a lady tries to appear her best at all times." She looked down at Megan as they went out into the hall. "Which is more than I can say for you, young lady. I want you to find Mary and the two of you go get dressed."

At that moment, Sandford's door opened and he stood there, elegantly garbed for the day. He smiled at Kate, then transferred his gaze to Megan, slowly looking at her from her disheveled hair all the way down to her bare feet. Kate was horrified to see a large tear in the hem of Megan's nightgown. "Is the child ill?" Sandford asked.

"Uncle Barton's going to London," Megan announced.

Sandford looked at Megan, then up at Kate. "Really?" There was a wealth of meaning in the word and in his lifted brow. Most of what he seemed to be implying was that Megan had terrible manners.

"Go on, sweetheart," Kate said, giving Megan a pat on the shoulder. "Find Mary and the two of you get dressed. I'll come have breakfast with you if you like."

Instead of quietly trotting off, Megan gave a war whoop and dashed off down the hall, yelling for Mary. Kate could have cheerfully strangled her.

"Mrs. Armitage is right, I think. It's time to begin thinking of a boarding school," Sandford said, falling into step beside Kate. "And aren't they getting rather familiar? *Uncle* Barton? They certainly don't call me uncle."

"They . . . they . . . After all, Barton *is* my fiancé," she said, staring straight ahead.

"Really?"

Kate turned sharply on the stairs to look at Sandford. She opened her mouth to say something, but no words came. She turned to walk on down the steps, when Megan and Mary came hurtling out of the breakfast room and dashed up the stairs. "He's going to get us a present!" Mary told her, grabbing Kate around the knees.

101

"One for each of us." Megan looked at Mary. "And something else special."

Mary reached over to clamp her hand over Megan's mouth, and they lost their balance and started to tumble down the stairs. Mary still had one hand around Kate's knees, so she went down with them. There were arms, legs, and bare feet flying everywhere. All Kate could think of was wrapping her arms around the girls so they wouldn't get hurt.

They reached the bottom in a heap. There was no sound for a moment, and Kate was terrified that one or both of the girls was hurt. She herself had a sharp pain in her ankle but she ignored it. "Megan, Mary, are you all right?" She tried to stand up but her ankle didn't seem to want to hold her. Tears came to her eyes, but she turned her head and wiped them away. Kate couldn't let Sandford know the twins had caused her to hurt herself. She sat down hard on the bottom step.

Barton came running to the bottom of the stairs and knelt down beside them, while Megan took Kate's face in both her hands and looked into her eyes. "Hurt? Are you hurt?" Megan looked ready to burst into tears.

Sandford grabbed Megan by the shoulder and pulled her away. "Someone ring for the nurse to take these children to the nursery where they belong," he said sharply. He started to reach out for Kate, but looked at Barton kneeling beside her and stopped.

Kate reached for Megan, but Sandford stepped between them and motioned to a maid. "Take the children away," he said. "They are not to be downstairs for the rest of the day. They will stay in the nursery."

"No!" Kate couldn't stop herself. She scrambled to her feet, hanging on to Barton's arm. "They didn't do anything. I . . ." She averted her eyes from Sandford's. "I slipped."

"Don't be ridiculous, Kate. You're only hurting them when you mistakenly try to protect them." Sandford's voice was cold. "I'm their guardian, and it's time I stopped you from

102

spoiling them." He looked at the girls standing on the stairs, both of them now sobbing. "Go upstairs and I'll deal with you later. You are not to leave the nursery." He looked back at Kate and smiled. "That's all it takes, Kate. A firm hand."

Kate started to speak, but Barton nudged her. "Let me take you upstairs, Kate," he said, holding her around the waist.

"I really don't . . ." she began, but Barton gave her a nudge and a smile.

"Your fiancé wants to say good-bye," he said with a smile as they walked by Sandford and went up the stairs. Kate tried to make her steps firm, but every one hurt.

As soon as they rounded the corner at the top of the stairs and were out of sight, Barton let her go and turned her to face him. "You did hurt yourself, didn't you, Kate? I could feel you hesitate every time you put your foot on a step."

She sagged against the wall. "My ankle."

Before she could move, Barton had dropped to his knees and was running his fingers over her ankle. "Barton!" she gasped, looking around. "What if Mrs. Armitage comes by?"

He chuckled. "A fiancé's privilege, Kate." He stood up and put his arm around her waist. "You've twisted your ankle, but it's not broken. You'll need to stay off it for a day or so and keep it propped up." He laughed. "It'll give you a good excuse to stay in your room with the twins."

"It'll delay our escape to America." She made a face.

Barton laughed and put his fingers under her chin, lifting her face to meet his eyes. "Promise me you won't worry. Or escape to America." His eyes became serious. "I'm going to London for two or three days. It's about last night's business. I hate to leave you now, but I'll be back and have, I hope, good news."

"What kind of news?" Kate had a mental image of an engagement announcement telling the world about the up-

103

coming nuptials of Barton Rush and Amalie Armitage. "You don't have to come back, you know."

"But I do," he said with a grin. "I wouldn't miss Christmas here for the world. The twins are expecting me, and besides, I want to be here. I'm going to London for a reason—actually, two reasons—but I don't want to say anything until I get back."

Kate allowed herself to put her hands on Barton's chest. She spread her fingers apart and felt the warmth of him through her fingertips. The large sapphire gleamed dully against the dark blue of his coat. "Do you want to take this?" she asked, pulling the ring from her finger. If he was going to announce his engagement to Miss Armitage, she shouldn't be wearing it.

Barton took the ring, then held her hand and slipped the ring on and off twice. "All right," he said finally, pocketing the ring. "If you want me to do this, then you must have a clue about what I plan to do in London."

"I think I do." She forced herself to smile at him. "I think it's probably the right thing for you to do."

He broke into a grin. "You do? Kate, that's wonderful! I had no idea you felt that way. This puts all my fears to rest." He gave her a sheepish grin. "I was worried, especially after last night." He looked at her bare hand. "If anyone asks, tell them I took the ring to London to be repaired. That's close enough to the truth."

"I will." Kate looked at her bare hand and thought her heart would break. To her surprise, Barton put his arms around her and pulled her close to him. "Don't let Sandford bully you or the twins while I'm gone," he whispered in her ear. "I think I can work everything out so that it's best for all of us."

Kate pulled back to look at him. Before she could say anything, Barton bent his head and kissed her lightly on the lips. "I've got to be gone or I'll never get there." He smiled

104

at her. "Remember, Kate, hold your ground. I'll be back before Christmas."

In a flash, he was down the stairs and gone. Kate stood at the top of the stairs and watched him take his many caped coat from Wallace and go out the door. She looked down at her finger, remembering how strange the ring had felt there when Barton had first given it to her. Now her hand felt bare without it.

She swallowed the lump in her throat and started to go down the stairs, but changed her mind. She simply couldn't face Sandford or, worse, Miss Armitage. Instead, she went to the nursery and sent down for breakfast for herself and the twins. They all sat—Kate with her foot propped up on a small footstool—around the small table and ate. They were still there an hour later, Kate in a chair with the twins wedged in on either side of her. She was reading a book aloud to them when Sandford appeared in the doorway.

Chapter 8

"Are you all right?" he asked pleasantly, coming into the room and looking around.

"I'm fine." Kate put her finger in the book to keep her place. "I was reading to the twins. Do you want to hear our story as well?"

"You know good and well that I don't." Sandford paced around and stopped by the window. "I need to have a serious discussion with you. I wanted to speak to your brother as well, but he seems to have gone off for the day." He glanced at the twins. "A private discussion."

Kate got up and gave the book to Nurse Freeman. She went down the stairs without answering Sandford's comments about the weather. It was enough to walk without grimacing. They went to the study, where she sat down in a chair by the fireplace. Instead of sitting, Sandford stood by the mantel and pulled a letter from his pocket.

"I've made a decision about the twins. Mrs. Armitage is right: They need to go to a good school until they get older. I'll make the decision later about whether they need to stay in school or if something else should be done."

"They're just babies!" Kate cried. "They'll be lost at a school."

Sandford looked at her. "They'll get the discipline they need. If they're not taken in hand now, Mrs. Armitage is right: They'll be nothing but hoydens by the time they're fifteen. I'm going to have to think about marrying them off, and I can't risk having liabilities on my hands."

"Liabilities?" Kate couldn't believe her ears.

Sandford nodded and looked at his letters. "Exactly. I received replies to inquiries I made about schools and discovered it's going to cost much more to keep them in school than I realized. Then there will be the cost of wardrobes and seeing that they have the right social come-out and so on. William's allowance to them won't cover all the costs." He looked at her and frowned. "Still, I'm prepared to do the right thing since they are my responsibility. Do you think your father might want to contribute?"

Kate tried to hang on to her temper. "He's contributed to this point, hasn't he? I'm sure—"

Sandford interrupted her. "I know he's contributed. Still, if this is done right, the cost will certainly be more than William left for them, not counting their marriage portions. I really can't touch that for their upkeep and education." He sat down in the chair across from her and smiled. "I've thought about this, Kate. We could get married and then you could take care of them. I think you could do a credible job of educating them—and any children we would have, of course. It would certainly cost much less." He paused. "Of course, if we had male children, they'd have to go off to school. That's very important for men; they need that background. It really doesn't matter for girls, but since boys do make connections at school, I could justify the cost."

Kate tried to breathe. "Is this an offer, Sandford? Are you suggesting we marry or else you're going to send the twins off to a boarding school?"

"I thought this was what you wanted, Kate." He shrugged slightly. "Barton is, I understand from Miss Armitage, gone, and I see you're no longer wearing your ring." He frowned. "Right now, I'm not really sure if this is a formal offer, Kate.

Your father and I would, of course, have to discuss the financial arrangements before I could decide."

Kate closed her eyes and thought about the twins. She had to do what was best for them. "What about Miss Armitage?" she asked. "I thought you planned to offer for her."

"It is an option," he said, looking at the figures in his letters again. "However, Miss Armitage is an expensive woman, quite accustomed to the best and to frivolous living. Also, I understand her father's pockets are to let."

"So I'd be a better choice." Kate tried not to allow sarcasm to come through her voice.

"Exactly," he said, smiling. "One of the things I really like about you, Kate, is that you grasp reality. I like that in a woman." He glanced back down at his letters. "I have replies from two schools. One is Miss Finchley's near here— it's much cheaper—and the other is Miss Bramley's in Bath. Your father would have to help with the expenses if the girls go there." He folded the letters and repocketed them. "Of course, I'll write your father before I decide. May I tell him that we've had this discussion?"

"By all means." Kate stood up, not bothering to hide the pain that flashed across her face. "I'll write him as well."

Sandford smiled at her. "We match well, don't we, Kate? Both of us look at reality and make the best decision under the circumstances." He hesitated. "I'd appreciate it if you didn't mention this conversation to Miss Armitage. At least not until I've had a chance to discuss it with your father."

"I wouldn't dream of it." Kate gave him a false smile and went out the door. She had to find her brother.

Robbie didn't return until late. He came up to her room to find her packing a trunk. "What are you doing? Surely you're not planning to run to America with the twins in a trunk." He peered down into the interior of the trunk. "It won't work, Kate. You can't stuff both of them in there." He looked at her again as she fought back tears. "Exactly what *are* you doing, Kate?"

"I'm looking at reality and making the best decision under the circumstances," she said, trying to smile at him through her tears.

Robbie gave her a strange look. "That sounds like Sandford. What's going on here?" He put his arm around her shoulders.

"Oh, Robbie," she wailed. "Barton's gone to London to see about marrying Miss Armitage, and Sandford wants to take the twins and put them in a boarding school. And he wants to marry me, Robbie!" She dissolved into tears.

"Well, up until last night, I was under the impression that marriage to Sandford was what you always wanted." He handed her his handkerchief. "Except for the part about the twins in boarding school, of course."

"He wants me to keep the twins if we get married."

Robbie smiled and took back his handkerchief. "Then that solves everything, doesn't it? You'll have Sandford and the twins as well, although as I recall, you plan to make his life a living hell. Am I correct?"

"It isn't funny, Robbie." She wiped away a tear. "It doesn't matter anymore. Barton's going to marry Miss Armitage," she wailed. "He's gone to London to take care of it." She looked down at her bare fingers. "He took the ring with him."

"And that isn't all right?" Robbie gave her a teasing smile. "I realize that wasn't the original plan, but isn't this better? You get the twins and Sandford, while Barton gets Miss Armitage. It seems to me that all's well that ends well."

"Oh, shut up!" Kate broke into fresh sobs. "You don't know anything!"

He turned her around to face him and wiped her eyes. "Oh, but I do, Kate. Tell me, have my suspicions been verified? Have you fallen in love with Barton?"

Kate blushed and turned away from him. "Of course not. That is . . . not precisely in love with him, Robbie. Barton's

109

a wonderful person and he deserves better than Miss Armitage. He's . . . he's . . . I just think that . . ."

Robbie turned her around to face him. "I just think that you're in love with Barton Rush. And, for my money—bad choice of words there," he said with a grin, "Sandford is a dead bore and not nearly good enough for you, Kate."

"But Barton's in love with Miss Armitage," she said wearily, shifting her eyes from Robbie's. "He told me so."

"He did?" Robbie sat down in a small chair by Kate's dressing table. "Surely you misunderstood, Kate. I think Barton has seen Miss Armitage for what she is. I certainly don't think he cares for her, despite Miss Armitage's games. She's been trying to play off Sandford and Barton, you know. I hear she's desperate to get married before her father's a known bankrupt."

"That wouldn't matter to Barton if he loved her."

Robbie nodded in agreement. "Yes, but it would to Sandford." He grinned at Kate. "At the risk of sounding like Sandford, Miss Armitage would be much better off with him than she would with Barton, as far as fortune goes."

"Yes," Kate agreed, "but she'd be better off with Barton in other ways. She'd have to account to Sandford for every farthing she spent."

Robbie thought a moment. "I doubt that." He sat up and took Kate's hand in his. "Don't leave in the middle of the night. I won't allow Sandford to do anything about the twins for a while. I give you my word on it. In the meantime, I'll go to London to talk to Barton."

"There's nothing to talk about," Kate said with a sigh. "Anyway, you don't need to go to London. He said he'd be back before Christmas. I suppose he wants to come back here and make his arrangements with Miss Armitage."

"He is coming back? For Christmas?" Robbie thought a moment. "That's very interesting, Kate."

Kate leaned up against the bed and rubbed her ankle. "I don't find it interesting at all, Robbie. Actually, if I live through this Christmas, it'll be nothing short of a Christmas miracle."

He stood and pulled her hair playfully. "It'll work out. The twins have been bothering me again about the animals talking in the stable. They even made me promise to take them out there tonight and sit for an hour or so. Do you want to go along? I could use some company, and you seem to be the one who started this whole thing."

Kate laughed. "That should be something. You sitting in the stables waiting for the animals to talk. The only thing you're likely to hear is Ben muttering to himself as he finishes up."

"I've already warned him. There'll be no language to sully female ears." Robbie laughed. "Be sure to wear warm clothes. It'll be cold out there."

They sat without incident for almost an hour in the stables before it was time to come inside and dress for supper. "I think," Megan said, skipping along in front of Kate and Robbie, "that we came too early. Aren't they supposed to talk at midnight?"

"Midnight. Didn't you say Christmas Eve?" Mary asked. "Does that mean the midnight before Christmas Eve or the midnight of Christmas Eve?"

Kate looked at Robbie and he shrugged. "Don't ask me." She took the twins' hands firmly and guided them around to the back door. She didn't want to chance running into Sandford.

"It isn't magic if we listen to it," she told them. "That's why it's special. They're never going to talk while we listen." She shooed them up the back stairs. "Now go on and get ready for bed."

"I like your style, Kate," Robbie said with a grin. "When in doubt, tell them to go to bed."

"It's better than your style," she said with a laugh as they walked into the front of the house. Too late, she noticed that she had straw and worse on the hem of her gown.

111

The next two days passed uneventfully, and then it was Christmas Eve. Kate's spirits were low, but she did her best to keep up appearances and try to be as involved as the twins. Unfortunately, the girls were overexcited, so Kate was trying to do several things at once: keep the twins away from Sandford; pretend to be happy and excited about Christmas; and put up with Miss Armitage's comments about the girls' rowdy behavior. The last was the hardest to do. With every comment Miss Armitage made, her mother nodded in agreement and added her own comment about how wonderful her children were. To hear Mrs. Armitage tell it, her children were all paragons.

The twins got even more excited as the afternoon wore on. Sandford kept frowning at them, his disapproval quite evident. It was the custom at Falwell Hall to have an open house and presents for all the servants and villagers on Christmas Eve. Kate and Robbie stood in the hall welcoming everyone, while Mary and Megan helped hand out the gifts. They were so excited they were almost dancing. Worse, almost everyone who came in asked Kate when she and Barton were planning to marry. Mrs. Linwood stared pointedly at Kate's finger and was rude enough to ask where her ring was.

"My fiancé took it to London for repair," Kate answered automatically, looking elsewhere. Her gaze fell on Miss Armitage, who regarded her in a strange, speculative way.

"La," Miss Armitage said, laughing as she smiled at Mrs. Linwood, "and here I thought we'd had a lover's quarrel and dear Mr. Rush had gone."

Mrs. Linwood looked quickly at Kate. "He's just gone to London," Kate said, riveting her attention on the floor. "He's planning to return for Christmas."

"Of course," Miss Armitage said, linking her arm through Mrs. Linwood's. "My dear Mrs. Linwood, you must have refreshments with me and tell me all about your charming village."

Robbie came to stand beside Kate and extend a welcome

to the next guest. "It takes one gossip to know another, doesn't it?" he whispered, glancing at Miss Armitage and Mrs. Linwood.

Kate sighed. "I love being an on-dit almost as much as Barton does." Robbie laughed as they welcomed the next guest.

By suppertime, Kate was exhausted and her ankle was hurting. To her surprise, she had no trouble persuading the girls to go upstairs to bed. "I had a little talk with them," Sandford told her as they watched the pair go up the stairs. "I think their behavior will improve markedly."

"I wasn't aware it needed improvement," Kate answered acidly.

Sandford offered her his arm to take her into supper. "I know you weren't, Kate. That's why I took matters into my own hands."

Kate bit her lip to keep from replying as Sandford helped her to her seat.

"I thought," Miss Armitage remarked casually at supper, "that Barton was going to return before Christmas."

"He'd better hurry," Sandford said. "Christmas will be here shortly.

Almost as if on cue, they heard Barton come into the front hall. He looked in the dining room and smiled at them. "If you don't mind my being late, I'll change and come down in a few minutes."

When Barton joined them, he smiled at Kate but sat down in an empty chair next to Miss Armitage. Kate tried to tell herself that with Robbie sitting on her left and Mrs. Armitage on her right, Barton had no choice except to sit beside Miss Armitage. But no matter how hard she tried to convince herself, it still did bother her. Barton was still sitting beside Miss Armitage, and they were laughing and talking as he told her all about the latest doings in London. Kate didn't think she had ever been more miserable in her life.

What little hope she had held that Barton would fix things

113

evaporated as he laughed and talked with Miss Armitage. There was, she realized, only one thing for her to do: She would see Sandford and tell him that if the financial negotiations with her father were satisfactory, she would marry him as soon as possible. She was, Kate reflected, assessing the realities and making the best—the only—choice under the circumstances.

Chapter 9

To Kate's dismay, Barton asked Robbie and Sandford to join him in the study after supper. He apologized to Miss Armitage and promised to join the ladies as soon as possible. He gave Kate what she thought was a tight, small smile, then left. As the study door closed behind the men, Kate could almost hear her hopes crashing. Barton was, she knew, going to tell them that he planned to marry Miss Armitage. At least, that would force Sandford to offer for her. There was no one else.

Before the men returned, Kate went up to her room, pleading a headache that was very real. She didn't want to hear any of the congratulations or comments. Instead, she waited in her room until she heard Miss Armitage and her mother go to bed. It was a few minutes after midnight—Christmas, she thought dully. Her favorite time of the year would be forever marred by the thought that this was the day she had committed herself to a life of misery. "Another realistic assessment," she muttered to herself as she took one last look in the mirror at her appearance and went downstairs to find Sandford. She hadn't heard him come up and was almost sure he was still in the drawing room, smoking and perhaps sipping port.

Sandford was there, sitting in front of the fire. He was neither smoking nor drinking, but was just sitting there in the semidarkness. She had been afraid that Robbie and Barton might be with him, but he was alone.

Kate almost asked where Barton and Robbie were, but at the last moment she checked herself. If Sandford had not taken Barton's news well, then Barton's whereabouts would be the last thing he wished to discuss. Instead, she feigned a happy mood. "What, Sandford, alone on Christmas? Let's begin to celebrate." With that, she took a candle and lit several of the tiny candles on the tree. They shimmered against the brass of the candleholders like stars in the darkened room. "There. Doesn't that make you feel like Christmas?"

Sandford shrugged. "I never feel like Christmas. It's just another day and a complete waste of money."

Kate kept smiling as she sat across from him. She tried to think of a way to broach the subjects of marriage and the twins, but she didn't have to. Sandford brought it up himself. "Speaking of money, why didn't you tell me about Barton's plans? Late this afternoon, I finally had a conversation with your brother, but he seemed singularly uninformed about the family finances. He didn't seem to think the costs involved in the upkeep of the girls were worth discussing. However, when Barton discussed it with us in the study, he seemed . . ."

Kate couldn't bear to discuss Barton. She didn't want to hear about Barton and Miss Armitage. "What did Robbie say?" she asked.

Mercifully, Sandford's reply was drowned out by a commotion from the front. Kate stood up just as the door was thrown open and Barton came in, carrying two very cold, very dirty girls. He had one under each arm, and their arms and legs were flying. "Kate! It's true! It's true!" Megan shouted as Barton put them on the floor. They were dancing with excitement.

"What is?" Kate looked anxiously at Barton. "What? . . ."

"Don't ask," Barton began, but it was too late.

"The animals talk," Mary said, running to Kate. "We

slipped out and heard them. We could hear them right through the wall of the stable.'' She danced around Sandford's chair. "Kate, you said they'd talk on Christmas Eve and they did.''

"And what did they say?'' Sandford asked.

"Oh damn! Oh hell! Oh damn! Oh hell!'' Both girls shouted out the words together.

"Girls!'' Barton's voice was sharp. "Sit down!'' To Kate's amazement, both girls sat immediately and looked at Barton. Sandford started to speak, but Barton stopped him. "Just a moment, please. I need to say something to the girls.'' He turned to the twins. "Girls, you didn't hear the animals talking. That was Ben trying to take care of my horse. Ben says things girls shouldn't repeat.'' He looked at Kate. "My horse pulled a muscle, so I went out to check on him before going to bed. Ben had promised to look at him. When I came out of the stable, I found these two huddled against the side, their ears to the wall. Do you want to take them up to bed?''

With a horrified glance at Sandford, Kate nodded and herded the girls out the door. This had to be the final straw. Sandford would probably send the twins to a convent to clean up their language. Kate tried not to let her gloom show. After all, it was Christmas now and the girls were entitled to one last happy day. She washed them off and put clean nightgowns on them. When they put their arms around her neck and kissed her good night, she thought her heart would break.

"Did Uncle Barton give you your present, Kate?'' Megan asked. "He said we couldn't have ours until tomorrow.''

Kate couldn't even look at them. "I'm sure I'll get my present tomorrow, too. We'll open them together.''

Megan looked at Mary. "Didn't Uncle Barton say he was going to give Kate her present tonight?''

Mary nodded in agreement. "Go get it, Kate, and come show us.''

"Absolutely not.'' She tucked the covers around them. "We'll all find out tomorrow.''

Slowly, she went back down the stairs and looked at the drawing room door. She could hear Barton and Sandford talking to each other. She closed her eyes and inhaled the spicy scent of the evergreens and burning candles. Christmas and her life might as well be over. She didn't want to go back in there and see Sandford, much less hear him prose on about finances and liabilities. It was all too much to bear. She sat down on the bottom step, put her head on her knees, and cried.

"What's this?" Barton sat down beside her and put his arm around her shoulders. "Crying on Christmas?"

"It's the worst Christmas I've ever spent," she sobbed, putting her head on his shoulder. He tightened his arm around her and pulled her closer. "It's all right, Kate. Everything's all right."

"No, it's not," she said, sobbing. "You heard how the twins disgraced themselves. Now Sandford will send them away and I'll have to marry him if I ever have a chance of seeing them again. I don't want to marry him. And worse," her voice broke into a wail, "you're going to marry Miss Armitage."

Barton turned her face up to his and wiped her eyes with his fingertips. "Miss Armitage? Wherever did you get that idea, Kate?"

"Because"—she paused and hiccuped—"because you went to London. I know you went to make all the arrangements."

He smiled at her. "Oh, sweetheart, how could you think that? I went to London to talk to my solicitor about William's will. I wanted to find out what legal aspects were involved in Sandford's guardianship. I thought you knew why I went."

"Then I don't have to marry him?" She looked at Barton and blinked away the tears. "I don't want to."

He pulled her close to him and kissed her hair. "I'm certainly glad to hear that, because I want to marry you myself and I can't do that if you're promised to Sandford."

Kate drew back so she could see his face, and she blinked hard. "What?"

He grinned at her. "Why can't I ever do this right? I had

planned the perfect romantic scene in front of the Christmas tree. I just don't have the touch, do I?''

"What did you say, Barton?" Kate sat up to look at him. "Not about the tree. About marrying me."

"I want to marry you, Kate. I want to adopt the twins and I want us to be a family. I've already talked to Sandford."

"And he said?" Kate held her breath.

Barton laughed, the dimple in his cheek deep. "What do you think he said? I told him that as soon as we were married, I'd adopt them and release him from any expense or obligation. He can even keep the allowance William left the girls."

"He agreed!" Kate flung her arms around Barton's neck and kissed him on the cheek. "He agreed!"

Barton moved her arms and held them. "Yes, he agreed, and if truth be known, I think he was glad someone else was going to take the responsibility." He chuckled. "I don't imagine I'll ever see a moment's peace again, will I?" Then his brown eyes darkened and he became serious. "There's just one thing, Kate." He hesitated a moment. "I want you to marry me, but I want you to be sure about my reasons. It isn't just the twins, although I've come to love them." He paused and looked at her. "I wish I could say this in a perfect way, but I'm not really that good with words so I'll just be plain." He took a deep breath. "Kate, more than anything else, I hope you'll come to care for me. I want to make a home for the twins and for you, but I want you to know that I've . . . I've come to love you very much. I suppose I've always loved you, but this time it's different." He paused a moment. "I really can't explain it, but . . . ."

"You don't have to explain, Barton," Kate said, her green eyes shining. "I know exactly how you feel because I feel the same way. I can't think of anything better than spending my whole life with you." She put her hand on his cheek and traced the mark of his dimple with her fingertip. "The reason I didn't want to marry Sandford was because I'd fallen in love with you. I couldn't admit it because I thought you were in love with Amalie Armitage. After I saw you two the other night . . ." Her voice trailed off.

"Ah, that. I was afraid that you had gotten the wrong impression then. She came in to see me and she . . . she suggested that we might want to take up where we left off." He grinned broadly, his dimple quivering. "I told her I was an engaged man." He turned his head and kissed her fingertip. "Now that I'm really in love, I realize my feelings for Amalie were merely infatuation. Thank God she turned me down last year. If she hadn't, I might never have known just how wonderful love with the right person can be." With that, he pulled her toward him and kissed her, softly at first, then quite thoroughly.

"Merry Christmas, Kate," he whispered. "I love you." He smiled. "Would you like your Christmas present from me now? That was also part of my trip to London. I wanted to get just the right present for you."

"I think I've already received the perfect present, Barton."

He chuckled and pulled a box from his coat. He flipped it open with one hand and pulled out a ring—this one a perfect single emerald the color of Christmas evergreens. He smiled as he slipped it on her finger. "A Christmas ring for my Christmas love," he whispered.

Kate started to reply, when she heard a noise on the stairs behind her. The twins were there, in their nightgowns, their eyes wide. They looked at each other. "Is that your present? Kate, did you get a present?" they asked as Barton held out his arms for them. In a second, all four of them were snuggled on the stairs together.

Kate held out her ring for them to see. "We're going to be a family. Forever."

Megan looked from Kate to Barton and then to Mary. "I told you it would happen," she said smugly.

"I knew it all the time," Mary said.

CHRISTMAS IN THE COUNTRY

by

Nina Porter

Chapter 1

"But Hector," said Galatea Haslett, eldest daughter of Baron Haslett, to her younger brother that November morning, "why on earth should *I* ask Papa to invite guests to a Christmas house party here?" She frowned, pushing her wire spectacles up on a nose that was actually rather cute but too small to properly hold them in place. "Papa knows I have no use for fashionable entertainments. Why, my translation of the *Aeneid* is only just begun. And out here in the Cotswolds, as we are, where shall we find enough people for such a party? No, I am not—"

"*You* are precisely the proper person," Hector insisted. "Please, just think about it. At least think about it."

He sighed. He didn't like deceiving his sister, even for her own good, but Papa had made it exceedingly clear. He must persuade Galatea to ask for this Christmas house party, and he must involve her in the preparations for it so that she would have to forsake her books—those stuffy old books that kept her out of the marriage mart—for at least a little while. That would not be quite so hard if he didn't, at the same time, have to keep her from discovering that the whole scheme had actually been hatched in Papa's fertile brain, a rather last-ditch endeavor to procure for Tea, who was already approaching four and twenty, a husband of the proper sort.

Hector swallowed another sigh. Papa had been adamant

about this, saying that if Hector wanted his last racing wager paid off—a trifling sum of a few hundred pounds, but more than his pocket could bear at the moment—he *must* persuade her.

Tea stood there, clutching one of those musty old books she so loved, her pale brow wrinkled into a pensive frown. The sunlight pouring through the breakfast room accented the ink stains on the front of her gown, the smudges on one cheek. Tea had always been something of a puzzle to him, engrossed as she was in the ancient past.

But she had been kind to him, always kind, even when he'd been a toddler and she'd found him playing with one of the old books that were already precious to her. Kinder than Mama, when he'd inadvertently defaced one of their mother's Greek texts by drawing a stick horse on it. Now if Tea were enamored of horseflesh, that would make some sense. But those dusty old books? How could anyone get excited about books?

She should have a husband, he supposed. There wasn't much else in life for a woman. Yes, a husband—a good one, of course—and some little ones to cling to her skirts. That would bring Tea out of her preoccupation with musty old times. Of course, it hadn't brought Mama out of hers. But it was worth trying. And Papa . . .

"Hector," Tea said, still frowning. "I *have* thought. And I just don't think I'm the person to do this. Ianthe is the one who knows about entertainments, balls, and that sort of thing. She's the one to ask. Not me."

Hector knew that as well as she did. But Papa had said Tea must ask, Tea and only Tea. "Perhaps," he agreed with a nod, "but Ianthe is always asking Papa for *something*. You know how she is. He says he's getting tired of giving in to her every demand." Hector looked around, then lowered his voice and added, "Just yesterday he told me he means to refuse any request of hers for some time. Just to teach her a lesson."

Tea nodded. No one in the family, even one as immersed in books as Tea was, could avoid knowing that Ianthe, though beautiful—very beautiful, Hector admitted—had a disposition far different from her looks. Truth to tell, Ianthe was shallow, all looks and no heart. And very vehement about having her own way.

And Hypatia—at fifteen Hypatia was horse crazy, which was fine with him—was just too young to be given responsibility for a party. Hypatia, he repeated silently. What a name for an innocent baby!

For the thousandth time, Hector wished Mama had never heard of the ancient Greeks. His own name had been a curse to him all through public school. Only since he'd attained manhood had he been able to give off bloodying noses and pounding heads in order to receive the respect he deserved.

But that had little to do with this. He'd best give off woolgathering and get on with it. "Please, Tea," he begged, putting on his most winning smile. "Do it for me? You know how deadly dull it can get here during the holidays. And Papa won't let me spend them in the city."

He held his breath. Would she give in? "Please," he begged, "do this for me. And after the New Year, when I go back to London, I'll—" He cast about in his mind. What could he offer her? A ribbon? A bonnet? No. He had it! "I'll look for a book for you, whatever book you wish."

Tea's face lit up with delight. "Really? You would do that for me?"

"Yes." Feeling guilty, he made his voice as sincere as possible. "Of course I would."

She gave him a sly look, accompanied by a sad smile. "But I have asked you before, Hector, and you always said—"

"I know. I know." She *had* asked and he'd made excuses, most of them really transparent. "But you know I always keep my word. And I give it to you now. Do this for me and I'll search out your book, whatever book you want, even two,

125

through all the dusty, musty, ancient and smelly shops of London. I promise," he finished fervently.

Tea laughed. For the first time he thought about her laughter, really thought about it. It was a lovely sound, sweet and trilling, not like the shrill staccato of young city women. And now that he looked at his sister closely, he was a little surprised. She wasn't actually bad to look at. If she were washed up and gowned proper, she might even turn a few heads. Her hair was blond, of course, and the fashion this year was brunette; she was tall, and the fashion was short. But still and all, properly groomed, she could be quite a looker. She might even snag a husband. Did Papa have someone in mind?

"All right," she said. "I'll do it. I'll ask Papa. But you must go with me."

Outside the door to Papa's study, Galatea paused. She didn't really want to do this; she wanted only to go back to her books, to a most intriguing passage about Queen Dido that she hoped to get just right. But there'd always been a soft spot in her heart for Hector, ever since that long-ago day when Mama had put the squalling red-faced infant in her four-year-old arms. So little and so helpless he'd been. Galatea had loved him from the first moment, wanting to keep him safe, to make him happy. But this—this was more than kissing a bruised knee, cleaning a scraped elbow, or telling an exciting story. This house party would take a long time, a lot of work.

"Hector, maybe I should go freshen up first. I mean, you know Papa doesn't like to see me with ink on my face."

Hector put on his little-boy-hurting look. "Please, sister dear. I ain't asked you for much."

"Really," Galatea said. "Why must you say *ain't* when you know better?"

Hector looked even more crestfallen. "All the chaps say *ain't*, Tea. It's fashionable."

"Oh, very well." Galatea sighed. She really knew very little about the ways of the fashionables. She much preferred her life in the country, alone with her books.

"Please, Tea," Hector begged again. "Please?"

Even though she knew better, she felt her heart softening toward him. And anyway, it wouldn't hurt to ask. More than likely, Papa would say no to the whole idea. Then she wouldn't have to do a thing; she could go right back to her books. And Hector would still be satisfied.

She took a deep breath and tapped tentatively on the door.

"Enter," Papa said. As she came into the room, he looked up from his desk and smiled. "Galatea, my dear, do come in."

"Thank you, Papa." Hector stood close behind her, so close it was a wonder he didn't tread on her heels or her hem. He must be terribly bored to want this party so strongly.

She took the large chair Papa gestured to, perching on the edge of it, and Hector took up his stand beside her.

"What is it, my dear?" Papa asked. "Did you wish to see me about something?"

"Yes, Papa." Now that she was here, she *knew* this wasn't a good idea. But Hector coughed and looked at her pleadingly, and not wanting to disappoint him, she forged ahead. "Papa, I was thinking, with Christmas coming and all, it would be nice to . . . maybe . . . well, maybe invite some guests."

Papa smiled. "Guests?"

"Yes, some guests." Beside her, Hector coughed again. "For Christmas. For a house party," she went on timidly. Surely Papa would say no to that. She knew he really didn't care to have noisy people about.

But to her surprise, he said, "Yes," his smile growing larger. "That's a good idea. It's time we livened the place up. You may enlist any of the servants to help you," he went

127

on. "And you may invite . . . oh, say, a dozen or so persons."

"A—a dozen?" Tea choked on the word. "Where shall I find—?"

"I have some friends," Hector interrupted, "who've been eager to see the place. I'd like to invite them up. That is, if it's all right with Tea."

Galatea swallowed, but before she could reply, Papa answered for her. "I'm sure she won't mind at all. Your friends will improve our holidays. And Ianthe will enjoy their company."

"Yes, Papa," Galatea said, feeling a little better. Perhaps a party would make Ianthe more charitable. Lately, deprived of her London friends, she'd been quite snappish. The other day she'd almost bitten poor Hypatia's head off. "I'm sure Ianthe will like that. I know! She can plan—"

"No," Papa said, his voice becoming stern. "You must manage the affair yourself."

Herself? "But, Papa, I know nothing about—"

"That doesn't matter," he said firmly. "It was your idea and you must manage it."

Hector lingered in the study after Galatea left. He waited till she had closed the door behind her, then turned back to Papa.

The old gentleman was beaming and Hector felt his spirits rising. Surely he wasn't the cad he'd been feeling. He hadn't done such a terrible thing. Tea needed to get away from her books.

"Very well done, my boy." Papa was actually rubbing his hands in glee. "Now, about those friends of yours . . ." He paused.

"Yes, Papa?"

"You may go into the city for a few days, but just a few.

To issue your invitations. But be sure to include Barnaby, Baron Tragon's eldest son.''

Hector felt a rush of cold dread. Papa couldn't mean . . . ''That bookish chap? The spindly one with the spectacles?''

Papa rubbed his hands again. ''Yes. That's him. He should suit Tea admirably, don't you think?''

''I—'' Suddenly mindful of his still-outstanding debt, Hector nodded, though feebly.

''See to it then,'' Papa said, turning back to his papers. He looked up again. ''Oh, by the by, my boy, I shall send payment directly to your bookie. *This* time.''

Hector stumbled out, shuddering at the vision of a houseful of miniature Teas and Barnabys marching solemnly about, their ink-stained fingers clutching moldy old books, their little noses supporting identical wire spectacles. Ghastly! Absolutely ghastly! He could not doom Tea to such a dire fate. Something must be done.

Chapter 2

The next week, with Hector gone off to London and Christmas only three weeks away, Galatea set herself, with some trepidation, to planning the house party. She tried first to consult with Mama about the menu, activities, and possible guests, but her mother was immersed in Ulysses's problems with Circe and only muttered, "Do as you please, my dear. I'm sure it'll be just fine."

Ianthe was eager to help, of course, quite full of ideas, but the menu she proposed, consisting of exotic dishes that Galatea could not recognize, was impossible, and the cost of the hothouse flowers she proposed would have sent Papa into apoplexy.

Hypatia was not even interested. She could speak of nothing but next spring and which mare would drop what kind of foal.

Her head ringing, Galatea repaired to the kitchen for a cup of strong tea and some comfort. "Oh, Cook," she complained, perching on the stool that she'd used since she was a little girl, "I am at my wit's end. I don't know a thing about organizing a house party. It's quite beyond me, I'm sure!"

Cook put a cup of steaming tea before her. "You just drink this, miss. It'll raise your spirits, it will."

Cook poured herself a cup of hot tea as well and took it

to the cane rocker by the hearth, the same rocker that had been exclusively Cook's for as long as Galatea could remember. "Now," Cook said with an encouraging smile, "let's just go at this a piece at a time. Ain't no different than planning a meal—only somewhat bigger."

For the first time since she'd left Papa's study the week before, Galatea saw a small ray of hope. Perhaps she *could* get through this thing without making an utter fool of herself. She leaned forward. "Thank you, Cook. Thank you so much."

When Galatea left the kitchen an hour later, she was clutching a sheaf of notes and wearing a smile. With Cook's help, she was going to carry this thing off. It was a tremendous undertaking, of course, but she would do it this once—and only this once—for Hector. She went to look for Hypatia. She would know where they should take a sleigh ride to find a Yule log to bring home.

In London, Hector was slumped in a chair at White's, staring into a glass of wine. This house party thing was enough to make a fellow take to drink. All the chaps he'd thought might make good—or even decent—brothers-in-law were already engaged for the holidays. His sisters, much as he loved them, were no lure to young males. No one even remembered Tea from her come-out—and he couldn't puff her charms too much. After all, these chaps were his *friends;* he had to go on living with them after the holidays were over. Unfortunately, everyone remembered Ianthe, though without much pleasure and with very little interest in seeing her again.

He sighed mournfully. The only taker had been that infamous sludge Barnaby, the next Baron Tragon. *He'd* pushed his spectacles up on his beaky nose, smiled shyly, and replied, "Kind of you, old fellow. Most kind. I'd be delighted."

Hector sighed again. Where could he find some more eligible *partis?* He simply couldn't let Tea get fianced to that bookworm Tragon. He was such a weak-kneed fellow, with no style to him at all.

"Mind if I join you?"

Hector looked up. Alexander, Viscount Kendall, stood before him in all his sartorial splendor.

"Not at all. Not at all." Hector motioned to a seat. "I warn you, though, I am quite in the dismals. I will not be good company."

Alec settled into the chair across from him and motioned to the waiter to bring wine. "I know precisely of what you speak."

"You do? That is," Hector went on in amazement, "how can *you* have any problems?"

Alec laughed. "Just because I was several forms ahead of you in school and knew how to keep myself—and you—out of the suds then doesn't mean that I can do it now."

Hector stared. He could hardly believe it. London's most eligible bachelor . . . with problems? "You haven't—" He halted. He couldn't ask Alec a question like *that*. Anyway, Alec wouldn't be that stupid. "What—" he began again, then ground to another halt. It was infernally hard to ask such personal questions. He'd always looked up to Alec, always admired him. But the fellow *had* said he was in trouble.

And they *were* friends. He'd never forget how Alec had saved him from being sent home in disgrace that time the vicar found the dead cat tied to the bellpull. No, Alec was his friend. It was his duty to help him. Hector took a deep breath and leaned across the table. "What's wrong?" he managed to ask. "That is, I'd be glad to help if I can."

Alec sighed, running a hand through the curly black hair that was reputed to send London's youngest ladies into swoons of rapture. He straightened the broad shoulders that affected older ladies in a similar, though perhaps more experienced, fashion. "It's those abominable Lindens," he said, his black brows meeting in a great frown. "They are driving me up in the boughs."

132

"The Lindens?" Hector sipped his wine, still confused. "What harm can the Lindens do *you?*"

"No harm," Alec said stiffly. "At least I hope not. But they're a most infernal nuisance."

"They're always a nuisance," Hector replied. It was clear, though, that there was more to this than a simple nuisance. "What are they doing now that is especially obnoxious, besides, of course, carrying their sordid on-dits about all of London?"

"It's the young one." Alec glanced around and, though their table was some distance from the others, lowered his voice. "She is after me."

Hector felt his mouth drop open. He closed it with a snap. Had something affected his hearing? Surely this couldn't be true. "After *you?*" he repeated in amazement.

Alec nodded heavily. "Yes, my friend. After *me.*"

Hector gulped and swallowed hastily. He couldn't laugh. He shouldn't laugh. Alec was rather high in the instep, a little on the prickly side; he might take offense at laughter. "But how can she—how can she think that *you—*"

"I don't know," Alec replied grimly. "But she's like a terrier after a rat. Everywhere I go she's there, hanging on my every word—indeed, hanging on my arm, even pressing that flat bosom against it—fluttering those ghastly eyelashes at me." He groaned. "I tell you, Hector, I'm afraid to open my lips. Everything I say, no matter how innocuous, she construes as some gallant compliment to her, some sweet words of love. I told her outright that I had no interest whatsoever in matrimony, and she laughed and said how sweet I was. She won't hear anything that says I'm not interested. And her mama . . ." He groaned again.

"Ah," Hector observed with deep sympathy, "I see." The formidable Lady Linden would give pause to any man, even one as high in society as Alec, Viscount Kendall.

"She stands there," Alec went on, "that huge bulk of hers

133

poised, watching my every move, till I feel like a mouse, waiting for the cat to pounce."

Hector smothered another laugh. This was serious business indeed, not a subject for amusement. "So what are you going to do?"

"That's just it," Alec said. "I don't know. The holidays are coming. I could run off to Sussex, to my estate, I suppose. But I hate to creep out of the city like a dog with his tail between his legs." He frowned fiercely. "No man has ever made me turn tail and run. Shall I run from a woman— a woman like *that?*"

He took a swallow of wine. "But come, Hector, enough of *my* troubles. Tell me, what has sunk *you* into the dismals?"

"It's this infernal house party," Hector explained. "Papa insisted that Tea manage it, though *she* doesn't know that. And *I* am supposed to provide the eligibles."

"Your father wishes to marry your sisters off?" Alec inquired with a wry smile, which showed he was well aware of the maneuvers of such fathers, having, indeed, been their object.

"Tea at least." Hector sighed again. "Ianthe is very beautiful, but her tongue . . ." He shook his head and motioned to the waiter to bring more wine. "She makes Shakespeare's shrewish Kate seem like a veritable angel."

"And Tea?" Alec asked. "I seem to remember her comeout. Tall, isn't she? And fair?"

Hector nodded. "Yes. Actually, she's a pretty good looker, when she's dressed proper. But she has no head for fashion nor any desire for it. I'm afraid she's just like Mama, her nose always in a musty old book. Why, you'd think all those ancient Greeks and Romans were something special."

Alec laughed. "I suppose some people do think so."

Hector snorted. "Well, I ain't one of them. And poor Tea . . . she's a kindhearted soul. My favorite sister, you see, 'cause she always took care of me when I was a sprout and

Mama had *her* nose buried in the books.'' He vented a sigh of mammoth proportions. "I can't see why a fellow should be burdened with such womenfolk. It just ain't natural.''

"You're right,'' Alec said. "But I begin to think all unmarried women are after but one thing: marriage to a man of title.''

"Not Tea,'' Hector protested. "That's just the problem. She doesn't think of marriage at all. And she hasn't any idea that this thing was a setup.'' He smiled a little sheepishly. "I even offered to search out old books for her. You wouldn't believe the affection that girl has for musty old books! Anyway, Papa found out about my last wager, and he kindly offered to pay it if I could—''

Alec chuckled. "If you could con your sister into arranging this house party.''

"Yes.'' Hector nodded. "It's for her own good, you know. Every girl needs a husband. But Papa insisted I invite Baron Tragon's eldest, Barnaby. You remember the chap, the one with his beaky nose always in a book?''

"I know him,'' Alec said. "Not a bad fellow.''

Hector snorted again. "Perhaps not. But Tea will never get her nose out of books, never get to *live*, with the likes of him. She needs a real man.'' He paused. "I got a soft spot in my heart for her, you see. So I invited all the chaps I could think of, hoping maybe one of them would appeal to her—and her to him, of course. But nobody can come. They're all already committed.'' He frowned. "And Papa's going to be unhappy with me, to say the least.''

"Hmmmm.'' Alec ran his hand through his hair again. "You know,'' he said thoughtfully, "I might just be able to help you.''

"You might?'' Hector eyed him hopefully. "Anything! I'll take any suggestion you can give me.''

"I am looking for a haven,'' Alec said. "A safe place to spend the holidays, away from you know who. So . . . why don't you invite *me* to this party?''

135

"You?" Hector gasped, hardly believing his good fortune. "I would have, of course I would have, but I thought—That is, a man like you—"

Alec waved his apologies aside. "Yes, I think that will serve admirably. I shall spend the holidays in the Cotswolds. And if you like, I could invite some others. Some more eligibles."

"Like?" Hector cried, so loudly that heads turned in recrimination and the older club members scowled at this rash disturbance of their peace. "Oh, I should be eternally grateful, most eternally grateful."

"Good then," Alec said, preparing to rise. "It is settled. Only one thing."

"Anything, my friend," Hector replied fervently. "Anything at all."

Alec smiled grimly. "Remember, I am not in the matrimonial mode. So do not expect *me* to be available to either of your sisters."

"My God, no!" Hector cried. "The thought would never have crossed my mind."

Alec smiled and left the room. *But it will cross Papa's*, Hector thought. *It will definitely cross Papa's.*

Chapter 3

For an anxious Galatea, the days passed in a whirl of frenzied activity. Never had there been so much to do and so little time in which to do it. Every time she so much as thought to steal a moment to work on her precious translation, something else came up. Reassuring Hypatia that though she was not yet come-out she *would*, since they were in the country, be allowed to attend all the functions. Soothing Ianthe because Papa only allowed her to get new gowns from the local seamstress, not from one of London's fashionable modistes. And worrying about Hector, who mooned around looking alternately elated and depressed but, when questioned, insisted he was fine, just a little anxious—that is, eager—to see his friends.

And so the dreaded day finally arrived. All Hector's friends—and Ianthe's—were expected by dinnertime. Thank goodness yesterday's snowfall hadn't made the roads impassable. Now that Galatea had done all the work, it would be dreadful if the party failed to happen.

Standing in front of her cheval glass while her maid, Peters, adjusted her hair ribbon, Galatea felt that she, like her namesake, had been transformed. The creature who looked back at her didn't look at all like the self she knew. Customarily, she wore gowns of dark shades and serviceable fabrics, which showed ink and dust less.

But this gown that Papa had ordered for her was of pale blue sarcenet. Gathered high under the bosom, it fell from there straight to the floor in graceful folds. Since it was an afternoon dress, it didn't sport ruching, dreadful stiff stuff anyway, but it was trimmed with ribbons of deep rose—a contrast she found quite lovely, especially since Peters had put a matching ribbon in her curls. She liked the gown's square neck and long narrow sleeves, too. Smiling, Galatea poked the toe of a blue satin slipper from beneath the hem, a slipper that was a perfect match. Well, she looked present-able, at least. Papa should have no reason to fuss about that.

She turned to Peters. "I still don't see why I can't have my spectacles. I feel so strange without them. And things far away look so fuzzy."

"Can you see the bed and the chair?" Peters asked.

How silly. "Of course I can see them. I'm nearsighted, you know. It's things far away that I can't see well."

"Then you won't be running into anything," Peters said. "That's enough."

"But—"

"Yer Papa sent word," Peters reminded her. "He said to leave 'em off."

"Oh, very well."

Sounds from outside drew Peters to the window, which overlooked the front lawn. "A carriage, Miss Tea. They're starting to come."

Galatea turned anxiously toward the door. "Oh, dear. Where is Hector? He promised to be here, to help me greet the guests and—"

"Miss Tea." Peters's firm tone halted Galatea halfway to the door.

"Yes, yes. What is it?"

"You got to calm down." Peters propped her fists on her ample hips. "These folks'll be here fer a whole week. You go on like this, and we'll have to put you to bed afore din-ner—all wore out already."

138

Galatea smiled and took a deep breath. "You're right, of course, Peters. Thank you."

Hector would be downstairs. He would help her get through the greetings. After that, it would be easier. The guests would know each other and . . .

Hector stood waiting at the foot of the stairs, as nervous as a jockey before a big race. If Alec and his friends didn't show up . . . No, no, he wouldn't think about that. That Tragon fellow would show, of course, no doubt about him. And Ianthe had been allowed to invite a couple of girls. They might . . . But of course, if they were *her* friends, *he* wasn't likely to be interested in them, even for the briefest flirtation. Tea had mentioned one of her friends, too, Celandine something or other. He'd been too worried about Alec to remember the correct name.

Strange, of all the chaps he'd thought to invite, Alec had never even entered his mind. It was true they'd been friends, of a sort, at school. But Alec had always been ahead of him, a big boy, feared and respected, though not as feared as some other big boys. But now Alec was the Viscount Kendall, top-of-the-trees Corinthian, the best catch in all of London, so the eager mamas said. And, if Hector read the matter rightly, the least likely to be caught. So for Alec to come to this house party was a real favor. Even if the man had his own reasons for attending.

Hector could hear the carriages rumbling to a halt outside. Where was Tea? He turned toward the stairs and gasped, his jaw dropping open. Could that be Tea, that vision of angelic loveliness at the top of the stairs?

"Oh, Hector," his sister cried. "I'm so glad to see you! The guests are arriving. They're here!"

Dismounting from his carriage, Alexander, Viscount Kendall, looked around him with some relief. It had been a long, cold ride. True, the countryside was enjoyable, even in the snow, and the golden stones of the Hasletts' manor glowed in the afternoon sunlight, but he was having second thoughts. He still had to face the sisters. And he'd been told enough Banbury tales about beautiful sisters—sisters who'd turned out to be closer to ugly—to fill a good-sized book.

Still, anything was better than being hounded around London by that horrible Martine. The girl was not downright ugly, but she *was* sticklike and he'd always preferred his women with ample bosoms. She wasn't completely lacking in intelligence, either, though he suspected her talents ran to tallying up a man's possessions more than discussing ideas with him. He supposed to some men she might even look appealing. But not to him. Certainly not to him. Besides, he was accustomed to choosing his own companions, male *and* female. And he certainly intended to choose his own wife. No matter the corpulent Lady Linden's hopes—or schemes.

But he had a week's respite from the gossipmongers. It would probably be a dull week in the sisters' tedious company, but at least he could relax here. He squared his shoulders. Time to meet his hostess—and assure Hector that the other fellows he'd been promised *would* arrive. Alec smiled. No need to tell Hector they were coming as a personal favor to him. The poor chap was worried enough.

The front door opened. "Alec," Hector cried. "How great to see you!"

"And you, too," Alec said, a trifle wearily. Stepping inside, he stamped snow from his feet. He shook Hector's hand and turned. My God! Who'd have thought Hector capable of snaring a woman like that!

Alec removed his curly-brimmed beaver and handed it to the butler. He did the same with his greatcoat. Then he turned again to Hector. "Hector, my boy, you didn't tell me the Christmas angel was making an early visit this year. Who is this lovely creature?"

140

The young woman flushed, raising a hand to her fair cheeks—cheeks now turning even rosier.

"This is Galatea," Hector said, his voice tinged with affectionate pride. Justifiable pride, Alec thought. "My sister," Hector went on. "We call her Tea. My nickname for her."

"Pleased to meet you," Alec said, raising the beauty's hand to his lips. Her fingers trembled in his. Her lips were trembling, too. How could they have trouble marrying off this divine creature? Were the men around here blind?

He remembered her come-out now. She'd been wearing those awful wire spectacles, looking deadly dull in a gown that was all wrong for her. Now she looked good enough to . . .

"You're very kind, I'm sure," she murmured, trying futilely to withdraw her hand from his. "I'm—I'm a trifle nervous, you see. I've never managed a house party like this and—"

"I'm sure you'll do admirably," Alec replied, reluctantly releasing her fingers. Prospects for the week were definitely looking up.

He turned to Hector and, noting his frown, hastened to add, "Conigsby and Douglass should be along soon. Varley may be with them, or he may come later."

Hector heaved a great sigh of relief. "Good job," he said. "Come along now. I'll show you where to bivouac."

"I shall see you at dinner, then," Tea said softly.

Alec decided her nickname fit her well. "Yes," he replied, giving her his best smile. "I shall look forward to it." Reluctantly, he followed Hector up the stairs.

Galatea stood there, staring after the viscount. Alec. She spoke his name silently. Alec. Even without her spectacles, she could see what a fine figure of a man he was. Tall, strong, handsome. And with such lovely manners.

He and Hector disappeared up the stairs, and she gave

herself a small shake. Dear, dear. She shouldn't be standing around in a daze. There were still more guests to come.

The sound of another carriage reached her ears, and she straightened her skirts and motioned Borden to the door. Time enough to think about Alec—the viscount, she should call him—later. She could not remember seeing him before, but then her come-out had been such an uncomfortable time. She remembered little about it except the foolish conversation of the few men who'd come to court her, men who didn't even know who Aeneas *was* and were obviously not suitable husband material.

Borden opened the door to three young gentlemen, who stood laughing and brushing off snow. One of them she recognized as Hector's friend, Peter Varley. No doubt Hector would be glad to talk horses the whole week. She'd seen him at it more than once.

Stepping forward, she extended her hand. "Peter, welcome to our home."

Peter turned, his eyebrows going up in surprise. "Galatea? Is that you?"

She flushed again. Did a new gown make that much difference in how she looked? "Yes, thank you. And these must be your friends."

"Yes," Peter replied, turning to the others. "This is Conigsby. That's Douglass."

Each of the men took Tea's hand in turn and raised it to his lips. "Enchanted," said the tall, thin one, Conigsby.

"Likewise," the short, stout Douglass purred.

She pulled back her hand. Strange, when Alec had kissed her hand, it had seemed quite different. "Borden will show you to—"

"Galatea, my dear, dear friend." Celandine came hurrying in, scattering snow from her hooded fur cloak and stamping her tiny booted feet. "Snow!" she cried. "Glorious, glorious snow. I love it!" And she rushed to envelop Galatea in a huge hug.

"Oh, Deenie," Galatea whispered. "I'm *so* glad to see you, so very glad. I don't know how to manage—"

"Nonsense," Deenie whispered back. "Don't you worry. We'll carry it off."

Deenie withdrew, smiling coquettishly at the young men. "Ah," she said. "Tea, you have worked a miracle! The cream of London's crop—and all in one place."

The young men looked extremely pleased and Deenie turned—and winked at her. Galatea felt the laughter bubbling up in her. This was going to be a good weekend after all. Deenie always made everything fun. Even the horror of Galatea's come-out had been eased somewhat by Deenie's contagious humor.

And then Galatea spied Barnaby, Baron Tragon's son, standing in the doorway as though he might take flight at any moment. Poor boy, he looked uncomfortably out of place. Extending her hand again, she hurried forth to greet him. "Come in, come in."

He took a hesitant step forward. "I didn't know . . ." He looked toward the others. "That is, I thought . . ." He ground to a halt, then mumbled on. "Perhaps I shouldn't . . ."

"Nonsense," Galatea said, taking his arm. "You come right in. Look, Celandine, here's Baron Tragon's son."

"Please, do call me Barnaby," he said, looking at Deenie with wide admiring eyes."

"Oh, I shall," Deenie said, deserting the others to tuck her arm through his free arm. "I certainly shall."

Dear Deenie, Galatea thought, watching the men cluster round her again. Deenie knew precisely how to attract men to her side and she obviously enjoyed their attention, so obviously that at four and twenty she hadn't yet decided which man to devote herself to exclusively. And no one seemed to care, no one even hinted at Deenie being "on the shelf," though other women her age, women like Galatea herself, were seen as being already unmarriageable—spinsters to be clucked at.

"There you are!" Ianthe called dramatically from the top of the stairs, striking a pose designed to show off her new muslin gown. Galatea swallowed a sigh. Things had been going along so well. Now Ianthe was going to spoil them.

"Do come down, Ianthe," Deenie called up gaily, not at all impressed. "Or we shall get cricks in our necks from gazing up at you."

Galatea chuckled, feeling better immediately. How could she have forgotten that Deenie knew how to handle Ianthe? She'd never been able to understand how the two of them got along. Usually, Ianthe was rude to everyone who was not her personal friend.

Ianthe swept regally down the stairs and embraced Deenie. And at that moment the door knocker sounded again. Borden opened it and the chattering group grew suddenly silent.

Chapter 4

Alec followed Hector back down the hall toward the stairs. Eager to see that lovely sister again, he'd decided to just dump his things in the room assigned him and then he'd voiced his desire to return to the lower floor with Hector. From the sound of the chatter rising from the front foyer, the other guests—or at least some of them—had also arrived. He quickened his step. Tea was too lovely to be left to the tender mercies of Varley and his cronies. Eager young bucks could be dangerous to lovely—and innocent—young ladies.

Hector rounded the corner, Alec close behind him. The chatter stilled—instantly, completely. Hector stopped dead in his tracks. "Oh, my God!" he cried, his words echoing in the sudden silence.

Now what? Alec asked himself. And then, reaching Hector's side, he had a clear view down the stairs to the front door—and the guests who stood expectantly there.

Great galloping cannonballs! Not them! How had they . . .

"How kind of you to invite us!" Lady Linden gushed, lumbering forward to embrace the beautiful dark-haired Ianthe. And close behind her minced that bane of his existence, the sticklike Martine, leaving a trail of wet footprints behind her and a cold chill up his spine.

Hector turned a pale face to him, extending a trembling

145

hand in supplication. "God, Alec!" he whispered. "I didn't know they were coming. Honest to God, I didn't know!"

That was apparent enough. No need to badger poor Hector about this ironic twist of fate. Alec squared his shoulders. There was no escape now. He must bite the bullet. "Easy, Hector, old boy. Hold on. We'll survive."

"But, Alec, you came especially—" Hector groaned. "Oh, God, I wish I was dead."

"Hector." The boy was carrying on too much. "Don't have an attack of the vapors on me. There's no putting off the inevitable. Let's go down and greet my nemesis."

"Oh, my God!"

Galatea turned from her guests to look up the stairs. That sounded like Hector. It was. What was wrong? Hector had turned dreadfully pale.

Then the viscount came to a stop beside him. And he, too, looked dreadfully pale. Something was definitely wrong. And from the way they were staring, it seemed to have something to do with these strange-looking ladies who had just arrived.

She turned to Ianthe. Perhaps she could explain. "Sister—"

Ianthe withdrew herself from the grasp of the huge lady in the brilliant orange cloak and dangerously large, outrageously purple bonnet. "Galatea, this is Lady Linden." Ianthe gestured to the thin girl. "And this is my friend, Martine, her daughter."

Martine's gaunt nose was bright red from the cold. It was the only colorful thing about her. Her lean lips were barely discernible in her pale face. And her cloak and gown were drabber than drab, not at all like her mama's blinding array.

What a strange pair they made. And why had Ianthe invited the mother to a house party like this? Mama had made it clear she had absolutely no intention of leaving her work to play hostess. And if this Lady Linden invaded the sanctity of her study, Mama would be irate, extremely irate. And Papa?

146

He, too, had said this was to be a week for young people, that he meant to stay out of it.

Well, Galatea reminded herself, she was hostess here and she must do something. The poor girl looked frozen. "Do give Borden your cloaks and bonnets, and come in to warm yourself at the library fire," she invited. "You must be dreadfully cold."

She risked a glance at Deenie, but though her friend's eyes were full of laughter, it was impossible to tell what had amused her so.

And then, before Galatea could usher her guests into the library and the warmth of the fire that burned there, Martine Linden squealed. There was simply no other word for it, Galatea thought. This thin, drab girl squealed exactly like a pig in the farmyard. And then Martine ripped off her cloak and bonnet, practically throwing them at an astonished Borden, before she rushed for the stairs. "Alec! Alec!" she cried. "How marvelous to find you here. When Ianthe invited me—"

"Don't come up," Hector called down rather rudely. "We'll be right there."

"Yes," Alec said, his voice strained. "Stay there."

"Isn't he the precious one?" Lady Linden gushed, fastening pudgy beringed fingers on Galatea's arm and drawing her close. "Dear boy, pretending to be so distant when all London knows he's mad about my little girl."

Perhaps it was the tightness of Lady Linden's grip or the overwhelming sweetness of her scent—it couldn't be the news that Alec was in love with someone—that made Galatea's stomach suffer an attack of instant butterflies. After all, *she* was not on the prowl for a husband. That was the last thing from her mind.

But Martine Linden was such an unattractive girl. And her dreadful mama's reputation . . . Galatea had placed them now. They were those awful gossip merchants Hector had told her about, going from house to house, spreading rumors and lies. Who would want such a creature in his family? Galatea eased her arm free and backed hastily away. Alec. Alec and Martine. Could it really be so?

Feeling like a felon on his way to execution, Alec descended the stairs. Tea looked delectable, even with her lovely forehead wrinkled in a perplexed frown. Now, marriage might—just might—be supportable, providing it was to a woman like that. But to Martine Linden? Never!

He risked a glance at the young bucks clustered around Celandine. Privy to his dilemma, they stood with expectant faces, waiting for the coming show. Obviously, the next move was his. Should he suddenly recall a pressing engagement, concoct a contagious illness? But if he did that, he must leave Haslett Manor, leave Tea, now, when he'd just met her. And already Conigsby and Douglass had shifted their attention to her. God, but she was exquisite—far more lovely than Ianthe of the beautiful form and foul disposition, who now stood glaring at her sister.

He had reached the bottom of the stairs and Martine pounced, practically throwing herself into his arms. Alec turned his head, evading her kiss, so that it landed harmlessly on his cheek. But though he tried to set her back, away from him, she persisted in clinging to him.

"Silly boy," she purred. "No need to be so shy. Mama knows about us."

Her mama approached them, her ridiculous purple bonnet bobbing like a garish scow on the Thames. "Dear, dear Alec," she gushed, her fat chins quivering in unison. "Why didn't you tell us you'd be here?"

Remaining silent, he counted to a hundred. Ten wouldn't do it, he knew. But even counting to a hundred couldn't quell his anger at this insufferable juggernaut. In his years on the town, he had encountered more than one prowling mama, but never had he tangled with one so impervious to the truth.

Lady Linden used words as a carriage maker used slats, bending each one to make it fit a preconceived idea. A carriage was a useful construct, of course, but this edifice of lies that Lady Linden was building could not endure. Nothing on this earth, not even the prospect of the most dreadful degrading disgrace, could persuade him to condemn himself to a lifetime with those two harpies.

Firmly—and it took firmness, since she stuck like a veritable leech—he extracted his arm from Martine's clinging grasp. "Hector, old fellow," Alec said, interjecting heartiness into his tone and hoping it sounded real. "The ladies look quite done in from their trip. Why don't you see them to their rooms?"

"Yes, yes," Hector mumbled, affixing himself to the Lindens but casting a longing gaze to where Celandine stood. "Come right this way, ladies."

"You all go ahead," Celandine cried gaily. "I am much too excited to rest."

The young bucks around her nodded in enthusiastic agreement.

Fine, Alec thought, slowly letting out his breath as he watched the Lindens until they were out of sight. Now, if he could just get Galatea alone for a moment . . . But how? . . .

Tea turned to Celandine. "Oh dear, Deenie, I've just remembered something I forgot to tell Cook. Will you take our guests into the library? I'll be back shortly."

"Of course," Celandine replied, smiling coquettishly at her entourage.

Without another thought, Alec followed Galatea down the hall toward the kitchen. When they rounded the corner and were out of earshot, he called, "Miss Haslett?"

She stopped, hesitating for a moment before she swung round. When she faced him, her cheeks were flushed again and she avoided his gaze, looking over his left shoulder instead. "Yes, Viscount Kendall? Can I get you something?"

"I—" For a moment he was silent, lost for words. "I—" he stumbled on. "I need your help."

She met his gaze then, incredulity in her eyes. *"My help?"*

And then what had started as a spur-of-the-moment subterfuge turned into a full-fledged plan. He searched her face. "Yes. I guess Hector didn't tell you."

She wrinkled her brow and pursed those delicious-looking lips. "Tell me what?"

He hesitated. It was demeaning, but he had to do it. "Lady Linden's daughter, Martine, you might have seen. She—she's set her cap for me."

Tea's face remained bland, expressionless—polite. "Well, I noticed that she seemed quite familiar with you."

He snorted. "Familiar? That's hardly the word for it." He drew closer, taking her hand in his. "You must understand."

She struggled to withdraw her fingers, but he held them tightly. "Please, Miss Haslett. I am terribly distressed. Miss Linden follows me everywhere, you see. I cannot escape her."

Tea ceased to struggle, letting her hand rest in his. "Escape?" she murmured, her green eyes widening. "You want to escape?"

"Of course I do." He drew closer still. "Surely you cannot imagine that I would welcome her attentions."

Tea smiled then, shyly. "I—I did not know. I mean, I have only just met you. And they do say love is blind."

He shuddered. "Not that blind. You must believe me," he insisted. "She is driving me quite wild. And I thought"—he squeezed the fingers that rested so trustingly in his—"I thought maybe you would help me."

She frowned in puzzlement. "Of course I would—if I could. But what could I possibly do?"

He took a deep breath. "You could allow me to court you."

Shock turned her cheeks even redder. "Court? Me?"

"Yes," he said. "Oh, I know you don't wish to marry. Neither do I, though I have the devil's own time trying to convince certain mamas of that fact. But we could pretend. We could live in each other's pockets—bill and coo. At least for this week. And then perhaps Martine would set her sights on one of the other eligibles."

He heaved a mournful sigh that was only partly theatrical. "You've no idea how dreadful it is to be constantly hounded. She has chased me over all of London. Every time I turn around, she's there, waiting to entrap me. And that mother of hers. . . . She's even worse. Please, Miss Haslett, please help me."

Galatea stared into the dark eyes so near her own. She could see his pain. The poor man. How awful it must be to be hounded like that. She would like to help him.

"But I—I know very little about being courted," she said. "I am a scholar, a scholar of ancient Greece and Rome."

"I know. I know the stories of your namesake," he said. "Both of them. The nymph and the statue."

"You do?" She could hardly believe it. A man who knew something about her beloved ancient history, a personable— a very personable—man. "Perhaps," she began, "if you tell me what to do, perhaps I could help you."

His smile was brilliant. It warmed her whole body, making her cheeks burn even hotter.

"Bless you," he said. "You're a real angel. It'll be easy. You'll see. And fun."

He raised her trembling hand to his mouth and put a lingering kiss there, a kiss that she could feel long after his lips had left her skin.

Chapter 5

By the time the guests gathered in the dining room for dinner, Galatea had succeeded in cooling her fevered cheeks. Alec was a very persuasive man, but she was not at all sure this plan of his would work. How could one simulate love? Of course, she had never paid much attention to the subject, her only experience with it occurring in the pages of her beloved books. And there, quite often, lovers came to bad ends, very bad ends. But she *had* promised Alec and so she would do her best to help.

She glanced around the table at the others. After her talk with Alec, she'd gone on to the kitchen and instructed Cook to change the name cards so that he would sit to her right. On his other side sat Deenie, then Hector, then Martine, then Conigsby, then Hypatia, then Peter Varley, then Ianthe, then Douglass, then Lady Linden, and finally, rounding out the circle, Baron Tragon's son. True to his word, Papa had advised Cook that he would take his meals with Mama in her rooms, leaving the dining room to the young people. And Lady Linden of course. With her there, no other chaperone was necessary.

"A lively group," Alec commented, leaning close. "We should have a fine week." He leaned closer still, to whisper, "Smile at me now, laugh gaily."

Galatea tried to laugh, but it sounded strange in her ears, strange and affected.

Hypatia looked up. "Oh, Tea, Peter is just telling me the most exciting stories about horse racing! About a great stallion named Waterloo. You really should hear them."

"I will," Galatea said. "But later, dear."

"Horses!" Miss Linden snorted, an unfortunate action that didn't at all improve her looks—looks that were particularly drab that evening. "Stupid creatures."

"They're not!" Hypatia cried indignantly. "They're very intelligent and—"

"Easy little one." Peter chuckled. "Not everyone's lucky like us. *We* know what's important."

Galatea breathed a sigh of relief. Dear Peter would keep Hypatia busy—and he could be trusted not to bruise a green girl's feelings.

Thinking of green girls, she swallowed a sigh. She was rather green herself. One season in London was all she'd had. And even then, neither she nor Mama had had great expectations for her. They'd really only bothered with a come-out because Papa had insisted. But he'd been most kind afterwards, not berating her when she turned down the two men who had proposed marriage, then allowing her to return to the country—and her books.

On her left Barnaby coughed nervously and scratched his nose, then toyed with his soup spoon. Such a shy fellow he was, even shyer than she. She must do her best to put him at ease. "What are you studying at present?" Galatea inquired politely.

He almost dropped his spoon. "Me? Oh, a new translation of the *Iliad*. A fascinating approach. I—Oh, I forgot. Excuse me, please. I know ladies do not care for ancient texts."

"I do," Galatea said firmly. "I am a scholar of the ancients. My mama is one, too, you know. I am presently working on a translation of the *Aeneid*. I'm at the section where Aeneas meets Dido and—"

153

"Oh, Tea," Ianthe cried. "Please, don't go on so about such dreadfully dull stuff. No one wants to hear about those boring old ancient people." She laughed shrilly. "Why, they've been dead for hundreds of years."

"*Au contraire,* Miss Ianthe," Alec said. "The ancients are quite interesting féllows. And Dido—"

"Dido?" Ianthe wrinkled her nose. "What an ugly name!"

Alec smiled. "Dido was the queen of Carthage, a beautiful, powerful woman."

Ianthe's eyes sparkled. "Really? A queen? Why haven't I ever heard of her?"

"Because," Douglass said, "you're too lovely to bother your pretty head about such ancient things."

For once, Ianthe ignored a compliment. "Did this Aeneas marry the queen and become king then?"

"Unfortunately not," Barnaby said with a frown. "She died for love of him. Killed herself when he left her."

Galatea turned to him in surprise. His shyness seemed to have vanished, but of course he was talking about his beloved studies.

"How romantic," Hypatia breathed.

"How stupid!" Deenie cried. "I should never kill myself over a man. They simply aren't worth it."

Galatea looked around the table. All the men were beaming at Deenie. Strange how that girl could say the most outrageous things and get away with it. All she had to do was flutter her lashes and men would forgive her anything. It was hard to understand, but it had always been true.

Galatea cast a sidelong glance at Alec. Was he fascinated by Deenie like the others were? Why hadn't he asked *her* for help? But Deenie's reputation was well known. Perhaps this Martine would not believe in a love match between Alec and someone like Deenie. That was good because . . . Galatea stopped. She didn't care to explore that thought any further.

"So," Lady Linden observed, sauce dripping down her several chins. "What is the schedule of events for the week?"

"I have planned a sleigh ride," Galatea said, "to bring home the Yule log. And if the weather permits, perhaps a visit to the Rollright Ring."

"More ancient things." Martine sniffed, her long nose twitching. "So dreadfully boring."

"Now, my dear." Lady Linden smiled at her daughter. "I'm sure Miss Galatea has in mind to put on a delightful Christmas play for us."

Galatea's heart dropped plumb into her blue satin slippers. "Play?"

"Of course," Alec interjected, coming smoothly to the rescue. A pleasant task, considering the smile of gratitude Galatea immediately lavished on him. "We'll each be doing our favorite stories from mythology. Tea and I," he returned her smile, "are going to do the story of her namesake. You know, Galatea and Pygmalion. Perhaps, Lady Linden, *you* would consent to play Venus for us?"

For once, the fat old shrew fell silent. She gaped at him while her chins quivered in surprise. Finally, she collected herself enough to speak. "Of course, of course. I shall be delighted."

He noted the bewildered glance Galatea gave him. She was so innocent she didn't understand the advantage of a rear attack.

"Yes," he went on, seeing the question in Varley's eyes, the surprise in Hector's. "Tea and I have given the matter a lot of thought. Haven't we, my dear?"

Tea managed to nod, to smile, but she said nary a word. So he went on. "We thought you would enjoy pairing up and picking your favorite stories to act out."

"I want one with horses in it!" Hypatia turned to Peter. "You must know a story with horses. Tell me you do."

While the others babbled, Alec smiled to himself. That was a capital idea he'd had. He'd surprised even himself with

155

it. He would make an adoring Pygmalion. And the lovely Tea . . .

She put a tentative hand on his sleeve. He covered it with his fingers before she could pull away. "Viscount?" she whispered, leaning close.

"Alec," he reminded her, leaning closer. "You must call me Alec."

"Yes, yes, Alec. But I don't think—That is, I have no experience in acting and—"

"That will hinder nothing," he said. "Remember, Galatea is a statue through most of the story. You won't have that much to do."

"Yes." She looked relieved, but then she added, "Yes, but there will be so much managing to it and—"

He smiled. "Galatea, my dear, you must learn to use your authority. *You* are the hostess. Ask one of our guests to organize things." He laughed. "Ask Martine."

He could almost see the wheels turning in Galatea's pretty head, could see her weighing the pros and cons of such a strange request. Finally, she nodded. "Very well, I will do it." She turned to the group and raised her voice. "Please, everyone. May I have your attention?"

Almost all the heads turned. Galatea smiled. "Miss Linden?"

The sticklike Martine turned from an argument with Hector to demand, "Yes? What is it?"

Alec swallowed a curse. Not only was the chit a confounded nuisance, but she was also entirely lacking in manners.

"I was wondering," Galatea continued calmly, politely, "could you possibly see your way clear to organizing the scenes? It's a lot of responsibility, I know. And perhaps you would rather just relax. I'm sure I can ask—"

"No." Martine looked around the table in triumph. "I will do it. And a good job, too."

"Of course," Tea said. "Now, shall we present our scenes on Christmas Day or—"

"Christmas Eve," Martine announced, already warming to her position of authority. "After dinner."

"That sounds fine." Alec reached under the table for Tea's trembling fingers and gave them a reassuring squeeze. "Just fine."

Now he had Martine occupied. And when the redoubtable Lady Linden saw the affection and esteem he lavished on Tea, even *she* would understand that her schemes were useless . . . that Martine hadn't a chance with him.

Hector kept a smile on his face and nodded, but he heard little of the steady stream of words Martine was pouring into his ear. He was aching to turn his attention to his other side, to the lovely Celandine. Her brunette beauty made even Ianthe's look second-rate. And, from what he could tell, Celandine's disposition was as superior to Ianthe's as her looks.

"Yes," he told Martine firmly. "That sounds quite right, but why don't you explain it to Conigsby? Perhaps he can suggest something additional."

And having done his duty, he turned gratefully in the other direction. "Miss Celandine. I have not seen you much about town."

She tapped him coquettishly on the arm. "Then, dear boy, I'm afraid you haven't been looking. I have been all about for several seasons now."

Hector swallowed. Lord, but she made him feel like the greenest schoolboy. "Still, I can't imagine I have seen you," he insisted. "For if I had, I should never forget it. How could anything erase from my memory such a vision of loveliness?"

To his surprise, this quite genuine compliment was received with a trill of girlish laughter. "Oh, Hector, how you do go on."

But she didn't turn away, even though she had Alec on her

other side. And so, emboldened by her smile, Hector ventured on. "Do you suppose— That is, I should like—"

Her eyes were full of laughter and she leaned closer, so close that her scent made his head spin. "Come, Hector, spit it out, whatever it is."

"The sleigh ride," he mumbled. "Would you allow me to—to escort—to sit beside— That is, I mean—"

"La, Hector! You must be more direct. If you wish to succeed with the ladies, you must be more forceful. Ladies like gentlemen who are strong, you know." She waved a delicate hand in the direction of Alec. "Why, look at the viscount. He hasn't been here above two hours, and already he's calling Tea 'my dear.' And she lets him." She frowned in puzzlement. "Now that I think of it, that is rather strange. Tea has so little experience with men and—"

Hector leaned closer. "I don't wish to talk about Tea," he said softly. "You are the one who interests me. And," he continued, "you have not answered my question. May I be your escort on the coming sleigh ride?"

"Well . . ."

"Please," he begged. "I would count it a signal honor."

Celandine seemed to be considering, pursing her little red mouth in a delightful pout. "Very well," she said finally. "Since you have asked me so nicely, I will go with you."

"Thank you!" Hector searched his mind. What kind of scene could they play together? But his brain would not cooperate. Why hadn't he paid more attention when the schoolmaster told his interminable dry-as-dust stories about ancient times? Blast it, the only story he could think of was Robinson Crusoe—and that had no part in it for a woman, unless he counted the one Crusoe left behind in England.

No, he'd better not suggest that. Better wait and think. Think hard.

Chapter 6

The next morning Alec woke early. Unable to sleep, he rose from his bed and went to gaze out the window at the snowy view in the courtyard below. This visit had certainly gotten off to a different start than he'd imagined. His plan had been to stay in the background, perhaps do what he could to get Varley or one of the others to notice the charms of Hector's poor sister, perhaps even get one of them to end up leg-shackled to her.

He chuckled. So much for well-laid plans. One look at Galatea and he'd wished he hadn't invited the others at all. He wanted to keep the lovely Tea all to himself. For this week, of course. He had no plans beyond this week.

For a moment, he felt a pang of conscience. Galatea was obviously an innocent. And he had been on the town for some time. He didn't want to turn her head with his attentions. But he *had* warned her, he had told her it was all a charade, an effort to free himself from Martine's unwanted attentions. And in the meantime, he could enjoy Tea's company. Such lovely company.

The early morning sun shining down on the yard revealed a red-haired figure in a riding habit crossing toward the stable. The little Hypatia hurrying to her beloved horses, no doubt.

Alec turned from the window. A ride would suit him right now. He certainly couldn't sleep anymore. He smiled. Yes, a ride would suit him very well. And as an extra benefit, he would be free of the presence of the abominable Martine, who by her own admission despised the equine breed and wouldn't be caught dead near a stable. Lucky, lucky horses.

First he'd ride, then he'd breakfast with the lovely Tea. Too bad they couldn't breakfast alone. But that wouldn't be wise. His intent was to avoid Martine, not to get involved with someone else.

Ten minutes later he was dressed and in the stable. The little Hypatia turned a beaming face toward him. "Viscount Kendall! Good morning. Are you looking for a ride?"

"That would be excellent," Alec said, "if you could arrange it."

Hypatia's smile faded. "Yes, of course I can. But—"

"But what?" Alec asked, wondering what was on the child's mind.

"But first I should like to ask you something."

"Yes. Of course. Ask me what you please."

"Well, you're being so attentive to Tea. No one ever has been before, you see." Hypatia regarded him solemnly. "And Ianthe . . . well, Ianthe says that you really don't care for our sister. That this is some kind of trick. And that Tea will be hurt by it. Hurt badly."

The horse behind her nudged her shoulder and she rubbed its nose affectionately. "Yes, Marigold, I know. I want a ride, too. But just a moment." She peered up at Alec, her innocent eyes reminding him of her sister's. "Viscount—"

"Please," he interrupted. "Call me Alec."

"Alec." She hesitated. "I shouldn't believe Ianthe, should I? I mean, I know she can be awfully wrong. And awfully mean sometimes."

She giggled, a little girl giggle that made her seem even younger than the fifteen he knew her to be.

"I just ignore her then. Or I run to Papa. Papa always takes my part. But you didn't answer me." She turned a sober stare on him. "You wouldn't hurt Tea, would you?"

160

"No," he said solemnly. "I wouldn't hurt your sister. I admire her a great deal." That was the truth, too.

"Good." Hypatia nodded vehemently. "That's what I told her. And Peter said you wouldn't do such a thing. He said you're a man of honor."

She looked him over carefully. "I believe him. I think you're a good man."

For some reason, he felt a wave of embarrassment. She turned back to the horse, checking the cinch. "Peter will be here soon. You can ride with us."

Galatea woke with a smile on her face and lay still for a moment, contemplating the sunlight on her pale blue bed curtains. For the first time in a long while, her waking thought was not of her work. She didn't think of Aeneas or Dido or of getting to her books at all. She thought instead of Alec—Viscount Kendall. And how nice it was to have him there—and paying attention to her.

Oh my! What made her think in such a peculiar way? She hadn't even wanted to hold this house party, and she certainly had never intended to wake up thinking about a man!

She threw back the covers and climbed out of bed. How Deenie would laugh if she knew about this. But then again maybe she wouldn't. Surely Deenie had been prey to such feelings. She was certainly more knowledgeable about such things. She'd been long on the town and she obviously enjoyed it. Perhaps she could explain these strange feelings— feelings Galatea had no name for and wasn't sure she should even admit to having.

She crossed the room to the armoire. Which gown should she wear today? The drab ones were all in a row near the front. She gave them a single glance, then shoved them aside and turned to the new ones Papa had insisted on ordering for her. Kind, helpful Papa. How grateful Galatea was that she could look as nice as the other girls.

She'd worn the blue yesterday, so it wouldn't do to wear it again today. What should she choose? The pink? The yellow? The pale green? Which one would Alec prefer?

Oh, dear. She raised a hand to her flushed cheeks. How had Alec managed to become so important to her? And so quickly. Before yesterday she hadn't even known he existed. And now—now she was committed to helping him evade Miss Linden. She wanted to do that, of course. She wanted to help him in any way she could. Certainly, she didn't want him to marry . . . Oh, Lord, he just couldn't marry Martine Linden, not that dreadful creature.

A brisk rap made her turn. "Yes? Who's there?"

The door opened a crack. "Galatea? Are you up and about yet?"

"Yes, Deenie. Come in. I'm just trying to decide which gown to wear. I can use your help."

Deenie was already dressed, in a gown of deep rose that set off her trim figure and dark hair. Deenie always looked nice, in the top of fashion. She would know what was most becoming.

Pausing before each gown, Deenie surveyed them thoughtfully. "I think I prefer the green. I believe it goes best with your eyes."

"Yes, I think so, too." Galatea took it from the hanger and started toward the bed. "Deenie, I need to ask you something."

Deenie turned, her face grave. "Of course, Tea. You know you may ask me anything."

When Galatea hesitated, Deenie frowned. "My dear friend, don't worry. I would never divulge anything you told me in confidence. Not to anyone. You can be certain of that."

"I know." Galatea enveloped her in a hug, almost crushing her gown in the process. "I do know. It's just that . . . well, I don't quite know how to ask—or even *what* to ask."

"It's about the viscount, isn't it?" Deenie inquired, her eyes twinkling merrily.

162

Galatea was startled. "Yes. But how do you know?"

Deenie laughed. "I know. Believe me, I know. Has he kissed you yet?"

Shock took Galatea's breath away. She clutched the gown to her. "Oh, my no! Why, Deenie! What a thing to say! Kiss me? I only met the man yesterday."

"Really?" Deenie raised an eyebrow in surprise. "Only yesterday. Well, that puts quite another complexion on the matter."

Galatea laid the gown on the bed. "It does?"

"Of course. I thought you were already quite familiar with each other. I mean, he called you 'my dear.' And in front of all of us."

"Yes, yes, he did." Now what should she do? *She* trusted Deenie, but that didn't mean she could divulge Alec's secret to her.

Absently, Deenie unscrewed the stopper from one of the few perfume bottles on the uncluttered vanity and sniffed it. "Not this scent, my dear," Deenie said. "No, no. It's simply not you. Too cloying by far."

"I don't use scent much," Galatea said, stepping out of her nightdress. "And I never use that. Papa gave it to me last year."

"That explains it," Deenie said. "Men have no understanding of these things."

"What things?" Feeling thoroughly confused, Galatea pulled on her chemise.

Deenie shrugged. "Take your pick. Perfume. Clothes. Love."

"Love?" Galatea paused with her gown half over her head, almost choking on the word. "Are we talking about love?"

"Of course."

"But love?" Galatea pulled the gown down and struggled to fasten it. "Really, Deenie. Why should we talk about such a thing? I know nothing at all about the subject. Not a thing."

163

"Then," Deenie said with a mischievous smile, "don't you think it's time you learned?"

That made a certain sense, she supposed, but to imagine that a man could fall in love with her, that was impossible. "But Deenie, how— That is, it's easy for you to say that. You know so much." Should she tell Deenie that this was all a charade, that she and Alec were putting on their own little play for the benefit of Lady Linden and her overly ambitious daughter? But did she have that right? A confidence *was* a confidence after all.

Deenie turned from admiring her reflection in the cheval glass. "The sleigh ride is an excellent idea," she said. "I hope you arranged to have it occur after dark?"

"After dark?" Galatea asked in surprise. "But it will be hard to find the Yule log in the dark and—"

"Tea, Tea." Deenie shook her head. "Think, my girl. A sleigh ride—in the dark."

Galatea frowned in puzzlement. "I'm sorry, Deenie. I just don't understand."

"The gentlemen will accompany us, won't they?" Deenie asked.

"Of course. At least, I had thought so."

Deenie nodded. "Yes, they will. And in the dark we can sit a little closer. They can—"

"Deenie, stop! You're embarrassing me."

Deenie frowned. "Nonsense. It's necessary to know these things—and to use the knowledge if we wish to snag a husband."

Galatea stared in surprise. "But I thought— That is, everyone says—"

Deenie smiled sadly. "That I don't wish to have a husband?"

Galatea nodded. "I'm sorry. I shouldn't repeat gossip."

Deenie shrugged. "Don't worry about it. I know what they're saying. But it isn't true. I *do* want a husband. But I want a husband I can love. And I haven't found him yet."

"Oh, Deenie, I am sorry. I shouldn't—"

"Yes, you should. Now forget that and tell me, where do you plan to hang the mistletoe? I'm surprised you don't have it up by now."

"Mistletoe? I didn't plan to hang any." Galatea frowned. "Papa has never hung it and I didn't think—"

Deenie looked at her severely. "You *must* think of such things!"

Galatea felt her cheeks burning again. Mistletoe! If Alec surprised her underneath it, would he . . . "But, Deenie—"

"You must!" Deenie repeated. "And believe me, all your guests will appreciate it." She smiled slightly. "I can vouch for that."

Galatea considered. After all, a good hostess should try to please her guests. And mistletoe was a tradition. Surely Papa wouldn't object to a tradition. "All right, Deenie. I'll ask Cook."

Deenie nodded. "Very good. But we should be getting ready for breakfast. The men will be down soon, if they aren't already. And we should be there." She chuckled. "We don't want them to forget about us."

Galatea hesitated. "Do I—do I look all right?"

Deenie slowly surveyed her from head to toe. Then she nodded. "Yes. You will do. You will do very well." She grinned. "I'm sure Alec will think so, too."

Immediately after breakfast, which she and Deenie ate alone because no one else was about, Galatea went to the kitchen to speak to Cook about the mistletoe. "And so you see," she finished, "Celandine says the guests expect it."

Cook nodded. "She's right, Miss Galatea." Cook grinned. "Everyone likes fer to have the mistletoe up. It gives a good holiday feel to things."

And so shortly before lunch, the mistletoe was up. After supervising its hanging, Deenie and Galatea stood back to gauge its effect.

"Yes," Deenie said, nodding vigorously. "We have chosen an excellent spot, right over the door to the dining room.

Everyone will have to pass beneath it.'' She paused to consider. "Of course, we could use another bunch over the study door.''

"Another?'' Galatea asked. "Wouldn't that look a little . . . forward perhaps?''

Deenie laughed. "My dear Tea, it would simply look like we are celebrating the holiday as we should. But we shall make do with one, I suppose.''

Galatea kept silent then, but she was feeling more and more confused. Why should a young woman want to be kissed by just any man who happened to catch her at the right place? She herself couldn't imagine being kissed so indiscriminately.

She felt her cheeks heating up again. Truth was, she had never imagined being kissed at all. Until lately. But sad to say—though she wouldn't have admitted it to a living soul— ever since Deenie had questioned her about Alec and kissing, Galatea had been unable to erase the thought from her mind. What would it be like to be held in Alec's arms, to have his mouth pressed against . . .

She turned away quickly. She must stop this ridiculous kind of thinking. Alec had no intention of kissing her. Alec didn't think of her in that way. He'd told her plainly, very plainly, that the whole intent of his plan was to foil Miss Linden in her matrimonial machinations. So she, Galatea, must not let her imagination run away with her. She *must* not. Because in a few days, this holiday week would be over and Alec would be gone. She might never see him again. And so she must not allow herself to form any kind of attachment to him.

She told herself that very thing, over and over, through the rest of the morning. But unfortunately, it didn't do a whole lot of good. She was afraid that her heart had already betrayed her and, though it seemed quite illogical in such a short space of time, had already given itself to Alec.

Chapter 7

Alec hurried toward the dining room, hoping he wouldn't be late for lunch. When Peter and Hypatia went for a ride, he had learned, it wasn't for an hour or two but for an entire morning. And though Alec had fretted a little at being so long away from Tea, wondering what the other male guests were up to, he hadn't thought it fair to ask such horse lovers to cut short their pleasure on his account.

He had enjoyed the ride, too. But now he wanted to see Tea. He'd hurried to get through his ablutions and change his clothes, hoping no one would usurp his place beside her before he could get to the table.

He quickened his step, rounded the corner, and skidded to a sharp halt. Good God! There, in the doorway to the dining room, in full sight of all the guests, stood Peter. And standing on tiptoe and kissing him right on the mouth was the little Hypatia! Had the man lost his senses? To so abuse the hospitality of his host?

"Peter!" he cried. "My God, man! What are you doing?"

Hypatia turned and smiled, the grin of a mischievous child. "Lord Kendall! There you are! We wondered how long it would take you to get down here. You mustn't be mad at Peter. I kissed *him,* you see."

"You *what?*" Alec asked, wondering if the ride had affected her brain. Or his. Or had the whole place gone crazy?

167

Obviously pleased with herself, Hypatia giggled. "I kissed *him*. Look up there."

She pointed above their heads—to a clump of mistletoe hanging from the door frame.

Alec let his breath out in relief. Thank God! For a while there he'd thought Peter was really in the suds, kissing a child like that—and right where everyone could see.

Peter grinned at him. "Don't look so grim, old man. It's all Christmas fun. She took me by surprise, the little minx." He smiled at her affectionately. "One of these days she's going to set all the men's hearts aflame. You wait and see."

Suddenly realizing that the mistletoe could lead to someone kissing *him*, someone he didn't care for, Alec glanced around warily. "Have either of you seen Miss Linden lately?"

Hypatia sent him a startled look. "No, not today."

Tragon came meandering from the other direction in time to hear his question. "I believe Miss Linden was in the library," he offered tentatively, "consulting certain volumes on Greek mythology." He coughed apologetically, scratching his beaky nose. "I offered her my assistance, but she seemed determined to manage on her own."

The poor chap looked so crestfallen that Alec felt sorry for him. And with good reason. Martine had a tongue that could cut a strong man to ribbons. He'd heard her do it more than once. "I shouldn't worry," Alec told him. "Miss Linden sometimes suffers from a bad disposition. It's best just to ignore it."

He stepped back, allowing Tragon to pass through the doorway—and under the mistletoe—before him. Just in case.

And Tragon did so, going on toward the laden sideboard unmolested by any young women. Alec heaved a sigh of relief. With luck, he should be able to get past the mistletoe before the abominable Linden showed up.

He'd like to catch Tea in that doorway—oh, would he like to! But instinct told him that the delightful Tea would not understand a make-believe kiss—no matter what their supposed plan to foil Martine. And besides, he wasn't at all sure that he could keep any kiss he gave her make-believe. He was feeling rather more toward her than was sensible for a man who had no intention of being leg-shackled for some years yet.

But this was hardly the time to examine his feelings on the subject of matrimony. Where *was* Tea, anyway?

Alec stepped through the doorway . . . and was enveloped in a cloud of feminine scent and rustling skirts, startled by a female body pressed against his own, female lips against his. For the barest second he thought—hoped—the female might be Tea, but almost immediately he knew better. Tea was too shy to do such a thing. Besides, he recognized the scent that Ianthe wore. Far too heavy, too sweet, to be Tea's. He eased away as best he could, trying to evade Ianthe's grasp.

"Now, Alec," she cried, coquettishly tapping him on the arm. "You act as though you've never been kissed before. But we know better—a man-about-town like you!"

Alec managed a feeble smile. Ianthe was right, of course. He'd been kissed many times and never been embarrassed by it. Indeed, he was known to relish the attention of women—women of all kinds.

"Now you may kiss us all," Ianthe pointed out with a smile that struck him as almost malicious. "As is your usual wont."

A wave of embarrassment rippled through him. How could this one be a sister to the gentle Tea? At least Tea wasn't there to hear her. "I believe you are mistaken," he said, making his tone icy in hopes of discouraging her. "Someone seems to have given you misinformation about me. *Much* misinformation."

Ianthe's laughter was shrill, too shrill for male ears. No wonder she was unwed. But Tea—he couldn't understand Tea being still a spinster, unless she'd been so sequestered with her books that she'd remained unnoticed by neighboring men.

Ianthe's glance conveyed her scorn for him, but suddenly

Alec sensed more than scorn. Her kiss still burned on his lips. Lord! Not another matrimonial-minded maiden on the prowl!

Little Hypatia looked from her sister to him, then back again, her face reflecting bewilderment. "Really, Ianthe, you are unkind to His Lordship. Why are you so rude?"

"Rude!" Ianthe raised a beautiful black eyebrow.

Lord, Alec asked himself, how could such a beautiful woman be so shrewish?

"One can't be rude to *him!*"

"Of course one can!"

Alec swung round. Tea stood in the doorway, beautiful Tea in a gown of sea-foam green. Her lovely forehead was wrinkled in a frown of annoyance. Her gaze went to Ianthe and back to him.

"Ianthe, that's enough. I'm sorry, Alec." She moved forward, tucking her arm through his. "Come, it looks like the meal is ready."

"Of course," he agreed. She was every inch the lady, but Tea was trembling. She had come to his rescue. Even though the action made her fearful, she had stood up for him. His brave Tea.

"Did you enjoy the morning?" she asked politely.

"Very much," he replied. "I took a ride with Peter and Hypatia." He laughed. "A *long* ride."

Tea laughed, too, and he sensed some of the tension leaving her. "Yes, I can imagine. Those two are both horse crazy."

"I like horses myself," Alec said. "But there *are* other things in life." He leaned closer. "Other pastimes to enjoy."

Her eyes widened slightly, those lovely green eyes, and he wondered if he'd said too much, offending her.

"Yes," she murmured. "I suppose so. I'm not particularly fond of horses, but I believe I can understand Peter and Hypatia—somewhat. My books on ancient history, you see, are as important to me as horses are to those two."

"Yes," he said. "So I suspected. There are many different interests. But yours is rather rare. I don't suppose you know many scholars of ancient studies."

She sighed. "None but Mama—and Tragon . . . Barnaby." She nodded toward the fellow, busy filling his plate at the sideboard. "He's doing a translation of the *Iliad*. He's conversant with all the central texts and—"

She rattled on, telling him about the wondrous learned Barnaby, but Alec hardly heard a word because he was experiencing a sudden rush of . . . My God! Jealousy! He couldn't be jealous of that spindle-shanked, beaky-nosed fellow. But he was. He *was* jealous. He wanted to show the scholarly Barnaby out the front door. In fact, he'd like to help him on his way with a good swift kick.

Alec swallowed a regretful sigh. He couldn't do such a thing, of course. It was stupid and ridiculous. And besides, insulting her guest would not endear him to Tea.

"Yes," he agreed when she paused for breath. "I'm sure that's true. My, what a great spread your cook has prepared. Shall we taste it?"

Galatea enjoyed the luncheon meal. Deenie had been right about the mistletoe. It added quite a festive mood to the meal. Everyone seemed much at ease, laughing and talking. Even Barnaby appeared less shy, more willing to converse. She felt a pleasant glow. Amazing that this business of hostess could be so pleasant.

She glanced toward the doorway where the mistletoe hung. If only *she* had Ianthe's nerve, *she* might have kissed Alec, might have felt his arms around her. She couldn't do a thing like that, of course, couldn't throw herself at a man. It was unladylike. Unthinkable, really, for someone of her nature.

But perhaps on the way out Alec would . . . She shoved the thought to the back of her mind and looked around at her guests.

171

Across the table, Hector was gazing at Deenie with adoring eyes. And Deenie . . . It was hard to say, but her eyes were sparkling and she was devoting all her attention to him.

Galatea frowned. She did hope Hector wasn't developing a *tendre* for Deenie. Much as she loved Deenie, she knew her friend's character, knew she was not a woman for constancy.

But then perhaps Hector wasn't really enamored of her. Perhaps he was just enjoying himself. Young men were reputed to do that, to flirt with young women and not mean a thing by it. Still, she would have a talk with Hector. Deenie couldn't be hurt by such behavior, but other young women might be.

When it looked like everyone was finished eating, Galatea announced, "The Rollright Ring is about an hour's drive away. I had thought we might take an outing there this afternoon, but I should like to know how the rest of you feel about it."

"It's too cold," Ianthe declared with an exaggerated shiver and a sly glance at Conigsby. "I don't care to go."

"Nor I," said Hypatia. "Peter has promised to help me chart my mare's genealogy. And we are still looking for a horse story for our scene."

"Hector?" Galatea asked.

Hector tore his gaze from Deenie's laughing face long enough to say, "Whatever Miss Celandine wants."

Deenie laughed a little louder. "I believe I prefer to stay in. The cold is so hard on one's skin."

"Your skin is quite perfect," Hector began.

Lady Linden looked up from her fourth dish of blancmange, apricot sauce dripping down several chins. "I do admire ancient things," she declared. "But stones? I mean, of what use are stones? Except perhaps to build fences. And really, in this dreadful wet weather, who wants to go gadding about?"

"Mama's quite right," Martine said firmly. "And besides, we can use the time to good advantage."

"How so?" inquired Douglass, his tone rather grim.

"We must get our scenes chosen," Martine declared. "And we must rehearse."

"Of course," Conigsby agreed with a sly smile at his friend. "Rehearse."

Galatea looked to Barnaby, then to Alec. Barnaby said nothing, gazing down at his plate.

Alec leaned closer to her. "I should like to see the stones," he said. "But perhaps in warmer weather. I would not want you to take ill from the cold."

She heard all the words, but when he said "warmer weather," her heart leaped up in her throat. Did that mean he meant to come back in the summer? Come back to see *her?* No, no. That couldn't be. He was just being polite.

She looked around again. The guests had all finished eating, even Lady Linden having evidently filled her stomach— for the time being at least. Galatea rose. "Then if everyone is agreeable, we'll stay in this afternoon. And those who wish to can work on their scenes."

She watched the guests make their way out. Hector looked up at the mistletoe and then at Deenie, but he let her walk through the doorway without stopping her for a kiss.

Galatea stared after him with a frown. It looked as if Hector were heading for heartache.

Heartache. There might be more than one heartache in this house before the week was over.

"Tea?"

She almost jumped. "Yes. Yes, Alec. What is it?"

"Nothing." He smiled gallantly. "I just thought I'd walk out with you."

"Yes, yes. I suppose you might."

When he offered her his arm, she took it, her heart pounding. They passed under the mistletoe and she almost faltered,

173

hesitating, but Alec appeared not to notice. And so they walked on, out into the hallway.

She'd been right. He didn't want to kiss her. She was nothing to him, nothing but the means to an end—the end of ridding himself of Miss Linden's unwanted attentions.

Very well, Galatea told herself, swallowing over the lump in her throat. She would help him, and when he was gone, she would . . . But she wouldn't think about that now.

Chapter 8

After they left the dining room, Alec turned to Galatea. "If you are free this afternoon, perhaps we could talk a little about how we're going to do our scene. Where we'll stand. What we'll wear. You know, such things as that."

For a moment, her disappointment under the mistletoe rankling, Galatea could not answer him, but then her good sense came to the rescue. There was little point in getting angry with Alec. It was hardly his fault that he was a personable man or that his charm had affected her so strongly. He was only doing what any sensible man would do—trying to escape the odious attentions of Miss Linden. He could hardly help it if his partner in the deception was so foolish as to wish their playacting were the real thing.

She cast a worried look toward Hector and Deenie, their heads much too close together, going slowly down the hall. That looked too much like the real thing. She was worried about those two, but her talk with Hector would have to wait a little.

Summoning her best smile, Galatea turned to Alec. "Yes, I am free for a while."

"Good," Alec said. "Very good."

"Shall we go into the library?"

Deenie and Hector turned the corner, and looking back

over her shoulder, Deenie sent them a mischievous smile and a wink.

Alec chuckled. "We appear to have convinced at least one person of our esteem for each other."

"Deenie just likes to tease," Galatea said, feeling her cheeks flame. "It is rather embarrassing."

"Nonsense," Alec said briskly. "You have nothing to be embarrassed about. But come, we must get to work."

Some time later, Galatea stood in her little sitting room. Her favorite grandfather clock ticked away in the corner, echoing the beating of her heart. "It is difficult to stand so still," she complained from the footstool where Alec had positioned her. But actually, it was not the standing still that she found so disturbing as it was the being alone in the room with him. They'd left the door open, but . . . "I don't see how anyone can be still for so long."

"But you can," Alec soothed. "Just think how lovely you look. The beautiful Galatea."

"But I am *not* beautiful," she protested. "My mother—my mother gave us all Greek names. Because she was so fond of her Greek studies. But just because I'm named for some girl—some statue—in an old story doesn't mean I look like her."

"But you do!" he insisted. "You are so beautiful it will be easy for me—for Pygmalion—to gaze at you with eyes of adoration."

To her amazement, he dropped to one knee, right there on the Persian rug, his hands clasped over his heart, gazing up at her from heated eyes.

Her own heart started to pound, faster and faster. Was it with eyes like that that Aeneas had looked at Dido? Was that how he had captured her heart, only to break it later by leaving her? "Really, Alec," she said, her cheeks growing even hotter. "How can you pretend to—to be devoted?"

He laughed a little. "I can see you've forgotten much about your Season. In the city, pretense is the essence of life. We all pretend—and much of the time. But that aside, actors always pretend. It's their livelihood. And while we're in the theater watching, we believe them."

She considered this for a moment. "I suppose you're right," she conceded finally. "But this—this is not a theater. And we are not actors. At least, *I* am not."

Galatea looked down at him, still on one knee before her, and her whole body seemed to grow hot. If only the adoring looks he directed at her were real. If only he really . . . She couldn't stand this pretense any longer. "Alec, please! You must get—"

"Oh! There you—"

Startled by Lady Linden shouting from the doorway, Galatea whirled about, lost her balance, and toppled off the footstool. To her chagrin, she fell directly onto Alec, knocking him flat on the Persian rug and taking the breath out of her own lungs.

"Well!" Lady Linden rolled into the room like a huge yellow cannonball and stood staring down at them. "What is *this?*" she demanded, her crimson mouth agape.

"This," Alec said, calmly gazing up at her over Galatea's shoulder, "is the result of your popping unannounced into our rehearsal. You startled poor Galatea and she fell from her footstool, from her pedestal, as it were."

In great confusion, Galatea discovered that her head was lying against Alec's waistcoat. She struggled to remove herself from him, to untangle her limbs from his. How dreadfully embarrassing to be found like this—and by London's most garrulous gossiper. But even more disconcerting than being found so was the realization that she was lying on his chest, as close to Alec as it was mortally possible to get, so close she could feel the beating of his heart beneath her ear. And that she wished she could stay that way!

Though she was all confusion, Alec appeared completely

unperturbed. Very calmly, he helped her roll off his chest. She sat back on her heels, her hair tumbled in dreadful disarray around a face she was sure reflected acute embarrassment. "Thank you," she murmured. "I'm sorry, I—"

Lady Linden took a step toward the door.

"But Lady Linden," Alec called, "now that you're here, we must talk about your part in our scene."

Lady Linden cast a longing look toward the door, but she didn't move. "What did you have in mind for me?"

Alec got to his feet and extended a hand to Galatea, helping her rise, too. "I had thought to give a speech, declaring my intense desire for Galatea. As Pygmalion," he added, as the lady's face began to change color alarmingly. "And then perhaps you could say something—if you wish to, of course."

"Oh, yes!" Her distress forgotten, Lady Linden positively glowed at the thought of a speaking part. "I should love to." She raised a hand to her hair—hair so brilliantly red it couldn't possibly be the color she had been born with—and struck a majestic pose. "You probably don't remember it," she gushed. "But in my salad days, I was much in demand." She smiled coyly. "For amateur theatricals."

"I'm sure you were magnificent," Alec said. "You will make a splendid Venus/Aphrodite."

"Yes." Lady Linden accepted his compliment with a complacent smile. She must actually *believe* it! Galatea thought with some shock.

"I will write my own speech, if you don't mind," the lady went on.

"No, I don't mind."

Galatea stared from one to the other. What was going on here? Lady Linden and Alec should be at odds with each other, shouldn't they?

Alec turned to her. "You don't need to stay for this part, Tea. Didn't you say you needed to talk to Cook? Something about dinner, I recall."

For a moment she stared at him, not comprehending, then

178

something in his look registered. For some reason, Alec wished to be alone with Lady Linden.

"Yes, yes," she hurried to say. "I will see you both later."

But it wasn't Cook whom Galatea went looking for, it was Hector. Now it was more imperative than ever that she find out what was going on. With Hector looking at Deenie like that . . .

She found the two of them in the foyer, Hector about to help Deenie into her cloak and bonnet.

"You are going *out?*" she asked, looking at Deenie for confirmation.

But it was Hector who nodded. "Yes, Miss Celandine expressed a desire to see the stables. So I'm going to—"

"See *what?*" Galatea was aware that her voice had gone quite shrill, but to her certain knowledge Deenie had no interest in horses, no interest whatsoever.

"You needn't look so shocked," Deenie said, her eyes gleaming with suppressed laughter. "I have discovered a late-blooming interest in horseflesh. Especially horseflesh belonging to Hector. And we are going out to view it."

"Ain't she the grandest?" Hector asked, grinning at Galatea stupidly.

She could see it all now, she thought in dismay. It wasn't Hector who needed speaking to, it was Deenie. Deenie who was leading poor Hector around by the ear.

She composed herself. "Deenie, when you return, if you've a moment, I need to speak to you."

"Of course," Deenie replied, looking a little worried. "We could put off our visit to the stables and—"

One look at Hector's pained expression and Galatea hurried to say, "No, no. Go ahead. When you get back will be soon enough. I'll be in my room."

Galatea turned away and headed up the stairs, but she could still hear Deenie's trills of laughter and Hector's delighted

179

chuckles. If only *she* knew how to behave as Deenie did, to enchant Alec as Deenie so clearly enchanted Hector. But such a wish was sheer foolishness. She knew nothing of female tricks or how to use them.

She could do nothing to ensnare him. For her such a thing was impossible. As long as she lived, Alec would hold her heart.

You are being so foolish, she told herself, going into her room. *But at least you're not as foolish as Dido. When Alec leaves you, you will go on living. In a way.*

An hour later, Deenie knocked on Galatea's bedroom door.

"Come in," Galatea called, sitting up against the pillows and removing the cool cloth from her eyes.

"What is it?" Deenie wore a worried frown. "You look dreadful. All upset. I would have stayed and—"

"I know." Galatea motioned to a lyre-back chair, but Deenie remained standing. "I didn't wish to upset Hector."

Deenie nodded. "Poor boy. He is much taken with his horses."

"And with you." Why must her voice sound so cold? She didn't want to offend Deenie, she only wanted to spare Hector pain.

Deenie stared at her. "Surely that does not upset— Ah, I see that it does. It upsets you very much."

Galatea searched for the right words. "It's just that his devotion to you seems so real. And I am afraid he'll be hurt because yours is not."

Deenie frowned. "He's a nice boy, Tea, but really, there's no need to be so distraught. It is only a game we play."

Galatea pressed a hand to her throbbing forehead. "It's a game for you. It's not a game for Hector."

Deenie looked startled. "My dear, are you quite sure?"

"Quite sure," Galatea said. "I know my brother. And I know that look in his eyes." She laughed, a brittle sound.

180

"That is the look he gives his horses. You *know* what horses are to him. He is not feigning this, Deenie. He means what he says."

"My word!" Deenie sank onto the chaise lounge. "Are you—? Yes, I can see you are sure. Oh, Tea, I am sorry. I didn't mean to hurt anyone, least of all your beloved brother. We get caught up in these games—all the fashionables play them, you know—and we forget that not everyone knows it's a game."

She settled back. "Don't worry, Tea. I'll see that Hector isn't hurt. I think I can do that. I can protect him. But I'm not so sure about you."

Galatea gasped. "About *me?* What about me?"

Deenie smiled sadly. "You forget . . . I am your oldest and dearest friend. I *know* you. Now, what can I do to help you?"

Galatea swallowed over the lump in her throat. "There is nothing anyone can do. That is, nothing is wrong and I—"

"Tea!" Deenie cried sharply. "Stop spouting drivel, stop immediately. Of course something is *wrong*. I am not stupid. I see the way you look at Alec."

How embarrassing! Did everyone know? "Oh no! I thought—I thought I was hiding my feelings."

"From him," Deenie said. "And from the others perhaps. But not from me. Never from me."

Galatea swallowed again. There was no need for tears, but a few managed to trickle down her cheeks before she could stop them. She straightened and fished for her handkerchief. "I feel such a dreadful fool. It's all pretense, you see. All his warm attentions to me are subterfuge, designed to convince Lady Linden that she will never snare him as a son-in-law. But I—"

She gulped and hurried on. She might as well tell Deenie the whole sorry tale. "The thing is, I have formed a partiality for him. Already! I know it's foolish, but I couldn't help myself. And oh, Deenie, in a short time he'll be leaving.

And I shall never see him again! Oh, what am I going to do?''

"First," Deenie said briskly, "leave off this blubbering. It does you absolutely no good, and besides that, it'll make your nose all red and your eyes all puffy. Not the best way to attract a man, I can tell you.''

Galatea sniffled and wiped her eyes. "You are such a good friend. But I don't see how anyone can fix this awful bumble broth, really I don't.''

"Well, don't count me off too soon." Deenie sat erect on the edge of the chaise. "Now, let me see if I have this clear. You have a *tendre* for Alec.''

Galatea nodded dumbly.

"And you say that his attentions to you are—"

"False," Galatea interjected sadly. "All false.''

"All false," Deenie repeated in wonderment. "But they seem so real.''

Galatea shook her head. "All pretense. A plan to rid him of Miss Linden's unwanted attentions.'' 3

"I see." Deenie leaned her head in her hand and looked at her friend thoughtfully.

If only Deenie could help. But no, that wasn't possible.

"All right," Deenie said, straightening again. "I take it that you wish for Alec to regard you seriously. You want to bring him to the sticking point—that is, to making an offer of marriage for you.''

"Marriage!" Galatea started. "I—I am not sure. I mean— You put it so—so brazenly.''

Deenie snorted. "How do you suppose a woman snares a husband? She must be a little brazen. But if you aren't even going to admit—"

Galatea straightened. "All right, Deenie, I admit it. It's very soon to know my mind, but I do know it. I want Alec to make an offer. God help me, I want to be his wife.''

"Very well," Deenie said. "That's settled then. Now we must *think*." After a few moments, she smiled and held up three fingers. "Well, we have three things in our favor, at least."

Startled, Galatea asked, "We do?"

"Of course." Deenie counted them off. "First, there is no one else."

"But how do we know that?"

"Because, silly, if there were, he would have gone to her."

"Yes, yes, of course," Galatea replied. "He would have."

"Two," Deenie went on, holding up another finger, "he is here. In your house. With you."

Galatea nodded.

"And three"—the third finger went up—"his plan is still in effect."

"His plan—?"

"Yes, his plan. You *must* continue with his plan."

"But—"

"Because," Deenie said briskly, "it's your best chance. It's obvious he doesn't actually *dislike* you, otherwise he would have asked someone else to be his partner in this."

Galatea nodded again. She wanted to believe all this, but . . .

"And there is this curious thing about human nature," Deenie went on. "When people *pretend* at feelings, those feelings sometimes become real." She paused as though struck by a singular thought. "Yes," she repeated softly, a curious smile crossing her face, "they sometimes become quite real."

Chapter 9

The next day passed uneventfully, the guests each going about his or her own employments. Galatea spent part of the day with Alec, part with the others. In the late afternoon she retired to change, then shortly before the dinner hour she went hurrying down the hall. For this meal, as for the previous ones, she wanted to get to the dining room before the others. Her heart was pounding in her chest and her hands had gone all sweaty. Just thinking of the mistletoe put her into a kind of panic.

It was all well and good for Deenie to offer advice. It was probably *good* advice. But how was she to follow it? How could one *pretend* to a feeling that was already so real? It was all most confusing. And if Alec should ever discover that her feelings were *not* pretense, that she actually *had* formed a partiality for him, it would be terribly embarrassing. She would simply shrivel up and die. Or wish to.

She paused outside the dining room door, trying *not* to look up, not to even think about the mistletoe. Then pulling in a deep breath, she hurried into the room.

There! She let her breath out in a whoosh of relief. Thank goodness the dining room was empty. She'd been early enough. Again no one had stopped her, no one had kissed her. She swallowed hastily. It was Alec she was thinking about. Alec who hadn't kissed her . . . who *wouldn't* kiss her.

Ianthe came hurrying in, looked around the almost-empty room, and smiled. "Good," she said. "He isn't here yet."

Galatea's heart rose up in her throat. "He?" she asked, her voice quavering in a maddening way. If she wasn't careful, Ianthe would guess the truth.

"Yes," Ianthe said with a strange smile. "Isn't he the handsomest man you've ever seen?"

Galatea swallowed hastily. "Well, I—I think Alec is—"

"Alec!" Ianthe snorted. "Alec is all right, I suppose. But I'm speaking of Douglass." She lowered her voice. "He has been most attentive to me, don't you think?"

"I—I—" Galatea floundered. "I don't know. I've been so busy I haven't had—"

"Well, he has," Ianthe insisted. "And I'm going to wait right here, by the door, and—"

"You wouldn't—you wouldn't kiss him?" Galatea breathed in dismay.

Ianthe tossed her dark curls. "I might," she said, her voice defiant. "I just might. But perhaps he—"

"Shhh," Galatea hissed. "I hear someone coming."

Ianthe nodded and stepped closer to the door. "Is it—?"

"Yes," Galatea breathed.

Douglass came through the doorway. "I say, Miss Haslett, have you seen—? Ah, there you are!"

Ianthe stepped forward, brazenly forward, stopped under the mistletoe, and smiled at him. "Have you been looking for me?" she asked, batting her eyelashes furiously.

"Yes," Douglass said. "And I've found you in just the right place!" He pulled her to him and kissed her soundly.

Heat flooding her cheeks, Galatea turned away, pretending to survey the food set out on the sideboard. They were *all* playing that game Deenie had talked about. By now, except for their talk, Deenie would have kissed Hector. Martine, if

185

she could, would have kissed *any* of the men. Even Hypatia, fifteen-year-old Hypatia, had ventured to kiss Peter Varley.

Galatea frowned and tugged at her hair. *She* was the only one who didn't know how to play the game. She was the only one who felt stupid, foolish.

"Miss Galatea?" said a timid voice she recognized as Barnaby's. Well, perhaps there was one other person who didn't know how to play. Forcing herself to smile, she turned. "Yes? Can I help you with something?"

He actually blushed. "I . . . well, I was wondering if you might have a Greek dictionary I could borrow. I . . . there's a word I want to look up."

"You brought your *Iliad* with you?" she asked in surprise.

Barnaby moved a little closer, lowering his voice in embarrassment. "Yes . . . well, I really hated to leave it behind. My work is rather like a drug, you see. Like that opium I hear people talking about—which, of course, I would never use." He smiled at her sheepishly. "But I find that if I don't work on my translation every day—you may laugh if you like—but if I don't work on it every day, I can't go to sleep at night."

She did laugh, but only a little, and mostly at herself. "Do not worry," she said softly. "I quite understand." She leaned closer. "You know, I am much like that myself. After dinner, I'll see that you get the dictionary. Don't let me forget."

Across the room Alec frowned. Tea hadn't even seen him come in. There she stood, laughing with that Tragon fellow, laughing and leaning close to whisper in his ear. A wave of anger swept through Alec. How could she prefer that—that stripling to him? It was true that she and Tragon shared an interest in the ancient Greeks, but that was hardly a foundation on which to build a marriage.

Marriage! Why in God's name was he thinking of *marriage?* He certainly had no intention of . . . But yesterday, when she'd fallen onto him . . . Lord! It had taken every ounce of will power he had to keep from dragging her even closer against him and planting a kiss on those lovely lips.

He sighed. Lucky the old harridan had been there, otherwise his control might not have held. Galatea was so lovely. Tonight she had worn to dinner a gown of pink satin, which set off her fair beauty, a plain gown adorned only with narrow white ribbons.

He let himself feast his gaze on her while he mused. Why did she appeal to him so? She practiced none of the subterfuges, none of the coy laughter and languishing glances that the women he knew used to lure men to their sides. Tea was all honesty, all naivete. Yes, for a woman her age, she was exceedingly green.

Strange, he thought, that before this week he had actually preferred women of experience—had, indeed, eschewed the company of young women newly out, finding them dull and boring. But Tea was different. She was not a green girl, not in age at least, and she had ample intelligence. But she also had that refreshing honesty—and innocence.

Tea laughed again, and before he could stop himself, Alec had moved across the room to stand by her side.

"Your cook has outdone herself again," he said, feeling like a veritable fool. How much conversation could one hold on the matter of food without looking inane?

"Yes," she said, turning a bright smile on him. "Did you finish your conversation with Lady Linden?"

Tragon blanched and backed a step away, almost colliding with the sideboard. He looked as though mentioning her name might make the Linden dragon appear right there, breathing fire.

"Yes," Alec said, moving closer to Tea and noting with pleasure that she did not retreat from him. "Lady Linden has agreed to play Venus for us."

Tragon gave a snort of disbelief. "Venus! Her!"

Tea looked around quickly. "I'm sure Lady Linden does the best she can."

Tragon backed down deferentially, murmuring, "Yes, of course."

Alec swallowed again. It looked as if what he'd feared was true. Tea definitely had an admirer in Tragon. Of course, the fellow could hardly help being drawn to her. She was a beautiful, desirable woman. Any man worth his salt could see that.

Alec took another step closer to Tea. He would like to get very close. He would *like* to take her in his arms and kiss her passionately. He would like . . .

"Alec! There you are!" Martine Linden came sweeping through the doorway in a blinding gown of yellow silk, which made her sallow complexion even more gray than usual. She was smiling, however, that false smile that turned his stomach inside out and set his teeth on edge. She clutched his coat sleeve. "Dear, dear Alec! And how is your scene coming? Have you given up yet on making our sweet Galatea into an actress?"

With great restraint, Alec refrained from yanking his arm out of her grasping fingers. Instead, he eased himself away. "Tea will never make an actress," he said. "She hasn't a pretending bone in her body. But she makes a most admirable statue of her namesake."

Tea's eyes widened at his use of the word *pretending*, but she said nothing. Perhaps she was thinking of *their* pretense, of his plan to convince Martine and her formidable mama that he had set his matrimonial sights on another target. That must be the reason Tea smiled and moved closer, tucking an arm through his.

"Alec is right," she said brightly. "I am not an actress. But I find that I *can* stand still. And it seems that that is all the part requires."

"Indeed." Martine gave a sniff of disdain. What on earth

188

had convinced this chit that she was so superior to everyone else? Had she no sense? Couldn't she see what she was?

He watched with distaste as Martine's fingers came again to rest on his sleeve. "Did you know? I am doing a scene, too. With Conigsby and Tragon."

"Oh," Tea said, and dutifully asked, "What is the subject?"

Martine laughed, a laugh that if he hadn't been fond of horseflesh and loathe to insult it, Alec would have characterized as horselike. "I decided it would be useful to do the other Galatea story. Sort of a contrast, you know. So, I am going to play the nymph Galatea. Conigsby will play Acis, my lover. And Tragon will be Polyphemus."

The prospect of the shy and retiring Tragon playing a one-eyed monster almost sent Alec off into whoops of laughter. He turned to Tragon, expecting a blunt refusal, but to his surprise, the man was actually nodding—nodding and smiling.

"I thought it might be instructive," he muttered, "to play at raging and roaring for once."

Galatea, ever polite—Alec hoped it was only politeness—smiled warmly. "I'm sure you'll enjoy it." She flushed a little. "I imagine playing a part can be fun."

Martine laughed again. "Conigsby makes a most excellent lover."

Watching Tea's face, Alec saw her blush deepen. What an innocent she was!

Hypatia bounded into the room, trailed by a smiling Varley. That man had better beware, Alec mused. Hypatia might be young, but . . .

"We have found our story!" she cried, pushing at an auburn curl that had fallen over her forehead. "The Pegasus story!"

Tea smiled—such a beautiful smile.

Alec frowned. How could a woman's smile melt a man's insides like this?

189

"That sounds nice, dear," Tea said. "But what part do you play?"

"I am the horse," Hypatia cried, flapping her arms. "The horse with wings. And Peter is going to play Bellepheron, my rider."

Lord! Alec thought. The chit didn't even see the implications of being a horse that Varley would 'ride.'

Or did she? After all, Tea wasn't her only sister. Ianthe had had a Season or two in the city. And she obviously knew her way around. Had she been instructing the little one in how to set out lures?

Really, he told himself, almost snorting aloud, this business with Martine had given his mind a suspicious turn, far too suspicious probably. Little Hypatia was only enjoying herself, consorting with grown-ups, so to speak.

But Tea . . . Something was wrong with—or at least different about—Tea. Her lower lip had a tendency to tremble when she wasn't smiling. And her smile looked somehow forced.

But he had no time to think of that because Lady Linden sailed in, a bright blue frigate under full sail. And behind her, mere ripples in her wake, came Conigsby, followed by Hector with Celandine on his arm.

"Shall we take our seats?" Tea said, smiling at them all. "I believe dinner is ready."

Chapter 10

After the meal, while the gentlemen enjoyed their port and cigars in the dining room, Galatea led the ladies to the drawing room. But to her surprise, Lady Linden stopped her at the door. "I wish a word with you."

Galatea couldn't think of anything she wished less than a word with Lady Linden, but propriety had to be observed. And so she nodded. "Perhaps we could take a seat in the corner."

Lady Linden shook her brilliant curls. "No. I mean privately. We must go to another room."

Galatea's heart sank. What did this woman want with her? "The library then," she murmured, leading the way.

When Lady Linden closed the door behind her, Galatea felt a very real urge to yank it open and run out, back to the safety of the others, but she told herself she was being foolish. Lady Linden was a picky guest. She probably wished to complain about some inconsequential thing, something one of the servants hadn't done quite right. She turned to her guest. "Shall we sit down?"

Lady Linden lowered her ponderous bulk onto a large sofa and Galatea took a nearby chair, folding her hands calmly in her lap and presenting what she hoped was an attentive face to the other woman. "Yes?" she inquired pleasantly.

Lady Linden pursed her scarlet lips. "I have a matter of

great import to discuss with you.'' She scowled. ''I tried to approach your own mama, but she was too busy to heed me.''

Galatea allowed herself a small sigh. Mama must have been quite irate to be interrupted about some trivial household matter, and by such a garrulous and offensive person.

Lady Linden adjusted a ring on one pudgy finger. ''It pains me to bring up such a delicate matter,'' she continued, though she didn't look at all pained. In fact, she looked rather fiercely triumphant. ''But it must be done. And since your own mama refused to do it, I must take the task, onerous as it is, upon my own already-overburdened shoulders.''

Galatea stifled a sigh. It had been a long and trying day. What on earth was Lady Linden babbling on and on about? Would she never get to the point?

Lady Linden fixed her with a piercing stare. ''I'm sure you're aware of the matter to which I allude, a very serious matter indeed.''

Galatea tried to think, but she hadn't the faintest idea what the lady could be driving at. How was she to know about some servant's supposed effrontery? ''I'm afraid . . .'' she stammered. ''I'm afraid I have no idea what you're talking about.''

Lady Linden bridled. ''Of course you do, you silly girl. I'm talking about your setting out lures for the viscount.''

A wave of heat spread over Galatea's body and for a moment she found it almost impossible to catch her breath. Lures for the viscount! What a thing to say!

''There's no use denying it!'' Lady Linden sputtered. ''I've seen it with my own eyes—the way you look at him. It's—it's quite disgusting!''

Disgusting! Galatea thought. What about Martine's behavior? Now, that was disgusting. Even if there were some truth in what Lady Linden said, she had no right . . . Good manners at least . . .

Drawing herself up, Galatea looked the old harridan right

in the eye. "Lady Linden, that is enough. I cannot see that how I look at people is any concern of yours."

"It is! It is," the lady cried, "when you're making eyes at my daughter's intended husband! It must stop! It must stop right away!"

"Indeed," Galatea said, putting all the frost she could into her voice. "Then perhaps you should talk to Alec." She laid delicate stress on his Christian name and saw by the response in Lady Linden's eyes that she noted it. "Because I very much doubt that he is aware that he *is* her intended."

Lady Linden's face turned pale. "Well, perhaps he hasn't asked her just yet. But he will. I know he will. And it isn't right for you to interfere. Besides," her tone turned wheedling, "you are not the sort to suit the viscount. You must know that." She smiled again, though feebly. "He requires a worldly woman, one versed in the intricacies of the *ton,* and you—" The smile turned to a smirk. "You know none of these things. You would be an encumbrance to him, and if ever you managed to get him to the altar, he would shortly be looking for more sophisticated company."

Galatea felt her cheeks reddening, but she held her ground. Alec needed her help and she had promised to give it to him. That was all that mattered here. "I thank you for your concern, Lady Linden. But it is unfounded. Let me assure you that I am not the innocent you believe me to be."

Lady Linden's beady eyes gleamed with unconcealed malice. "Very well. But beware, you are bringing this disaster upon your own head. Don't say I didn't warn you."

"If you'll excuse me," Galatea returned, "I must get back to my guests." Carefully, then, she got to her feet and, with her back ramrod-straight, left the room. *Would* Alec really do a thing like that? Would he marry a woman and then turn away from her? Such an awful thing. How could anyone . . .

Her heart threatened to stop. Dido! This sounded so much like Dido's story. Dido loved Aeneas. Aeneas loved her. He *said* he loved her. But still he left her. Galatea put a hand to her head. It was all too confusing. She would have to think about it later. Now her guests were waiting.

But before she could rejoin the women, Galatea was approached by Hector.

"Tea," he said, his face turning scarlet, "can I have a word with you?"

Galatea swallowed a sigh, but she said, "Of course, Hector."

"Private," he mumbled. "Need to be private."

Now what! "Come down here," she said. "To my little sitting room. We can be alone there." The library was too big for such a private talk, and besides, it would make her think of Lady Linden.

With Hector following meekly at her heels, Galatea went in and closed the door carefully behind him. When he stood before her, her heart rose up in her throat. He looked so strange. Was he in some awful trouble? "Hector, for heaven's sake! What is it? What's wrong?"

"You like Miss Celandine, don'cha?"

"Deenie? Of course I like Deenie. What have you done? You haven't—"

"I have," Hector said sheepishly. "I have fallen head over heels in love."

"In love!" Galatea's legs refused to hold her and she sank into a chair. For a moment there she'd thought Hector had . . . But she should have known that Deenie wouldn't allow liberties like that. "In love?" she repeated.

She stared up at him. "Oh, my dear, you don't love Deenie."

Hector straightened and eyed her as though she'd suddenly taken leave of her senses. "I don't?" he mumbled.

"No, no," she faltered on. "It's all a game—a game the fashionables play with each other."

"Play?" Hector repeated. "Tea, this ain't play." He

squared his shoulders. "I'm dead serious about this. I mean to marry the girl."

"Marry?" Galatea repeated. That couldn't be. Deenie would never . . . "Hector have you—have you asked her yet?"

Hector hung his head. "No, not yet. Truth is, Tea, I'm scared." He frowned. "She ain't like the other girls I know. She's a real sport."

"But Hector, marriage? I mean, marriage is very serious business."

"And didn't I just say that?" Hector demanded. "That's why I came to you."

"To me." Galatea frowned. She must stop repeating everything he said like some foolish child. "Hector, my dear, you haven't known Deenie long. How can you be sure that—"

"Oh, I'm sure," he said fiercely. "I've never felt like this before."

"But . . ." Galatea stumbled to a halt. How could she convince Hector that love didn't happen so quickly when she knew it did, when it had happened to her?

"I thought you'd be pleased," Hector said truculently. "You being her friend and all. To have her in the family, I mean."

"I would be. But Deenie is older than you and—"

"Only a couple years. 'Sides, I don't care about that. I love the girl."

Galatea nodded, searching vainly for something to say. How could Deenie have let her games come to this? But she'd said she would handle it. Maybe . . . "It's a little soon," Galatea said. "You don't mean to declare yourself yet."

"Well . . ." Hector stared over her shoulder. "That's why I came to you. For some advice. And for help with Papa when the time comes."

"I should wait a little, then," Galatea said. "Till the week is more nearly over. Give Deenie more time to get to know you." *And to let you know she's not interested,* she thought.

Hector smiled, his first real smile since he'd entered the room. "I'm a lovable sort, ain't I? She's bound to care for me."

Galatea swallowed hastily. "*I* care for you," she said, "but you know I can't speak for Deenie."

"I know," Hector said, "but she'll come to love me. She's got to."

When Galatea came into the drawing room, Alec felt her presence. Though he had his back to the door, he sensed that she was there. He half turned, wanting to go to her immediately, but the little Hypatia was relating, with much gusto, a story about her childhood pony. And so he forced himself to remain there, nodding and at least *trying* to listen to her story.

But his eyes kept returning to Galatea. She was making her way from guest to guest, seeing, no doubt, that each was comfortable. When she reached that Tragon fellow, she smiled sweetly, sending a wave of jealousy pulsing through Alec. After a brief discussion, Tragon got to his feet and offered her his arm.

"Alec!" From the look on Peter's face, this was not the first time he'd called his name.

"Yes, yes. What is it?"

Peter followed his gaze and then smiled. "It looks like the beautiful Galatea is going for a stroll with Tragon."

"Damnation!" Alec muttered, rather louder than he meant to.

The little Hypatia's eyes widened. "Why, Alec," she said, "what a thing to say." She frowned. "Why do you—? Are you—?"

Peter smiled. "I believe the green-eyed monster has a hold of our Alec."

Hypatia frowned in puzzlement. "Green-eyed . . . Oh! You mean Alec is jealous—jealous of Barnaby?"

196

"Nonsense," Alec said, ignoring Peter's knowing grin. "It's just that I wished to discuss something with her, something about our scene."

"Of course," Peter said in disbelief.

"Shame on you, Peter." The little Hypatia stood, hands on hips, glaring. "You mustn't tease poor Alec so." She turned. "He's an awful tease, Peter is, and besides—" She grinned. "I think you're sweet on Tea. That's nice. That's very nice." She put a hand on his sleeve. "But don't worry. Tea hasn't got a partiality for Barnaby."

"And how do you know that?" Alec growled in mortification.

Hypatia grinned smugly. "Because I know where they're going. Tea told me. Barnaby wants to borrow a Greek dictionary and she's taking him to get it."

"A dictionary!" He might have known. Sheepishly, he pulled at his cuffs. "Of course. I understand Barnaby is quite a scholar."

Peter chuckled. "So they say."

Alec glanced at the Sevres clock on the mantel. He would give them ten minutes—no more—and then he would look for her.

The next minutes passed like hours. Alec tried to remain calm, to make conversation, but his gaze was always on the door, his ears always pricked for the sound of her voice.

Eight minutes passed—eight long interminable minutes—and then Galatea returned to the drawing room, blessedly alone.

Quickly, he excused himself and went to join her. "Tea! There you are. I've been missing you."

She smiled at him. "Barnaby needed a dictionary. You see, he brought his translation along."

Alec nodded. "Of course."

Something in her eyes, some longing, alerted him. "Have you been able to work on your translation?" he asked gently.

"What?" She started. "Oh, no. I've been too busy with our guests."

"And do you miss it?" he inquired.

Tea blushed, putting a hand to her cheek. "Yes, I rather do. You see, I had just gotten to this most interesting part."

"Aeneas and Dido," Alec said.

"You remembered!"

"Of course. When I was in school, I spent a lot of time studying ancient history." No need to tell her he had done it against his will. "Fascinating people," he went on. "Very heroic."

"Yes," Tea replied. "But difficult to understand."

"How so?" he asked, genuinely curious. "Seems to me honor is much the same in any time or place."

She shrugged. "For men, perhaps it is. I was thinking of Dido. Of course, she wasn't Greek. But for her, honor seemed to demand she kill herself."

Alec scowled. "Aeneas was a fool. He should never have left her."

"But *his* honor," Tea protested. "Didn't he have to?"

Alec yearned to wipe the puzzled frown from her face. "I don't know," he said softly. "But I would never desert a woman I loved."

Her gaze searched his face. "You . . . would . . . not?"

"I would not," he repeated gruffly. "But enough of this sober stuff. We're supposed to be festive. Let's gather round and sing some carols."

Her face lightened and she tucked an arm through his. "Yes, yes. Let's sing."

Chapter 11

Another day passed. Galatea hustled about, seeing to the comfort of her guests and rehearsing her scene with Alec. Whenever they were with the others, she did all she could to further his plan, to convince Martine and Lady Linden that Alec's heart had been given to her—Galatea Haslett.

But Martine refused to notice what she didn't want to see. Continuing to regard Alec as her personal property, she latched on to him every time she came into the room, fawning over him in a most disgusting fashion.

Galatea did her very best to help Alec, to make the Lindens believe he was already ensnared by her charms. For the next several days she hung on his arm—and his every word—sending him languishing glances, lavishing him with sweet smiles. And in the process feeling rather like a fool.

Still, fool or not, she persisted in her efforts. As Deenie had pointed out, Galatea was committed to helping the man. And *if* that helping served their purpose, too . . . well, so much the better. Besides, if she didn't do her best to get Alec to form an affection for her, she would no doubt regret it all the rest of her life. Or so Deenie had reiterated, and with great emphasis.

Galatea reminded herself of this very fact as she left another rehearsal with Alec and went to change for dinner. But just before she reached her room, Ianthe called from the doorway of hers. "Tea, come here. I must speak to you."

Galatea considered ignoring the summons, for a summons it clearly was. She was heartily tired of being 'spoken to' by all and sundry. But Ianthe was nothing if not persistent, so perhaps it was better to get it over with. Swallowing her sigh, Galatea crossed the hall.

As always, she entered Ianthe's room with a feeling of distaste. The room was so excessively feminine, so filled with frills and furbelows, that she felt almost smothered. Not that she didn't like feminine things. She did, but not in such excess.

"Come in," Ianthe repeated with an exasperated sigh. She closed the door briskly and turned. "I absolutely must talk to you." Her eyes gleamed. "You must stop this, you know! You're making a perfect cake of yourself over Alec."

"I . . . what do you mean?"

"I mean," Ianthe said, venom lacing her voice, "that you are absolutely throwing yourself at the man. And it is most unseemly, believe me."

Galatea's cheeks burned, but with righteous indignation, not shame. "That is not true," she retorted. "Why, I have not even kissed him."

Ianthe snorted. "You mean he has not kissed you."

"However you choose to put it." Galatea steeled her voice. "It doesn't matter. I enjoy his company and he enjoys mine. And if something more comes of it . . . why, surely that is *our* business. No one else's."

Ianthe's beautiful face twisted into a frown. "How can you be so cruel? I never thought you would steal my friend's intended like this and—"

"I am not stealing him," Galatea declared, overcoming the urge to scream. "There . . . is . . . no . . . understanding between them. Not at all."

Ianthe had the grace to look startled. "But Martine says there is."

200

"And Alec says there is *not*. Certainly he should know." This conversation had already gone too far. Galatea started toward the door. "You have been listening to Lady Linden's lies." She threw the words back over her shoulder. "Really, Ianthe, how can you believe a woman like that . . . a woman who lives on others' misfortunes?"

Ianthe's face turned pale. "Perhaps you're right," she conceded, her conciliatory tone halting Galatea. "Perhaps I did listen too much to Martine's mama. But Tea, dear Tea, you must believe me when I say that Alec is all wrong for you."

Not again! Why didn't these people mind their own business? Galatea stopped and turned. "You don't know—"

"Tea! Please!" Ianthe looked genuinely concerned. "I know Alec. He's talked about all through the *ton.*" She raised a hand, fending off Galatea's protest. "This isn't just Lady Linden talking. Everyone knows Alec is a Corinthian of the first stare."

"So," Galatea demanded angrily, "what is wrong with that?" Of course Alec was well-known. Such a tall, handsome man, with that curly black hair. And such charming manners. Why shouldn't women be interested in him?

Ianthe shook her head. "Tea, think! Please! He's been on the town some years now. He has kept women—*kept* them—actresses, singers, ladies of the night. Many, many of them."

Galatea stood silent. Why must Ianthe say horrible things about Alec? Next she'd be saying he'd seduced innocent young girls. And Galatea would never believe that!

"You do understand?" Ianthe cried. "You know what I mean by *kept?*"

"Of course I understand. Of course I know." She straightened her shoulders, trying to look unimpressed. "I am not a complete innocent. I have heard of such women. But what has that—or Alec's former life for that matter—to do with me?"

"What!? What indeed!" Ianthe planted her fists on her

hips. "You must know the man is only toying with you. He has no intention of making any honorable—"

Galatea's heart plummeted to her slippers. Ianthe was the fashionable one, the one who knew the ways of the *ton*. But then common sense reminded Galatea that Alec was *not* toying with her. How could he be toying with her when he was counting on her to help him?

From somewhere inside herself, she pulled a shrill laugh. "I can play the game as well as any fashionable."

Though she had never been nearer to tears, she smiled and tried to look coy. "And that is all it is to me—a game." And smiling a dreadfully false smile, Galatea turned away from her sister's shocked face and marched off to her room. Her very best gown—the royal blue one—that was what she'd wear to dinner tonight. And if she wanted to smile at Alec and lean on his arm and . . . well, that was *her* business.

Galatea donned the royal blue gown. It was cut a little lower in the bodice than she was comfortable with and its bottom third was stiff with ruching, but it should certainly draw a man's eyes. Alec's eyes, she told herself with some dismay. Alec's dark, dark eyes were the ones she wanted to draw.

She might, possibly, convince Ianthe that her heart was not involved in this charade. But there was little point in trying to fool herself. She had lost her heart to Alec. Who wouldn't love a wonderful man like him? But could she do what Deenie had just lately advised? Could she lie in wait for Alec? Surprise him under the mistletoe? Actually *kiss* him?

A shudder sped over her, but she kept on toward the dining room. She must not let her fears overcome her. She must act! That's what Deenie had said when she proposed this kiss. Act! Act now!

There were people already in the dining room. Galatea

could hear them talking as she approached. Relief and disappointment warred in her breast. Was Alec already in there? Was she too late to kiss him before dinner? Certainly she didn't want to wait till after they'd eaten. To have that hanging over her throughout the entire meal . . . She wouldn't be able to swallow a bite.

And then she gulped. Alec was coming down the hall from the other direction. From this distance and without her spectacles, she couldn't see his features clearly, but she would know him anywhere from his special way of walking, that strong masculine swing to his stride. And some paces behind him came someone whose features she couldn't make out at all. She should have insisted on wearing her spectacles from the first. But no, she didn't want Alec to see her in them.

He raised a hand in a wave. She waved back and hurried through the dining room door. She *would* do it! she told herself. In a few moments Alec would come through the door. And she would be waiting for him. She would kiss him.

Her heart pounding in her chest, Galatea took up a station to one side. How did the fashionables take kissing so lightly? She could scarcely breathe at the thought of what she was about to do.

And then she heard male footsteps approaching. Closer and closer, down the hall they came. Closing her eyes, she jumped forward, threw her arms around the startled man in the doorway, and plastered her mouth to his.

Oh, Lord! This was all wrong. He wasn't kissing her back at all. He hadn't even put his arms around her. He didn't even *feel* like . . . She pulled back and opened her eyes.

"Barnaby!"

His face ashen, he stared back at her. "M—M—Miss Haslett!" he stammered. "My word!"

All the blood rushed to her face, leaving her red and breathless. Galatea cast about in her mind for something—anything—to say. "I thought it was time someone kissed

203

you,'' she said with brittle gaiety. "Come, shall we take our seats?''

And then, as she took his arm, she saw Alec staring at her in utter amazement. Lord! To think that he had witnessed this embarrassing fiasco! But why hadn't *he* come through the door? Had he suspected she'd be waiting and sent Barnaby in first? Oh dear, it was all too humiliating to think about. In confusion, she led the others toward the table.

His feet rooted to the floor, Alec stared. Good God! Tea and Barnaby? Together? How could that be?

You know how, he told himself angrily. *It's those damned ancient Greeks. That's what they talk about.*

But Tea? He'd never imagined Tea would *kiss* a man so boldly. What had made her do it? Tea catching a man under the mistletoe. Could he have mistaken her innocence?

The question gave him pause, but he had to answer it negatively. Hector wouldn't have lied about his sister. Not to his friend Alec. Tea couldn't be casually flirting. Could she possibly feel a real interest in this Tragon? In such a mooncalf? Could she possibly be considering matrimony, actual matrimony, to that fellow?

The thought sent a cold wave of shock through Alec. Not Tea. Not to Barnaby. Not to Douglass or Conigsby, either. Not to anyone!

Alec forced his legs to carry him into the room before he stopped again, and he was almost run over by Hector and Celandine, who had eyes for no one but each other.

Good God! He didn't want Tea to marry anyone but him! In a state of shock, he advanced toward the table. In the space of a few short days, Tea had brought him to contemplating matrimony, an institution he'd been devotedly evading for years.

Still in a daze, Alec considered his options. He could walk away when this week was over, let Tea go, keep his long-cherished freedom. That was clearly the thing to do, of course. He'd had no thought of marrying, no idea at all. But . . .

"Alec! Dear, dear Alec!" Martine Linden's fingers closed around his wrist.

When he turned to her, she leaned against his arm, ogling him. And suddenly he couldn't take any more of her machinations. "Excuse me," he said, pulling out of her clutches. "Tea is calling me."

Martine's mouth opened, but before she could say anything, he had crossed the room.

Tea looked up at him, her cheeks still rosy, her eyes somehow wounded. "Alec." The word was a mere whisper.

"Tea." He wanted to think of something—anything—to say. All he could think of was the prospect of life without her. Everything he'd enjoyed in his years on the town—horses and racing, prize fights and betting, bits of fluff and their enjoyment, even his precious freedom—all meant nothing without her sweet face across from him in the morning, her golden hair on the pillow next to his at night. He swallowed a sigh. That was it, then. He was actually smitten with Hector's sister! The humor of it! The absurd humor of it!

London's most notorious man-about-town head over heels in love with a country girl—and a scholar at that! How the *ton* would talk! With the Lindens there to fan the flames of gossip, they would burn ever brighter. But suddenly he didn't care.

"Alec?"

Tea's voice was so low he could barely hear it. "Is something . . ." she stumbled over the word, "wrong?"

"Wrong?" he asked, throwing a dark look Tragon's way. "What on earth could be wrong?"

Chapter 12

The meal was far from a success. Uncomfortable in her fetching blue gown, Galatea still endeavored to play the hostess. But both Barnaby and Alec were behaving strangely. Barnaby wouldn't meet her eyes at all. He stared down at his plate, barely nodding when she spoke to him.

And Alec . . . Alec was very attentive, leaning over to speak to her softly, helping her with this dish and that. But his voice sounded hoarse and his face looked almost feverish.

Something was wrong with him. Surely it couldn't be that kiss . . . Her face heated at the very thought of that awful misdirected kiss! Of course, Alec might be upset because of how the kiss would look to Lady Linden, because it might interfere with his plan to escape Martine's clutches.

He couldn't be jealous of Barnaby. She wished Alec *could* be jealous. But he had given no evidence of partiality toward her, nothing but the false imaginings that were supposed to impress Martine and instead had accidentally won Galatea's ignorant heart.

Still, she managed to eat most of her dinner and, the meal over, stood to lead the ladies toward the drawing room. At least she thought she was leading the ladies. But just after she passed through the door, a murmur behind her made her turn. And what she saw sent her already-sinking spirits spiraling further downward.

Hector had stopped Deenie under the mistletoe—and he was kissing her quite thoroughly. Even worse, she was kissing him back—and just as thoroughly.

Galatea turned away, a sob catching in her throat. So Deenie was turning on her, too. How could she possibly dissuade Hector, protect him from hurt, when Deenie had gone back on her promise?

Galatea started down the hall, her eyes filling with tears, and stumbled over her own feet. Stupid, she thought. She was above all stupid.

But there was no time to think of her stupidity, for at that very moment a strong hand fastened around her elbow and Alec asked, "May I help? We gentlemen decided to join you ladies immediately."

"I—I am fine," she murmured. The biggest lie she'd ever uttered.

"Your brother is quite taken with Celandine," Alec observed, his voice low.

Galatea turned to him. "You see it, too, then." She hesitated. "It's not just—" Embarrassment overtook her, but Hector's happiness was at stake. She pressed on. "I have been so worried about him. I mean—"

Alec was looking at her so earnestly that she faltered again. "That is—"

Alec smiled sadly. "What you mean is, the boy's in danger of being leg-shackled."

"Leg—leg shackled?" she repeated, not understanding.

"Brought to the sticking point," Alec went on. "Contemplating matrimony."

"Oh." So that was how men spoke of marriage. Leg-shackled. But Alec was looking at her expectantly. She would have to reply. "Yes, I'm afraid so."

"Is marriage so dreadful, then?" he asked softly.

She ignored that question. In her present state of mind, she dared not attempt an answer. "I'm afraid—that is, Hector is serious, but—but Deenie—I'm afraid that to Deenie it's all a game."

207

"I see." Alec's face darkened. "You disapprove of those who flirt too freely, then?"

"Of course. That is, they should at least have a care for others. For their feelings."

"Yes," he said, his face darkening even more. "A fellow's feelings can be hurt easily."

"Hector is young, you know, and—"

"Your concern for your brother is very touching," Alec said. But why should his voice seem to hold a sneer? "Are you also concerned for Tragon's delicate feelings?"

"Barnaby?" she asked in surprise. "Why should I be concerned about him? Barnaby is not—"

Alec positively scowled.

"Oh!" She swallowed over the lump in her throat. "You mean the . . . that kiss?"

Alec nodded, his black brows coming together fiercely. "Yes, that kiss."

"That was just—" She couldn't tell him that it was a mistake, that she had meant to kiss *him*. He would think her a real noodle-wit then. "I—I just wanted him to feel part of the company. Not—not neglected, you see."

"Not neglected?" Alec repeated. "I think you have been more than friendly to him."

She managed a smile. "Well, I hope so. I want everyone to have a good time."

Alec swallowed an oath. A good time, indeed! Too bad his hostess didn't have such concern for *him*. For a moment he lived that horrid second when he had watched her throw herself into Tragon's arms, cover his mouth with hers. And this she considered a gesture of hospitality! That was the outside of enough!

He wanted to drag her off somewhere private, and then—then he wanted to kiss her as he had never kissed any woman before. What would she do? he wondered ruefully, if he fell to his knees right there in the hall and asked her to become his wife?

Good Lord! He was really, actually contemplating matrimony. And with a certain sense of anticipation. Did he have bats in his attic? The bucks at White's would never believe this! Kendall brought to bay! And walking willingly into the trap, yet!

"Excuse me," Galatea said, disengaging her elbow from his grasp. "I must speak to Deenie."

"Of course." From the look on her face, Tea meant to take the flirting Celandine to task. But was Celandine really just flirting, or had she at last found a man who made her heart pound and her blood sing?

Good Lord! He was beginning to rhapsodize like one of those poet fellows—all roses and blushes and such trash!

Hector, on the other hand . . . Now, Hector might be driven to such lengths, spouting love and dove, and heart and apart. But the Viscount Kendall was cut from different cloth. If he loved a woman—his heart skipped a beat—if he loved a woman, he would come right out with it, tell her so man to man—that is, man to woman—and . . . Good grief! He'd better go off for an evening walk in the snow. His blood needed a good deal of cooling!

Galatea turned back to where Deenie and Hector were proceeding, at a snail's pace, toward the drawing room. "If you please, Hector," she said, "I should like to speak to Deenie."

Hector smiled, obviously believing she meant to put in a good word for him. "Of course, of course. I'll see you both later." And off he went, smiling broadly.

But Deenie wasn't smiling. "All right," she said, "what's wrong now?"

"Not here," Galatea whispered, casting an anxious glance after Hector's retreating figure. "Come with me."

209

Deenie followed her into the little sitting room and closed the door. "What is it? Has something gone wrong with Alec?"

"Oh, no!" Galatea cried. "Except that your advice was completely off! And it has gotten me in a great deal of trouble! Awful trouble!"

"How?" Deenie demanded.

"I—I kissed the wrong man," Galatea admitted, sinking into a chair.

"You what?" Deenie paced back and forth thoughtfully.

"I—I saw Alec coming down the hall. I knew it was him from his way of walking. It's so masculine and strong. So I went into the dining room." She paused.

"Go on," Deenie urged, her eyes bright. "What happened then?"

"I—I heard him coming—heard his footsteps, that is—and I closed my eyes, jumped out, and kissed him."

"And?" Deenie's eyebrows shot up.

"And it wasn't Alec," Galatea wailed.

Deenie shook her head. "My dear, you must never close your eyes till you're sure of your man. Who was it?"

"It was Barnaby."

"Merciful heavens!" Deenie put a hand to her heart.

"And—and just as I drew back, all confused, I looked over Barnaby's shoulder. And there was Alec, positively glaring at me."

"Good," Deenie declared.

Galatea started in surprise. "What are you talking about, good? He saw me—he saw me kiss Barnaby!"

"Good," Deenie repeated complacently. "A little competition is just what he needs. You did say he glared?"

"Yes, but that's because of his plan—Miss Linden—" But wait. Why was she going on about herself? This wasn't what she meant to discuss with Deenie. Not at all! "But I didn't ask you in here to speak to you about Alec."

"You didn't?" Now Deenie looked really surprised.

"No." Galatea tried to remain calm. "It's about Hector.

Deenie, you promised! You told me Hector would not be hurt." She took a deep breath. "But I saw you. Under the mistletoe. You kissed him back. He's going to be just miserable when you refuse him."

A strange look crossed Deenie's face. "Who said I mean to refuse him?"

Galatea gasped. "Deenie! You can't mean—you aren't—"

Deenie smiled. "I know it seems strange, after all the men I've refused, to accept Hector. I mean, there's nothing wrong with Hector . . ." She stopped in obvious confusion. "What I mean is, there's a lot right with Hector, but people might be surprised and—"

Galatea could control herself no longer. "Do you mean that when he asks you'll accept him?"

Deenie nodded. "So tell me, how would you like to have me for a sister-in-law?"

Galatea got to her feet and enveloped her friend in a huge hug. "Oh, Deenie, I should like that above all things! And Hector—Hector will be so happy!" But wait! Deenie hadn't said . . . Galatea sobered suddenly, drawing back. "But are you sure? Are you quite sure? I mean, Hector is deeply in love with you."

"I know," Deenie said. "And that is my first prerequisite for a husband. He must love *me*. Not my connections. Not my dowry. Just me."

Galatea nodded. "I understand that. But Deenie, do you love him?"

Deenie smiled wistfully. "How could I not? He is very lovable. And I think we shall deal quite well together." She frowned a little. "But don't let on to him that I mean to accept. Not yet. I have waited a long time to enter the state of matrimony. I don't want to rush things."

"I won't tell a soul," Galatea promised. "And especially not Hector."

211

Chapter 13

The next night after dinner, Alec dressed warmly for the sleigh ride. He didn't know why Tea wanted to bring home the Yule log in the dark, but he was thankful. Darkness was more romantic, more . . . suited to his purpose.

He buttoned his greatcoat and put on a muffler over it, wondering whether she would wear a fur-lined cloak. If she got cold, she might draw nearer to him for warmth. But on the other hand, he didn't want her to take sick. She seemed like a healthy girl in spite of her preoccupation with books.

But something else had been on her mind the last few days. She'd been acting strange. In fact, since that curious kiss she'd given Tragon under the mistletoe, she'd been smiling a lot. Throwing strange looks at her brother. Had she confided in him? Did she think Tragon was going to offer for her? Had she already given that bookworm her heart? That had been her father's plan, of course, and they did have much in common.

But Tragon wasn't going to win her that easily. No one was going to sit beside Tea tonight except Alec, Viscount Kendall. Once he got her beside him in the darkness, he meant to take advantage of the situation. He meant to kiss her. He'd waited long enough, respecting her shyness, thinking he might offend her by moving too soon. Pray God he hadn't waited too long!

When Alec descended the stairs to the front hall where the

others were gathering, he found Hector holding out Celandine's fur-trimmed cape for her, and from the fatuous look on his face, Tea had judged rightly. Her brother was irredeemably caught in the clutches of love.

Alec swallowed a sigh. The rest of the crowd was fairly much obliterated by the bulk of Lady Linden, practically filling the hall herself in a fur wrap dyed bright purple and wearing what looked like an upended fur muff pulled down over her orange curls. Beside her stood Martine, her drab mantle dragging on the floor, her false curls squashed beneath a huge fur hat of indiscriminate color.

If those two managed to crowd in the same vehicle with him and Tea, all would be up with his plan. Lucky he'd been able to enlist Hypatia—that girl was going to be a charming schemer—and Varley to help him. Fortunately, Tea had asked Hypatia to arrange for the vehicles for the ride. And she had planned . . .

When Tea came up the hall from the kitchen wing, his heart actually beat faster. She was wearing an old fur cloak, very unfashionable in cut, but she was beautiful, her fair hair shining against the dark fur hood like an angel among mere mortals. Lord, he was waxing poetic again!

She looked around, counting the guests. "Well," she said. "I guess everyone is here. Now, we have a wagon on runners that holds eight and a sleigh that holds four. There are plenty of lap rugs and—"

"And we hope you all enjoy yourselves," Alec added, grabbing her arm and starting toward the door.

"But, Alec," she began, "shouldn't we decide how to divide up? Who's going to ride with whom?"

Alec shook his head. "No, no," he whispered. "Come on."

She lowered her voice. "But won't Martine—"

"Martine will be taken care of," he insisted. "Come along."

He hustled her out and down the walk, Hypatia and Varley

hard on their heels. "Really, Alec," Tea insisted as they reached the outdoors, "I should be seeing to my guests."

"Your guests will be fine," he soothed, helping her into the sleigh rather urgently, lifting her almost bodily. He settled himself beside her and tucked the robe over her knees.

"But—"

"Tea?" Hypatia's voice carried just the right note of child-ishness. The little schemer should go upon the stage. She would be a great success there.

"Yes, dear?"

"Peter and I—we have to ride with you and Alec. Mama said so. She said that's the only way propriety can be preserved, if you're my chaperone and all."

Tea sighed.

In spite of her studious bent, she must have been called on often to mother the other Hasletts, Alec mused. It must have been rather hard on her, but it boded well for the future.

The future of what? he asked himself sardonically. But he knew the answer. If Tea responded to his kiss, if he thought he had even the ghost of a chance with her, he meant to spring the question. And before this Christmas in the country was over.

"Very well," Tea said. "I suppose Mama is right. You're young to be going on such an excursion. But since you're with me, any irregularity will be overlooked."

"Thank you, Tea." Hypatia leaned over to give her sister a hug, casting a triumphant look over her shoulder at Alec.

"Well!" Lady Linden and Martine had reached the sleigh. "I must say that this is hardly polite!" Martine's nose was already turning bright red and she sniffed emphatically. "My mother can't ride in a wagon. And she needs me with her."

"Well, then," Tea replied in a voice of controlled politeness, "we shall *give* you the sleigh. Come, Hypatia."

Alec was out of the sleigh instantly, handing down first Tea, then Hypatia. The little one couldn't help grinning at the success of their ruse, but fortunately Tea was looking the other way.

214

When they reached the wagon filled with hay, Alec looked the guests over. "Perhaps Tragon and Conigsby would ride with the Linden ladies," he suggested. "Conigsby is quite a hand with the reins. They'll be safe with him."

As he'd hoped, Conigsby swallowed the compliment and clambered down with a smile. Tragon wasn't as enthusiastic—and who could blame him—but he was too polite to object and followed Conigsby to the sleigh. Alec helped Tea up and settled her in the hay, tucking the woolen rug carefully around her knees. Then he settled back himself, trying to keep the smile of satisfaction off his face.

The little Hypatia had done more than arrange the means of transportation. Much more. *She* had contrived it so that the Lindens would not be in the same vehicle with him and Tea. And *she* had suggested that if they protested—as they'd been fairly sure would be the case—Tragon and Conigsby would be the obvious choices to share the sleigh. So not only was he rid of the Lindens, he was also rid of Tragon.

Hypatia had even come up with the chaperone idea. When she got a little older, that girl was going to get the man she wanted. He'd lay odds on it.

Inhaling the sweet fragrance of the hay, Alec shifted slightly, allowing himself to come to rest somewhat nearer Tea. He held his breath but she didn't move—or even lean—away.

Galatea breathed a sigh of relief. She'd been so afraid the Lindens would find a way to spoil this trip for the Yule log. There was so little time left; this week was her only chance. She had to make Alec care for her. The only trouble was, she didn't know how to do it.

It seemed to come so easily to some women. Deenie knew just what to do. And Ianthe . . . she was always comfortable with men. Even Hypatia knew more about how to treat men than she did.

"Are you warm enough?" Alec asked, bending so close she could feel his warm breath on her cheek and tucking the woolen rug solicitously around her.

She wasn't cold, not at all. But perhaps that was because he was so close to her. "Yes, yes," she murmured. "Thank you."

He shifted again, putting his arm behind her nonchalantly, as if he didn't notice what he was doing. Trying to remain nonchalant herself, Galatea leaned back, resting against it as though it were just hay and not his arm at all.

He wasn't doing this for the Lindens, she told herself happily. They couldn't even see. This was—was . . . well, because he wanted to. That was all she knew—and right then, all she wanted to know. If he was playing the game, if tomorrow she meant nothing to him . . . But she wouldn't think of that now. She couldn't.

On her other side, Hypatia was giggling, leaning up to whisper in Peter Varley's ear. Hypatia was getting to be quite a young woman. Mama ought to be paying more attention to her. Before many years, Hypatia would have her come-out and choose her husband. And she would get the one she wanted, too. There was no doubt in Galatea's mind about that.

Ianthe seemed to have enchanted Douglass. Perhaps he would offer for her. Deenie would be with Hector, of course. They would all be married and *she* would be the only spinster.

A long, low sigh escaped her. This house party had been a mistake. Why had she ever listened to Hector? She'd been quite content before with her studies. Reading about Dido and Aeneas had been enough love for her. Puzzling over the exact translation of a word had been excitement enough, too.

But now—now she was afraid her studies would never be enough. For the rest of her life she would be thinking about Alec, longing for him and the life that might have been.

"Tea," he said, startling her.

"Yes. What is it?"

"Perhaps you should tell the driver we're ready."

"Ready? Oh, dear, yes." How embarrassing. She felt like

216

diving under the sweet-smelling hay and hiding. Imagine woolgathering at a time like this! "Driver!" She leaned forward. "Let's go."

The driver spoke to the horses and the wagon creaked forward. Galatea leaned back and found that Alec had moved closer still. Now his arm was most definitely around her, his body close to hers.

"The stars are out in full force tonight," he said, looking up to the heavens. His cheek brushed hers, causing her heart to catch in her throat.

"Yes," she breathed. "It's a lovely night. Just cold enough, but not too cold. The stars sparkle so."

Alec chuckled, and somewhere inside Galatea felt a burgeoning bud of joy. How good it would be to sit like this often, to feel his arm around her and know that it would always be there. She let herself sink into the most pleasant dream, surrendering to her need to be close to him, settling back against his strong masculine chest.

They rode in silence for some moments, silence broken only by the sound of the horses' hooves on the snow, the muted whispers of the others, and an occasional giggle from Hypatia. But though she heard these sounds, Galatea was scarcely aware of anything but Alec's nearness. She was pretending that he loved her, that he was her husband. It was such a lovely dream.

"Tea?"

He said her name so softly, so tenderly, that still in the dream, she turned her face to his. "Yes?"

His mouth was only an inch from hers, but she didn't turn away. She didn't move at all. Now that they were away from the house and its lights she could see very little, only the vague outline of his head, dark against the blackness of the sky. But she knew with some inner certainty that he meant to kiss her. Still, she didn't move away. Like a moth to the flame, she leaned slightly toward him.

His lips covered hers in a kiss that was at once tender and

compelling. Without even thinking about it, she slid a mittened hand up around his neck. His lips moved on hers and her body flooded with the certainty that this was meant to be. Her entire life seemed to have led to this moment in his arms.

Why had she ever thought that studies were important? The ancients were long gone—nothing but dust and memory, stories in old books. But she was alive—very much alive—and she wanted to stay that way. She pressed closer, kissing Alec back, letting him know that she cared.

Alec deepened the kiss. He could hardly believe it, but she hadn't rebuffed him. When her mouth softened beneath his and her mittened hand stole up around his neck, he gathered her closer. She didn't dislike him, then! He had a chance with her.

He kissed her thoroughly, blessing the darkness that covered so much. But then, when he realized that she was kissing him back—and with such fervor—a cold shiver wriggled down his spine. The *ton* was always circulating stories about so-called innocents who had turned out to have rather more experience than they should and the surprise of the men who had taken them to wife. How did Galatea know to kiss like this?

He drew back a little, took his mouth away from hers, and settled her into the crook of his arm. She nestled there without a murmur, leaning against him all soft and warm.

And he cursed himself for being a cynical fool. Tea was just what she appeared—innocent and trusting. She kissed him as she did because she didn't know the dangers. She expected him to take care of her. Sighing, she nestled even closer, turning her face again to his. But he restrained himself. She was inexperienced. It was up to *him* to have sense.

In the darkness he smiled. Tea loved him and she trusted him. He would be worthy of that love. Tonight—and forever.

Chapter 14

The next day Galatea hurried about, finishing the preparations for Christmas Eve and the Christmas Day celebration. Sometimes she felt she hardly knew what she was doing. She hadn't slept much after last night's ride, her mind going back to Alec. Alec *had* kissed her. Not once, but several times. He'd held her close, kept her warm, been very devoted to her.

If she closed her eyes, she could still feel his arms around her, his lips on hers. The memory was a joyful one, but it was already the day before Christmas. In two more days the house party would be over. Alec would go back to the city. If he waited that long.

Just this morning she'd seen him in whispered conference with his groom. And then Hypatia told her the groom had ridden off posthaste—to London on an errand for his master.

Why should Alec send a groom to the city? Was someone expecting him there? Someone he didn't want to disappoint?

Such thoughts tormented her throughout the day and even while she dressed for dinner. She'd saved her nicest gown for this occasion. After all, when dinner was finished they would be performing their mythological scenes. For a moment she wished there really was a goddess of love, someone who could give her sound advice. But of course there wasn't and she would just have to muddle through.

Her gown was of creamy ivory satin, decorated with the narrowest of crimson ribbons. The same kind of crimson ribbons were twined through her curls. She looked quite attractive, except that she was inordinately flushed. She wouldn't need to pinch her cheeks; there was more than enough color in them. But what had Alec been thinking last night? Did he mean something by those kisses? Or was he only playing the game?

She went down to dinner, her color still high. It was hard to imagine that people did this sort of thing just for fun. Kissing, of course, was very pleasurable. But that was because it was Alec she was kissing. Kissing Barnaby had not been the same thing at all. And as a game . . . No, she wouldn't find it very amusing. But then, as Deenie had often told her in the kindest way, she was not like ordinary females.

Alec came down the hall toward her and she felt her cheeks growing even hotter. He'd been looking at her strangely all day. Did he think she'd been too forward last night, kissing him back like that? She really didn't know what had gotten into her. The Lindens hadn't even been in the sleigh to be impressed. But the dream of being loved had been so real. His kisses had seemed so real.

"You're looking lovely tonight," Alec said when he reached her. "But then, you always look lovely."

How she wished she could get into his mind and know what he was thinking. Was he only mouthing pretty words? Playing the game as it should be played? Or did he really care about her?

Galatea swallowed a sigh of exasperation. Why couldn't a man and a woman just come right out and say what they felt? Why must they dance around and around the subject? And why must she feel so embarrassed by it all? As though she'd been caught doing something wrong?

Alec was so handsome in his evening clothes that her heart

220

caught in her throat. No wonder so many women wanted him.

"You look just right for the part," he said, his voice husky.

She shook her head, more in bewilderment than in denial. She had never *felt* lovely. She had never been sought after by men. "Thank you," she murmured. "I—I hope that I will do the part properly."

"You will." He took her elbow and guided her through the doorway. And then, in the middle of it, inexplicably, he stopped and turned, brushing her lips with a kiss. She was so startled she almost swooned.

Well, she really wasn't one to swoon, but the shock of it— and he was so quick, the kiss there and gone before she could really respond to it. She felt the blood rush to her cheeks, but Alec seemed unperturbed, guiding her expertly toward the table.

He was like that all through dinner, solicitous, helpful, friendly—and yet somehow removed from her. She thought she knew him and yet . . . did she really?

The thought of standing there before the others while Alec gazed at her with burning eyes put her in such a state of confusion that Galatea could scarcely speak. By the time the meal was over, she was feeling such agitation that she wasn't sure she could manage a sensible word.

How would she be able to dissemble when, at the end of their scene, Pygmalion took the statue-come-alive in his arms? Alec had told her, quite seriously, that the story really called for such an ending. And she had believed him, perhaps because she wanted to. But now, thinking of it made her go hot and cold by turns.

After dessert, Martine looked around the table, her eyes alight with power. "There will be no port for the gentlemen tonight. We'll go directly to the library for the presentation of our scenes." She scoured them all with a penetrating look. "I expect you all to be properly prepared."

"Of course, of course," everyone murmured. Galatea

hoped Martine wouldn't be too overbearing about this. Ianthe, for one, was not apt to take kindly to being ordered about by another woman, especially one without good looks. And Deenie wouldn't put up with it, either.

Galatea rose, preparing to lead the way, and was pleased to find Alec right there beside her, offering her his arm.

The library had been decorated by the servants, writhing under Martine's caustic tongue, no doubt. But the room did look nice, festooned with red ribbons, the Yule log burning brightly on the hearth. And in front of the area designated as the stage, the chairs had been arranged in a semicircle.

Galatea turned. "Thank you, Martine. Everything looks lovely."

"Of course," Martine said with a sniff. "Now, everyone take a seat. We'll start with Ianthe and Douglass."

His hand on her elbow, Alec guided Galatea to the chairs in the front row. Evidently, he meant to stay beside her through the entire evening. But that didn't give her quite the pleasure it should have. After all, the Lindens were there. It was probably all part of his plan.

Ianthe and Douglass, Martine and Conigsby and Barnaby, did their scenes. But Galatea saw very little of them.

She did note that the scene Hypatia and Peter had chosen really did have to do with a horse. A beautiful horse with wings, as Hypatia kept explaining.

Then Martine said, "And now Galatea and Alec will do their scene."

Alec helped Tea to her feet. Numbly, she allowed him to lead her to the impromptu stage. While he positioned the footstool, she stood by. When he extended a hand to help her up, she accepted it. And there she was, being stared at by everyone. But it wasn't everyone looking at her that made her feel so strange. It was the thought of Alec . . . Alec and his burning eyes.

* * *

Alec positioned Tea on the footstool, draping the skirt of her gown in classic folds. She was so lovely, the most divine-looking woman he'd ever seen. And soon he would ask her . . . But would she accept?

He pushed the thought out of his mind. Time enough for that later. Right now he had to concentrate on the scene.

"Smile now," he said. "Remember, you're absolutely lovely."

She nodded but she looked scared, almost too scared to speak. He launched into his monologue, telling the story of the beautiful statue he'd created and how he'd fallen hopelessly, madly in love with it.

Through it all Tea stood, two spots of red high on her cheeks. He finished the monologue and went into his supplication to Venus/Aphrodite. But the last word was barely out of his mouth when Lady Linden entered from the far door.

Stunned silence fell upon the group. Her costume for the evening outdid all of her previous ensembles. She had draped herself in brilliant pink satin, which together with her orange hair, rolled into great sausage curls, created an unforgettable sight.

"Ah, Pygmalion," she cried, in tones that would have made an ordinary man run for cover. "Poor Pygmalion, loving cold marble."

She swayed down the aisle, which knowing her mother's girth, Martine had kept wide enough, and joined him on the stage.

"On your knees, mortal," she commanded.

He saw Tea's expression of revulsion and for a moment he hesitated. The old harridan was carrying this goddess thing too far. But then he caught sight of Tragon's face, the look he was directing at Tea. Alec went to his knees.

Lady Linden expanded her part, ranting on and on until even Martine began to squirm restlessly. Stealing a look at Tea, Alec was alarmed to see that she was looking paler by the second. And then, just as he opened his mouth to interrupt, Tea gave a little sigh and began to crumple.

Pushing the old bitch aside, he lunged forward, just in time to break Tea's fall with his own body.

"Some statue," Martine hissed. But he had no time for her inanities.

"Tea?" he begged, gathering her to him. "Tea? Are you all right?" He straightened her limbs, chafing her wrists lightly.

Her eyelids fluttered. Once, twice. The third time they stayed open. She gazed up at him in bewilderment. "What? What—what happened?"

"You swooned."

"I . . . what?" She came suddenly erect in his arms. "I never swoon. How could I—"

"It's all right," Alec soothed. "It was just too much for you, all that standing."

"Of course," Lady Linden cried, rustling her pink satin imperiously. "Now, let us get on with the scene."

Alec shook his head. "No. Tea has done enough for today. We're finished."

Lady Linden sniffed and looked about to explode, but Hypatia—blessed little Hypatia—came rushing forward, exclaiming in her little girl voice, "Dear Tea, you must listen to Alec. You know he always knows best."

And Tea nodded. She was willing to let him care for her! If only he could do it forever. If only she said yes.

"Yes," Celandine said. "Come sit here on the sofa. Alec, help her over."

Galatea frowned. They were making far too much fuss over a simple spell of fainting. And what was Hypatia doing, saying things like Alec always knows best—as though he'd been their friend for years. Had Alec told her about the ruse to fool the Lindens? Or had they fooled Hypatia, too?

224

She allowed Alec to help her to her feet. "I—I'm fine," she protested. "Quite able to walk. It was only a momentary weakness."

But he was frowning, looking concerned.

"Really," she began again, but before she could finish, he swept her up in his arms and carried her to the sofa.

"That's the way to do it," Hector said with an approving smile. "Treat her like a lady."

"She *is* a lady," Alec replied, looking at her in a way that made her blush.

"Really," Lady Linden tittered, "my dear, you are the best actress of us all. Seldom have I seen such a convincing swoon."

Alec scowled, but Hector was before him, actually glowering. "Now see here. My sister don't fake swooning. Some ladies might"—he directed a glance at Martine, who looked away quickly—"but not Tea."

"Very well," Lady Linden replied. "Whatever you say." But it was clear she didn't believe him.

"Please," Galatea begged. "Go on with the scenes." She hated being the center of attention. It was too embarrassing. "I shall be fine."

Martine sniffed again, but she turned to Hector and Celandine. "Your turn now." She gave them a disapproving look. "Their scene will be a surprise even to me."

Hector led Celandine to the stage. He was beaming as he had at the age of ten when he'd gotten his first pony for Christmas.

Alec leaned closer. "Looks like he's done it," he whispered to Tea.

"You mean—"

Alec chuckled. "If ever I've seen a fellow in the throes of love—"

"He does look happy, doesn't he?" She sighed. "Do you think— That is, I know very little about marriage, but— I mean, Mama and Papa are hardly an ordinary couple." She faltered. Alec was looking at her so intently it was hard to think. "Oh, dear, I'm not saying what I mean to. I just want Hector to be happy."

"I understand," Alec said, pressing her hand. "I believe some men are very happy in the state of matrimony." He paused, giving her a strange look. "If they choose appropriate partners."

Did that mean . . . "Do you think Deenie—"

Alec smiled. "I think Celandine will make your brother very happy. But listen, they're about to begin."

Galatea tried to listen, but it made very little sense because Hector grinned through even the most serious parts. Finally, Peter cried, "Give off, Hector old boy, and tell us why you're grinning like a cat in the creamery."

Hector looked to Deenie and she nodded. "I'm getting . . ." Hector began. "That is, we're getting hitched. Soon as I speak to her father and do all the proper stuff, you know."

"Congratulations!" Alec called. "I'm sure you'll be very happy."

Galatea swallowed a sigh. If only *she* could be so happy, but . . .

Later that evening, when the scenes were all finished, Galatea suggested they retire to the dining room for refreshments before bed. Alec went to give further congratulations to Hector, and Deenie and Galatea started off together. Halfway down the hall, they were stopped by Lady Linden. "My apologies for my earlier remarks," she said, fastening pudgy fingers on Galatea's arm. "But you must admit that your swoon was most fortuitous and—"

"Come along, Tea," Deenie said, taking her arm and sending Lady Linden a cool look. "I want to discuss marriage dates with you."

"If you'll excuse me," Tea said, easing away.

"Now, May," Deenie began as they moved on, "is a good month for flowers and—"

"Oh!" Galatea stopped in her tracks. Some feet ahead of

them, Hector and Alec were entering the dining room. Just as Alec stepped through the door, Martine ran up and threw herself into his arms, pressing her lips to his.

He put her away from him almost immediately and she came running past them, tears coursing down her cheeks. "You're cruel," she cried at Galatea. "You've stolen the man I love. How could you?"

And then she was gone, running down the hall, her sobs echoing behind her.

Deenie snorted. "Now *that* is a performance. And not a very good one."

Chapter 15

Christmas Day brought a fall of fresh white snow, but in spite of its beauty and the joy of the day, Galatea stood staring down at the yard with heavy heart. Alec and Deenie had both assured her that Martine's display of emotion had been counterfeit, put on to impress the guests and make her back off from Alec. Galatea thought she believed them, but she was still sad. There was going to be heartache. For her, at least.

She started, stepping back a little. Oh, no! Riding into the courtyard on a horse that drooped with weariness came Alec's groom. He threw the reins to a stable boy and stumbled toward the house.

She knew it! Alec had sent him to London and from the looks of it, the return message had been urgent. She turned from the window and went down to breakfast.

The others were already gathered, all but Alec, who was late. Galatea sighed and fixed her plate. Soon he would come in and tell her he must leave early. Even the fresh snowfall wouldn't keep him here.

Composing herself, she took her seat at the table and exchanged the day's greetings with the others. Hector and Deenie positively glowed. Ianthe smiled continually at Douglass—and he smiled back. And with Peter's help, Hypatia was relating some horse ancestry to Barnaby and Conigsby, who—

to give them credit—actually looked interested. Lady Linden had already emptied one plate of food and was engaged in filling another. And Martine was pushing eggs and ham around on her plate.

Suddenly, the hair on the back of Galatea's neck prickled. Alec! Though her back was to the door, she knew Alec had come into the room.

"Good morning," he said, slipping into his chair beside her. He smiled. "Isn't it a lovely morning?"

"Yes," she murmured, trying to smile back.

Alec leaned closer. "After breakfast," he whispered, "I should like a few minutes alone with you."

"Of course." She managed to get the words out, though she hardly knew how. This was it, then, their last meal together. After Martine's sobs last night, he must consider the Lindens convinced. They would bother him no more. So he was going back to London—to his life there.

Methodically, she ate the food she'd put on her plate, but she might as well have been eating straw. The food was tasteless. Would it always be that way? Would everything be colorless and lackluster because Alec was gone from her life?

She mustn't go sinking into the dismals now. All the guests would be leaving in a couple of days. And she would be glad—glad to get back to her studies. But perhaps she'd work on something else for a while, something not as tragic as poor Dido's story. Unrequited love was not the best topic for such a time.

The meal was finally finished. When the others got up and wandered away, Alec turned to her. "If we might go somewhere private?"

He looked rather nervous. Didn't he know how to tell her that now that his plan had been successful he was going to leave? Did he think *she* was going to run sobbing down the hall like Martine? *She* was made of sterner stuff than that.

"Of course," she said stiffly. "We'll use my sitting room." It seemed an appropriate choice. They'd rehearsed there so

229

often, it was there that she'd fallen onto him, and now he would tell her goodbye there. That room would always remind her of Alec.

Galatea tried to smile and look natural, but she had to blink to hold back the tears. Alec followed her in and closed the door. They'd always left the door open before. She really shouldn't be sequestered in a room with him with the door closed. Lady Linden would be sure to notice. Galatea swallowed, afraid to say anything for fear her voice would betray her.

"Please," Alec said, "take a seat. I have something for you."

"You do?" Surprise made her stare at him, but she sank into a chair, glad her wobbly knees didn't have to hold her up any longer. The grandfather clock ticked merrily away. If only her heart felt that merry.

He reached inside his jacket and pulled out a thin, flat package, brightly wrapped. "This is for you," he said, putting it in her hands.

"I—" She didn't know what to say. "Thank you."

"Open it, please."

The tears were threatening to spill over, but she managed to pull off the bright paper. "Oh my!" Galatea lifted the precious book carefully. "Oh, Alec, you shouldn't have. This is old, so rare. However did you—"

"It's been in my family for generations," he said. "I thought you might find it useful."

"Oh, I would. But this book is valuable. Very valuable. I can't accept it."

"But, Tea—"

"I helped you as a friend," she hurried on, praying she'd say this right. He mustn't suspect her true feelings. "You don't owe me anything."

"Owe you?" Alec cried in a strange voice.

"Yes. I understand you feel gratitude for my help with the

230

Lindens, but you mustn't give away your family heirlooms,'' She managed a feeble smile. "They're too precious."

Alec swallowed a curse. Did she really not know what he was trying to do? Or was she trying to spare his feelings? Either way, he had to go on with this. He had to have an answer.

"Tea, you must accept the book. It belongs to you now and—"

"No." She got to her feet. "I cannot accept such a gift. I was happy to help you, really I was. It was fun, and a simple thank-you is enough."

Good Lord. What a mess he was making of the thing! "Tea, please, the book is yours." Why the hell was he carrying on about a musty old book? He must get to the point. "Tea, I want—"

She lowered her head and started for the door. "No, Alec, I simply won't accept—"

This was the outside of enough! His first and only proposal of marriage, and he was botching the job!

She paused, her hand on the doorknob. "I want to thank you, too, for helping with things. The house party would not have been—"

Good God! Would she never leave off talking? She was starting to turn the doorknob. It was now or never. "Tea!" He covered the distance between them and swept her into his arms.

And then, just as his lips covered hers, the door flew open. Lady Linden stood there, staring at them, her face almost as scarlet as her ridiculous gown. "And what," she demanded in stentorian tones, "is going on in here?"

"It's very simple," he said, smiling down into Tea's dazed eyes. "I am proposing marriage."

"Pro-posing?" Tea murmured, tears running down her cheeks.

231

He closed the door in Lady Linden's face. "Tea, Tea darling, don't cry. I didn't mean to make you cry."

He kissed the tears from her cheeks. "I want to make you happy. For ever and ever. And this"—he indicated the old *Aeneid* she still clutched—"I meant it to show you that I won't interfere with your studies."

When she didn't reply, he swallowed hastily. Maybe he'd been right before. Maybe it was Tragon she loved and she was too tenderhearted to say so. "But if you really can't love me, if you really want that Tragon chap . . . well, I guess I can't do anything about it. But—"

"You can kiss me," Tea said.

"Kiss you?"

"Yes." She sniffled. "Because I accept your proposal."

"You do?"

"Yes. My tears"—she brushed at them—"they were because I thought you wanted to tell me you were leaving."

"I'll never leave you," he exclaimed. "Never!"

The door swung open again to reveal all the guests, a beaming Hector standing in the forefront. "I'm glad to hear that," he cried, "us being friends and all. Say, maybe we can make it a double wedding. We're planning for May and—"

"Hector," Tea said firmly, "we'll talk about that later. Kindly close the door and leave us alone."

Grinning, he did.

"Now, Alec," she said, "kiss me again. Please."

HOME FOR CHRISTMAS

by

Alicia Rasley

Chapter 1

Near Plymouth, December 22, 1818

"Captain Randall?" The ostler blinked up at him in the predawn dusk, then bent down again to tend to the chestnut's hoof. A stone had lodged under her shoe, in the first mile of road she had run in three months, poor girl. "Of Rose Cottage? Captain Randall's been at sea this past year or more. The Indies. Or whaling. Something. Never met him, I ain't. Sorry, sir."

Disappointment stabbed him, sharp as anger. The notice had appeared in last week's *Exeter Mail,* and yet the man who had placed it, by this account, had been gone for months. He pulled the crumpled piece of paper from the pocket of his greatcoat, stared again at the precise description of the dagger, and remembered the sense of destiny that had struck him when he first saw it. Someone had placed this notice, just for him. "He has family?"

"A wife. Pretty little thing, aren't you?" This last was apparently meant for the mare, not her rider or the wife of Captain Randall. The ostler rose, stroking the mare's nose, tugging at her ear, smiling at her. Absorbed in his flirtation, he added absently, "Leastways, she calls herself Mrs. Randall. Out past Kingsand, on the coast road. Rose Cottage. You'll see it. Covered in—"

Roses. It was a pretty trick of the sheltered Cornish coast that roses bloomed in December, long after the trees had lost their leaves. The cottage was twined in roses, pink and cream and golden, profligate as on Midsummer Day. The sun was just rising, though it was eight o'clock by his watch; he had chosen one of the shortest days of the year to buy back his past.

He tied his mare up on the road beside the cottage, well out of range of the team hitched to a post chaise in the yard. A driver sprawled on the box, his peg leg stuck out before him and his stick beside him on the bench. His posture proclaimed that a poor cripple could not be expected to load baggage as well as drive.

He must have won his argument. A red-cloaked young woman came out of the cottage, her arms full of luggage. With her hood pushed back in the early sunlight, she glowed pink and cream and gold like her roses. She was small but lithe, tossing a portmanteau into the chaise with the ease of a longshoreman, then gathering up her blue woolen skirts in one hand and dashing back through the open door of the cottage. She emerged a moment later with a bag in each hand and a pink baby blanket thrown over her shoulder. It must be Captain Randall's wife or his daughter, on her way somewhere else.

He intercepted her on yet another trip back into the house. "Miss Randall?"

She turned in the doorway, startled, ready to run, her long, dark braid whipping round to fall over her shoulder and onto her breast. But he was a gentleman, at least as far as appearance went, and her tense posture relaxed a bit. Still, she did not come off the step to meet him. Her words came out a cloud in the frosty air. "I am Mrs. Randall."

"I saw a notice in the *Mail*. For a dagger . . ."

"The Lionheart?"

Now she came to him, eager and bright like a bride on her wedding day, her bare hands held out in welcome. For a

236

moment he could not breathe, then he realized her hands were seeking not him but the dagger. "I don't have it."

She stopped a few feet short, the expression on her face flashing from pleasure to loss to anger. "You don't have it?" she echoed. "Then why are you here?"

It was a moment before he could recall the quixotic impulse that had brought him back to these rocky shores after so many years away. "The notice said the dagger was one of a pair. I presumed you owned the other one and might sell if you couldn't buy."

"Well, I don't own either one of them." Crossly, she slammed the carriage door shut. "And if I did, I wouldn't sell. I meant to purchase the second one as a gift."

Another fruitless quest. A fool's journey, this meeting with his past. Better that he leave it behind again, sail off, and forget it. He glanced back across the road to the pewter-gray Channel, wishing he could see his *Carrara*. But she was moored several coves away and invisible to him, as well as to the revenue agents. An hour ashore, he was, and already longing to leave.

Something held him there, though. Perhaps it was this young woman, with her bright eyes and her welcoming arms and her disappointment as apparent as his own. And then he took a breath and held it, thinking of what she had said, the description in the notice, and what he knew of this pair of daggers. "You wanted to purchase the second as a gift. You knew precisely what it looked like, though, for you had it described in the notice."

"I wrote it myself," she said, with a tilt of her chin.

"Then you've seen the first of the pair. You know, don't you, where at least one of them is?"

"I might. Why do you want to know?"

Just his luck to need information from that rarity, a woman who knew when to keep her mouth shut. He got a grip on his patience and replied softly, "I thought you understood. I

237

want to purchase one—just one—of the daggers. I'm willing to pay one thousand pounds.''

She took a quick breath, then released it, her face enigmatic and wary. "Then if you find it, you will doubtlessly win it. You must know I can't afford that sum. You must''— she looked down at the hands she had clasped at her chest, as if in supplication—"you must want it very badly.''

"I want it enough.''

She had changed, suddenly. He sensed no more despair, only a cunning she was trying to conceal by bending her head so he couldn't see her eyes.

"Tell me where I can find it.''

Then she raised her head and studied him, this time letting him see the calculating expression on her face, the appraisal that narrowed her dark eyes. She was a young wife, if wife she was, he thought, remembering the ostler's cryptic comment. Still, she looked too innocent for a courtesan or whatever the ostler thought her to be, with that spray of freckles over her nose and cheeks flushed bright from her exertions in the cold.

That gaze she aimed at him, however, was all woman— assessing, aware, apprehending. Not so innocent after all.

His disappointment drifted off, leaving in its wake a slight tingling sense of anticipation. He was no more superstitious than the next sailor, but he knew an omen when he felt one. Destiny flickered in this elfin girl with the innocent face and bold looks. His destiny. She would lead him to the dagger and that would lead him home.

"If you want it,'' now her voice was only a whisper, throaty and enticing, "you must follow my lead. Starting right now. Tie your horse on the back of the carriage. It's only a short journey, so she'll be fine.''

He was not used to being ordered about, much less by a woman who barely topped his shoulder. But he reminded himself of destiny and did as she bade.

238

Then she grabbed his hand, and still considering his destiny, he followed her toward the coach door.

"You are a sailor, aren't you?"

It was no more than a good guess; sailors were everywhere on this coast, few of them Navy and thus few in uniform. "Why do you say that?"

"Your hand."

She stroked it between her small, cold hands, teasing the hard spots on the palm, the jagged scar along the back, with gentle brushes of her thumbs. Then she released him to pull open the door. No, she was not innocent at all.

"Callused, but not by reins. By rope. And you are so tanned and yet so blond. Like a Viking. Like Eric the Red."

He didn't like being so easily identified, but he knew that his fifteen years at sea had left their mark on his body as well as his spirit. And she was, of course, a sailor's wife. She wore a gold band on that teasing hand. She had already known a sailor's touch. Annoyed, he halted there, refusing to get into the coach. "When can I see the dagger?"

"You shan't ever see it if you don't follow my lead." She smiled reassuringly at him and called back to the cottage, "Lucy! We're ready to leave!"

"Where are we going?" he demanded.

"Don't talk that way, sir. You'll frighten the baby."

Before he could respond, that baby was before them, swaddled like a parcel and held in the arms of a nurse whose disapproval was etched in every line on her careworn face. "Mrs. Randall, are you sure—"

"Of course, I'm sure," the girl said gaily, taking the parcel, hoisting it up, cooing at it, and then handing it to him. It was the size and heft of a rolled-up jibsail, but no jibsail squirmed and uttered inarticulate sounds of rebellion. He was too busy juggling it to protest, until he heard Mrs. Randall tell the nurse, "You see, Captain Randall has made it home after all! He will be escorting me to Porthallow, so you may visit your sister now in good conscience, without the slightest

239

worry for Beth and me. For you may be sure, my husband will keep us safe!"

Lucy was gazing suspiciously at him, as well she might; his incomprehension must be plain to see. Then some childhood edict against calling a lady a liar made him assume a neutral mask. He didn't even flinch when the madwoman took his arm and smiled up at him possessively.

"I am so happy to see you again, darling! And just in time. Another minute and you would have missed us! Now you go on into the coach with Beth, and I'll just get the hot bricks for our feet. . . ."

She disappeared back into the cottage, leaving him to look down at the wriggling bundle in his arms and wonder if destiny was worth the trouble.

"Baby's getting cold," Lucy said, her voice tight with reserved judgment. "Shouldn't be out in the chill."

During his years at sea, he had survived hurricanes with his ship intact by accepting that events were more or less out of his control, that he had to go with the storm to get out of the storm. Now he saw another storm coming toward him, her face alight, her arms full of flannel-covered bricks, and shoving the parcel under his arm, he climbed into the coach.

It was just a job-coach, but a well-appointed one and quite clean, fit for the most respectable matron. Mrs. Randall's unostentatious traveling garments were also entirely proper, the bonnet she loosened and the leather gloves she removed being of the finest quality. It was incredible that this perfect lady had flat-out abducted him—incredible, that is, till he saw the impish, excited glitter in her eyes whenever she stole a glance at him.

But there seemed to be no escape, no awakening from this strangely realistic dream. As the carriage lurched into the road, Mrs. Randall arranged the hot bricks artistically on the floor, spread the baby blanket over her lap, and held out her arms for the parcel. He was glad to be relieved of it but angry

240

at her blithe manner, and he didn't allow her crooning to the child to divert him. "What was *that* about?"

Mrs. Randall laid the parcel on the seat beside her and gently unswaddled it. Eventually, a little face emerged, red and pugnacious. "Oh, Lucy has been combing my hair with a three-legged stool, telling me I shouldn't take Beth on a journey by myself. So now she will be happy. Won't she, sweeting?" This last she crooned to the child, who regarded her quite as warily as he did himself. "We're just going to your Grandpapa's home, aren't we? And that's not even a day's journey." She looked up at him with that radiant smile he was learning boded trouble. "Do you know Porthallow, sir?"

Grudgingly, he nodded. He'd grown up not far from here and had been a privateer half his life; he knew every hidden cove in Cornwall. "It's on Talland Bay. But I have no desire to go there."

"Of course you do. Otherwise, you will never see that dagger you want so much. And as you are escorting us, Lucy will have no fear for our safety, for how could we be in any danger when my husband is along?"

He hated pointing out the obvious, but with this woman nothing was really obvious. "I am not your husband."

"No," she said thoughtfully, to his immense relief, for he had been infected by her madness and for just an instant wondered if on some drunken night in Plymouth a couple years ago he might have somehow debauched and married this woman and then forgotten all about it.

"No," she said again, adding, "But you might be." She opened her cloak and unfastened the top of her blue dress, and before he could explore exactly what he wanted her to do next, she withdrew a necklace from her bodice and awkwardly, with one hand, pulled it over her head. "Look and see."

One long, dark hair was caught on the chain. He twined it around his finger as he opened the locket. There was more

241

hair inside, but this time blond, a wisp of curl about the size of his thumbnail.

"See?" she said triumphantly. "Almost precisely the color of yours."

He almost retorted that any blond sailor ended up with hair that sun-bleached shade, hair that moreover resisted any comb applied to it and curled mostly because it was deeply imbued with salt. "Is this Captain Randall's?"

"No." She tugged the knit cap off the baby's head, revealing hair as golden and soft as a sunbeam. "Her father's. She got her curls from him."

He took a deep breath, counted to ten, then said as unaccusingly as he could, "Captain Randall is not the child's father?"

"Her father was only a lieutenant." She seemed to think this sufficed as an explanation and went back to unwrapping her daughter. "Lucy always bundles her up like this. I think children need fresh air, and I always unbundle her. It's rather amusing, but poor Beth has never gotten used to being trussed up and hates it." Revealed, Beth turned out to be a child rather older than he had thought, old enough to sit on her mother's lap and put her thumb in her mouth and stare suspiciously at him.

"Don't worry about me, child," he told her, unnerved by her big unblinking eyes and the vigor with which she sucked her thumb. "I'm not the lunatic in this carriage."

Mrs. Randall looked startled and then laughed. It was a pretty sound, low and husky, and when she replied her voice still shimmered with amusement. "Do I confuse you? I always do that. But I am not a lunatic. I just don't explain things well."

"That I believe." He looked back down at the locket, at the blond curl that could have been his own, and marshaled his thoughts. "Answer my questions and only my questions," he said sternly, as if he were talking to an errant cabin boy.

She settled her child into a more comfortable perch on her lap, the head resting against her breast, and said meekly, "I will."

"Where do you mean to take me?"

"To my father's house."

"In Porthallow?"

"Yes." She started to say something else, then remembered her promise and pressed her lips together ostentatiously.

"He has the dagger?"

"One of them. He's always wanted to complete the pair, but he could never locate the other one. I thought it might have come on the market since he quit looking. And I wanted to buy it to give to him at Christmas. I thought that he would be more than likely to— Oh, I forgot, I was only to answer your questions."

"More likely to what?"

She bent her head, kissing the child's golden locks. Her voice came muffled; she no longer sounded so blithe. "More likely to accept Beth. I was supposed to bring my husband with me on this visit, so Father could meet him. But I couldn't. So I hoped the dagger would—might appease him."

He shook his head, as if that might dislodge the cobwebs. "I don't understand. If Captain Randall is in the Indies, how can you father expect him to escort you on a Christmas visit?"

She cast him a sidelong glance. "My father isn't quite convinced that Captain Randall exists."

This took a moment to absorb. "Why?"

Mrs. Randall looked around, as if afraid that she might be overheard. Then she covered her daughter's ears, and while the child removed her thumb from her mouth to protest, she whispered, "Because he doesn't."

Suddenly, he understood. There was no captain, but there was a lieutenant; no husband, but a lover. The advertisement in the *Mail*, the Rose Cottage, the child, were all attributed to the name of a mythical man. "Where is the lieutenant?"

"Dead." She held out her hand for the locket, and when he gave it to her, she closed her fingers around it. He saw her knuckles go white before she loosed her grip and pushed the necklace into her pocket. "I thought it best not to let his family know about her. They—they had been unkind to him, and I'd no reason to think they would treat Beth any better. So I needed a husband with a different name. Captain Randall came along, then."

He knew she had left a lot out, but he couldn't decipher what. "You mean you invented him?"

Her eyes shone with relief at his understanding. He must be going mad, to understand one like this. "Precisely. Eric Randall. It sounds rather seafaring, don't you think? And a captain of a merchant vessel has some standing in the community, even if he is merely the son of a third son of a noble family. I wanted Beth to have a bit of an entrée, at least. Perhaps she'll do better with it than I did."

Captain Randall, he sensed, was rather better known to his wife than most real husbands were. She had invented a history as well as a name. And he understood why well enough. A young lady known to have run off with her lover, left with only the one token of his affection, would never be accepted in any community. He couldn't condemn her, really, but he couldn't trust her, either. And what her plans were for him he didn't like to imagine. "How have you supported yourself?"

"Oh, I inherited a bit from my mother, and I give lessons in drawing and music and Italian to local girls. They would never be allowed to come to me, you understand, if there weren't a Captain Randall."

"And he's been in the Indies?"

"Since we came here, when Beth was but a babe. Once I made a trip to Portsmouth to meet him, but I've never brought him here."

It was disorienting, the way she spoke of this husband as if he really existed, only a moment after admitting she had

244

made him up. But he understood, in a way. He had done much the same fifteen years ago, taking a new name and a new role and almost coming to believe that it was true. He had to believe it was true, or he wouldn't have been able to make it work. And because he knew how many adjustments maintaining this role required, he anticipated her answer to his question before he asked it. "What need have you of me?"

Again she cast him that sidelong glance, not sly, precisely, but knowing. Somehow she had sized him up and decided he was just the man she needed.

"You must take the place of my husband. Just for this one visit. Just until after Christmas. Not even a week. So my father will no longer wonder if Beth is a—" The word hesitated on her lips, then was swallowed back, and she tightened her arms around the child. "My father is the only family we have. I would like my daughter to be accepted by him."

He had to look away, out the window, at the bay glistening now in the pale winter sunlight. He wondered what it was like to be as close as this mother and child, Beth nestling into the curve of her mother's arm, warm and secure as if nothing in the world could touch her now. But there were limits to the security a young mother could provide, and he feared they had already been tested. Life for a bastard child— a girl, and the bastard of some undistinguished lieutenant, no less—would be bleak. Mrs. Randall's blithe way with deception made him wary, but he could not fault her maternal love. There was little enough of that in the world, in his experience.

But he did not trust her. She seemed harmless, but her cheerful manner masked a tigress's ruthlessness. "What do I get in return for playing this part?"

She looked disappointed. Perhaps she thought he would agree out of mere gallantry to give her a week out of his life. But then she smiled, as if in recognition of their essential likeness. They were neither of them the gallant sort. "The dagger."

"But you haven't got it."

"My father does."

"I can't think what good that will do, since you admit yourself that he is displeased with you." His voice was hard, but to his surprise she took no offense.

"That is nothing new." She laughed again; this time it wasn't such a pretty sound. "I have ever found it easy to displease him. My natural state, I think, is displeasing to him. But—" she paused, and then added firmly, as if she meant to persuade herself as well as him, "but I am grown now, and he is old, and Beth is his grandchild—the only one he is likely to have. And he can't help but be pleased with her, don't you think? Even if she's not a boy."

He spared a glance at the child, who had been lulled to sleep by the rocking of the carriage. She was angelic enough, at least as she slept, especially when her mother gently tugged her thumb out and her bow mouth went on sucking. But the angel's effect on her grandfather was none of his concern.

"What is to keep me from approaching him on my own?"

Judging from the frown that creased her forehead, it appeared Mrs. Randall hadn't thought of that. But then she laughed with a childlike triumph. "You don't know who he is!"

"He's your father. In Porthallow."

"But you only know me as Mrs. Randall. My father's name is quite unknown to you."

"I could find it out. There can't be that many collectors of martial antiquities in Porthallow."

"He does not live in Porthallow. Nearby. And his collection is not generally known. My father, you see"—with an innocent air she bent to kiss her daughter on the head—"is usually quite scrupulous in checking the provenance of his acquisitions. But with this dagger, his methods might have been a bit . . . unorthodox."

246

"A family trait, it must be, unorthodoxy." He could not doubt what she said was true. Fifteen years ago, at least, her father must have had dealings with a broker no scrupulous collector would know, one who hadn't blinked at buying the Lionheart dagger from a desperate fourteen-year-old boy. "If he is such a collector, why do you think he would sell it to me?"

She busied herself arranging the folds of her cloak over her sleeping child, even as she arranged her answer. "You'll have no chance at all without me. But *with* me, as my husband, you might persuade him." She looked away, out the window, at the misty landscape passing by. "That dagger has given him little joy all these years. He wanted so to complete the pair, but he could not advertise openly without calling attention to himself. It's almost been a reproach to him. And a thousand pounds . . . that will buy him many more antique arms." She shrugged, a concession that she had no more arguments to marshal. "If you want it so badly, you must take the chance. It is only for a week, after all."

"And then?"

"And then what?"

"What happens when he wants to see you and your husband again? What then?"

"Then you will die."

Her voice was low, pleasant, matter-of-fact. She had been planning that all along. Eventually, of course, Captain Randall would have to die. Even a sea captain's absence would be remarked after a few years. And the pretense of a widow would be less a strain than the pretense of a wife.

And yet it chilled him, the casualness with which she disposed of him—no, not him, but that Captain Randall he hadn't yet agreed to be. "What about a grave? A stone? A—a body?"

He didn't really think her capable of—of whatever strange notion had glimmered in his mind when she had said, so matter-of-factly, "you will die." But she was so unknown to him, this woman who invented men. Something lightened in him when she said, "No stone. No grave. Sailors die at sea, and their bodies are committed to the deep. 'My soul fleeth onto the Lord . . .' "

Before the morning watch, I say, before the morning watch. Silently, he finished the prayer she began; he knew it well, having heard it spoken and spoken it himself over the bodies of shipmates dozens of times. It seemed almost as if they were pronouncing Captain Randall dead. . . . But that was nonsense, of course. This odd young woman was disorienting him, that was all. Captain Randall hadn't even come to life yet.

The child murmured in her sleep, and Mrs. Randall bent and whispered something to her, making tiny adjustments in her position to make her daughter more secure.

"Her father died at sea, I take it."

Mrs. Randall glanced up. "Yes." For an instant there was bleak memory in her eyes, then she looked back down at her daughter and tried to smile. Her voice, when it came again, was determinedly bright. "She isn't usually this good, I must tell you. She's been awake for hours as we prepared to go, and so she needed a bit of a nap. But usually she has much more to say and do."

"What part will she play in this—this charade?"

"What part?" She looked blank for a moment. "It's *for* her, don't you see? So that her grandfather will accept her. Sponsor her. I wouldn't care so much except that . . . I could die."

The genuine surprise in her voice as she spoke of her own mortality almost made him smile. He had been surprised, too, when he first conceived death as an inevitability. And it was hard to imagine this mercurial woman dead, her bright spirit extinguished; her child orphaned and alone.

He wondered if she were exaggerating for effect, to persuade him into compassion. Her father was hardly one to cast the first stone, judging from his collecting techniques. But then again, fathers were like that, weren't they? Righteous. Self-righteous. "Is your father truly so harsh?"

She frowned; he sensed her trying to be fair, objective. "I don't know. We were never close. We never—never knew how to speak to each other. He cast me off the one time. Good riddance, he said. And didn't answer my letters . . . oh, till the last one. And even then it was just to challenge me. He wants to meet this husband of mine, that is how he wrote it: 'This supposed husband of yours.' "

"What about your mother?" Mothers were more merciful . . . or so he once believed.

"She died when I was seven. There is only my father." She met his eyes then, but all the boldness was gone. "When I saw you and you looked so very like the man I described, you seemed almost a gift from fate. As Beth is a gift. I could not refuse it."

She was a tenacious creature, for all her swift changes. She always came back to that point . . . that he must come with her. Somewhere he had lost that initial objection, the one about the child. Oh, yes. "But you want me to pretend to be the child's father?"

"Oh!" She smiled, as if relieved it wasn't more than that. "Oh, you needn't worry that I will thrust her upon you. I shan't require any help with her. And my father would never expect you to pay any mind to a child. Not a girl-child, anyway. You've been at sea most of her life, after all."

It seemed so easy. He could have a chance at the dagger, his only chance, and the payment was merely pretending to be another man for a week. He need not be bothered by the child or consigned to support them for the future. He needn't even see them ever again once Christmas was over. "What have you told your father about Captain Randall?"

She had won, she knew it, but she concealed her triumph courteously, only her shining eyes betraying her. "Not much. He was in the Royal Navy until '12, then joined a merchant

249

fleet as a first officer, and recently got his own command on the East Indies route. The *Tescador* is his ship.''

"Wouldn't your father have made inquiries with the East India Company if he doubted your word?''

She flushed, as if confessing a fault. "Captain Randall's not with the Company. Too many officers wanted those posts. So he's with a new group. An informal arrangement. Not yet incorporated.''

The story was plausible enough, and his respect for her ingenuity went up a notch. There were plenty of such merchant fleets on the seas since the war, scavenging off the remains left by the East India Company. His own fleet had begun the same way, with a few privateers agreeing to sail together for mutual protection. "What does he ship?''

"The usual. Spices, silk . . .'' She met his gaze levelly. "I have done my research, sir. I know the customary sea route and the ones that aren't so customary. I know how much he can expect to make from a voyage, after his crew and the shipowner get their portions. I had all sorts of emergencies that would explain his delay this holiday, but I shan't have to use them, shall I?''

He didn't answer her directly, looking away instead out the window. They were approaching the cove that hid his ship. "We'll have to stop here.''

"Stop?'' Her bright look dimmed; she thought he was refusing.

Gently, he asked, "Do you have a few sets of clothes for Captain Randall? Or did you expect me to wear this one for a week?''

Mrs. Randall must not have considered that problem at all. She frowned, but her relief broke through and curved her mouth into the smile he had already become accustomed to. "You have a thousand pounds, don't you? I thought you could buy whatever you pleased in Porthallow.''

"I do not buy my clothing in Porthallow,'' he replied. "God forbid.'' As they rounded the curve, he tapped on the wall against the driver's box. The carriage clattered to a halt; he rose and stretched and opened the door.

It was full daylight now, and the *Carrara* could no longer be hidden in her anchorage off the cape. But she needn't be hidden any longer, he reminded himself as he called down the hill for his boatman. She was as respectable as an Indiaman now, her crew all peaceable sorts, her cargo entirely legal, her captain released by the fall of Bonaparte from sinister missions. It was only habit that anchored her here instead of at the Plymouth docks—and her captain's superstition about the ghosts of the past.

Mrs. Randall—he couldn't help thinking of her as that—had left the child in the coach and come up to stand beside him. "Oh, what a pretty ship she is. Is she really yours?"

"Yes." One of three, he almost added, but the coxswain had clambered up the hill and was waiting for his orders. Within a few minutes, he had dealt with the mare and his baggage, and his first officer was waiting for orders, his speculations about the captain's companion written all over his young face.

A week, at least, away from the ship. "Take her into Plymouth and let the crew have leave—a week, except for a dozen or so to guard the ship. You and they will get leave when I return. If you need to reach me, I'll be at—" He turned to Mrs. Randall, waiting.

She set her lips tight, as if torture wouldn't force her to divulge the address.

"As you wish." He turned back to his officer. "Belay those last orders. I'll be rejoining you after all."

"Morrell Hall. South of Porthallow." Mrs. Randall spun on her heel and climbed back into the carriage, yanking the door shut behind her.

She was over her pique by the time he rejoined her on their journey. She greeted him with a smile and the news that the angel had awakened and was feeling rather demonic. That he could observe for himself. Little Beth was engaged in the

251

annoying game of dropping her mitten and whimpering until her mother picked it up. Mrs. Randall, ever cheerful, ever resourceful, eventually pulled a ribbon off her braid, loosing a cloud of dark curls, and tied it to the mitten's thumb so she could retrieve it without bending over.

Once it was easy for her mother to play, however, Beth tired of the game, taking again to sucking her thumb and staring at him balefully. It challenged him, that suspicious stare from an innocent child, as if she had no confidence at all that he could do the job he had been hired to do. She would think differently, he thought, matching her stare for stare, if she knew him better.

Fortunately for the future of their relations, he found in his pocket a marble one of the ship's boys had left on the deck. It had nearly cost its owner his young life when it got under the heel of the boatswain. He rolled it in his fingers, until the child dropped her unblinking gaze to the green glass ball, then tantalizingly, he dropped it onto the floor. The carriage obligingly hit a pothole and the marble rolled loudly down the floor, ricocheting off the warming bricks. Beth scrambled out of her mother's arms and chased after it on her hands and knees, batting it back up the incline and crowing when it rolled back.

Beyond sternly warning the child not to put that in her mouth, Mrs. Randall voiced no objection to Beth's new game. "How very inventive of you," she added, sounding surprised. If she knew him better, she would not be so surprised; inventiveness had ever been his besetting sin. It was something else they had in common.

These last miles along the coastal road, past tumbledown cottages and fishing shacks, were all too familiar to him. At Downderry, he thought he recognized a cassocked man who raised his hand in blessing as they clattered past the tiny old church. Werton, that was his name; he had been a curate back then, picking up spare silver tutoring bored young lordlings in Latin. But though the vicar smiled benignly as they

252

passed, he could not have recognized the man in the coach as the worst of his Latin pupils—not after so long, not now that he was grown taller and stronger than anyone then would have guessed. He was safe enough, in yet another identity—his third or fourth, perhaps, since he had last read Latin.

This was all familiar to her, too, he realized. She was peering out the window, her forehead pressed against the glass, one hand trailing down to clutch Beth's petticoats. It was strange to think they had grown up within a dozen miles of each other, only to meet under these incongruous circumstances.

"Do you know," he remarked, watching a clutch of schoolboys erupt from the little dames school, "I don't think we have ever been formally introduced."

She had stolen the marble from Beth and was holding it up to her eye to survey her daughter. "Beth, sweeting, you are all green! No, sir, we haven't been." She gave the child back her toy and added, "Though I feel I have known you quite well for a long time!"

She had, it was true, behaved with a familiarity beyond what their short acquaintance would warrant, abducting him and extorting him and smiling at him as if he were a willing conspirator in this scheme of hers. He could not find it in his heart, somehow, to resent this; she had such a roguish smile, after all, which produced a deep dimple in one cheek and glints of laughter in her dark eyes.

"Not so long nor so well. You don't even know my name."

"No! Don't tell me!" In a more reasonable tone, she explained, "I mean, if I know your real name, I might accidentally call you by that instead of Eric or Captain Randall. It would make my father suspicious."

He smiled, but with an edge to his voice, he remarked, "Perhaps then you should call me only darling, as you did when your nurse was about."

That made her shy, or at least pretend to be shy. She ducked

253

her head and applied herself to spit-polishing Beth's smudged cheeks. "Lucy is a romantic. Father, I'm certain, is not."

"Tell me your name at least. He will be quite suspicious if I don't know that."

"My given name?" She held her protesting daughter between her knees and rubbed the cheek dry, then dropped a kiss there. Then she released the child and smiled to herself. "My name is Verity."

"Verity." Truth. "How appropriate."

Chapter 2

Morrell Hall's only concession to the holiday season was an evergreen bough tacked onto the great oak door. Otherwise, it stood as stern as ever on the windswept bluff. I'll soon see to that, Verity thought as she knelt on the flagstone walk to tidy Beth's apparel. "We'll put up holly and ivy and candles in every window," she promised, straightening the little pink bow in Beth's golden hair. "And a Yule log and plum pudding . . . a real country house Christmas, just as we had when I was a little girl. My own mama used to let me stir the plum pudding, and so I shall let you."

She rose and looked back to see Captain Randall paying off the coachman, just as a real husband would have done. She felt in her pocket for her purse, reminding herself to keep an accounting of his expenditures on her behalf. Of course, a man who thought nothing of spending one thousand pounds on an antique dagger probably didn't worry about a couple sovereigns here and there. Still, she had been saving her pennies, hoping to come home, and she needn't get herself any more obligated to this man than she already was.

He was, she thought as he directed the groom to take care of their baggage, very good at this pretense. She could not have asked for a better conspirator had she had the prescience to plan this scheme ahead of time. He had agreed almost straight off, though he obviously thought her half-mad, and raised no tiresome objections about sin and crime and fraud. He even looked the part of the successful sailor; indeed, he was well used to that role, judging from his pretty frigate. He was of the right class—or seemed to be, anyway—with his cool unaccented speech and expensive dress—a bit too expensive, she thought; Weston must have tailored that well-fitting gray coat, and few sailors could afford Weston. She would have to tell her father that the last voyage had been a rousing success and all their financial worries solved. That would pave the way for the moment when this half-pay sailor offered one thousand pounds for an old dagger.

He came up now and offered her a quick smile, meant, she supposed, to reassure her. She smiled back; he was rather kind, in his oblique way. As she bent to pick up Beth, she gave last instructions in an undertone, "Remember, my father is Sir William Morrell. He's originally of Hampshire but didn't like the crowding. I have said that your people are from Dorset but that they are all dead."

"Yes, dead relations are so much more convenient, aren't they?"

That made her chuckle, and so it was a merry face she presented when the door opened and the elderly butler beckoned them in. She kept the smile bright, though merely entering the shadowy entry hall had the effect of depressing her spirits. She had forgotten how magisterial, how dark this house was, with the suit of armor guarding the entry and the pairs of crossed lances all the way up the stairwell wall. How had she ever managed to grow up here?

But she remembered her part and forced herself into it. It must be a pleasing family portrait that greeted her father coming down the great staircase—the tall handsome husband, the happy wife holding the pretty child, outlined artistically in a shaft of weak sunlight. No prodigal daughter repentant and returned in this picture, no supplicant grandchild begging for crumbs of recognition.

She felt her smile waver as her father stopped halfway down

the steps, the shadow lines from the leaded window above emphasizing his frown. It was characteristic of him to remain above, apart from her, too far to touch, too silent to address. She had never in her life known what to say to him, and though she had been rehearsing her lines for thirty miles, the words rang in her head now, tinny and revealing.

Captain Randall—Eric—must have sensed her momentary weakness. He took Beth from her arms, murmuring an answer to her instinctive protest. "Come, Beth," he told the child, "you must meet your grandfather. He owns this house and that set of armor you are admiring. Perhaps if you are very good, he will let you go a bit closer to it."

He wasn't an experienced parent, and he held Beth as if she were some slippery fish hauled up from the deep and eager to jump back in. But Beth was an experienced child. She gripped him with her knees—he had a boyishly slender waist for a tall man—and leaned perilously out, stretching her hands toward the knight's armor. "Pretty," she said; that was her universal word for approbation, applied to dolls as well as armor.

That did not make Sir William happy, Verity knew as his frown deepened, the prospect of a child roaming through his antiquities; he would likely have them thrown out. She was seized by the urge to hand him the gifts she had brought, bid him a happy Christmas, then turn around and go back to the little cottage that seemed suddenly so much more of a home. That would be reconciliation enough, with no chance for additional angry confrontations.

But Captain Randall was braver than she. "Don't worry, sir," he reassured the silent figure above. "We shall keep Beth out of mischief. Verity mentioned a sun porch, I believe . . ."

She hadn't, but it was an easy guess, as most houses in this area were built to take advantage of the gentle breezes and sea vistas. He would know that, she thought, for it was apparent he was familiar with this coastline. He secured Beth's scrabbling hand in a gentle grasp. "We'll confine her to that area when she is not outside or abed. Isn't that right, darling?"

Only Verity heard the slight emphasis on that last word, and despite her anxiety she felt a spark of amusement. She had taken him by surprise this morning, calling him darling, calling him husband. And some of the dawn's optimism rose again in her. He had decided, for whatever reason, that he would do his part. She had only to match his performance and hold her breath for a week or so, and they would come right about.

So as a clean-conscienced daughter might, she came to the bottom of the stairs and held out her hand to the man above. "Father, dear, come meet Eric and our little Beth. I am so glad we can all finally be together, as a family should."

Likely it wasn't the sentimental words that wooed him, but rather the presence of the butler at the door watching the proceedings with an interested air. "Verity," her father said, taking her hand for a moment, then releasing it.

What had she expected, after all? A kiss? A "welcome home"? No matter. She didn't need him for herself but for Beth. And no one, *no one,* could know Beth long without loving her. It was a settled truth, just as Christmas followed the winter solstice, love followed Beth. She turned to the man holding her child.

"This is—" the faintest of pauses, then it came easily to her tongue, "my husband, Eric Randall."

He shifted Beth to the crook of his left arm and reached to take her father's hand. "Sir William."

"And this is Beth. Elizabeth." Verity's voice stopped working right, taking on that pleading note she hated. "After Mother."

Her father cast a cursory glance at Beth. "She hasn't the look of your mother."

When Verity could not answer, Eric said with a smile, "No. She is her father's daughter, I'm afraid. Look how well she clings to the rigging." Experimentally, he withdrew his

258

hand from Beth's back; she grabbed his expensive coat and hung on, laughing.

She's so funny, Verity thought, stealing a glance at her father to see if he appreciated this. But Sir William was asking Eric about his voyage, and Eric was replying with just enough technical detail to sound convincing without giving much away.

At least he hasn't denounced us as impostors and slammed the door behind us, Verity thought as her father turned to order their luggage taken away. He meant for them to stay. As they followed him up the stairs to the drawing room, Eric reached out to take her hand. It was an unnecessary gesture— her father was ahead and couldn't see—but his firm, rough clasp reminded her that, for the first time, she wasn't alone in her father's house. She had Beth, and she had this enigmatic man and his temporary support—and her own not inconsiderable resources.

Sir William could be a good host when he wanted to, and he provided a light repast of tea and bread and butter in the formal drawing room. Beth ate only a few bites of her mother's bread, then demanded to be set down on the floor. Verity glanced warily at Sir William but could not read his expression. So she let Beth slip to the floor, and Eric proved himself yet again to be a quick study. In a marvelously authoritative father-voice, he told the child to stay between him and her mother.

So Beth crawled back and forth the short distance between their legs, rolling the green marble ahead of her. Verity took up her tea with a silent sigh of relief. That marble diverted Beth far more than the familiar doll that Verity had stuffed in her reticule.

There was an awkward silence, broken only by Beth's murmurs to the marble. Verity was usually at ease in a social setting, but with her father sitting in his wingchair like a judge at the bench, she couldn't manage more than a few questions about the house and the village, before she took up her teacup again. Her father kept glancing down at Beth, as if worried she would become sick on his Axminster carpet.

Just to break the tension, Verity gestured to the portrait over the hearth. "That's me at Beth's age. With my mother."

Eric studied the painting as if it really mattered to him. "I don't see much of Beth there—except that smile. You look as if you were contemplating running away from your mother and engaging in some mischief. You haven't changed very much, have you?"

It was true; she had been a mischievous child, with an excess of high spirits, too much for her gentle mother. A hot flush rose in her cheeks. Eric grinned at her, as if this discovery amused him.

But her father only harrumphed and asked, "How old is she, the child?"

Verity answered quickly, in case Eric had forgotten any of the facts she had coached him on as they journeyed. "She'll be two on Twelfth Night." She added proudly, "She speaks very well for her age. Fifty-seven words and more each week."

Sir William's lips moved in silent calculation. "Two at Twelfth Night. That means . . . when were you wed?"

The abruptness, indeed the rudeness, of his question did not unnerve Verity. She had been expecting this and had already worked out a plausible wedding date, somewhere between the time she had run away from her aunt's house in Plymouth and the night Beth was conceived. "February 22."

"1816," Eric added helpfully. "It was a fortunate accident. We'd never have met if my ship hadn't been damaged from the big Christmas gale in the Bay of Biscay. I brought her in for overhaul and saw Verity . . ." He gave Verity a fond husbandly smile. "Hard to believe it's been near three years we've been married. Sometimes it seems as if we have only just met."

Verity glanced quickly at her father, but he had never been sensitive to tone and had not heard that sardonic note. Why,

Eric was enjoying this! No wonder he was so adept at masquerade; he had to be a pretender at heart. He only grinned as she frowned warningly and replied, "That's because you have been gone most of the time we have been married. It is a difficult life, married to a sailor."

"But such rewards there are!" He reached over to take her hand and raised it to his lips. There was the surprising heat of his mouth on her skin, then a playful nip before he let their clasped hands rest on the arm of his chair. She resisted the urge to snatch her hand back to see if he had left a burn mark or the imprint of teeth. "Especially after a voyage to the Indies! Wait till you see what I brought you for Christmas."

His kiss was so casual, his warmth so believable, that even Verity, who knew better, felt a connection between them, something warm and taut and strong. And Beth, looking up from her marble at that moment, rose to her feet and tottered over to put her hand on top of theirs, as if ratifying this union.

It was the perfect picture, the three of them together, and for just a moment Verity let the warmth of his hand on hers warm her all the way through. Then she glanced up to see the ironic glint in his gray eyes and gave herself an inward shake. It wasn't true, and just as well. She and Beth were fine alone. She just had to make sure she didn't start believing the drama they were performing so well.

Her father wasn't as persuadable. He leaned back in his chair, eyeing their pretty tableau skeptically, until Beth drew back and climbed into the safety of her mother's lap. "You don't wear a wedding ring," he said to Eric, accusation plain in his voice.

Verity was about to remind him that he never had, either, that few men did. But Eric beat her to it. "I did, in the beginning. Verity insisted. Said she wanted the women to be alerted." He gave her that quick, boyish grin. "I don't know why she's worried. I might as well have *tamed* written on my forehead."

He made it sound as if he were almost proud to have a possessive wife. Now that had to be an act. If a man like this had such a wife, he'd never come back from the Indies. She knew little of him, but she knew that much: Shackling would drive him mad.

But now he was talking to her father with that easy man-to-man air, inventing what she hadn't thought to coach him to say. "Then it caught on a nail forty feet up the mizzenmast, and I almost twisted the finger off. They had to cut the ring off, with my finger so swollen." He detached his left hand from hers and held it up, displaying a ring finger that was indeed bent a little at the knuckle, as if it had been broken. That whole hand was battered, in fact, with the long scar along the back and a black blood-bruise on the thumbnail. A sailor's hand, it was, capable but inelegant. She dropped her gaze to her own hands, now holding Beth still, and recalled how firm and warm his grasp had been only moments ago.

But her father hadn't ceased his interrogation. "I don't imagine you have your marriage lines, do you?"

Even the imperturbable Eric was silenced by so blatant an insult. She suddenly recalled she had never described the wedding to him. He was just saying, "Well, you can't expect us to travel with them," when she broke in.

"But, darling, I don't think we ever *got* marriage lines." She turned to her father with a light laugh. "We were married at sea, you know. It seemed rather havey-cavey to me, but Eric assured me it was entirely legal."

"It is." Eric answered his cue immediately, in a tone that suggested they had had this discussion too many times already. "A captain is king and judge and bishop on his ship and may marry passengers as long as he is outside British waters. We were halfway to France, you'll recall. And no, he didn't give us marriage lines, come to think of it. No doubt he recorded the marriage in his log book. At the time, I recollect, you thought it all vastly romantic. It's only since

262

that you have decided the wedding was insufficiently respect-able.''

His aggrieved expression was so consummate that Verity almost believed he was annoyed with her. And her father surrendered, though he made one last broadside. ''This captain . . . he still exists, does he?''

''Still exists? Unless he's had some accident in the last two days. I passed him Saturday coming round Ushant into the Channel. Captain Bering, of the *Myland.*'' To Verity, he said, ''Asked to give you his regards, in fact. At least, I think it was his regards. His signal flagman isn't much of a speller.''

To her very great relief, Sir William apparently decided to accept this man, this marriage. He rose and crossed the room to pull the bell-rope. ''I'm sure you'll want to get settled. I've put you in the guest suite in the north wing. I'll assign a maid to help with the child.''

The gesture was a considerate one, and as Verity rose with Beth in her arms, she felt relief and happiness fill her. He was going to recognize them. He wouldn't turn them away after all.

Indeed, he even nodded toward Eric, almost genially. ''I expect I should welcome you into the family. After you've settled in, perhaps I could show you around Morrell Hall. As a military man, you might appreciate my collection of antique armaments.''

She saw the leap of interest in Eric's eyes and hoped that, after he had done so much to help her, he would not be disappointed in his own quest. But he showed no untoward eagerness as he replied, ''I should like that, sir. In an hour, shall we say?''

A few moments later, she understood how successful their imposture had been. ''Look!'' she told her conspirator, spinning around in the middle of the blue bedroom, gesturing to their bags heaped on the floor. ''You did wonderfully well. You've convinced him entirely!''

''What do you mean?''

Verity smiled at him, grateful now for that instinct that had made her trust her fate to him this morning. "Don't you see? If he doubted our marriage, he would never have put us in a single bedroom!"

Chapter 3

Eric's thorough exploration proved Verity correct. A small sitting room was accessible through a connecting door, and Beth was settled by the maid in a room just across the little hallway. But there was only one assigned bedroom and, more to the point, only one assigned bed. As he stood in the sitting room doorway, Eric's gaze was drawn magnetically to that bed, heaped high with pillows and half concealed with draperies, large enough for two; indeed, cozy to the extreme.

He glanced appraisingly at his companion, who was singing softly as she put a stack of nightgowns away in a drawer. She had loosed her dark curls again, and they danced around her pretty face as she rose and shut the cupboard. With quick grace, she crossed to the hall door and looked out, as if wary of eavesdroppers. But they were quite, quite alone in their marital quarters.

A thought had glimmered in his mind since she had first come toward him, eyes alight, hands outstretched, and now it crystallized: This radiant girl, with her songs and laughter and inventiveness, would be lovely in bed.

"I know what you're thinking," she said, closing the door securely behind her.

"You do?" He was glad for the deep tan that hid his hot flush, glad that he was grown and his voice no longer broke when he was startled.

"You're thinking that my father wasn't really very welcoming."

Disappointment struggled with relief and won. She hadn't been thinking about the bed at all. He'd have to be the one to bring that up. But not yet. Better wait till evening, when the soft moon was rising and the child was fast asleep.

"Well, he didn't kill the fatted calf. But I think we were let off easily." Odd, how easily the *we* came to him. With luck, she would feel just as familiar come nighttime. "From what you had told me, I was expecting moral outrage personified."

She slanted him an amused look, one that made her dark eyes glint with irony. "I am sorry to disappoint you. He does moral outrage very well. But the important thing is, we have persuaded him that we are indeed man and wife! You were wonderful, truly! You behaved just as I would expect a husband to behave. When you chided me . . . oh! I almost felt sullen, as if you were forever taking me to task that way! However did you manage the pose so well?"

"Just the way you did. I invented Captain Randall."

"You must have a vivid imagination, sir. For you have imagined him better than I ever did."

She dropped onto the bed, kicking off her slippers and drawing her feet up under her skirt. It was a casual pose, unself-conscious, and his pulse quickened. Already they dealt so well, anticipating each other's responses, as if their roles had become so believable that they almost fooled themselves, too. But it had ever been too fertile, this imagination of his. As she sat cross-legged, her hands busy rolling a pile of cotton stockings into neat spheres, he almost imagined he knew her as well as he pretended to, as if he had shared many bedrooms, many days, many nights with her. He remembered the way her hand had stroked his and could almost feel it again . . .

He had been too long without a woman, that was all. If he had taken the time when they docked to visit a house of pleasure, his mind wouldn't be reveling so with plans for this pretend-wife of his. At the very least, however, he could wait until nightfall. A sailor learned restraint early on—and he would need every ounce of it, if this Mrs. Randall insisted on looking quite so fetching on the marital bed.

He turned away from her bright face, her slender form, her adept hands, and began pulling shirts out of his seabag. "Tell me more about how your father got the dagger."

She was silent for a moment. He looked back over his shoulder to see that her hands had stilled in her lap. The bright light had gone out of her eyes. She shook her head, as if dispelling cobwebs, and looked down at the white cotton stocking wrapped around her hands. "I don't know. He brought it home from Plymouth one Christmastide. I remember that he showed it to me and told me that he was giving it to my mother. She loved to read stories of Richard the Lionheart."

It was true, then. This was no fool's errand, his venture into Morrell Hall. The Lionheart dagger—the second of the pair—was here. "When was that?"

"Christmas. I don't recall the year . . . oh, yes." Slowly, she wound up her stocking, took another from the pile, studied it abstractly, then put it aside for darning. "It was the Christmas before she died. My mother, I mean. I must have been seven. So it's been fifteen years."

"Did he buy anything else from that broker?"

"Oh, I don't think so. He was so furtive about this purchase, I shouldn't think he'd be likely to do that again. He must have wanted the dagger very badly." She added, with an innocence that didn't fool him for a moment, "Just as you do."

He refused to satisfy her curiosity. It was none of her affair why he would go to such lengths for a bit of military history. She would find that he was more reluctant than she to involve others in his past.

He halted his irritated searching through his seabag and

267

stood up straight to take a deep breath. His annoyance with her was due less to her inquisitiveness than to his own frustrated desire, and it was unfair to let that affect his behavior toward her. Impolitic, too. She couldn't help the radiance that made him want to kiss her every time she smiled, or the quick graceful movements that made his imagination run riot. And besides, there was no reason to alienate her, not with the night still ahead.

So he tamped his irritation and his desire alike, and pulling out his watch, he said, "It's time for me to meet your father. Where should I go?"

She jumped down from the bed, scattering all her stockings on the counterpane. "Oh, I will take you."

"No!" His objection came out more emphatically than he intended, and he saw the flash of hurt, quickly extinguished, in her dark eyes. But the last thing he wanted was her escort. He could hardly go to meet this woman's father with his thoughts still running rampant. Deliberately, he gentled his voice. "No, thank you. I'm a sailor, you see, and I shan't feel right till I navigate my own way through my surroundings. Just point me in the right direction. And you needn't fear," he added, "that I shall make a mistake that will ruin your plans. I am not given to making mistakes." Not in the last decade, at least, he concluded silently.

"Oh, I shan't worry about that at all," she exclaimed. "Why, you have already proved far better than I could have hoped." She glanced quickly at his face and then away. "But—but if he should agree to sell you the dagger, you will stay, won't you? I mean to say, you *should* stay, just through Christmas. Or . . ." Her voice trailed off, then with a determined brightness, she added, "Or if you must leave, I hope you will pretend you have received some urgent summons from your ship—perhaps that the shipment has been confiscated by the excise authorities or that your first officer has been injured in a dockside brawl; something my father will believe."

268

There was a quaint courage in the way she kept improvising, as if she had learned to expect trouble and to scramble to deal with it. Watching her eyes, Eric said dryly, "I take it he hasn't many illusions about the decorum of sailors in port. But you needn't worry. I have signed onto your command until after Christmas, and you can trust me to keep my word."

Her eyes flashed her relief, and she declared, "Oh, I knew from the first that I could trust you!"

And on that disconcerting pledge of faith, she flung open the door for him, giving him one of those radiant smiles in lieu of the conjugal kiss he half expected and fully craved.

If Eric had any last doubts about the dagger, they were dispelled when Sir William led him into the armaments room hidden behind the library. The very surreptitious nature of Sir William's posture was enough of an alert. First he showed Eric the tournament lances, the old maces, the fearsome crossbow, hung on the half-timbered wall. He lingered by the glass-cased Saracen swords and British longbows, explaining the history of each in detail. He even pointed out the Algonquin tomahawk. Finally, after circling the large room twice, Sir William stopped in front of a teak cabinet and regarded him rather belligerently.

"Know you anything of blades?"

The particular blade in question Eric knew all too well, but he only shrugged. "I've used cutlasses and sabres, a machete or two. Daggers, of course; they are useful in close combat."

"Come see this one then. But . . ." Sir William glanced around him and, in a conspiratorial voice, added, "I don't show this to very many visitors. But as you're part of the family now . . ."

He took a key from his pocket and opened the front of the cabinet. It must have been specially made, because behind the wooden door was another door, this one made of glass. A hidden display case. Paradoxical, but suitable for the object within. This was a weapon of war, but inappropriately ceremonial, a meld of the primitive and the ornate. The blade was rough-hammered, with a vicious-looking but impractical serrated edge; the hilt was elaborately worked in gold and silver, mounted with an emerald, featuring the head of a lion with rubies for eyes.

"The Lionheart dagger." Sir William's tone was reverent, proud. "Brought back from the Holy Land by Richard Plantagenet himself in 1190. I was fortunate enough to find it a decade or so ago and bring it here to Morrell Hall."

Sardonically, Eric noted that this account was silent on the whereabouts of the dagger in the intervening six centuries. "May I hold it?"

Sir William hesitated, then nodded and opened the case. Eric took the dagger from its black velvet setting and closed his hand around it. The last time he had gripped this dagger his hand was so small that the emerald had cut into his wrist. But this was a man's weapon, and he had become a man in the interim. The hilt now fit easily into his hand, the jewel scarcely noticeable against his callused palm.

He held the blade up to the light from the nearby barred window. It gleamed silver, the grain of the hammerstrikes reflecting curves of light against the cabinet. He waited for the memories to flood him and they did, as if the last fifteen years had been merely a moment. But instead of the triumph he expected, he felt only emptiness, the emptiness of completing a voyage that had claimed half the crew.

He replaced the dagger in its case. "A fine piece, that one." He forced casualness into his voice. "I have always admired Richard I, and I would like above anything to start collecting items of his. Would you—" he took a deep breath, then went on, "would you consider selling this to me, to become the center of my collection?"

Sir William was shaking his head even before Eric had

completed his sentence. "No. No. Not for any price." He closed the glass door, then the wooden door, and locked it up.

"Why not?"

"I don't sell my pieces. Especially not this one."

Eric could not mistake the other man's adamancy, and for a moment he let the despair fill him. But then he gathered up what remained of his resolve. A week ago, he had never thought he would see the dagger, much less touch it again. He would be here for several days, and that gave him time to be persuasive or, if necessary, more innovative.

"I did well on this last voyage, you know. I can afford to pay you far more than you must have paid for it."

Sir William led him back down the hall, as if removing him from the room would remove him from temptation. "I am sorry, but I cannot sell it. I am pleased you recognize its value. But there is no price that can be placed on it. It's the centerpiece of *my* collection, you see."

"Then why don't you display it openly?" They were back out in the entry hall, and Eric gestured at the suit of armor. "That's Norman, isn't it? It must be worth more than the dagger, and yet you don't keep it hidden."

"You know your armaments, I'll give you that." Sir William touched the handle of the Norman mace with the gentleness most men reserved for their lovers. "This is a valuable piece. But the Lionheart—there's another, do you know? I learned that investigating its history. The pair got broken up at some point, and—and I acquired this one. The other dagger's owner might be willing to sell to you, and then"—a gleam appeared in his eyes—"then both of the pair will be in the family."

Wonderful idea, Eric thought sardonically. "Why haven't you tried to buy the other, then?"

"I don't want to call attention to my ownership of this one." Sir William shot a wary glance at him. "These artifacts sometimes come with—with uncertain provenance.

271

That's the reason it can't be displayed openly. And why I would be beholden if you kept it to yourself."

Eric shrugged, deciding to let it go for the moment. "As you wish. But if you should decide it's not worth the trouble, remember my offer."

That was the way his luck went on this first evening at Morrell Hall. After a light supper was served in their suite—Sir William said he knew they would be too tired to dress for dinner—and Beth was put down for the night, Eric entered the bedroom to find Verity with an armful of bedlinens. She flashed him a smile and moved past him to the sitting room door.

"What are you doing?"

"I am making up the couch in the sitting room."

Eric put out a hand to stop her. Holding her arm firmly, he said, "You don't have to do that."

"Oh, but you are too tall to be comfortable there. I shan't mind a bit, I promise you."

"I meant—" He took a deep breath to slow down his racing pulse. "I meant that we can share the bed. It looks big enough for two."

She still had the smile, but it wavered uncertainly. "I—I don't think that will be necessary. Father won't come seeking us. We need only make it seem as if nothing is untoward for the maids—and I have already made it clear to them to stay away unless we ring for them."

It was another lost cause, but he gave it a final try. Eric slid his hand up her arm to cup her shoulder, and he felt her tremble through the thin muslin. "I could sleep atop the blankets, you know."

She broke away from his hand. "Oh, but then you would get a chill. The nights are cold here in Cornwall, you know."

"I know." He sighed and gave in to inevitability. "I will take the couch." Her pretty mouth opened in protest but he cut her off ruthlessly. "No arguments. This is your home and you should be comfortable. And I—" he swallowed back a sigh, "I am used to narrow berths. I don't know if I could sleep in a real bed."

Not with her next to him, at least.

And not with her in the next room, either, it turned out. The moon had long set over the harbor before Eric found a comfortable position on the couch and his brain became too weary to imagine which of the angels the lady next door resembled in her sleep.

Chapter 4

December 23

No boots. Verity checked under the bed, under the chair, inside her portmanteau. But her sturdy walking boots were missing.

"Mama, hurry!" Beth cried imperiously. She at least was fully outfitted for a morning's tramp in the woods, in two petticoats, woolen pullover and leggings, and sturdy stockings and boots. Actually, Verity thought with a smile, Beth looked rather like a hedgehog, so roundly and warmly wrapped up was she.

"Just a moment, sweeting. Mama can't find her boots."

On a hunch, she went to the sitting room door and tapped lightly. When she got no answer, she slipped in. Only a sliver of early light pierced the drawn drapes, and she could hardly make out the blanket-wrapped form on the couch. Poor man, she thought, sparing him a glance as she located her carriage bag under a chair. His gallantry must have given him a very restless night, but he was certainly fast asleep now. Only the back of his golden head was visible, that and the outline of a slim but strong form under the blankets.

She found her boots and drew them out of the bag, careful not to make a sound. But it was all for naught. From behind her Verity heard the peal of a child's laughter, and she turned to see Beth in the doorway, pointing at the shaft of light on the floor. "Sun, Mama!"

Verity grabbed up her boots and her daughter's hand and went back through the door. But she wasn't quick enough. "Don't bother, I'm awake," came the resigned voice from the couch.

Guiltily, Verity retraced her steps. "I am sorry, sir. I've promised her a walk in the woods, and she's a bit impatient."

"Just as well. I should be rising, anyway." He sat up, keeping the blankets tight around him. It was too dark to make out his expression, but she saw that his hair was ruffled by sleep, and she imagined he had that drowsy, vulnerable look that even a grown man must get when awakened too soon. "Where are you going?" he asked.

Beth was tugging at her hand and whispering "mama," so Verity replied quickly, "We're looking for holly and evergreens. My father has not had the staff decorate, you must have noticed. So Beth and I are going out to gather some, and I hope we will be able to bring a little holiday cheer back with us."

Her voice sounded foolishly bright in her own ears, as foolish perhaps as her hope that she could brighten this dark house with holly and pine boughs. But he shook his head as if to shake away the remaining drowsiness. "If you will wait a bit, I'll come with you. I expect it would be more persuasive to your father to see us all tramp out into the woods."

"You needn't really," she said, but he waved her away. And indeed, as she left him to dress, she felt a warmth steal through her that had nothing to do with the merino wool pelisse she donned. It was kind of him to keep up the appearance of a happy family, even if her father was already persuaded. Just as well, a little voice inside said, that Sir William hadn't been willing to sell the dagger. Now she needn't worry that Eric would accomplish his own mission and vanish before she accomplished hers. As long as he was

275

set on gaining her father's goodwill, both their purposes would be furthered.

Her father was in the breakfast room, bent over the news-paper with that absolute concentration that she remembered from a thousand breakfasts in the past. And as she had finally learned to do, she said no more than "good morning" and gently hushed Beth's exuberant gurgling. Gathering up apples and scones and crumpets into a napkin, she urged Beth back out the door to the hall.

"Where are you off to?"

Startled, she almost dropped the napkin full of breakfast. She put on a smile before turning back to her father. "Eric and Beth and I are going to take our breakfast to the woods. We mean to gather up some greens as decoration for the Hall. Then I must go into the village for some wool—I've just a few more gifts to knit. And then—"

Her father's gaze had returned to his newspaper, as if he had already forgotten that his daughter and granddaughter were standing before him. That annoyed Verity so much that she made the request she had earlier decided not to make. "Father, Dolly told me that Isabelle is visiting her parents for the holidays. I'd like to invite them to dinner tonight, if you don't mind."

The Revlings lived a quarter mile down the road, and she and Isabelle had spent their childhoods trading dolls and having spats and making up, only to fight again. They hadn't seen each other in more than three years, since Isabelle's wedding to a wealthy Sussex baron. But Verity knew if her conscience had been entirely clear and her marriage entirely authentic, she would not hesitate to introduce her husband to these neighbors and friends. It was only lingering shame that made her anxious about the prospect—shame that she needed no more, now that Eric was here.

Her father rumbled negatively, but Verity pretended not to hear. "Oh, good! I'll just send a note over to Lady Revling and speak to the cook, also. You needn't worry about anything, Father, for I will take care of it all. Come, Beth, we must hurry now.''

"Just a minute. If you will, tell your husband that I am going to ride around the estate later and that he's welcome to come along. After all''—her father shrugged and went back to his paper—"it will all be his eventually, and if he's the man I think he is, he'll want to know how best to administer it.''

All his eventually. Verity took Beth's hand and went back to speak to the cook. Even later, as she sent off a note to the Revlings, she felt a bitter amusement. How very fitting that her father had finally found something to approve of in her— her choice of a husband. And that was the one thing about her that was entirely false.

But she could hardly blame Eric for the sharp sense of injustice that stabbed her. He was only doing the job she had asked him to do . . . and very well at that. She was glad her father liked him and she was not surprised, either, Verity decided as Eric joined them on the terrace. She liked him, too, for he had been nothing less than exemplary since that first moment she had come up with her scheme. A lesser man might have dismissed her outright or failed miserably at pretending to be a husband. And a more venal man might have taken this pose of husband too literally. But Eric—or whatever his name was—greeted her this morning with a light comment, as if he had never for a moment imagined that they might share the bed assigned to them jointly.

She was glad he had taken no offense. Still, she glanced covertly at him as he slung over his shoulder the bag of tools he had acquired. Perhaps he was sorry he had come, since he had so far gotten neither dagger nor bedmate from this effort. At least he seemed resigned to it, striking out into the forest in the direction she indicated.

The sun was brighter than it had been in weeks, as if to proclaim that winter had not arrived, contrary to the calendar. So even in the depths of the home woods, it was light

277

and not very cold. The brisk walk brought a flush to Verity's cheeks and must have warmed Eric, too, for he started whistling "Heart of Oak" softly in time to his strides.

Beth had decided that she liked him, too, and Verity was amused to see that he didn't quite know what to do about it. The little girl trotted along beside him, pointing at every bird and plant and keeping up a steady stream of chatter.

"Am I supposed to understand what she is saying?"

Verity laughed at his puzzled look. "No. Oh, she does speak some English words, you've surely noticed. But she makes up her own more often. Oh, there's a likely tree. Let's take a few of the lower branches."

He pulled out a handsaw and began trimming the branches she pointed out. "Beth *sounds* as if she is speaking full sentences, but I don't recognize any of the languages I know in there. It's disconcerting, for she obviously knows what she's talking about."

"It won't last." Verity gathered up the boughs that fell from his saw and tossed them onto the sheet she had spread out in the clearing. "Soon she will speak only English—and not very well—and she shan't remember a word of this language she's devised."

"It sounds a bit like Mandarin, now that I think of it." Eric paused in his work and studied Beth, who was sitting on the ground arduously stripping the needles from a twig. "Rather a singsong."

"Do you know Mandarin?"

He laughed and moved to another tree. "No. But I've heard it often enough. Two of my best foretopmen are from Peking, and when they get excited, they sound very much like Beth."

With a bit of coaxing, he told her how he had come to employ these Mandarins, then about other exotic seamen he had known over the years. As they finished with the evergreens and started collecting holly, she asked more about his crew, intrigued by his spare explanations of why Malays made the best watchmen and Danes were best at the helm. This led

278

to more questions about his many voyages, as they prowled the woods with Beth in tow. Finally, they emerged onto the bluff overlooking the bay, and Eric walked to the brow and looked out east, as if he might see the ship he had left thirty miles away.

Holding tight to Beth's hand, Verity joined him at the edge of the cliff. Sixty feet below the sea was choppy, though there was only a light breeze. Beth pointed to a large ship bound for Plymouth, laboring a couple miles offshore. "Boat."

"Ship. A boat's not so big," Eric corrected. "Here, I'll show you."

Verity bit back a protest as he effortlessly lifted Beth to his shoulder. No longer was he tentative about how to hold her; just hoist her up and let her hold on seemed to be his attitude. And Beth loved it, crowing with delight and waving to the ship with one hand, while grasping his arm with the other.

"One of His Majesty's ships of the line. A triple-decker, do you see? Seventy-two guns. You can't see them, Beth, but there are more than five hundred men on that ship."

"Did you serve on a ship like that?"

It was a harmless enough question, but as soon as the words were out of her mouth, Verity regretted them. His eyes had been alight with pleasure at the pretty ship, but just like that they clouded over. "No." He set the protesting Beth on the ground and picked up the knotted sheet that held their morning's haul. "If I'm to ride out with your father, we'd best get back."

Verity, trailing a bit behind with Beth, cursed herself for ruining their amity. He'd already made it clear that he didn't want to talk about his past. And yet she couldn't still her curious mind. He was an enigma, and she hated to let him go unsolved.

But he was also her fellow conspirator, and she needed him. She would be stupid to alienate him by asking questions he didn't want to answer.

Verity spent the afternoon making gifts and decorating the

drawing room and the front hall, even festooning the suit of armor with a sprig of holly. But she couldn't keep her mind on her work. Her thoughts were following Eric around the estate, speculating on what he might be saying to her father. I should have gone along, she told herself. But her father would have thought that very odd, indeed, and might have refused outright.

No, she just had to trust Eric not to betray her. And he wouldn't. She might know nothing else about him, but she knew that much. He had promised to see this holiday week through, no matter what.

So when he returned from the ride, she greeted him affably. As her father went up the stairs, Eric pretended to wipe his brow in relief, then grinned at her. "Your secret is safe," he said in a stage whisper, and ran up the stairs two at a time to dress for dinner.

Verity had been looking forward to seeing her old friends again and introducing them to Eric. But when the Revlings arrived, Isabelle had a bright, hard smile on her face, one Verity recognized with a sinking heart. Even as a little girl, Isabelle had looked just that way whenever she decided to regard her best friend as a rival.

It was a silly competition, for they weren't much alike. Isabelle had always been an acclaimed beauty, the only daughter of adoring parents, the county's leading belle. And Verity had never been more than pretty, lacking the toys and gowns that an indulgent father might have given her, and popular more because of her skill at devising games than because of her looks. She was too willful, however, to stay in Isabelle's shadow, and the older they got, the more they argued.

Even now, Verity couldn't help but notice that Isabelle's lilac gown was in the height of fashion, while she knew from her friend's sharp glance that her own second-best dress wasn't. "You haven't been up to London lately, have you?"

Isabelle asked with a pitying air as they gathered around the roaring fire in the drawing room. "You should go, you know. Do remind me to give you the name of my dressmaker. She could work miracles for you."

So she couldn't help a spurt of glee that Isabelle was accompanied only by her parents, her husband having elected to remain in Sussex for the holiday. Perhaps he preferred his own company. Perhaps they weren't happy together. Perhaps Isabelle was being so catty because she was even now envying Verity this man who was so undeniably *here*.

Verity slanted a look at the man standing next to her and, for the first time, saw him the way a woman might see him, a woman who didn't need him but might want him anyway. Yes, she decided, a woman would want him—if she liked a bit of mystery. He was tall and lean and impeccably dressed, yet somehow dangerous, with his golden curls haloed by the firelight and his face half in shadow. The perfect corsair, Verity thought, and slipped a wifely hand into the crook of his arm.

After the slightest hesitation, he covered her hand with his own and smiled down at her. To Isabelle and her parents, this probably looked like a fond husband's smile; only Verity could see the ironic glint in his eyes that said both that he knew what she was about and that he understood. Simultaneously annoyed and pleased with his assumption of camaraderie, she told Isabelle, "My husband is just back from the Indies. Isn't it fortunate that he arrived in time for the holidays?"

A slight pressure on her hand told her that Eric at least had heard the edge in her artless comment. A glance up at him told her that he liked that show of spirit—he was a rogue, she told herself, and shouldn't be encouraging her. But it warmed her to think that he was so obviously on her side. She wasn't used to having allies.

It was only when Beth was brought in that Verity wondered if the battle were worthy of her. Prompted by her nursemaid, the child came over to sit on Verity's lap. She was already dressed for bed in a pretty flannel nightdress, her blond curls peeping out from under a lacy cap. With her drowsy eyes and quiet murmurs, she appeared the perfect angel, and if Verity—and now Eric—recalled the mischief she could get into, they knew better than to say so. No one would believe them, anyway, with Beth cuddling against her mother and sucking contemplatively at her thumb.

Lady Revling exclaimed at Beth's sweetness, adding archly, "Well, she certainly takes after her papa, doesn't she, Captain? Such lovely golden hair . . . and those big eyes."

Verity heard Eric's indrawn breath, and she hoped that he would understand. Ladies always liked to attribute a child's looks to one parent or the other, so Verity had always been a great disappointment, being dark-haired and dark-eyed. It meant nothing, really. But after a moment's pause, Eric replied just as he ought; she liked to think that his quick responses were the result of military training. He was never at a loss for long, she thought admiringly.

As Eric listened gravely to Lady Revling's further comparisons between daughter and father, Verity turned to draw Isabelle into the conversation. But then she saw the longing expression in the other woman's eyes and remembered that Isabelle, three years married, was still childless.

Her petty sense of rivalry now seemed mean-spirited. Impulsively, she said, "Would you like to hold her? She's quite good at cuddling, especially when she's sleepy."

Isabelle hesitated, then held out her arms, and Verity gently deposited the child into her care. Beth, as she usually did in a new situation, gazed up suspiciously at Isabelle's face. But then she withdrew her thumb from her mouth and reached to touch Isabelle's diamond necklace. "Pretty," she said, nodding approvingly. "Pretty."

"Careful," Eric broke in. "She'll be persuading you to give it to her if you're not careful. She's got her mother's charm, and she isn't above exploiting it."

"Oh, she's a darling." Isabelle took the plump little hand and kissed it, then reluctantly released the child to her nurse.

Verity felt warmed, as if she were the one being praised; she was always more proud of Beth than she was of her own accomplishments. She felt Eric's hand on hers and knew he understood. It wasn't that silly competition with Isabelle anymore, one that she no longer really cared to win. It just made her happy to see her daughter appreciated.

But the peace couldn't last. As soon as Beth was taken off to bed and they adjourned to the dining room, Isabelle recalled that they were rivals. She dipped her spoon into the chestnut soup and inquired sweetly, "Are you in the Royal Navy, Captain Randall?"

"No longer. I am with a merchant fleet now."

"Oh, a *merchant* fleet." After her slighting tone elicited no more than a grin from Eric, Isabelle turned to Verity. "I imagine you have a lovely manor overlooking the Channel, so you can watch for your husband's ship."

Verity gritted her teeth, but following Eric's example, she showed no offense. "Well, it's on the Channel and I like to think it's lovely, but it's no manor. Just a cottage near Plymouth. Tell me about your home, won't you? I collect it's near Brighton?"

And on it went, with Verity deflecting each of Isabelle's little barbs with a smile that grew more and more fixed as time went on. She received no help from her father, who was deep into a political discussion with Lord Revling. And Eric was occupied with Lady Revling, who had taken quite a liking to him and wanted to hear all about his voyages.

So Verity could only nod and smile and wonder why she had thought she wanted to see Isabelle again. No, she didn't have a large staff, only a maid and a nurse. No, she hadn't seen the Regent's Oriental renovation of the Brighton Pavilion. No, she hadn't yet ordered a ruby and lacquer bracelet that was all the rage in London.

Verity had to remind herself that generally she liked her

life, liked taking care of her little home, liked giving lessons to the local girls, even liked making her own clothes. She had coped the best she could, and longing for a life more like Isabelle's was shortsighted and frivolous. Just once, her resolve wavered, when Isabelle spoke of her travels. That was something Verity had always dreamed of—travel, adventure, distant lands. And that was something a solitary young woman with a small child could not expect to attain.

But as it turned out, the only road Isabelle wanted to take was the one that went to London. She spoke archly of the balls and routs and theater parties that awaited her. "Surely you will be in Town this season, Verity?"

Unexpectedly, Eric broke off his conversation with Lady Revling. "This season? No, I think not. I mean to take Verity abroad this spring. Paris, perhaps, then, if she likes, Italy and Greece. You haven't ever been to Greece, have you, darling?"

The casual, slightly ironic endearment, the suggestion that Greece was one of the few places she hadn't visited, made Verity look down at her mutton with a secret smile. "No, I haven't," she replied innocently. "Though you've said it's very lovely. I do so long to see the sights you've described, darling."

Their exchange of amused glances was interrupted by Isabelle. She closed her hand on her diamond necklace and sighed almost as if she meant it. "Well, I shall miss you. What fun we had our season after the war ended. Do you remember, Verity? Of course," she added after a tiny pause, "I don't know that you will recall those weeks with quite as much fondness as I do. I vow, I felt as if I were in a whirlwind of pleasure—all the invitations to the *best* parties, all those lovely dresses, all the beaus . . . Sometimes I thought I would dance my feet right off, and yet even after a whole night without sitting out a single dance, I rose happy as a lark to see my morning callers. But I don't know that you had *quite* as lovely a time as I did."

Verity couldn't help herself. With a light laugh, she admitted, "No, I didn't! Why, that season wasn't by any means the xenith of my existence. In fact, my life has done nothing but improve ever since, and I'm so glad I can look back and see how much happier I am now."

It was unforgivable, really, but with a start, Verity realized it was true. No doubt Isabelle's happiness had peaked those few months in London. But Verity, always the optimist, had a strong sense that her own life would only get better, at least now that she could be welcomed back home with Beth.

Fortunately for her future relations with her old friends, Lord Revling sniffed rain in the night air and determined to return home before the clouds broke. Isabelle's manner was a bit chill as they took their leave, but Verity told herself it didn't matter. She was doing this for Beth, to secure her future. And all that was necessary for that was the assumption of respectability and a grandfather's sponsorship.

Sir William grunted with relief when the door closed behind his guests. "Thank God that's over. Revling thought he could convert me to the Whigs if he had another quarter hour. He's bored me so, I'm ready to retire early." He started up the stairs, then looked back over his shoulder at Eric. "Lady Revling certainly had a lot to say to you, didn't she? Prettiest girl in the country when she was young. Still a handsome woman—and still with an eye for the good-looking young Navy officer."

Verity thought her companion might be flushing, and she wondered if he were so unused to observations like that—or if it was the reference to the Navy that unnerved him. Surely Lady Revling wasn't the only woman to find him compellingly attractive. Isabelle's gaze had lingered on his bronzed face so frequently that Verity was almost annoyed. But here Eric was, disconcerted enough that she was led in sympathy to change the subject.

"I'm not tired, are you? Perhaps we can do a bit more with the greenery," she suggested, leading the way back to their suite. "With so little time left till Christmas, I hate to lose a moment. Isabelle made me realize how much I have yet to do—the evergreen ropes, the holly wreaths, the berry sprigs."

She had left a heap of evergreen and her sewing supplies on the couch, and here they tacitly decided to remain, next to the fire that had already warmed the sitting room. Verity was uneasy, sitting on the couch where he would be sleeping in a couple hours. It made her heart quicken to look across at his lean form and remember it blanket-wrapped on this couch. She could almost imagine that the leather against her was still warm from his body.

But she forced such visions away. There was no evidence that this had served as a bed, for neat as all sailors must be, he had stowed away the linens and it looked quite as innocent as any other couch in the house.

He made it easier on her by taking a seat at the desk as soon as she settled on the couch amidst the boughs of pine. He had instructions to send to his first officer, he said, and shipping contracts to review. He remained a dozen feet away, and as long as he did, she could pretend they were sedate married folk, too long acquainted for any sudden acceleration of the senses.

Chapter 5

His correspondence completed, Eric stood at the window, hearing, if he could not see, the great waves battering this battered coast. Isabelle, that little bitch, had been chagrined to find her girlhood friend married, if only to an inconsequential sea captain. Her catty comments about a London season had rankled Eric rather more than they should have, with their implication that Verity had been a failure as a girl and perhaps just as much so as a woman.

He recalled, from another life, the year his sister had gone off to London to make her debut. He never saw her again; he went off to sea a month later, when he turned twelve, and she married a Scotsman and moved to Edinburgh. But he recalled the breathless anticipation, the extensive preparations, and could envision Verity at that age in alt, in her element, preparing for a month-long party.

He glanced back over his shoulder at Verity, her head bent low over yet another rope of evergreen, the candlelight gilding her dark hair and the sweet curve of her neck. "So you had a season in London?"

She looked up from her work and studied him for a moment before answering, "Not a regular one. I was supposed to come out in the spring of '15, but Bonaparte had escaped and everyone was in a quiz. So I attended the Little Season that fall, after Waterloo."

"Did you enjoy it?"

She wrinkled up her nose, an ambivalent expression from a usually positive woman. "Oh, I had a deal of fun. But I didn't take, you know. That's what Isabelle was saying, in her nasty little way."

"You didn't take?" It was hard to believe, looking at her now, with the shawl half dangling from her slender arms, a full lip caught in her teeth as she rethreaded the needle. "Were all the bucks blind that year?"

A quick smile, a quick shake of her head, then she went back to her wreath. "Oh, they liked me well enough. As a bosom beau, that is. I was always the one chosen to help them rehearse the proposals they were making to Isabelle." She sewed on a berry sprig and automatically tied off the thread, before adding wryly, "It was because I was ever the organizer of our entertainments. While I was making sure the picnic was going off without a hitch, she or some other girl would slip off into the woods with my favorite. I just couldn't learn to be less capable." She smiled, shook her head, and bent to bite through the thread. Whatever pain she had felt then had softened into mere rueful remembrance.

"Is that—?" He broke off, annoyed with himself, annoyed with her for coming to him so complete, with a past he wasn't part of no matter what he pretended. He wondered what had become of that locket she had showed him, the one with the blond curl; the square-necked gown was bare of adornment, not that the gentle swell of her breasts wasn't enough. "Is that when you met Beth's father?"

Verity glanced around, startled, and only when she had listened hard, head cocked, to make sure they were quite alone did she answer. And even then she spoke so quietly he had to come back and sit near her to hear.

"No. I met him just after Christmas." The wistfulness in her eyes did not escape him. She was remembering that Christmas three years ago, when her life had changed.

"Not in London."

"No. I was staying with my aunt in Plymouth."

"And it being winter, you hadn't any picnics to organize when he came into port. So he ruined you instead."

She drew back at the hardness of his voice, but he didn't care. He didn't care for that other sailor, either, the one with the same light hair and lighter morals, who had taken such advantage of this lonely, laughing girl.

"It wasn't really as you are thinking," she said, her equanimity regained, her hands busy again with the pine branches.

"How do you know what I'm thinking?"

"I can tell. Your jaw is clenched tight as a fist." Boldly now, as she might have done with that other sailor, she reached over and drew her fingers lightly against his jaw. He closed his eyes for a second, breathing in the piney scent of her hands. Then the scent, the touch, was gone, and he opened his eyes to find her looking down at her wreath, her mouth curved in a smile.

"What is so amusing?"

She shook her head. "Oh, just the thought of Billy as a vile seducer."

Billy. A stupid name. He took the crooked end of her long rope and twisted it backward to straighten it out. "Wasn't he?"

"Not at all. He was only a boy. Only eighteen—two months older than I. He'd never been in love before. Neither had I."

The springy branch broke in his hands. Murmuring admonitions under her breath, Verity took it from him and began the laborious process of putting the rope back together.

He watched her hands weaving the thread around the greenery and saw them moving so deftly over the buttons of a man's shirt, undoing them. . . . "What else did he tell you?"

"What do you mean?"

"Did he promise to marry you?"

Her hands stilled their activity, and when she spoke there was no laughter in her voice. "He did. We meant to marry.

But we were underage and had no funds with which to bribe a parson. He did try, though . . ."

"You believed him."

For the first time ever he felt her anger, hot and sudden, flashing toward him like a flame. "Yes, I believed him. I *knew* him. He wasn't—he wasn't some hardened rake. He'd never had anyone before, no one who loved him. All he ever wanted was a wife and a family. And if he hadn't been called back to his ship, we would have gone to Scotland and married. Don't you try to tell me any differently, for you didn't know him. He loved me and he would not have hurt me for the world."

She rose, spilling the evergreen rope to the floor. Her eyes in the candlelight were dark and fierce, but then her dark lashes swept down to hide them and she crossed to the door. His anger melted in the heat of hers. This is what she needed to believe, and what harm was there in it, after all? Perhaps it was even true. She would be a great temptation for a lonely man, that much was clear.

Before she could leave, he said, "I'm sorry. You are right. I did not know him."

Slowly, she turned and retraced her steps. When she was back at her chair she didn't sit down, but only knelt on the floor and began to wind up her evergreen rope. "It is only what most people would think. I know that. They would think the worst. That is why—why I thought of Captain Randall."

He went back to the window and looked out, so that he wouldn't have to look at her, kneeling there, her arms full of evergreen and her eyes full of hurt. "Do I look like him?" When she made a questioning sound, as if she didn't understand, he added, "Lady Revling said that Beth certainly had her father's looks. She meant that Beth looked like me."

"I think she just meant Beth doesn't look like me. Oh, I suppose there's a resemblance. But—but he was a boy. You're grown. I can't tell; he wasn't so tall. And he hadn't your air of command. I always wondered if he was different at sea,

f he grew into his role. Because with me he was . . . just
Billy."

That wasn't really what he wanted to hear, that he was an
older and not so endearing replica of her dead love. But then,
"just Billy" didn't seem as formidable a rival after all—if
rival he was. He was just a boy, and this woman wasn't just a
girl anymore.

So he could afford to be more generous now. "We judge
others by our own behavior, I suppose. The wicked among
us impart wicked motives to everyone else."

He heard her laughing and turned unbelievingly to see.
The wretched girl was incapable of maintaining anger or sadness or any serious emotion for more than a moment or so.

"Well, I am wicked as can be, aren't I?" she said gaily,
rising with evergreen trailing like a scarf over her shoulder.
"And I impart wicked motives only to the wicked."

"How would you know the wicked from the well-
meaning?"

"I am a good judge of character. I am, you know," she
said, serious again, for the moment. "I had to learn to read
expressions very early, to know if my father was amenable
to being approached. For if he weren't, I'd never get what I
asked. I developed a sixth sense about people." She went to
the door, and, juggling her greenery a bit, managed to turn
the handle. Just before she closed the door behind her, she
looked back. "For instance, I knew that I could trust you to
be my husband. As soon as I saw you, I knew that we would
be safe with you. And I was right, wasn't I?"

No. But he didn't say it aloud, and she was gone at any
rate, through that door to her bed. No. She couldn't trust him
to be her husband. If he were, she wouldn't be sleeping alone.

No. Then she would be sleeping with a man who had no
claim on the name she claimed, nor his own name, either.
And a woman like her deserved better than that.

Chapter 6

December 24

The whole house was redolent with holly and evergreen
and Eric was congratulating them both on a good morning'
work and speaking longingly of lunch. But Verity wasn't don
yet with her holiday decorating. The entry hall might be fille
with Yuletide spirit, even the suit of armor sporting a bit o
holly in his visor, but the front door was still unwelcoming

As Verity inched the library stepladder along the marbl
floor to the threshold, Eric eyed it dubiously. "Why don't w
get one of the footmen to put up the rest of the greens?"

In a low, reproving voice, meant to reach only him an
not the footmen, whose feelings might be hurt, she said
"There isn't a footman in the house younger than fifty, an
this would doubtless bring on an apoplexy."

She wrestled the ladder out onto the front steps, then stoo
there hugging herself and shivering as the chill worked it
way through her wool crepe gown. The sun was trying bravel
to pierce through the clouds, but all that was emerging wa
a weak ray that glanced off the copper hinge on the ladder
"Eric, let's hurry. It's cold out here."

Eric sighed deeply and emerged. Despite the chill, h
stripped off his coat and draped it over her shoulders, the
stood beside her in his white waistcoat and shirt, appraisin

the ladder as if it led all the way to the sky instead of just to the top of the door frame. "If I break my neck, it will be on your head."

She pulled his coat tighter around her; it was still warm from his body. The thought of his neck on her head made her chuckle, but she sobered when he made no move toward the ladder. "For pity's sake, Eric, and you call yourself a sailor? Oh, I'd forgotten. You get others to climb the rigging for you. You are a *captain.*" She invested that dignified term with the scorn due something like *poltroon,* and predictably he rose to the bait.

"I'll have you know, my girl, that before I was captain of a ship I was captain of the foretop and spent most of my youth aloft."

"A time long past, I take it, and fortunately so."

He was a good man to tease; he scowled deliciously and reached out a hand as if to cuff her. Laughing, she danced out of the way and down one step, so she could see the whole door frame. "Come, now, Captain, your manhood is at stake here. You have climbed a mast, surely, if you were a fore-topman?"

"A thousand times. But—" He took hold of the old ladder and shook it, and it creaked in answer. "But a foremast, even in a gale, is sturdier than this contraption. Come here and hold it for me."

"Let me get the rope first." She dashed back into the house to get the evergreen rope she had made the previous night, then made a great show of wrapping it around him. She let one end dangle over his shoulder, then she wound the rope round his chest, under his arms, and again around his slim waist.

He stood quite still, one hand on the top step of the ladder as if he needed that for balance. He made no comment as she tied him up in Christmas greenery. But every time she looked up, she saw the ironic quirk of his smile. They were friends again, for all that she had lost her temper with him the previous night.

As she came to the end of the evergreen rope, she let her hand linger on the smooth fabric of his waistcoat, only a few layers of fabric from the taut muscles of his side. It had been a lifetime—Beth's lifetime—since she had been so close to a man that she could touch him like this. And so for a moment she let herself enjoy this contact, her hand, bare but for a simple gold band, curved around the curve of his waist, warming where it touched his warmth.

She stole a glance up at his face and found all the irony gone. In his eyes instead was pure silver flame, desire so naked she felt naked herself, felt against her hand the tightening that meant he was holding his breath. This was no pretense, no husbandly pose. He wanted her, and he waited only for her to raise her hand to his face to tell him she wanted him, too, wanted his kiss, his caress.

I don't even know who you are, she thought, and his eyes, his desire, answered back, Does it matter?

Once it might not have. Once she would have moved closer to him, breathed in the piney scent of the evergreen, trailed her hand up his chest, lifted her face for his kiss, been as wild and wicked as only she knew how to be. But not now. Not with a man who could only pretend permanence, however real his passion.

She dropped her hand, stepped back, managed a smile. "Now you are properly rigged out for Christmas, Captain."

He turned swiftly away, but not before she saw the anger, the disappointment on his face. It was a moment before he looked back with that ironic expression. "I think I prefer to tack it above the door as we'd planned. You hold the ladder and hand me the tacks. They're in the pocket of my coat there."

At least he isn't pressing me, she told herself. He's a gentleman at heart, whatever else his life has made him. So she held the ladder steady with one foot on the bottom rung and one hand on the side near his booted calf, and with the other hand she passed the tacks up to him. He must not have wanted to prolong this painful proximity any more than she did, because he took only the time necessary to tack the rope around the door frame and then, with an impatient hand, waved her away so he could climb down. "We are done finally, I hope?"

Verity felt in her pocket for the last bit of greenery; there was still the mistletoe to be hung. But suddenly a kissing bough seemed too dangerous a temptation. "All done," she replied brightly, and then, as he started pulling the ladder back through the door, she added, "Except for the Yule log, of course."

He wasn't angry; he was just cool and remote, the way he had been those first few moments she had known him. "After lunch, I hope."

"Of course, we'll eat lunch first. Beth isn't finished helping the cook with the plum pudding, anyway." She followed him through the door and called to the footman to take the ladder back to the library.

Eric held out his hand for his coat, and she felt a premonition of loss. The cheer they had been tacking up all morning had no effect on the chill in this hall. But she shrugged off the coat and gave it to him, then located her gray wool shawl trailing from a chair. Tying the ends into a bow over her chemisette, she realized the futility of all her pretense: pretending that this house could be a holiday home; pretending she had a family; pretending this man was her husband when he wasn't hers at all.

Subdued, she started back toward the dining room. "You needn't come with us into the woods. My father's in Portmallow, so he won't be there to see us, anyway. And half the staff will be along, to help out. I think even our antique footmen can wield a hatchet. And if they can't, I can."

Eric gave her a sharp look as he held open the door. But he waited till they were seated and served before he replied,

"Verity with an axe. I shouldn't miss it for the world. I shall be sure to stay out of range, of course."

Her momentary sadness dissipated when he kept up the same teasing attitude as, booted and cloaked, they marched out into the woods, trailing a troop of servants. She studied him as he directed one group of footmen along one path, another to the copse. He looked every inch the commander, even in his riding clothes, even with Beth perched on his shoulder, her hands securely tangled in his hair. The brisk weather had put a flush into his bronzed cheeks and a sparkle into his eyes; she could imagine him just like this, steering his ship on some winter voyage through the Strait of Magellan.

Of course, this was a simple country excursion, not the great adventure he was used to. But after that single moment of resistance, he had joined in the fun as if it had been his idea all along. Verity couldn't help but be touched by his kindness, especially since she must be a great disappointment to him. He had come expecting to acquire the dagger and, perhaps, to bed her—a reasonable enough assumption on his part, considering what she had told him of her past. Last night she had tried to explain that, wild as she was, she had never been wanton, that Billy was special, and that she would not do that again. But he was a man, and perhaps he did not appreciate such distinctions. No matter; he was not holding her belated chastity against her, nor her father's reluctance to sell the dagger.

It took most of the afternoon to find just the right log for the Yule fire, for Verity was an exacting mistress of Christmas celebrations. But no one complained, though the more arthritic footmen spent most of the time huddled around the small campfire Eric built with the logs Verity disdained.

The weak winter sun was low in the sky when the youngest of the footmen, a mere stripling of fifty or so, found a log smooth enough to pass her test, a long, thick branch broken from a birch tree in a recent storm. He signaled to Eric to

296

bring Beth over, and after some quiet prompting, she sat down plump on the log and cried out, "Mama! Look! I find it!"

True to his word, Eric let Verity chop off the smaller branches, but then he took the hatchet from her hand to trim the ends of the log. Three of the footmen vied for the right to drag it home, one holding the single length of rope obstinately against his meager chest, the other two arguing seniority or superior strength.

In the end, Eric rigged up a three-part harness of rope, so that each volunteer could tug without too much fear of his heart giving out. As they started back, Eric hoisted Beth onto his shoulder, warning, "If you pull my hair again, little one, I shall set you right down again."

They had gotten far ahead of the servants and were just emerging from the woods when the maid Dolly started singing an ancient carol. Her voice was thin but pretty, and when the men joined in, it carried through the crystalline air. It was a country song, translated from the old Cornish tongue, and Verity had learned it at her nurse's knee.

> "Mary had a baby,
> A sweet baby boy.
> And that babe of Mary's
> He brought the world joy.
>
> "Joy in the morning,
> God's sun comes to rise.
> Joy in the evening,
> And in the baby's eyes."

Eric paused for a moment, his head cocked to the side. Verity saw the memory dawn in his eyes, and she realized that once someone had sung this song to him, years and years ago, before he had left his childhood home. She reached out and took his hand, and even through two layers of glove she felt the tingle as he pressed her hand.

But then Beth, excited by the song, took a handful of Eric's thick hair. "You little wretch," he cried in mock anger, and letting go of Verity's hand, he swung the child down in a great swoop. She shrieked in delight as he cradled her in his strong arms and pretended to toss her into a bush.

"She's terrified of me," he assured Verity, and Beth begged him to do it again. By the time they found their way back to the house, the child had laughed herself weary and fell asleep while Verity and Dolly were giving her a bath.

She'll sleep till midnight, Verity thought, miss all the Christmas Eve fun, and wake up ready to play. But it was useless to try to wake a sleeping child, and she resigned herself to a sleepless night. That would be nothing new. She thought back to other Christmas Eves, when her mother was alive and her father still enjoyed the festivities. She was always too excited to sleep on those nights before Christmas, when the carolers came and the staff worked late and merrily, preparing for the next day's dinner.

Verity wandered around the house, a bit at loose ends. There was nothing left to do for Christmas, really, except to celebrate it. All her packages were wrapped in the colored paper she had been saving the whole year, and all the decorations were hanging jauntily in their places. Now she had an entire evening yet to get through with no activities to fill her time.

She found Eric in the armaments room, standing in front of the glass case the held the jeweled dagger. He turned when she came in, and for just an instant she saw despair in his eyes before he smiled and asked about Beth. She kept forgetting that he was here not only to help her, but also because he wanted that stupid dagger. And even as she explained about Beth nodding off in the middle of her bath, she determined to help his cause as much as he had helped hers.

As soon as her father returned from Porthallow, she asked

him to join her for tea. They had spent little time alone these last two days; she wanted him to come to know Beth better, so she usually brought her along. Now she was annoyed to find her hand shaking a bit as she poured his tea, but she nerved herself to ask him for that which she had no reason to expect.

She knew her light manner annoyed him, so she schooled her features into a somber expression as she handed him the cup. "Here you are, Father. We are nearly ready for the holiday tomorrow, I think. I have wrapped gifts for everyone on the staff. Eric sent back to his ship for a whole casket of tea and I divided it up into little packets, and of course I have stockings for the maids and new hats and gloves for the men."

Her father only nodded, and she swallowed a frustrated sigh. Had he always been so taciturn? No, it was his isolation here on this remote coast, in this gloomy old house, she decided, that made him so unreachable. But she persevered. "Did you go to Porthallow to purchase a few gifts?"

"And to consult my attorney." He drank his tea and set his cup down on the table, then fixed her with an assessing stare. "I got the child a top."

"She'll like that." Her name is Beth, she wanted to add, but held her tongue.

"What would you like?"

Although this was exactly the opening she wanted, his question was so unexpected that she could not answer immediately. It was a measure of their distant relationship that she wasn't sure he really wanted to know. Perhaps it was some sort of trick. But she had little to lose, after all. "Oh, do you know, I've been away from home for so long, I sometimes wish I had something to remind me of Morrell Hall, some memento."

Sir William glanced around the drawing room, no doubt surprised that she would feel nostalgic about this place. But then he shrugged. "You will inherit it all eventually, anyway,

299

you and Captain Randall. If you want something particular, you might as well take it.''

Verity took a deep breath. It couldn't be so simple, not with her father. "The Lionheart dagger. It—it is a lovely object. And''—the falsehood stuck in her throat, but she forced it out—"I've always admired it.''

"The dagger?'' He drew back, his expression wary, dismayed. "Why that?''

"I remember that—that you gave it to my mother for Christmas, when I was just a girl.''

For a moment, a smile flickered on his face, and Verity was too surprised to go on. Sir William was not one to laugh, especially about her mother.

"Come, my dear, do you really think I purchased it for her?''

Verity shook her head in confusion. "But, Father, I recall distinctly when she opened it. You said that you knew Richard the Lionheart was one of her heroes and that he had held this very dagger in his hands. She was very pleased.'' Slowly, she poured another cup of tea, reviewing that vivid scene in her mind. "I know you think I am dreadfully fanciful, but I assure you I did not make that up. It was our last Christmas with Mother.''

"Yes.''

She must have been mistaken about the smile, for now he was somber, almost angry, the father she best remembered. He rose and went to stir up the fire. "Perhaps she did like it, as she pretended. Do you think?''

Verity stared at his implacable back, wondering if her father were really asking for her reassurance. It was so unlikely, and yet, reassurance was one of those gifts that she was used to giving. And so, warmly, she said, "Of course she liked it, Father. Don't you remember how she sewed a velvet lining for the case?''

The fire was burning merrily again, but still he did not turn around. "Perhaps you are right. I have often wondered since then if I should have gotten her something else . . . a diamond necklace, perhaps. Most women would have preferred that.''

"Mother was not most women.'' Verity nodded for additional firmness, though he could not see it. "She shared your interests, I think.''

"So she always said. I never questioned that while she lived.'' Incredibly, there was a catch in his voice as he went on. "She was so good. I fear I thought that her goodness would make up for the way I acquired the dagger. That if she touched it, it would be clean again . . .'' He gave the fire a last stab, then turned to Verity with a forced laugh. "It is not unknown for husbands to give wives what they most want for themselves. Hasn't Captain Randall ever done that?''

She was too unused to the role of her father's confidant to invent some reassuring story of such a husbandly trick. "No. But—but perhaps when we have been married longer he will do that.''

And then her father smiled at her, for the first time, really, since she had come home, the first time in years. "Probably not. He seems remarkably considerate of your feelings, that husband of yours.''

Filled with confusion, very near tears, Verity returned a tremulous smile, then excused herself and fled from her father's presence. It was only when she was back in her own room that she remembered that her father had not promised her the dagger. No matter, she told herself, rubbing away a few treacherous tears. That he would confide in her that way meant—meant what? That he was glad she remembered those days when they were a family? That he had accepted her with her husband and child as his new family? That he would grant her request?

She heard the door open in the next room, heard Eric moving about getting dressed for dinner. "He seems remarkably considerate of your feelings, that husband of yours,'' her father had said, almost as if he approved. That was not so

301

strange, was it? Sir William, distrustful of his daughter's judgment, had probably expected the worst of her chosen husband. And Eric, confident, considerate, must have seemed, in comparison, an ideal addition to the family.

But how fragile it was, this new family. It rested entirely on a man who didn't exist and yet had become so essential to them all.

She worried that her father would make up for his unusual candor by being aloof again at dinner. But he was obviously trying to assume the holiday mood. And Eric showed yet again how adept he was at the art of conversation, asking about the local Christmas customs, describing a holiday he had passed in Hawaii, when the missionaries staged a nativity play with a native Mary in a grass skirt.

After dinner, he suggested a walk, and as he was settling Verity's heavy cloak on her shoulders, he said, "You were very quiet."

She pulled her hair out from under the cloak and shook it free. Glancing back to make sure her father had retired to his sanctuary, she replied, "I don't want to alienate him, when there's still your dagger to be bought. I've finally learned that keeping still works best with my father. Children should be seen and not heard, even when they are adults."

He bent close to fasten the cloak at her neck, and so his words were low and gentle, almost a caress. "I'm glad you didn't learn that early enough to silence you. And I hope you unlearn it very soon."

As they emerged into the night, Verity slanted a glance at him. "But you are very good with him. I think he truly likes to converse with you."

She saw a flash of white in the darkness and knew he was amused. "And you can't imagine how a rough sailor learned to be so civil? Well, sweeting, more than navigation, a captain must learn conversational adroitness."

302